SHIFTERS OF BLACK ISLE

THE COMPLETE COLLECTION

LORELEI MOONE

eXplicitTales

CONTENTS

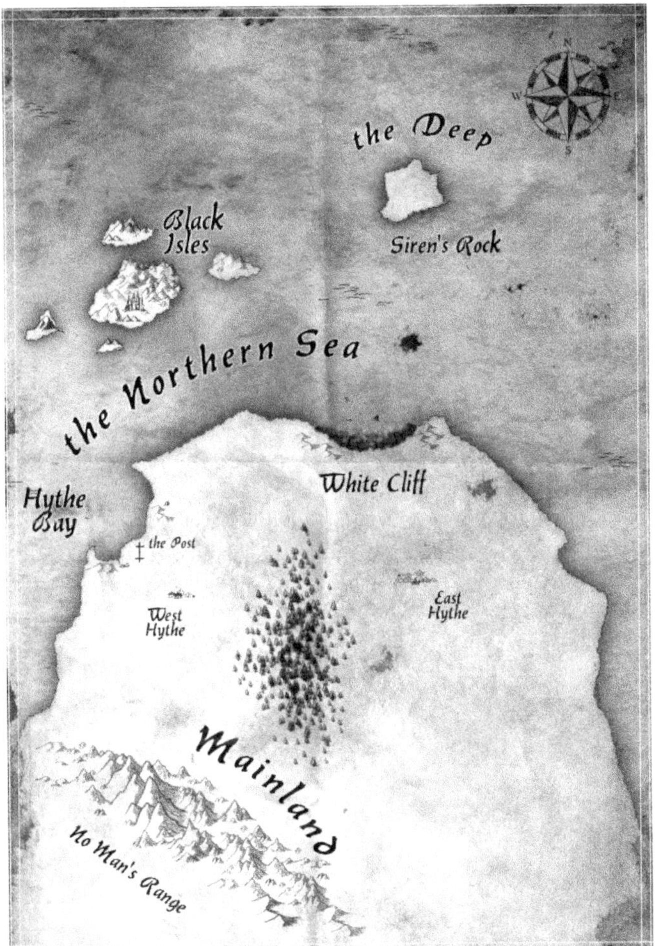

the Deep
N
W E
S
Black Isles
Siren's Rock
the Northern Sea
White Cliff
Hythe Bay
the Post
West Hythe
East Hythe
Mainland
No Man's Range

Claimed by the King

CHAPTER ONE

Once in every eight springs, a girl will be put forth by one of the coastal regions. A peace offering, a condition of the truce between the Giant Warriors of Black Isle and the men of the mainland.

1. No one shall remain with the offering when the time comes.

2. No one shall attempt to lay eyes on or follow the giants.

3. No girl shall ever come home, or her village shall feel the giants' wrath.

By this ritual we are bound, so long as our truce may last.

*M*y life is over.

Kelly sat down with her head in her hands, making sure she could no longer see the eerily dancing shadows created by the candle on the kitchen table.

They never did waste much time between the lottery and the banishing.

Perhaps that's for the best, Kelly thought. *If I had a lot of time to think about this, perhaps I'd be less likely to cooperate.*

Of course, she still wasn't willing to accept her fate, no, she had other plans.

After dusk, she would be left on the shores of the Northern Sea, tied up to the strong wooden post erected solely for this purpose, until the giants claimed her.

Perhaps they wouldn't like her. Perhaps they'd leave

her behind, demanding a prettier, daintier candidate? Kelly could only hope as much. Or perhaps her ties would be loose enough to wiggle free, allowing her to run before the giants even arrived.

Ever since her mother passed when she was only eight years old, she hadn't felt this alone in the world. Her father had betrayed her. He was meant to keep her safe, those were her mother's last words. *Keep Kelly and Ferris from harm, swear it to me.*

Instead, what had happened under the watchful eye of their father? She'd been chosen in the lottery.

It's an honor, he had said. *Your sacrifice ensures the safety of our people for the next eight summers.*

Kelly was to be made into a prisoner and slave, never to be seen again by her people, all of whom were just pleased none of their own daughters were chosen. She'd never gotten along with most of the villagers, most of whom took great pleasure in pointing out that her mother's death was God's punishment or other such nonsense. Kelly wasn't lady-like enough apparently. As a child she'd played with the boys out in the field rather than stayed at home and helped with the housework. If that was sinful enough to warrant her own mother's death, then she wanted nothing to do with such a God, or the feeble-minded people who believed in him. Of course, she could have never said that aloud, or they would have branded her a witch and punished her. So she had kept these thoughts to herself all these years.

And yet, she was chosen to protect those same people. Oh, the irony. She would love to see their faces when they realized that there'd be hell to pay for her upcoming escape. All those years playing with the boys would pay off. Now that she had reached a full eighteen years of age, Kelly wasn't half as weak as most girls she'd grown up with.

A horn blew in the distance, signaling that her wait was over.

It was time.

Her father opened the kitchen door, his weather beaten face tense - the only indication so far that he even cared what happened to her. *An honor.* What a joke.

He'd get over the loss of his first born daughter soon enough, at least he still had a son to focus on.

Ferris would miss her the most. Two years younger than she was, he'd always looked up to his big sister with admiration rather than the disdain others had shown her. She had been there for him more like a mother than a sibling, making sure there was food to eat, clothes to wear, even toys to play with.

Their father had never realized that he had been suffering the most after their mother had passed. While Father had stuck to his same old routine; heading off to the tavern after nightfall, as though nothing had ever changed, *she* had been there for Ferris.

Yes, Ferris would come looking for her as soon as he

realized what had happened.

Father had conveniently sent him off on some merchant ship as a deckhand only weeks before the lottery. As if he'd known what would happen…

"Kelly. Our fate lies in your hands." Her father waved Kelly forward with an outstretched arm.

She hesitated for a moment, but took a deep breath and finally got up.

"Yes, Father."

Mother, I wish you were here. Kelly swallowed hard.

"Come in," Father called out.

A group of villagers made their way inside the cramped little kitchen. They surrounded Kelly, who had already assumed the position expected of her: her arms were crossed behind her back, ready to be tied. They wouldn't take any chances, because in the heat of panic, many an offering had attempted to flee in the past.

Oh, Mother. Why did you have to leave me to this fate?

Kelly's eyes stung uncomfortably, though she tried not to let it show. A cold gust of wind from outside dried her tears.

As soon as the rough ropes were tightened uncomfortably around her wrists, it was time to head towards the shore. A long procession had already formed outside Kelly's modest family home, which in this dimmed light looked like nothing more but a dilapidated shack.

Of the sun, already vanished behind the mountain ranges towards the west, nothing remained but a reddish glow.

Fittingly gloomy, Kelly thought.

A few wisps of clouds did nothing to conceal the full moon shining down on Kelly's march towards her doom.

Towards the front of the procession two drummers would set the pace for everyone. Some of the villagers carried torches, deep shadows cast over their solemn faces, making it seem like they were wearing masks. These were not the features of the ordinary folk of West Hythe. Tonight, everything had changed. More change was yet to come.

Kelly lowered her head as she stepped forward, positioning herself between the butcher and the tanner, two of the strongest, and tallest men of her village. Their function was ceremonial as well as practical during this ritual: supposedly they'd ensure she was delivered to the right people, and not snatched by anyone on the way to the beach. Actually, it was more likely they were there to prevent her from bolting out of fear.

The drums started to roll, before settling into a comfortable marching pace, and the procession started to move. Kelly resisted for a split second, before being hauled forward by the butcher on her right.

Fine. I'm going.

The march was short, as Kelly's house was one of the few outside the village limits nearer the shoreline, and yet in her perception it seemed to last forever. With each step, her legs felt heavier.

But soon enough, the outlines of the misty Black Isles came into view in the distance, illuminated only by moonlight. The crisp, cold sea shimmered in the light, like diamonds. Not that Kelly had ever seen a real diamond before, but she'd heard it said they were even shinier than fresh ice.

A glimmer of curiosity overcame her. That was where she was headed; if she was to believe the stories. What secrets did those dark rocks out in the Northern Sea hide? Nothing good, for sure.

The villagers surrounding her had initially seemed calm and reserved, but now on the rocky beach, their faces had become tenser, more nervous. *Typical,* Kelly thought, *I'm the one being served up to the barbaric giants, and they're the ones who are scared.*

The butcher's large, calloused hands seemed to be trembling slightly as he attached the rope from Kelly's wrist to the huge iron ring on the half-eroded sacrificial post. He didn't even meet Kelly's gaze, which despite the incoming darkness was burning with anger and betrayal. Her earlier tears had long faded in the harsh wind. All that remained was a growing urge to fight.

She'd find a way to escape. She had to.

"Sorry, lass. May God be with ya," he whispered, before joining the procession again, ready to retreat back to the village.

Kelly pressed her lips together. God had nothing to do

with what was happening here. She watched scornfully as everyone backed away.

It was one of the rules of the ritual. No one shall remain with the offering. None shall lay eyes on the giants when they collect their prize.

Those rules were now etched into Kelly's mind, so often had she heard the stories. Every eight years, one of the coastal villages would put forth an offering. As prescribed, none of the girls had been seen since they were left at this exact spot.

This had been going on for as long as anyone in the village, even the elders, could remember.

All those lives ruined by such an archaic and stupid ritual!

There hadn't even been any sighting, any evidence that giants still roamed the Black Isles. None, except that the sacrificial post was always found empty the morning after an offering. Anyone could have taken those girls. Who knew what had become of them.

Kelly glared at the retreating villagers, last of whom was her father, who looked back once, but then hurried on home, or more likely, towards the tavern.

Bloody cowards, the lot of them.

How convenient to have a rule that nobody was allowed to stay and watch. Who knew who these giants actually were? Whether they even existed.

The last torch flickered away over the dune

surrounding the beach, and the sound of the drum faded into the distance. The ritual was over, and life could go on as normal until eight years from now when another girl was to be chosen from a neighboring village.

But for Kelly, the night was far from over.

A dense fog had rolled in from the Northern Sea, covering the beach like a damp blanket. Kelly blinked a few times, but was unable to see a thing. How long had she been here for? Minutes, hours? It was impossible to tell, although dawn still seemed impossibly far away.

Mother, don't leave me here.

Kelly's eyelids grew too heavy to remain open.

My darling, rest. You'll need it, a familiar voice seemed to say.

Mother! Was she dreaming already?

The regular crashing of waves had already hypnotized her. One could only be upset for so long, until it took a toll. Kelly tried her best to lift the heavy blanket of exhaustion; to stay alert. But it was hopeless. It would take a lot more than some fog to scare her awake.

CHAPTER TWO

roc held on to his sword tightly, the leather of his gloves creaking loudly under his powerful grip. He could hear it, despite the screeching winds and waves battering the wooden boat.

Although they were at peace with the men of West Hythe, one could never be too careful.

Every eight years, the humans had held up their end of the bargain, though. They had left a suitable young woman behind on the shore near their villages, and nobody had stayed behind to watch the giants' arrival or possibly interfere.

In any case, the timing of this exchange was carefully thought out: nights on the Northern Sea were always foggy this time of year. If anyone had stayed behind, they would have to be very nearby indeed to be able to see a thing. Looking around the wooden longship, Broc could see a lot of his people were much more excited about tonight's festivities than he was. Their chatter was even louder than the rhythmic drum setting the speed for the rowers. He hated to have to do this; to tear a young girl away from the only life she had known and take her to the Isles against her will. Sadly there was no other way to ensure the survival of their bloodline; without this tradition, Broc's people might become even extinct.

After the Great War, many of their number had fallen. Outnumbered, and overpowered by the sorcerers who had sided with humankind, their kind had retreated to the Black Isles and left the mainland to be ruled by men. However, their reduced numbers had meant that they would need fresh blood to replenish their line.

One can only interbreed for so long before things start to go wrong and madness sets in.

He had seen it happen with his own two eyes. If he squinted, he could just about see the shore through the dense fog. Luckily, his people had a lot better vision than the humans, meaning they could safely navigate the treacherous waters around Hythe Bay to collect the latest addition to their clan.

Broc had first pick, as was tradition.

There was no way he could get out of it either. He'd been king of the Black Mountain and surrounding isles for seven years, ever since his father had sailed off into the next realm.

It was time to start thinking about an heir, whether he liked it or not.

"Wonder what this one's going to be like," Rhea next to him remarked, her tone sharp with spite. Her comment was a reference to the trouble they'd had last time. Transitions could be difficult.

He glanced over at the strong young princess, his cousin twice removed, as she stared darkly over the water leading to the coast. It was obvious she'd wanted to be his queen, but it wasn't meant to be. A union between them would have been forbidden, in any case.

They were too closely related. And they even shared the same animal form.

Broc had always aimed to be a fair ruler; he could not make an exception to such an important rule for himself. The consequences would be too severe; the islanders' mating rules existed for a reason.

A king must do everything within his power to ensure a healthy heir is produced. In his case this had meant taking a human as his bride instead of the relative he'd grown up with. Although he hadn't made his intentions about this Reaping public yet, Rhea had guessed. And she had made it a point to openly express her displeasure.

Shortly before the keel of their ship threatened to hit ground, Teaq, Broc's half-brother and commander of the Black Isle armies, gave the order to steady the oars and drop anchor. Impeccable timing as always.

Broc observed as Rhea and Teaq shared a dark look. It was obvious they each disapproved of tonight's goings on for their own reasons.

"There she is," Teaq spat, unable to disguise his disgust.

His tone rubbed Broc the wrong way. It wasn't the girl's fault she had been sent to them as an offering in the Reaping. And what exactly had sparked Teaq's dislike of human females, Broc had not yet understood. "Remember, she will be shown the respect deserving of any citizen of the Black Isles," Broc spoke in a low, determined tone.

Teaq's jaw tensed, but he did not respond. "Yes, my king." Rhea averted her eyes from the shore and retreated to the back of the ship to stand watch over the waters behind them. As commander of the royal guard, it was her duty to ensure Broc wasn't ambushed.

"Just remember what we discussed," Teaq grumbled. "These are troubled times. The last thing we need is further complications within our own walls."

Broc nodded.

When their father had conducted the last Reaping ritual, the girl had found it incredibly difficult to adjust to her new surroundings. For some time it was feared they'd lose her to madness, but thankfully she had recovered and integrated into their way of life some months later.

They'd instituted a new rule; the newcomer would not be fully introduced into their ways until she had obviously adjusted to her new circumstances. Teaq had wanted for things to go much further; including keeping the girl on house arrest for the first month; something Broc had vehemently disagreed with. As king, the final decision had obviously been his.

They would keep her in the dark, figuratively, but she would be as free as any of the other inhabitants of the Black Isles. At least as far as her movements within the castle on Black Mountain were concerned.

Still, it was for the best to be cautious. She did not need

to know the truth about everything from the start. Humans did not handle it well when their views of the world were challenged.

"I wish you'd reconsider and at least let me put a watch on her. We do not know of her intentions," Teaq added.

Broc scoffed. *Her intentions.* This was just going to be some unfortunate girl who thought she was being sent to her death.

Just like the last ones.

Lately Teaq had grown more and more paranoid. They had enough to worry about with the threats from further out at sea. As long as the humans continued to hold up their end of the truce, their peace would hold.

"Alright. That's enough of that," Broc said. "We've laid down the rules already. But I won't have her treated as a prisoner under my rule. Let's get on with what we came here to do."

The many dozen or so soldiers onboard held their heads bowed as Broc strode past towards the port beam, which was by now perfectly lined up with the shoreline. Teaq signaled the all clear and jumped over the side, landing squarely on his feet in the waist-deep water. Broc followed.

They were back on track, but this wasn't the end of that particular discussion; Broc was certain of it. Teaq's stubbornness was in part because as the older brother he'd always expected to get first right to the throne. He wasn't good at following orders.

Too bad for him that their father, the late King Ryk, hadn't seen it that way. They had fought it out just like in the old days. Hand-to-hand combat.

Obviously, it was Broc's victory that had earned him the honor of ruling over the Black Isles. Whether Teaq liked it or not.

The salty water of the Northern Sea was close to freezing, but Broc—as well as the rest of his clan—were used to it. They were much better suited to cold temperatures than humans were.

Despite the saltiness in the air, Broc could smell the human from across the stony beach. Her scent was sweet, almost floral, with a hint of something sharp. Fear, perhaps.

His inner beast stirred. A new sort of sensation came over him. Although he hadn't even seen her yet, he knew how this Reaping was going to end. She would be his. And she would give him his much awaited heir. It was a bittersweet prospect.

The poor girl had no idea what was in store for her. Teaq took the lead, and Broc, flanked by two of his guards, followed towards the wooden post in the distance. Rhea stayed behind the men, keeping watch over the waters that separated them and the ship. The guards as well as Teaq had drawn their swords, just in case. Though the girl's was the only human scent in the air, they were trained never to make assumptions when it came to the king's safety.

Eight years since they'd last come here. King Ryk had been in charge of the last Reaping. How much had changed. Broc could now see the outline of a figure through the fog. She was tall for a human, though still a good two feet shorter than him, and clad in an ankle length cloak of some sort. Her curly hair blew wildly in the harsh wind, but there was no movement in her otherwise. Still, he could hear her heartbeat over the loud breeze. It was strong and regular; indicating that she was in good physical health.

As they covered the last few feet between them, her sweet scent almost overwhelmed his senses.

"Hold on." Teaq gestured at Broc to wait behind him, but Broc was similarly bad at following orders. "What's your name, girl?" Teaq demanded, as he towered over her.

The general's harsh tone startled the girl, causing her to let out a quick yelp. Although she was now shivering in the cold wind, she didn't cower like Broc had come to expect from previous offerings. After the initial shock of finding herself no longer alone on the windswept beach, she had recovered quickly.

Broc suppressed a smile. Teaq's attempt to intimidate her had failed.

"Kelly," she said in a firm voice. "Kelly Chaslain."

This was ridiculous. There was no threat here. "Well then, Kelly Chaslain of West Hythe." Broc stepped forward, and signaled Teaq to remove her bonds, who grudgingly obliged.

"I am Broc Bearclaw, King of the Black Isles." She blinked at him a few times, her eyes glazed over and dull; her eyelids were heavy with exhaustion. Poor girl, she must have had quite the ordeal behind her already. Still, she was in excellent shape, all things considered. "And now you are coming with us," Broc said. "So it's true," she whispered, before her eyes closed and her knees gave way underneath her.

Broc reacted quickly and caught her, just about. He wrapped her up in her woolen cloak and lifted her up in his arms.

How tiny and fragile she was.

Just at that moment, the fog lifted just enough to let some moonlight filter through. Her complexion shone almost white, her face flawless and unscarred, surrounded by a fiery red mane the likes of which Broc had never seen before.

Of all the human women he had ever laid eyes on, not one had been as enthralling.

The vision before him almost made him forget his reservations about the Reaping ritual. *Almost.*

He caught himself a couple of seconds later, and forced his gaze away from Kelly's unconscious form.

Broc nodded at Teaq and the guards.

It's time to leave. They turned, retreating towards the ship with their latest clan member: Broc's new queen, Kelly

Chaslain of West Hythe. Undoubtedly the most beautiful human alive.

Would she adapt to their ways? Would she accept her role by his side as queen of the Black Isles? Would his people accept *her* as such?

Only time would tell.

CHAPTER THREE

hadows circled Kelly. Inhumanly large figures, entirely in black. The clanging of weaponry and armor. A flag, flapping overhead, attempting to compete with the crashing waves.

But among all the confusion, there was something familiar. A smiling face. Red hair like her own.

You're not alone. You're safe here.

"Mother?"

Kelly startled awake, and covered her mouth with both hands to stop herself from screaming. Her heart beat so hard, the sound of it seemed to echo against the walls of the cell she found herself in.

She closed her eyes again and inhaled deeply. The memory of her dreams was already fading. Where was she?

Kelly blinked a few times. Her surroundings were unfamiliar. The dark, almost black stone walls looked like they belonged to a castle, not an ordinary building like the ones in her village. The bed she'd found herself in was much bigger than normal, both in width as well as length, meaning she had at least three feet of space below her feet despite being fully stretched out.

Even the heavy wooden door was impossibly tall. There was not much light, no windows that she could see, just a flaming torch attached to an iron fitting on the wall.

They had taken her. The giants that came to the beach.

She was on the Black Isles somewhere. A barren rock in the middle of the Northern Sea.

Kelly rubbed her eyes, and tried to remember what exactly had happened. The last thing she recalled was a face appearing above her in the dark of the misty beach. Two black eyes, set deeply in an angular, masculine face. His full beard covered part of a scar that extended from his high and pronounced cheekbone down to God only knows where.

It was the face of her captor: Broc Bearclaw. King of the Black Isles.

Everything after that was so fuzzy, it was beyond her reach.

Remembering his introduction gave her shivers all the way down her spine. She had tried not to show fear, to appear brave, but his deep, almost threatening voice had made her weak inside. And that was ignoring how impossibly tall he was.

Of course they're tall. They're giants, after all!

Now that she was alone, recounting these events in her head, she was second-guessing everything that had happened during their first encounter. Why on earth had she introduced herself with her mother's maiden name rather than her own family name? What difference did a name make when you were going to be a prisoner, anyway?

All she could recall was that saying her mother's name aloud had given her some semblance of strength. If only she had still been alive today, she would have never allowed Kelly to be taken as a sacrifice. All Kelly had for support was that name.

Kelly shook her head. She had to focus, if she was going to get through this somehow.

She looked around again.

This room where she had been left almost seemed too comfortable considering her desperate situation. She was their prisoner now, their slave, and yet, the bed on which they laid her down was more comfortable than the small cot she'd shared with Ferris for as long as she could remember.

She leaned up on both elbows and noticed that she was no longer wearing the same clothing as last night. Instead of her sensible long frock, with the woolen cloak, she was now clad in a soft, shimmery nightgown. The thought of someone taking her clothes off while she was unconscious made her feel even more vulnerable. She could only hope these people—no, these giants, had made a female perform that particular task, otherwise the shame would be unbearable.

They *had* females here, didn't they?

Her thoughts were interrupted by a loud metallic click and the creaking of the door. Quickly, Kelly dropped back into her soft pillow and closed her eyes, pretending to still be sleeping.

"Aw, look at that, she's still resting," a deep, yet unmistakably female voice said.

Kelly breathed a near silent sigh of relief. At least it wasn't the king, or the other, even scarier giant who had collected her from the shore.

"Humans… And to think that *they* won the mainland, whereas we have to live on this miserable rock in the water," another female sneered.

Kelly's heartbeat sped up so much, it was almost deafening in her own ears. Still, she didn't move a muscle.

After she heard the clanging of metallic objects near her, two sets of footsteps shuffled away and the door creaked again, shutting with the same metallic click.

Carefully, she opened her eyes and noticed a platter with a dome shaped cover on the table beside her. She lifted it and immediately the delicious scent of bacon entered her nostrils. Her stomach spasmed painfully, reminding her of how hungry she was. Although she had planned to be cautious, she couldn't resist.

She'd need her energy if she wanted to escape later. At least that was her justification. Surely they wouldn't have brought her here just to poison her first meal?

So she ate like it was her last meal on earth, because perhaps, it would be. Once they noticed she was awake, who knew what would happen.

Surprisingly, the food was amazing. Kelly hadn't considered that a bunch of barbarians living out in the sea would know good food when they saw it.

Yet the bacon, as well as the bread, were as good, if not better than what she had grown up with. On those rare occasions her family could afford bacon, that was. Their staple fare had been eggs from their own chickens, and stew made of the various vegetables that grew on their land.

A pig was a rare and prized possession on the mainland. Not many could afford it.

As soon as she had finished dabbing up the last crumbs of food from the pewter plate with her finger tip, something stirred in the dark far corner of the room. She was so startled she dropped the platter, which made an almighty racket upon hitting the stone floor.

That part of the room was so dark, she hadn't noticed anything—or anyone—there before.

"Well," that same impossibly deep voice she'd heard when they picked her up at the beach said. "At least you've got a good appetite. Not like the last one."

With a loud creak, the figure stood up from what must have been a big chair or bench hidden in the shadows.

Kelly was breathless and terrified, as she tried to scurry away backwards. The headboard prevented any further retreat.

The large outline of the giant man came into view, details on his strange attire shimmering in the dim light of the torch on the wall as he approached.

Broc, the king of the giants, Kelly remembered.

"How long have you been watching?" Kelly stammered.

"I entered with Rhea and Bree when they brought in the food."

Kelly blinked at him in disbelief. He snuck in with the two females? She hadn't heard his footsteps, or noticed his presence at all.

"We can be stealthy when we want to be," the man grinned, making something inside Kelly's chest stir.

Although he was terrifyingly tall, and built like an ox, now in the privacy of this room, his face wasn't as menacing and scary as it had seemed in the darkness of the beach. The warm light from the torch on the wall helped.

"I see."

"Now that you're awake, perhaps you ought to get dressed and get to know your new family." The way he spoke suggested a certain unexpected warmth. After all the stories she'd heard growing up of the barbaric giants, she hadn't considered that they were capable of compassion.

"What's going to happen to me?" Kelly whispered, still confused about what fate would be in store for her.

"I understand this isn't what you wanted for yourself. Believe me if there was another way, we'd do away with the Reaping ritual." Broc paused for a moment, then added, "Where we take in a human girl once every eight years."

Kelly slowly shook her head, no, this wasn't how she'd

wanted her life to turn out.

"It's a necessity for us, for our survival. But you'll learn about that soon enough. What matters is that you're safe here. You'll not be harmed."

Another sigh of relief escaped her lips before she could regain her composure.

Kelly suddenly remembered the voice she'd heard in her dreams. Her mother's voice.

You're safe here.

He sounded genuine, and she desperately wanted to believe him. She had worried so much already. She was exhausted.

If he was speaking the truth, perhaps she should go along with it all to gain the giants' trust and an opportunity to escape would present itself soon enough. Whether they were compassionate or not, she still had no intention of staying on this island any longer than necessary.

Broc turned and reached the door in barely two strides, turning back just once. "Bree left a few things for you in the wardrobe. I can send her in to help dress you."

Remembering the sharp comments from the two women who had brought her food, she quickly shook her head.

"No, I think I'd prefer to get ready on my own."

Broc shrugged, then turned the iron handle on the door, opening it with the same almighty creak it had made before.

He'd lock it from the outside, no doubt. There'd be no point in trying to open it myself once he's gone, Kelly thought glumly.

As soon as the large wooden structure clicked back into place, Kelly attempted to stretch the lingering exhaustion out of her tired shoulders. Passing out from fear did not make for a good rest.

She turned, and hung her legs down the side of the bed, noting that it was quite a bit taller than beds were back home. *Of course it was.*

Everything was bigger here, including the people.

Kelly took a few careful steps towards the large wardrobe, also in the dark corner of the room, and waited for her eyesight to adjust. The cold of the stone floor stung the bottom of her feet, but at least the air wasn't too chilly, letting her take her time rifling through the unfamiliar fabrics hidden behind the wardrobe's beautifully carved doors. Eventually, she picked out a gown of sorts that wasn't as elaborate as most of the others, though without taking it over to the bed, she couldn't make out exactly what color it was. How did these people live in these dark and gloomy conditions? Did they not need to see?

She stumbled back into the light and lay the gown across her mattress to take a better look.

It was a deep burgundy, like poppies about to wilt. She ran her fingertips over the smooth fabric down the front, as well as the intricate metallic looking embroidery at the neck line. She'd never seen a dress this ornate and elegant before. It was certainly vastly different from the plain woolens she was accustomed to wearing.

Turning it over, she noticed there was a lace-up back, and suddenly Kelly regretted refusing the help she'd been offered. Disappointed, she went back to the wardrobe, picking out another two gowns, a black one and a golden one. Upon closer inspection the latter seemed a bit more loose fitting and easier to manage on her own.

Kelly put it on, and bemoaned the lack of a mirror in the room. She could only hope she looked somewhat presentable. The moment she had finished adjusting the braided belt around her waist, the door clicked again and revealed the tallest woman Kelly had ever seen.

"My name is Bree, I'm supposed to assist you in any way possible. Your name is Kelly Chaslain, am I right?"

The woman, Bree, towered almost a foot over Kelly, who was already above average height compared to the other girls from her village.

Kelly nodded, but was lost for words otherwise.

"Broc requests your presence in the main hall. I see you're already dressed. Good. Will you follow me?"

Looking back at the two discarded gowns on the bed, Kelly hesitated.

"Don't worry, I'll take care of those, Kelly Chaslain," Bree said with a smile.

"Thanks," Kelly mumbled, "You can just call me Kelly." She clumsily followed Bree toward the door. It took her almost four steps to cross the same distance the king had previously travelled in just two steps.

It occurred to Kelly that she had felt out of place most her life, because she was broader, taller and not as delicate as the other girls. Yet here, on the Black Isles, she felt so small. Under any other circumstances, the entire situation would almost be funny.

CHAPTER FOUR

roc's position at the head of the main banquet table was perfect to oversee the rowdy company he found himself in. His subjects were in a very good mood indeed.

He himself had been thoughtful, until movement at the other end of the hall caught his attention.

Suddenly it became easy to ignore the goings-on around him, as Kelly, his human, walked into the Great Hall. A vision in gold, the new dress she had worn had transformed her from the diamond in the rough they'd found on the beach to a jewel worthy of kings. Even her mannerisms had changed, or so it seemed, as she elegantly placed one foot in front of the other, reluctantly heading towards Broc's throne.

She was tall, for a human, and her figure was unlike any of the Black Isle females. Soft curves, rather than hard muscle, hidden underneath the delicate, flowing fabric of her gown… Watching her made him forget his aversion to this particular tradition.

She was to be his bride, no question about it, and at this time he did not feel unease, but pride instead. Through their interaction earlier, he had also seen that she wasn't as meek and fearful as he had expected human females to be. Of course his presence had startled her, but her questions suggested curiosity rather than despair. With a bit of luck she would adjust quickly; learn their ways and make them her own.

Then, they could learn all there was to know about one another. Even Black Isle's biggest secret.

Broc continued to watch as Bree guided the human through the crowd of men and women, who were already well underway in their celebrations. The Reaping had always been an occasion for everyone; an excuse for a lavish celebration that would last for days, commemorating the new addition to their clan and the promise of their continued survival.

It was a welcome change from their daily routine. It wasn't easy, feeding the giant appetites of the islanders. And on top of that they had to continue defending their territory, as well as the mainland, from the threats that originated further out to sea.

His people had a lot going for them, but an easy peace was not one of them.

"Please, join us." Broc waved Kelly over towards the seat to his left. The ornately carved chair wasn't as imposing as his own throne, but it was appropriate for her future position in his court.

The much cruder seat to the right of course was already occupied by Teaq, who despite the promise of ale to mark this joyous occasion could not stop himself from glaring at the human. Thankfully she seemed not to take notice.

Kelly nodded and clambered backwards onto her chair, her face reddening when she finally met Broc's stare.

"It's a little tall," she explained dryly, before smoothing down her dress and diverting her gaze toward the festivities going on in the rest of the hall.

Broc could not suppress a smile. The human, she seemed to have a sense of humor.

"Although the feast is about to begin, I felt it prudent to send you some breakfast. You had been sleeping for quite a while," he said, changing the topic.

Kelly looked up at him in surprise. "How long?"

"A day." Noting the shock in Kelly's eyes, he added, "Don't worry, it's not uncommon during the transition." She opened her mouth slightly, as though she wanted to say something, but their moment of quiet was interrupted by an outburst from the crowd seated in front of them.

"What are we waiting for?" someone shouted.

"We want more ale!"

The islanders roared and some banged their empty tankards rhythmically onto the battered wooden tables in front of them.

"And wine!" one of the older members of the castle guard shouted, while raising a pewter chalice up into the air.

Even the small group of normally very sedate Elders was starting to become vocal.

Broc got up from his throne, his hands raised in an attempt to control the commotion.

"My dear men and women of Black Isle. Settle down!" Broc spoke with authority, without raising his voice much. Still, quiet spread around the hall as his subjects found their way back to their seats.

"Tonight we celebrate a new Reaping!" Again, the crowd cheered, some of the more excitable men clanging the butts of their swords or axes against the tables and benches.

"As you know, it has been eight years since our people have been blessed with new blood. The last time the lucky man was Elog of the Shard." Broc raised his tankard, his gesture mirrored by his followers. "And we all know how that turned out!"

Broc's latter remark sparked cheers, whistles and laughter.

"Bastard hardly leaves the house, I hear," Teaq remarked. Despite his still grim expression, he got up and clanged his tankard to Broc's.

"To Elog!" Teaq cheered, before sitting back down.

"Five beautiful children!" Broc exclaimed, met by an even bigger ruckus from the crowd. "To ensure the future of our clan!"

"May all our unions be as fruitful!" a booming voice shouted from across the room.

"May our ranks swell to their former glory!" the crowd responded in unison.

"May our honor be restored!" Broc replied. "Let the

feast begin!"

As soon as Broc finished speaking and sat back down in his ceremonial seat, some of the seated giants got up and vanished through the double doors towards the side of the hall, before re-emerging with trays laden with roast wild boar, smoked whole fish, lobsters and other seafood, as well as breads of varying shapes and colors. Numerous barrels of ale and wine were rolled in, one of each per table, and empty tankards and platters travelled the lengths of the crowd back and forth until everyone's plates were full and the feast could begin.

"Here you go," Bree said as she approached Kelly, handing her a large chalice.

The latter seemed taken aback by the festivities unfolding in front of her. She was observing everything and everyone with wide, curious eyes.

"Don't worry." Broc leaned over and tried to reassure her. "They're a good bunch. Our circumstances don't permit celebrations like this too often so we try to make the most of it."

"What circumstances are those?" Kelly asked. Broc's expression turned serious. The firmness in her voice had surprised him.

"We may be in the midst of a truce with the people of West Hythe, but life on a rock in the middle of the Northern Sea is far from easy or peaceful." He averted his gaze from hers, staring darkly in the distance. "There are things out there which the humans on the mainland couldn't dream up in their worst nightmares."

Teaq, who seemingly had just begun listening in on their conversation, subtly shook his head, probably as a warning.

Broc responded with a very brief and very silent glare. He watched as Teaq got up and left the table to join Rhea, who had taken a seat at the other end of the hall.

Just as well. If the two of them wanted to brood throughout the Reaping feast, that was their own choice. They might make a fine couple one day, if only they could get over their stubbornness.

"We tend to be preoccupied with what's on the Black Isles themselves," Kelly remarked.

This single statement drew Broc back into their conversation. What did the humans know of the Black Isles beyond what had been written into the treaty so many generations ago? The previous offerings had precious little knowledge of where they were being sent.

"How so?" he asked.

"Only last year, a young boy vanished while out crabbing at the bay. All that remained of him was the jute sack containing his catch for the day. Blood stained."

"And your people believe *we* were responsible?" Broc squinted at Kelly, curious how she might respond. Things were getting interesting now.

"Well you like your meat, don't you? That's what's been

said. That after growing tired of the taste of fish, the giants of Black Isle have developed a taste for human flesh." Kelly spoke in such a matter-of-fact fashion it sounded almost flippant.

Broc was surprised at her candor. Who would willingly divulge such a terrible story to the very same people who were supposedly responsible? Or did she have her own doubts about the truth in her tale and was just testing the waters?

"Human flesh isn't all it's cracked up to be. We much prefer wild boar when the craving for meat strikes us." Broc kept his expression straight as he raised up his plate as a form of proof.

Kelly, who had just taken a sip of her wine, seemed completely unfazed by the turn of their conversation. "I'm glad to hear it."

When their eyes met, he thought he could detect a hint of amusement. This human sure was different. A morbid sense of humor was something usually reserved for those hardened in battle. And Kelly, much like the other women who had joined their clan over the years, did not look like much of a fighter.

"After the feast, I would like to show you around if that's agreeable to you," Broc said.

Kelly nodded, and broke off a piece of bread from the platter that was currently making the rounds on their table. "I would like that very much, thank you."

They did not speak much for the remainder of the meal; the loud celebrations surrounding them prevented it. When Teaq returned with a fresh cask of ale, Broc figured it was just as well.

Still, he caught himself glancing over at his future companion, wondering what was going on in her head. He hadn't mentioned his intentions to her, yet, instead reserving that topic for a more appropriate time. Would she be agreeable?

His inner beast insisted she would have to be.

A blush had crept over her cheeks and the sweet, floral scent he had first noticed on the beach continued to tempt him even now. The celebration had suited her.

Broc tried to shake these observations for the time being and instead enjoy the evening, as Kelly seemed to do.

By the time the food had all but been finished, and the casks of ale and wine were near empty, the Reaping feast had progressed to the next stage, song.

Ancient melodies flooded the hall and those with good singing voices added the lyrics. The songs told of legendary battles, of the invasion of the mainland by the humans. Of sorcery and monsters living deep underneath the sea.

Some even told of his own people and their secrets; though the words were poetic and deliberately vague. *Taming one's inner beast*, that could be interpreted in any number of ways.

He noticed Kelly softly tapping her fingers along with the rhythm of the music.

Did they tell these same stories in West Hythe?

Did the humans, Kelly included, realize they weren't *just* stories?

If Kelly had any suspicions about the true nature of the people of the Black Isles, she certainly knew how to hide it.

Some of the men and women got up to dance, but Broc himself was content as an observer. Maybe he'd have the opportunity to dance with *her* one of these days. Once the uncertainty was over, and there were no more secrets between him and his future bride.

This was not that day.

CHAPTER FIVE

W hat was she thinking? Kelly couldn't believe she had just told the story of little Timothy's disappearance, all but accusing Broc and his clan of eating the boy alive.

It must have been the wine. Surely that, or whatever strange exhaustion that had overwhelmed her on the beach. Apparently it was all normal during her transition, whatever that meant.

Thankfully it seemed Broc had taken it well enough. His remark about wild boar had almost sounded like a joke, though she couldn't be certain.

For the remainder of the feast, she tried to keep her head down, and her conversation to a minimum to avoid further awkwardness. Thankfully the crowd started to sing soon after, eliminating the chance for further chats.

She was surprised to find that these barbarians were seemingly less cannibalistic than the stories of the village elders had made them appear. They also had great taste in food and wine.

Especially the latter had a very agreeable flavor, not too much of a burn, certainly not as sharp as the stuff her father used to drink when he thought she had gone to bed already. After only a few sips, she stopped feeling the slight chill coming off the dark granite walls of the Great Hall, her body instead filled with a pleasing warmth and cheeriness that seemed completely inappropriate for someone in her situation.

From what she had gathered during Broc's speech earlier, it seemed her role was not at all like that of a normal slave or prisoner. She was going to be a kept woman, responsible for providing healthy heirs for one of these wildlings. The fact that Broc had taken a personal interest in her and even made her sit by his side suggested she was going to be his bride.

This thought ought to fill her with dread, but somehow, their interactions had had a calming effect on her.

He had been respectful and decent, not aggressive and intimidating like some of the others. *Imagine if it had been the other giant, Teaq…* Kelly shuddered at the thought.

She couldn't help but steal a glance at the huge man by her side. She had never met any nobleman, never mind a king, but she imagined in the human world a feast like this would be conducted very differently.

The giants seemed to treat each other mostly as equals. Everyone, even the men, served each other when another's plate became empty. They treated each other as a family, with Broc firmly at the helm yet not exempt from jokes or even criticism.

It was a strange sight to behold, especially when it was a male offering a refilled glass or plate to a female. This type of thing would never happen in her village. There, especially the tavern was off limits for females, except for the beer wenches that worked there, whose position was certainly not enviable or respected.

Women were expected to take care of the home, while men went out and reaped the benefits of their farming or fishing efforts. That was the way things had always been as far as Kelly knew.

On this dark, cold island in the middle of the sea, everything she thought she knew about the world seemed obsolete. Her thoughts were interrupted by the occasional loud remark or question directed at Broc, which he responded to in the same controlled, quiet manner he adopted in all of his interactions.

He seemed like a good leader, well respected by almost everyone except perhaps Teaq, who Kelly had learned was his brother.

After a few rounds of drinks, even Teaq had cast off his earlier bad mood and properly joined in the celebrations. The dirty looks in Kelly's direction had also subsided as the night grew darker.

Perhaps she had been too quick to judge the giants, based on the snide remark she'd overheard in her room earlier. And of course, the better part of two decades listening to stories the villagers of West Hythe had told over open fires.

All this could still be just a ruse to get her to feel comfortable. However, Kelly doubted anyone, especially these exuberant people, could act so well while imbibing this much liquor.

Just the one glass full had gone to her own head significantly.

After listening to the various conversations and introductions over the past two hours, she now knew a few of the faces surrounding her a little better. There was Teaq of course, the commander in charge of Broc's army, Rhea, Broc's cousin and the most fearsome female Kelly had ever seen. Rhea also seemed the most disapproving of Kelly's presence, though Kelly still had no idea what caused her offense.

Broc had introduced her to some of the others at the first table as well, but she couldn't recall their names anymore. They all looked and acted alike, the only notable differences between them their different lengths and shades of facial hair.

At one end of the hall sat a few white-haired men in pale grey robes. The giants' elders. Kelly couldn't help but wonder how old they were. Their skin was so wrinkled and fragile. Like flakes of ash, about to turn to dust. And their beards, white as snow.

None of the senior inhabitants of West Hythe looked nearly as old as these men.

"If you're ready," Broc asked beside her.

She looked over at his outstretched hand and paused.

"I can show you around your new home now. They won't miss us." Unlike everyone around them, Broc was still his calm, controlled self. Either he'd not fully given in to the celebrations like the others, or he must have had an incredible amount of self-discipline not to let it show.

Kelly nodded and slid off her chair, accepting Broc's hand to keep her steady.

That wine really had been quite strong. She took a deep breath and focused on placing one foot ahead of the other, while keeping her head high as to not show weakness. Thankfully the floor did not feel quite as cold as it had before.

In fact she could not really feel her feet at all anymore. It was like she was floating.

Broc adjusted his long strides to match her pace better as they weaved past the banquet tables where the other giants were still eating, drinking and making merry.

A guard opened the large double doors at the side of the main hall and Broc and Kelly stepped into a dark corridor lined with the occasional torch on the wall. These giants really needed to address their lighting situation. The dim glow of the torches was not enough for her poor eyes.

Kelly was apprehensive about where they were headed, but then reconciled herself with the fact that if Broc had any ill will towards her, there was nothing she could do about it. She was at his mercy, so she might as well not worry about it.

After making it to the end of the corridor, around a couple of corners, Broc led her through a doorway, where all of a sudden a gust of wind chilled her to her core.

The vista stretched out ahead of her was breathtaking. Dramatic grey clouds lined with silver where the moonlight passed by them; the gurgling dark waters below seemed to hide all manner of evil. They stood quite high up on a plateau of stone surrounded by a fortified wall just low enough for her to peer over, yet high enough to keep her from being swept up by the wind.

Despite the cold, and the powerful gusts, Kelly stepped forward and placed her hands on the cold stone wall, allowing her to lean forward slightly. Perhaps a hundred feet below the platform, Kelly could make out the rocky mass of the island which the fortress had been built upon. The seas ahead of them were broken apart by the occasional sharp cluster of rocks, shiny yet black in the subdued moonlight.

"It seemed prudent to take you here first. On a calm day the mainland is visible from here, but not on a night like tonight." Broc looked down at her.

Perhaps still due to the wine, she broke character and met his gaze directly. His eyes were still black, but there was nothing dark or ominous about them this time. She thought she could see a certain kindness in them, along with a fiery warmth that set her heart alight.

How was it possible that this giant, this warrior who should instill fear in her, seemed so welcoming and even friendly? How could she possibly continue to distrust someone with such honest eyes? And yet how could she possibly put her faith in someone who would abduct a girl such as herself once every eight years just because it was written into a treaty?

None of it made any sense.

Broc broke eye contact at last, and cleared his throat.

"You must be freezing. Let us continue on." Broc placed his large hand on the back of Kelly's shoulder, sending an even more intense shiver down her spine than the icy winds had already done. Although she found it hard to let go of the impressive view, she did allow herself to be guided back indoors.

The rest of their stroll around the imposing castle was mostly quiet, except for the occasional explanation from Broc. All of it, from the stairs leading down to the dungeons, the wing set into the mountain containing the chambers of everyone who lived here, right up to the drawbridge and gate that led to the harbor, merged into one in Kelly's mind. There was no chance of her ever finding her way around this place. There were no markings to remember anything by. All corridors, rooms constructed out of granite blocks, or sometimes hewn straight into the mountain itself, looked too alike.

And all of it was barely lit up.

Kelly felt her eyes grow heavier and heavier as they walked through the maze of stone. Her supposed new home, until she could find a way off the island, that was.

At last they stopped in front of yet another ten foot tall

wooden door with iron hinges that looked identical to all the other ten foot tall wooden doors with iron hinges Kelly had seen this evening.

"Your chambers," Broc said, as he turned the handle with the click and creak she had become familiar with earlier in the evening. "I'd lead you back to the feast, but you look exhausted."

Kelly stood confused for a moment, staring at the door first, then looking inside the room to convince herself that it was actually where she had woken up. No guards at the door? Not even a bolt on the outside? How was it possible that they'd kept her, a prisoner, here against her will, in a completely unsecured room on her own? What if she had tried to run immediately after getting up?

"Thank you," Kelly stammered, but suddenly her legs refused to move and she froze as if her feet had grown roots.

"Where are your chambers?" she finally asked.

Broc responded with a knowing smile and nodded his head towards a door just down the hallway towards the right of her room. The last door on this end of the corridor. "Only a few steps away."

Kelly bowed her head as she entered her bedroom, thanking Broc again for his hospitality, upon which he left, closing the door behind him.

The evening's events had sent her thoughts into a confused frenzy. She was going to be his woman, whether she wanted to or not. So why not just get right to it and claim her? Why all the politeness? If they hadn't shared that intense stare out on the lookout point earlier, she may have suspected that he had no interest in her. Clearly, he had.

Oh Mother, what is the purpose of it all?

Kelly closed her eyes and tried to make sense of everything that had happened to her so far. But this was not something she could unravel here on her own.

CHAPTER SIX

Broc knew his approach with Kelly was out of the ordinary. If for example Teaq been awarded a human bride, he would have just been his obnoxious self until she agreed to see things his way. He may have even forced himself on the girl if that was what it took.

His brother had never been the subtle kind. However, Broc could not bring himself to do it. He preferred to let nature run its course first to see where it would lead him with Kelly. There was no rush, yet. And if he had interpreted their moment on the Watch Point correctly, he was already gaining ground with her. When he surprised her earlier in the evening in her chambers, she had been afraid of him, obviously. But by the time he showed her the view from on top of the castle fortifications, something about her had changed. The way she had looked at him betrayed something other than distrust and hostility.

Perhaps all of this was just a fantasy on his part. A dream inspired by that first moment when he saw his future bride at the beach. An infatuation, mudding his otherwise impeccable perception and ability to read people—allies and enemies alike.

But there definitely was something about her that he

could not yet understand. For a simple farmer's daughter from the mainland, she had shown incredible resilience, and bravery. Many a human entering into their world had spent the first weeks in despair, mourning the loss of life as she knew it. Kelly had shown none of that so far. Perhaps it was too early to tell.

Broc's thoughts were interrupted by the distant click of a door. He knew it to be Kelly's, and he knew that anyone other than him - namely Teaq - would have locked her up or at least posted a guard outside.

What would be the point? Where could she run to? If she even found her way to the harbor, she wouldn't do so undetected. And then, she wouldn't be able to sail to the mainland in these stormy conditions. The weather on the Northern Sea was treacherous in early spring and human females did not know how to sail alone. No, it would be fine. Let Kelly roam freely inside the castle for now, let her get used to her new surroundings until she could fully accept her place here.

He listened out for further noises, but couldn't hear a thing, not even footsteps. She must still be barefoot. He'd instruct Bree to provide her with some suitable footwear before they ventured outdoors.

Soon after Broc gave up on trying to hear further signs of her movements, he heard the creak of yet another door. His own.

He opened his eyes, his vision already accustomed to

the darkness of his room, and found Kelly's silhouette pausing in the entrance. She wouldn't be able to see a thing beyond the dimly glowing torch on the wall, giving him the advantage in this case.

"Broc, umm, your majesty," her soft voice called out. "I do apologize for disturbing you."

He sat up, surprised that she hadn't intended to keep her presence secret. Perhaps the clever girl had realized that there was no chance of surprising a battle hardened warrior such as Broc in his sleep.

"Just Broc is fine. What's the matter?"

"Would it be permissible for me to ask a few questions? After sleeping for a day already, it's impossible for me to find rest now."

Kelly stepped inside his room, while keeping her head lowered.

Broc got up to light a candle on the glowing torch on the wall, and noticed her gaze wandering from the corner of her eye. She spent a few moments stealthily looking around the large yet sparsely furnished room, then finally lingered on him.

"Shall I wait until you're dressed?" she asked, still unwilling to look at him directly for a long time, yet seemingly unable to contain her curiosity at his half-naked form.

He had always favored sleeping in only his breeches. The cold air of the unheated room did not bother him.

"You *assume* I was planning to get dressed." Broc kept a

straight face, even though his comment was meant in jest. If Kelly was shocked at his candor, she didn't show it. Instead she stepped forward a couple of paces, her relatively short human legs carrying her about half the distance a giant's stride would have.

Curiosity overcame him. *What was she doing here?*

"Your questions?" Broc asked, before taking a seat on the heavy chair beside his bed.

"What is my purpose… here?" Kelly folded her arms in front of her, then unfolded them again. Clearly, the girl was nervous but trying very hard not to let it show.

"Every eight years a human woman is offered up by the men of the mainland." Broc's explanation was intentionally vague; he was trying to test her reaction. "You know this." It took a few seconds of stark silence for her to formulate a follow-up question.

"Am I to be *your* woman?" she finally asked.

Broc couldn't suppress a smile. Indeed this one was quite different. Cautious when necessary, but of strong character and unusually direct. In a way she was a good match for his people. Islanders who didn't care much for false niceties and play acting.

It was a relief that she hadn't asked anything he would be unable to share during the transition.

"That depends."

Kelly shot him a curious look, before averting her eyes towards the floor again. "I do apologize if that was too forward. It was the only thing that made sense. Since I was seated beside you at the feast."

She paused.

"But your behavior puzzles me."

Broc got up from his seat and stepped towards the girl, who instinctively flinched backwards only slightly. An involuntary reflex.

"*My* behavior, you say." He reached for her, guiding Kelly's chin up towards him until she couldn't help but look up into his eyes. There was something there, when their eyes met, a spark, a glimmer of something he'd first felt when he'd collected her from that dark beach, not even two days ago.

This mysterious force seemed to grow with every moment he spent in her presence, making him question his patience, second-guessing his plan to woo her slowly. It was a powerful sensation which normally only songs were sung about, but which was rarely discussed in the open. The sacred bond between a man and woman who were meant to be.

As she blinked quicker than normal, her thick lashes momentarily hid her light green eyes from view. He heard her breathing pause, then speed up again.

She felt it too. He could tell.

"How would you have me behave, my lady?" Broc shot her the swiftest of smiles, so quick it would be easy to miss.

"That I do not know. But I know I didn't expect...

this." The way her shapely lips moved with every spoken word all but drove him crazy. His inner beast told him to pounce; an urge that became harder and harder to ignore as he continued to look into her eyes. But at the same time she spoke to his protective side. Those instincts that had served him well as King of the Black Isles, that had ensured the survival of his people through many a battle. Kelly's heartbeat grew more frantic with every passing moment, Broc could hear it so clearly. At the same time her eyes seemed to turn a darker shade of green as her pupils dilated. Broc had seen that same look on other people's faces. Couples, who could or would not hide their feelings for one another from the rest of the world. He could no longer fight his desires, and leaned down, bringing his face closer to hers until her eyes fluttered shut. She wanted him too, he could smell the change in her.

His normally controlled demeanor made way for something entirely new and reckless. It had been his self-control which had won him the throne, seven years ago. But faced with her, alone in his chambers during this quiet hour, he became a different man.

Broc gently touched his lips to hers, then gathered her up in his strong arms and carried her towards the bed. She embraced him and pressed herself tightly against his hard, muscular chest, all the while returning his kisses with a passion he had not foreseen.

Full of surprises, this human. She was unlike anything

he could have imagined.

He laid her down on the plush pillows, her expression one of shock mixed with feverish anticipation. "I'm sorry, I don't know what came over me," she stammered.

Despite her initial protest, she embraced him again, running her hands over his shoulders and chest, down the trail of dark hair running along his chiseled abs. "No need to be sorry. I'm at fault." Broc leaned in again, tasting the sweetness of her lips until she instinctively parted them, allowing their tongues to meet for the very first time. Their tender, yet rushed explorations progressed until Kelly's touch lost all hesitation and reluctance and seemed to become one with her own base instincts.

It seemed that she didn't notice, or didn't care when he slipped the soft fabric of her nightgown off her shoulders, exposing more of her ivory skin. He could resist her no more, letting his hands explore the generous curves on her body which had enticed him from the beginning. All the women Broc had grown up with and lived amongst were hardened by battle, strong and capable fighters, just like the men. There was nothing soft or gentle about their bodies. He'd never thought about it before, but from the moment he'd seen Kelly, he knew he had been missing something.

By the way she moved against him, he could tell she was strong too, for a human. But she was also delicate, irresistibly fragile. Every fiber in his body was alerted to the fact that her safety and her happiness were now to be his first priority. He would protect her from harm, and do his best to give her anything she desired. At this moment, as he laid her down on her back, allowing her fiery red hair to fan out on his bed, he knew that she desired pleasure.

He climbed on top of her, taking care not to hurt her with his considerable bulk, and continued to kiss his bride as if it was the only thing that mattered.

Her arms surrounded him, pulling him closer against her, signaling she was far from satisfied yet. She seemed as fascinated with his physique as he was with her, tracing the outlines of his clearly defined muscles with her fingertips, gently scratching at the bit of hair running along the center of his chest and downward.

"I've never done this," she gasped in his ear, but her tone made it sound more like an invitation than a protest. "That's fine, my darling, let me show you," Broc responded.

There was much he still had to show her, but tonight he focused only on one thing. The secrets he continued to hide from her; they could wait.

He tore her nightgown open all the way, once again marveling at the extent of her beauty. Her soft curves demanded to be touched, to be worshipped by Broc's lips. And so he did just that.

They caressed, licked, tasted and loved each other's bodies until the first light of dawn made an appearance through the narrow window above the bed. They gave in to all their desires but one: the first time they'd let their bodies merge would be as tradition required it.

Once they were wed.

CHAPTER SEVEN

When Kelly finally awoke the next day, she found herself once again in the same room where she'd slept the first night. Somehow after all their illicit activity at night, Broc had mustered the effort to carry her back into her own chambers so she could rest late into the morning.

She stretched herself, finding her neck and parts of her shoulder inexplicably knotted and sore. By the time she got up, finding that she was indeed wearing the same nightgown again that had at some point been discarded on the floor in Broc's room, she couldn't help herself and let out a giggle, while wrapping her arms around herself.

But her visit to his room had left its mark; the gown wasn't quite the same anymore. In the heat of the moment, it had become torn at the neckline.

So this was what it felt like, to commit sin. But it hadn't made her feel weak and wicked, instead she felt powerful and re-energized. Perhaps her transition wouldn't be as bad as Broc had made it sound yesterday.

Kelly's night with Broc had been the stuff dreams were made of. Even though she had told herself at the start that she only intended to speak with him in his room, her mind was quickly changed by the half-naked giant she'd found after opening his door.

Never before had she seen a man whose body was so powerful and strong, yet who showed so much tenderness towards her. Some of the boys of her village had made attempts in private. They had teased and tried to tempt her, but she had never been interested.

She had never felt attracted to a man before.

And what a man he was.

Shortly after she sat up in the bed, her mind still reeling from the memories of their encounter, there was a knock on the door.

"Enter," Kelly said, in a tone that was surprisingly firm.

After the good old click-and-creak of the door, Bree appeared with breakfast and some leather strapped boots and other items she wasn't quite familiar with.

"Had a good rest?" Bree asked.

Kelly nodded, her face turning bright red in the process.

Bree squinted and gave her a long, good look, before letting her eyes rest on the torn seams of the night gown.

"I see," she said, and put the breakfast down on the table next to the bed.

Kelly's heart started to race with nerves as she waited for a comment or perhaps even a lecture.

"I've been requested to help you with these." Bree held up the boots, and something that looked like a brown leather bodice, with buckles and straps along the sides.

It seemed she was content to just ignore the evidence of Kelly's indiscretion. Did she not disapprove?

Kelly took a deep breath in the hopes it would get her nerves under control. "What are they?"

"The kind of attire needed to leave these walls," Bree clarified, without clarifying anything much.

Kelly decided not to question it, as her stomach had started to growl uncontrollably, so she focused on breakfast first. Perhaps food would help her ignore the aches she'd woken up with.

Bree busied herself with organizing the large wardrobe as Kelly ate, even though there hadn't been much time for things to get out of place. Perhaps Bree just enjoyed taking care of others. Kelly could understand, her mother had enjoyed that kind of thing too when she was still alive.

"Perhaps you would like to try this one," Bree suggested, after Kelly had finished her last bite and put the plate back down.

Kelly looked up to find her holding a dress much shorter and narrower than the gowns she was used to wearing at home. It also had a lace-up back, meaning it would be quite tightly fitted.

"Is that what those—" Kelly nodded at the leathers while speaking, "go with?"

"Indeed."

Although she wasn't quite certain she was ready to wear something so revealing, it did occur to her that a lot of the giant women at the feast had been wearing fairly similar dresses. In her village, a girl would be branded a harlot for less.

Then again, she wasn't in her village anymore. And last night's visit to Broc's room had been a lot more sinful than simply wearing a shorter dress. Kelly shrugged and nodded at Bree in agreement.

"I also thought you might want to take a bath first," Bree suggested in a tone that told Kelly this was yet another done thing on Black Isle. Fresh water was such a precious commodity on the mainland that Kelly had scarcely been afforded the opportunity to bathe every other week, and it had only been about four days since the last time.

Still, if she was going to fit into this place, she'd better behave like everyone else. Kelly didn't argue and followed Bree through a door off to the right of the large wardrobe, in that part of her room that was mostly too dark to see properly. She hadn't even noticed a doorway there before.

Of course she hadn't spent enough time in her room to properly explore it. A memory of the reasons why tickled her, making her smile as she walked through the hidden corridor, into a large square washroom.

Here the stone floor felt inexplicably warmer than in her bedroom, and the walls were adorned with glass shelves laden with strange little bottles in all shapes and colors. Kelly's eye was drawn to the door opposite to the entrance she and Bree had just come in from, which was opened to just a crack.

While Bree prepared her bath, Kelly decided to warm

herself by the fire pit in the corner and just observe. After filling water from a hanging metal tube into the large kettle shaped tub in the middle of the room, Bree collected a bucket full of glowing coals from the fire and placed them underneath. Clearly this was going to be a bath unlike any she'd ever experienced.

As they waited for the coals to do their job, Bree kept stealing glances in Kelly's direction until finally, Kelly caught on.

"What?"

"Oh I… I probably shouldn't pry. But those bruises on your neck…"

Kelly instinctively touched her neck where it still felt a little sore. How had this happened? Again, her lingering embarrassment about the previous night flared up.

Bree let out a laugh, which echoed against the stone walls of the room, making it sound even louder and deeper than normal.

"Don't be ashamed. You are to be wed, it's expected."

Kelly was well on her way to turning a deep crimson, not just on her cheeks but her ears as well. It had been a lot easier giving in to him than should have been the case. And she didn't intend for it to be discovered. She started to wonder if maybe the villagers, blaming her for her mother's death, had been right and there was something inherently wicked about her.

"We… Oh dear. I didn't realize I was bruised!"

"It will fade."

"How soon?"

"A few days perhaps, it depends. Humans heal slower, apparently." Bree still could hardly contain her amusement at Kelly's predicament. The tall female's smile was so contagious it didn't take long for Kelly to calm down as well.

"You say it's expected? Not where I come from." Kelly looked down at the coals, which were now covered with a sheath of white ash.

"No? Tell me." Bree stopped smiling, instead looking at Kelly with large, curious eyes.

It took around half an hour for the bath water to come up to a temperature Bree deemed acceptable, during which Kelly did her best to tell tales of her home. Of the rules, the way the villagers, including her father, treated their women, even of the observations she had made at the feast, where it seemed that everyone was more equal here.

By the end Kelly had Bree shaking her head.

"And they call us barbarians."

That last remark finally made Kelly smile wide, and she wondered if perhaps the giants ought to take girls from the mainland more often. Being stuck on this island didn't seem like such a bad thing after all.

Bree held out her hand, gesturing at Kelly to hand over the torn nightgown. Apparently she planned to stay while Kelly soaked in the warm water. She held back any protests about undressing in front of someone else, and took a deep breath before letting the soft, silky fabric fall down her shoulders and over her hips.

Although the female giant didn't say a word, Kelly felt her eyes darting back and forth between her, and the dress, as if she was trying not to look but couldn't help herself. Kelly awkwardly hurried into the tub, keen to be a little less exposed. The only other person to ever see her as she bathed had been her mother, and back then she'd only been a child.

As Kelly's body was enveloped by the warm water, she couldn't believe how wonderful it felt. Bathing had always been a necessary evil, and not very enjoyable during the colder times of year. Bree gathered up one of the glass bottles and returned to the tub, trickling a bit of the liquid into the water until the whole room was filled with the sweet fragrance of a summer meadow. It was magic.

Kelly closed her eyes, enjoying how her muscles—even her bruised neck—completely relaxed. Her thoughts travelled back to last night; how Broc had made her feel when he touched her so intimately. How everything she thought she knew about right and wrong suddenly seemed to fade until it no longer mattered. She wasn't in her village anymore. The rules of her people no longer applied.

Even though she knew Bree was still around, Kelly couldn't help but take some time floating like that with her eyes shut, thinking through everything that had happened so far. Only yesterday she had been focused on escaping at the first opportunity. But now, things didn't seem so clear cut anymore. The magnetic pull Broc had over her made her feel like becoming his wife was not so bad after all. Life in the castle seemed pleasant enough as well.

Today she was going to explore the rest of the island apparently, hence the boots. Kelly no longer felt the urge to run, but a little voice in her head still pressed her to keep the option to escape open, should she need it.

———— ◆ ————

"Whenever you're ready," a gruff female voice dragged Kelly out of her deep thoughts. She opened her eyes, blinking a few times to stop the damp steam from her bath from clouding her vision. Rhea.

"I'll ensure she gets dressed," Bree said. If Kelly had been uncomfortable getting into the tub in front of Bree earlier, she definitely didn't want to get out with Rhea watching now. Kelly shifted awkwardly in the water, looking around the room for something—anything—that would afford her some coverage. The tall blonde warrior had her arm propped up on her hip and kept staring down at Kelly.

She did not seem in a mood to leave.

Bree seemed to sense Kelly's discomfort and intervened. "Rhea, I said I'll ensure she gets ready shortly." Reluctantly, Rhea turned away from Kelly to face Bree, and shrugged her shoulders.

"Fine. Get her to the drawbridge in ten minutes." Rhea turned on her heel without even shooting another glance in Kelly's direction and vanished, pulling the door shut behind her with a loud thump.

"She doesn't like me," Kelly mumbled.

"Rhea can be peculiar. But she's not a bad person." Bree smiled at Kelly, but it didn't do much to reassure her. "Let's get you ready so we don't make her wait unnecessarily."

When Bree had come into her bedroom earlier, Kelly had hoped she was going to go out and explore the island with Broc, but as it turned out, she was to be accompanied by Rhea. Disappointing as it was, she tried not to let it show.

Bree handed her a large, soft cloth, and Kelly did her best to dry herself off without showing too much skin. Her shoulder felt a lot better after the bath, but the hot water had turned her entire body from a pale ivory to bright pink, making her feel even more vulnerable than before. Bree meanwhile brought in some alien looking undergarments, which Kelly clumsily put on, before they returned to the bedroom where the dress and leathers were.

It really was a rather short dress, unlike anything Kelly had ever worn even as a little girl. Even on top, she felt quite exposed, the deep neckline revealing a bit of cleavage, further accentuated by the tight bodice which Bree had expertly laced up from the back. Next, she put on the boots, which fit surprisingly well due to the many fasteners and buckles.

Next, Bree helped her put on even more leather over the dress, harder than that of her boots, as if it was meant to be some kind of protective plate covering her torso. A dark woolen cloak was to be worn on top as soon as she'd leave the castle. You never knew when the weather would turn during this time in early spring and it seemed much colder out here than on the mainland.

Kelly again wished she had a mirror, because looking down at herself, all she could see was bare skin. She felt ridiculous, but again kept her concerns to herself. The second Bree deemed her ready, after braiding her damp hair and pinning it upwards, she led Kelly through the door and down the various confusing corridors to where Rhea was waiting. The Drawbridge.

CHAPTER EIGHT

When Broc entered the large hall that only hours earlier had hosted the beginning of the Reaping feast, a small group of notable persons had already assembled. There was Teaq, of course, who had called the meeting, along with his right-hand man and commander of Black Isle's fleet of ships.

Then there were three elders; ankle length robes matched the pale grey of their thinning hair. The Black Isle way of life meant that surviving into old age was a luxury not afforded to many. When an islander reached a certain, ripe age, he either sailed off into the twilight or cast off his armor and weapons and dedicated himself to the study of their history and culture. Elders served as librarians, as advisors to the king and as developers of military strategy.

Yorrick, second in command of the castle guard, was present, though his superior, Rhea, was not.

So, nearly everyone who held an important position in his court was in attendance. Perhaps Rhea had better things to do this morning.

"Settle down, everyone!" As usual, Broc did not need to raise his voice much. The small group did indeed quieten down quickly and everyone found a seat.

The last one standing was Teaq, who held his position beside the entrance to the hall, with his arms crossed.

"Let us begin," Broc spoke up again, then turned to face Teaq. "Why are we here?"

Teaq cleared his throat. "The threat from the north is growing. We must prepare for war."

Broc frowned.

"Is there any particular reason for your suspicions?"

"The prophecy determines it, my king," one of the elders said.

Broc pressed his lips together. He did not rule based on guesswork and so-called prophecies. Stories and legends, that's all they were. Useful to learn from, in order to avoid making the same mistakes, but far from a roadmap for the future.

"There is something not right with the girl," Teaq said.

Broc felt the hairs on the back of his neck stand up. His patience for Teaq's growing paranoia was wearing thin.

Still, he composed himself before responding. "What exactly do you mean?"

"Call it instinct." Teaq straightened himself. "Something in her mannerisms. In her behavior. Remember I am more intuitive when it comes to reading body language. Benefits of my wolf lineage."

"It's all in the prophecy," the same white-haired man who had spoken a moment ago piped up again.

Broc shook his head. "Would you prefer if she spent her first days here, cowering in a corner, mourning the loss of everything she had known so far in life? Everyone's transition is different. The last one suffered exceptionally.

We've already taken steps to avoid a repeat of the same, and when clearly our new approach is working, you want to call it evidence of something—I'm not even sure of what."

Teaq glared at him. His brother wasn't accustomed to having his judgement questioned.

Then again, neither was Broc.

The two of them stared each other down for an awkward several seconds.

"I just want to make sure you know what you're doing. That you have thought things through," Teaq all but growled.

"We need fresh blood. That's not up for debate, just ask the Elders. And whether anyone here likes it or not, I need an heir."

"You seem to be liking it just fine in this case," Teaq mumbled.

"What? Speak up, so the entire council can hear," Broc warned.

"The girl has had an effect on you since the moment we collected her from the mainland."

Broc closed his eyes and inhaled deeply. His patience really was running out. Kelly was a beautiful woman, a fact he had noticed from the start. So what? He was king. Was he not deserving of a beautiful mate?

Had Teaq wanted her for himself? Was all this just jealousy on Teaq's part?

"An effect, you say. Is this all just preparation for a challenge? Let me know right now, so we can settle it."

"I just want what's best for our people," Teaq explained.

Broc raised an eyebrow. "What's best for our people is to have a stable rule, a royal union and hopefully soon after, an heir to the throne."

"You've made up your mind then. That you'll make her your queen," Teaq said.

Broc straightened his shoulders. "It is time we had a queen, don't you think? And the rules forbid me from taking one of our own as my mate."

"And I suppose you've had a taste as well. I can practically smell it on you."

Anger flared up in Broc's chest. "What of it? No rules were broken."

"What of the coming war?" one of the other elders interrupted.

Clearly it was only Teaq who was interested in dragging Broc's private affairs into this council meeting.

Broc forced his attention away from his brother. "What coming war? Do we have any proof of what's coming?"

"The prophecy…"

Broc sighed. "Fine. What does the prophecy say?"

"That during a time of great change, two moons before the summer solstice, a stranger arrives among our people who hides a terrible secret. a power that could win or lose wars, one that could destroy us or mean our salvation.

That this stranger's arrival brings with it the third great age of war as our enemies try to win this power for themselves."

Vague, as prophecies usually were. How convenient. Although he'd never voice these suspicions aloud, Broc had long wondered if the old scrolls contained so many riddles and vague language to keep the Elders busy during times of relative peace. One could debate for days about what a particular passage meant as everyone usually had a slightly different interpretation.

"And you're thinking the human is the stranger mentioned in the prophecy?" Broc asked.

"Who else?" The Elders had spoken in unison. So they were actually in agreement about something for a change.

"And her power?" Broc asked.

The Elders exchanged some looks among themselves. "We have some ideas, but we will find out for sure what it is only once it is too late," one said.

"So in short, there really is nothing we can do, except bar all *strangers* from the island. Something which we cannot afford at this moment in time, when we still need our arrangement with the humans to add some much needed variety to our blood line," Broc concluded. "Or is your advice to stop the Reaping ritual in its entirety?"

The Elders were silent for a moment. "Not exactly. The Reaping ritual is essential to our survival. We are not even certain the outcome of the prophecy can be affected as such. But we need to be aware and fortify our position nonetheless. The events leading up to the third age of war are set in stone. However, the outcome of the war is not yet foretold."

The Elders' position seemed a lot more nuanced than Broc had given them credit for. He nodded. "Very well. I see nothing wrong with being prepared for any and all eventualities."

"We should keep an eye on the human though," Teaq butted in.

"To what effect?"

"To learn of her powers, before anyone else does, of course!"

If she even has any powers. The notion that this innocent young woman hid a terrible secret was ludicrous. Her only power, as far as Broc could see, was her sense of reasoning and a certain level of intelligence which was sadly lacking in his current company.

As well as an amazing appetite for pleasure. The memories of last night lingered on Broc's mind.

"I ordered Rhea to take her out onto the plateau, to assess her fighting skills," Teaq added.

That explained why Rhea wasn't here this morning. The two of them were in on it together.

Broc slowly shook his head. He had been king for seven years now. Teaq hadn't liked it, but he had won the crown fair and square. Broc had always aimed to be a fair ruler; to listen to his people, and never let his emotions meddle in official business. This morning, things were not so clear cut.

He found it difficult to not let his feelings about Kelly influence the way he handled this latest development.

It was a load of rubbish, though. If you read through the old scrolls long enough, you'd find a prophecy or prediction for everything under the sun. Had the Elders really come up with this on their own, or had Teaq tasked them to look for something specific to fit his agenda?

And what had really sparked his paranoia about brewing wars and dangerous invaders into Black Isle territory? There had to be something more to this particular story.

Perhaps the explanation was as simple as Teaq finally losing his mind.

Broc had to find out what exactly was going on within these walls, but first he would make sure he'd get to know Kelly a bit more. His own instincts weren't usually so bad either, no matter what Teaq thought. Surely, if the human had any ill intent, he would have picked up on it by now.

"Regardless of what you and Rhea have come up with together, the transition is going ahead as planned. I expect that arrangements are made so that I may announce my intended union with Kelly Chaslain of West Hythe by the next full moon."

Teaq shook his head. "As you wish, but I—"

"It's not up for discussion," Broc interrupted. "You

heard the Elders. The events foretold in the prophecy cannot be stopped, so there's no point in trying. We *will*, however, prepare ourselves for the next great war. Build up our armory. Strengthen our castle walls. Test the war horns on all the Isles."

He turned to address the Elders. "If there is anything in our records to help us fight the Sea Folk… I don't have to tell you how helpful that would be."

"Yes, my king," the Elders spoke in unison. "We will read on it."

Broc finally turned to face Yorrick, who had stood by in silence, watching the entire argument with a pained expression on his face. It seemed obvious that this situation had been spearheaded by Teaq and Rhea, and Yorrick was just an innocent bystander, so Broc diverted his attention away from him again.

"And as we're preparing for a possible siege, I would suggest you, Teaq, take a group of our best hunters to the mainland to gather supplies. The Reaping Feast is continuing regardless, but it would be unwise to be left without any reserves after."

CHAPTER NINE

"Let's go," Rhea snapped, and signaled towards the guards to open the large gate. The huge wood and metal structure creaked into action, and soon they were able to walk out of the castle and onto the bridge.

Kelly was glad to have the woolen cloak, because the island was still being battered by freezing winds. Rhea, who was just wearing a short dress with a similar leather breastplate, didn't seem to mind the weather at all, and marched straight down the path carved out between the rocky mountain faces, heading towards the harbor hidden in between the cliffs.

Nobody could ever guess this was here, Kelly thought as she looked around. All one would be able to make out from the sea was the angular facade of the fortified castle, but the color of it matched the surrounding rocks so perfectly that it would be difficult for any human to distinguish from afar. The harbor was so completely surrounded by cliffs and spiky rocks, not only was it extremely well hidden, it would also be quite treacherous to sail in and out of.

"Are these all the ships or are there more?" Kelly asked, but immediately regretted it when Rhea gave her a foul look.

"What do you know of combat? Broc asked me to assess you, because any woman of Black Isle must be able to defend herself in battle." Rhea folded her arms as she waited for her answer.

This was a surprise. So they weren't exploring the island at all, but Kelly was meant to *fight?*

"Not much. On the mainland, women don't fight." Rhea scoffed and shook her head slowly, the disgust evident on her face.

"That does not surprise me. No problem, I'm supposed to teach you, follow me." Rhea turned around as quickly as she had initially stopped for her brief interrogation. Kelly just did her best, trying to keep up with the leggy female giant as she marched up the slight incline leading around the harbor, towards a door set into the mountainous rock.

"Wait here," Rhea barked, as she took a key from a little pouch on her belt and removed the lock from the heavy, weather damaged door.

Kelly observed her as she disappeared into the dark cavern beyond the door, reappearing shortly with two rather large sword-shaped pieces of wood as well as two metal weapons of a similar shape and size.

Mother, help me.

Kelly eyed the weapons glumly but tried not to let her apprehensions show. These were a lot bigger and heavier looking than the sticks she and Ferris had play-fought with when they were younger. At the time she had been able to keep up with most of the village boys in similar sparring games, but Rhea was a much more intimidating opponent.

"Follow me," Rhea said, marching back down the path, around the harbor, and up some winding stone steps leading higher up into the mountainous center of the island.

They hiked for a while, at least an hour at what was a brisk pace for Kelly, with not a word said between the two of them.

How long would this go on for? How would she have energy to spar with Rhea after such a long hike? By the end of it, they reached some kind of plateau, only partially screened off from the land below by low shrubs and the occasional tree that had clung on to the otherwise rocky ground. The landscape lower down was also mainly stony, except for a few patches of greenery which surrounded a couple of small huts that clung to the hillside. After seeing nothing but black stone ever since arriving on the island, Kelly felt a surge of excitement at the small glimpse of familiarity ahead of her. Although slightly different in style, the huts looked vaguely similar to the farm buildings used in her village.

Other than that, there was nothing of note in the landscape that Kelly could see. Just more sharp looking rocks and peaks, and just a small patch of pine trees lower down towards the shore. The waters surrounding the island looked as hostile and untamed as the sea in front of the castle, and spiky rocks stuck out of the surface all around the perimeter. There was no way one could swim to the mainland from here; anyone stupid enough to try would be smashed to death against one of those cliffs. After a few moments catching her breath, Kelly noticed that Rhea had been staring at her.

"It's quite different from the mainland, isn't it?" Rhea asked.

"A bit."

"You know before your people turned on us, we didn't have to live in this miserable place." Rhea's bitterness shone through in her tone, as she almost spat out her words.

Kelly reminded herself of Bree's words, that Rhea wasn't a bad person. That was why Rhea was angry, she felt the humans had taken her home away, no matter how long ago.

"We lived in peace, and then your King Edrick came over the No Man's Range to the south and burnt down our villages in order to take the mainland for himself." King Edrick, Kelly had heard of him in some of the ancient tales. The village elders had spoken of him like a great and fearsome warrior, who had banished all evil from the northern lands, making them a safe place for mankind to live.

"I didn't know…" Kelly stammered, not wanting to upset the female fighter beside her, especially while she was carrying all those weapons.

"Oh, it is true. That swine came and tricked us before he murdered our children and raped our women. At the same time the Sea Folk attacked from the water and we were overrun. The only way we could survive was by coming here."

"And the treaty?" Kelly asked. The treaty that everyone in the villages on the mainland was so disapproving of, the one that meant sacrificing a young girl—Kelly in this case—to keep the peace.

"That. That came after. The elders of the Hythe approached our king at the time, Nerys, one winter many years ago. They proposed an exchange, they'd choose one of their kin every eight years as an offering to our clan, in exchange for protection from the dangers that lie further out to sea." Rhea stared darkly at the waters that lay beyond the shoreline.

"I don't know why he ever agreed to it. He should have insisted on a safe haven for our people on the mainland, rather than fight to protect the cowards who put us here. Instead he accepted their terms."

Kelly was taken aback by Rhea's story. The events of the Great War between humans and giants had been a popular tale to tell at the occasional village feast. Only in the version of her childhood, King Edrick was a hero, and the giants were a fearsome evil needing to be wiped from this earth. The proper story she knew did not feature any enemy from the seas beyond the Black Isles. And the so-called Sea Folk, people who lived underneath the seas, were rejected as myth by most, including her father.

But what did she know. She'd only been on this island for a couple of days.

And before that, Kelly herself had been wondering if even the giants were only a myth. After all, no one in her village had ever seen a live giant before and lived to tell the tale.

Could it be that there are other strange beings out there? Right now, looking at the strange landscape surrounding her, flanked by a 6 and a half foot tall woman, it seemed entirely plausible.

"Enough talk. Let's start what we came here to do." Rhea turned to face Kelly, and threw a wooden stick in her direction, which Kelly caught surprisingly easily, before putting the real swords down on a flat rock beside her. "You're holding it wrong."

Kelly looked at the positioning of Rhea's hands and tried to copy her. She was somewhat in shock that they were actually going to *fight*. She wasn't ready.

"Better, now come at me and try to stab me with it," Rhea ordered.

Hesitating for a moment, Kelly tried to tighten her grip on the rough wood, but a few splinters cut painfully into her palm. "It's broken," she protested.

"It's broken," Rhea copied Kelly's tone and let out a loud, disingenuous laugh. "Try telling your enemy that in the middle of a battle."

When am I ever going to be in a battle with anyone? Kelly thought.

Rather than wait for Kelly to make a move, Rhea charged in her direction with her wooden sword held high up in the air. Kelly instinctively stepped aside, dodging Rhea's attack, then indeed tried to stab her, only to have her stick swatted away and out of her hand, clattering onto the ground several feet away from the two women.

Kelly was shaking and sweat broke through her cold skin.

"Now do it again."

Although the walk up the mountainside and back down again had tired her out quite a bit, Kelly rubbed her wrist, which ached from the impact of Rhea's disarming blow, and picked up her practice sword again.

Mother, give me strength!

She did not last much longer in the second round. Or the third, or fourth.

Throughout the practice session with Rhea, Kelly felt in conflict with herself and her upbringing. This wasn't the game she had played with Ferris when they were young.

If her father could see what she was doing, learning how to *properly* fight with a sword, he would drop dead of shock. At the same time, she understood that this was the way things were in this new world. Perhaps if she tried her best to grasp at least the basics of the training Rhea was trying to give her, Broc would be proud of her.

That was her main motivator now.

Only yesterday she might have considered how this training might help her escape this place. Now, she kept on catching herself wondering what it would be like to become Broc's bride.

In a very short two days, Kelly had completely changed her outlook.

After numerous rounds, during which Rhea managed to knock the wooden stick out of Kelly's hand every single time, they paused for a while. They sat down on the flatter rocks towards the edge of the plateau on which they stood and rested in silence. Despite the winds still battering the island from seemingly all sides, Kelly felt warm enough to remove her cloak.

Kelly remembered some of the things Broc had told her. About how hard life on these islands was. Seeing the scenery out here drove things home for her.

How did one feed so many hungry giants, when there was no land here suitable for farming?

Except for some seagulls circling the skies, Kelly hadn't seen a single animal on the way over here. No sheep; not even any chickens or rabbits.

And yet at the feast, they'd enjoyed a wealth of foods. They didn't trade with the mainland, except for the Reaping. And if these so-called Sea Folk kept on attacking them, they probably didn't trade with them either.

So where had all the meat come from?

Her curiosity was sparked yet again, but looking at

Rhea's grim expression, Kelly kept her questions to herself. Perhaps she'd get the chance to ask Broc about all this.

If indeed she was going to stay here, she might as well understand this place and its people better.

CHAPTER TEN

They ate, they drank, they made merry. The second night of the Reaping feast had gone by much like the first.

Broc admired the way Kelly carried herself. She was adjusting.

Even the long day of training with Rhea hadn't dampened her spirits.

"Everything is fine, isn't it? I mean, *you* are fine?" Broc had asked her when he first saw her, just to reassure himself. A day alone with Rhea... that could have gone any number of ways.

She had smiled and placed her hand on his briefly.

"I am," she'd said, before elaborating in a more playful tone. "Better now to be sitting here with you."

Now, as he looked down on her, naked and fast asleep in his bed, he could see that perhaps she had underplayed things a little.

She'd had a hard day. These marks on her arms and legs hadn't been there before. Red grazes covered her lower arms and her knees, down to her shins. They weren't deep, but they stood out starkly against her ivory skin.

His kind healed so fast, he'd never seen anything like it before. It stung, to see her this way.

Although she'd shown the same enthusiasm, the same

passion as the night before, her touch had changed. She wasn't as free in her movements. Had she been in pain?

He would ask her, except he didn't have the heart to wake her up. She so very clearly needed the rest.

If Teaq and Rhea's plan had gone too far, there would be repercussions.

Everyone on the island had undergone a certain amount of combat training. But this was different. Kelly was to be his queen.

He'd fight to the death to keep her from harm. She would never have to pick up a sword in battle herself; he would make sure of it.

As he continued to observe her, how innocently she lay there, he couldn't help but wonder about the things Teaq and the Elders had said during the Council meeting. Surely *he* was the one keeping secrets in this room, not Kelly.

This prophecy the Elders had dug up; either it was simply a misinterpretation, or there was someone else; some other outsider whom they all ought to worry about.

It certainly couldn't be Kelly. Not his queen.

She stirred and turned onto her side, moaning softly in the process.

"What is it, my darling?" Broc whispered.

He sat down beside her and gently rested his hand on her bare shoulder.

She sighed.

"Mother. Why have you forsaken me?" Kelly

demanded.

Broc frowned. Her eyes remained closed. A dream, perhaps? Or a memory.

"Nobody has forsaken you. You're not alone."

Despite his attempt to comfort her, she grew more restless, turning onto her back again and shaking her head vigorously.

"I don't understand. Why did have to you leave us?"

Clearly there was something eating away at her. Broc regretted not asking Kelly about her past and her family some more. That might have afforded him some insights now.

Broc lay down beside her, wrapping his arm around her and pulling her body against his.

This seemed to help. Kelly's breaths became deeper and more regular. Her formerly tense expression relaxed.

"You're safe now," Broc whispered in her ear.

"Mhmm."

"Sleep on." He rested his head on the pillow beside hers.

This was how they remained, side by side, until shortly before dawn. Broc gathered her up in a sheet, ever careful not to wake her, and carried her back to her own room. He paused for a moment, watching as she settled into her new position.

He couldn't explain it. How Kelly had awoken all these feelings in him.

It was his duty as king to take care of all his subjects,

obviously. And as his future queen, Kelly held a special position. But this wasn't about duty. It was about instinct.

Remembering the scars on her otherwise flawless skin, Broc balled his fists.

He wouldn't stand idly by as Rhea and Teaq conspired to make Kelly's life unnecessarily difficult.

But his responsibilities took him away from her most of the day. He needed an ally. Someone he could trust to be truthful with him, but who could move around the island unnoticed.

As he closed the heavy door to Kelly's room as quietly as he could, a shadow in the corner of his eye attracted his attention. Her scent was unmistakably familiar.

"Bree?" Broc called out.

The young woman appeared from around the corner. Her head bowed as a sign of respect. She'd always been a bit timid around him, but he trusted her. That was why he had assigned her to take care of Kelly during the transition. She was a born protector.

Who better to help him with his latest problem?

"There's something we must discuss," Broc started.

Bree raised her head and met his gaze. "Anything, my king."

"It's about Kelly…"

At the mention of her name, Bree's eyes lit up. It was obvious that the woman had developed a certain fondness for his future bride. Broc smiled. Bree was the perfect ally indeed.

"I would like you to make sure that nothing untoward happens to her. The training with Rhea is fine and well, but Rhea has never trained a human before. Their bodies... they work differently from ours."

Bree eyes darted back at Kelly's room, then lingered on him again. "She's fragile."

"She heals more slowly," Broc clarified.

"You'd like me to accompany them. Watch over her."

Broc nodded. "But it cannot be obvious. Use your powers. Stay out of sight."

Bree opened her mouth as if to protest, but kept quiet when another dark figure approached the two of them in the corridor.

"Up so early?" Teaq asked.

"There is much to do," Broc said.

He exchanged one last look and a subtle nod with Bree, who quickly turned around and made herself scarce. The woman had never been too fond of Teaq, whose gruff and direct nature was indeed something of an acquired taste.

"This is hardly the time, brother," Teaq remarked while nodding sideways at Kelly's door.

"Oh, no, I was on the way to the Watch Point," Broc explained.

"In your night clothes?" Teaq argued.

"I had a feeling. An instinct. We cannot afford complacency."

"Finally something we both can agree on."

The two brothers exchanged a long look. Teaq had immediately steered the conversation to Broc's presence in the corridor. But what was *he* up to so early in the morning? More conspiring and scheming, perhaps?

"Perhaps we could inspect the fortifications on the Eastern Isle today. The weather seems good for it." Teaq folded his arms in front of his chest.

"Very well. It has been a while since I've visited those parts."

Was Teaq actively trying to get Broc off the main island today? Refusing would only raise suspicions though. With Bree firmly on his and Kelly's side, Broc felt it safe to play along.

"We can join the morning patrol," Teaq said.

Broc nodded. "I'll be there."

Rather than go back to his room, he turned in the opposite direction and soon found his way to the Watch Point, just as he'd told Teaq. It was where he liked to come and think.

With everything that had been happening, he had a lot to mull over.

But as the cold sea winds hit his face, forcing him to close his eyes for a moment, there was only one thing on his mind: Kelly.

———◆———

"This part of the island has always been more vulnerable.

It's too remote. We need more guards here." Broc gestured at the wall surrounding the barren wilderness of the island before them. Then he turned to face Teaq, who had folded his arms.

"More guards. When the invasion comes, a few extra guards aren't going to help us." Teaq had to speak up to make himself heard over the strong sea winds. The boat they had sailed on from the main island was being thrown around vigorously on the waves surrounding the island.

"What would you advise, then?" Broc asked. His elder brother could be quite the know-it-all, but he did have a keen instinct when it came to military strategy.

"We need a better method for the guards already stationed here to signal in case of enemy sightings."

"Another lighthouse?" Broc asked, glancing over at the lone tower toward the westernmost point of the island.

"Perhaps." Teaq was acting unlike his usual self. His expression was thoughtful, and he was even more tight-lipped than normal. Had the prospect of war spooked him? Or was it something else?

Broc would have to find out.

"We should convene regular meetings with the Elders. Perhaps they have ideas that might help," Broc suggested.

Teaq nodded in silence.

For a moment, the two brothers stood quietly by the railing of the ship, still staring at the island. This was the land their father had left them. Now it was up to them to defend it from the enemies that surrounded them.

It wasn't a light burden to bear, the responsibility to keep all the islanders safe. But who else was there to carry it?

Broc sighed and closed his eyes. The salty air had a way of cleansing one's thoughts, just like he had attempted to do earlier on the Watch Point at the castle.

His thoughts were far from clean, though. They kept on returning to the illicit activities of the previous night, no matter how hard he tried to focus.

He glanced over at Teaq. Luckily Broc's thoughts were his own.

Even so, these emotions, they weren't a sign of weakness, were they? They felt like a powerful force, one that would enable him to move mountains if he had to.

He'd conquer worlds for her.

And when the time came, he would find a way to defeat Black Isle's enemies to keep her safe. If it was the last thing he did.

"We should go on land. Speak with the guards. See what we can learn that may help."

Broc turned to look at his brother again, but Teaq seemed distracted again. What on earth was going on with him? Was he jealous of Broc's newfound happiness, perhaps? If Broc didn't know any better, he might have thought it was time for him to find a bride of his own. Was that why he was trying to meddle in Broc's relationship with Kelly? Had jealousy inspired him to attempt to undermine her?

"Brother, did you hear me?" Broc asked.

"Yes… Yes, of course. I have some errands to run on the island as it is. I'll join you in the main watch tower once I am done."

Broc shrugged, but scrutinized Teaq's face for a moment longer. "Very well then."

Errands… It wasn't in his nature to make excuses, and yet Teaq was being uncharacteristically vague. So many secrets all of a sudden.

What on earth was Teaq up to on this remote and barren island in the sea?

CHAPTER ELEVEN

A nother morning, another day of training with Rhea. Kelly followed Rhea along the now somewhat familiar path across the drawbridge and up the hillside until they were once more on the plateau where they had trained the day before.

She was no weakling, but she was no giant either. Her body was still recovering from all the unfamiliar movements Rhea had taught her.

The stiffness she'd felt after waking this morning hadn't worn off yet. The walk had only made her muscles protest even more.

And her right arm. It felt like lead.

"Here, take it," Rhea ordered while handing Kelly the real sword.

"What? No, I'm not ready," she protested.

Rhea just glared at her. Clearly the female giant was in no mood to argue.

Kelly's palm burned when she closed her fingers around the handle of sword. Small blisters had started to form at the base of each of her digits. Her wrist still burned from the repeated impacts she had received each time Rhea had disarmed her.

She looked down at her weapon; crude and not very sharp. The blade had developed a bit of rust on one side.

It wasn't in the best shape, much like Kelly herself.

"Can't we train with the wooden ones again? It's only been a day."

"And tomorrow, we might all be dead. You'd better learn more quickly," Rea grumbled.

It wasn't that Kelly didn't *want* to learn. She did. She wanted to make Broc proud, after all.

But she wasn't as strong, and certainly not as experienced.

Oh, Mother. What do I do?

"Well? Are you just going to stand there? You're not going to cry, are you?" Rhea said.

Kelly bit her bottom lip. No, she was not. She wouldn't give her the pleasure of breaking down now.

Give me strength.

Kelly closed her eyes and inhaled deeply.

"So, attack me, then!" Rhea demanded.

Kelly raised her weapon high into the air just as Rhea had shown her previously, and charged as fast as her aching legs could carry her.

Rhea dodged her attack, prompting Kelly to turn on her heel and swing the sword downward. Yet another move they had practiced the previous day. She almost grazed Rhea's arm, but the latter stepped aside and raised her own weapon, bringing it down hard. Sparks flew as the two blades connected.

The impact was much harsher than what Kelly had expected from their previous session. She dropped the sword and grabbed her wrist.

"Bloody hell!" Kelly shouted.

Rhea chuckled. "Best get used to the pain. The enemy won't wait for your recovery; he'll just strike you down when he has the chance."

Kelly glared at the female giant. There was no need for this. The woman had one whole foot on her. And years of training.

Mother, give me strength!

Rhea raised her blade and held its tip to Kelly's throat. "The enemy would just kill you right here."

"Are you?" Kelly asked.

"Am I what?" Rhea's tone was still full of ridicule.

"Are you my enemy?" Kelly demanded.

Rhea smirked. "I'm just supposed to train you. Whether you like the lessons or not."

"There's a difference between training and taunting. Watch yourself," Kelly hissed.

She wasn't sure if it was the pain, or a lingering effect from last night's wine-fuelled festivities that had given her ill-advised courage.

"Or what, my dear? You'll tell our dear king that I've been mean to you?"

Kelly closed her eyes and tried to focus. For whatever reason, Rhea had hated her from the start. Getting into a confrontation out here alone with her wasn't just stupid, it would serve no purpose. The only choice she had was to play Rhea's game.

She pushed the weapon away from her throat and picked up her own sword again while trying to ignore the sting the blade's edge had left on her palm.

"I'm not going to let this happen again," Kelly grumbled under her breath. "I swear it on the graves of my forefathers. On my mother's grave."

"What's that?" Rhea asked.

Kelly shook her head. "I'm ready."

Sure enough, Kelly's body felt revitalized. It was amazing what a bit of anger could achieve.

"Better be," Rhea said, before initiating the attack herself this time.

Kelly swung as hard as she could, landing a firm blow on Rhea's sword this time. The pain in her wrist was almost blinding, but she didn't flinch.

"Not bad, but not good enough!" Rhea turned and struck Kelly's weapon in return; from the bottom this time.

Kelly wasn't prepared for that. She could no longer hold on.

Mother, save me from this pain!

With her weapon once more on the ground, and Kelly holding her hurt arm tightly against her chest, a peculiar sensation came over her.

Suddenly, she found herself afloat, looking down on her own crouching form as well as Rhea, who stood by with her hand on her hip.

Kelly was no tattletale, but did Broc even know about this? He'd told her she wouldn't be harmed. Her injured wrist. Was this not also harm?

Rhea raised her sword over Kelly's defenseless form.

How easy it would be to strike this coward down where she stands. A training accident. That's what I'll say.

Kelly's anger flared up again. She didn't know how she could see what she did, and hear what she had heard. It didn't matter.

Rhea took another step forward. *Soon, you'll no longer stand in my way…*

Oh no, you don't, Kelly thought.

A vision appeared to her; red, wavy hair, a familiar face.

Darling, is this what you want? the apparition asked.

Kelly nodded. *Yes, Mother. This is what is necessary.*

The figure vanished as quickly as it had appeared. All of Kelly's energy. All her focus was aimed at only one thing: survival.

Before Rhea's sword even had the chance of coming down on top of Kelly's back, a blinding flash of light surrounded the two women and Rhea was thrown backwards over the edge of the plateau.

Kelly gasped as she was sucked into her body again. She was completely unscathed. The powerful explosion she had just observed had not affected her at all.

Not so, Rhea, whose angry snarls could be heard some way down the hillside.

What had just happened? Had she imagined it?

Kelly scampered toward the edge of the plateau and peered down. A figure lay quite some distance away; Rhea must have fallen at least fifteen feet straight down, and then rolled the rest of the way. But the female giant was in no mood to stay on her back. She scrambled onto her feet and wiped a blood-stained lock of hair out of her face.

"I'll get you for this, witch!" Rhea threatened.

Her face underwent an otherworldly change. A grimace momentarily covered in fur. Sharp teeth. A snout.

Kelly stumbled backwards in shock

First the bolt of blue light and now this.

It had to be a trick. Somehow Rhea had manipulated her; maybe she'd put poisoned mushrooms into her breakfast that had given her these strange visions. *Maybe...*

It took Rhea less than a minute to charge up the hillside. She grabbed Kelly firmly by the shoulders and glared at her. Her face was once again normal. Human-like.

Kelly couldn't help but stare.

What on earth was going on here?

"You shouldn't have shown your hand so quickly! It's all over for you now!" Rhea hissed.

Kelly didn't know how to respond. There was nothing to say. None of what had happened made any sense. And she felt so drained all of a sudden, her mind was fogging over.

"You're under arrest for witchcraft. Good luck wooing

Broc from down in the dungeons."

Of course. All this time, Rhea had been jealous. Kelly couldn't believe she hadn't seen it before. She had wanted to be queen. And then Kelly had come along and messed up all her plans.

"He'll see through this, you know. Tricking me like this," Kelly whispered.

The fatigue threatened to overwhelm, but she couldn't show weakness. Not now.

Rhea scoffed. "Tricking *you*? You're the one who has been tricking all of us. Infiltrating our walls by pretending to be some helpless human, when in fact you're a most dangerous enemy yourself. Sorceress!"

Kelly groggily shook her head. If she got a moment with Broc, she'd be able to explain it all. Rhea's jealousy. Her crazy scheme accusing Kelly of witchcraft. There was no such thing, after all.

Darling, be strong, said that familiar voice in Kelly's head.

No, she was just imagining it. Mushrooms, or some other poison. Those gave you visions that could drive grown men insane.

She couldn't allow her mind to be corrupted like that. It was all a dream. A figment of her imagination. None of this was real.

Kelly's legs threatened to buckle but Rhea had other ideas and held her upright. Once her hands were tied firmly behind her back, she was prodded and shoved into motion again.

Kelly had come full circle. A prisoner. Just like how she had started out on the shores of Hythe Bay only days ago.

She struggled to keep pace with Rhea, who began dragging her down the mountain path and back toward the castle.

Nobody would believe this crazy story, surely. There were no witches anymore. They had died out a long time ago, if they ever even existed at all.

There was no such thing as magic.

Was there?

"I don't…" Kelly tried to speak. "I'm not…"

Rhea prodded her in the back.

One foot in front of the other.

Looking down at the ground, it all seemed so alien to Kelly. These leather strapped boots Bree had given her. They might as well have been made of lead, given how difficult each passing step had become.

In the distance, the castle came into view. But Kelly could give no more.

Her legs buckled and her mind sunk into a dense fog.

Rest, my child. You'll need time to recharge and recover.

Kelly tried to respond, to argue and question this voice in her head. But she was unable to.

Far away, another voice.

Rhea, cursing.

"Coward. Witch! You'll regret making me carry you!"

That was the last Kelly could remember.

CHAPTER TWELVE

A warning horn sounded in the distance, which immediately urged the guards on the fortifications into action. Broc and Teaq also pulled their swords and ran towards the group of men converging on the lower sea wall.

"What is it?" Teaq called out.

One of the guards; his horn still in his right hand, pointed at the water's edge. Two soldiers were in the process of hauling in a large net. Within it, a figure, flailing and writhing furiously.

Broc leaned across the wall to get a better look.

Greenish, shimmery skin, and long silver hair.

Well, I'll be damned…

"It cannot be," Teaq said. His voice was uncharacteristically thin, like for once in his life something had genuinely surprised him.

Broc inhaled sharply and straightened his back. If his brother wasn't in a mood to show decorum, at least he should.

"Well, let's see it," he ordered in a firm voice.

The guards looked up briefly, then dragged the figure fully ashore. One kneeled down, restraining the sea creature in something of a strangle-hold, while the other quickly tied it up.

Then, they removed the remainder of the net and forced her up. She stopped struggling immediately as she became aware of her new surroundings.

A fully grown mermaid.

Her eyes shone golden in the subdued sunlight attempting to break through the clouds. She looked at the two men with about as much consideration as one would give a cockroach, or a fly.

"Well, you don't see *that* every day," Broc remarked.

He'd seen Sea Folk before, of course. They were stealthy, and preferred to attack mostly from underneath the water. Prisoners of war were a rare occurrence in their bloody conflict with Weiland, King of the Seas, but occasionally one had been caught.

Sea Folk soldiers were all male, though, so no one on Black Isle had ever seen a female before.

She was, in her own way, exceptionally beautiful. And the coldness in her eyes was terrifying.

A stranger, with immense power... Broc didn't believe in prophecies and such, but it almost fit too beautifully.

"There's your intruder," Broc remarked, and gestured down at the mermaid. "Seems like the Elders might have been onto something will all their talk of prophecies."

Teaq didn't say a word.

The two of them watched as the guards tried to wrangle her up the slippery granite steps toward where the remaining soldiers were waiting. The Mermaid did not fight, but she did take a moment to spit on one of her captor's faces.

The latter cursed as he wiped his affected eye, then grabbed her by the throat.

"Don't lay a hand on me, wolf!" she hissed.

Broc raised an eyebrow. The guard hadn't transformed. How did she know about his inner beast?

The other soldier helped keep her contained. Meanwhile, Broc was mesmerized.

She wasn't as tall as most islanders, but the confidence and control with which she moved suggested that she was strong for her size. One thing was certain though; she acted entirely fearless. The predicament she was in— captured by her people's fiercest enemy—did not seem to faze her at all.

Sea Folk invaders had shown the same confidence in battle.

The enemy certainly knew how to make an impression. The entire incident was greatly worrying.

Perhaps her arrival was just the start of something much more ominous. After all, the Elders with their scriptures and prophecies had been on the lookout for the first sign of the upcoming age of war.

This was likely it.

Still, they couldn't very well let her go and wish this incident away. This was Black Isle territory. Intruders had to be punished. And she had been lurking around their defenses after all. They had to assume she was a spy.

"Lock her up underneath the deck so she doesn't dry out, then transfer her to a nice, cozy puddle in the castle dungeons at the earliest," Broc ordered.

He glanced at his brother, who was still frozen in place. What had gotten into him?

Teaq wasn't one to be easily startled, but this unexpected capture had clearly shaken him up. Was it the prospect of war that had him worried? This wasn't the Teaq Broc had grown up with.

"Brother?" Broc urged. "Will you accompany the prisoner transport?"

Teaq glanced to his side. His expression was even more serious than usual.

"Dark days are upon us."

Broc nodded. Once the Sea Folk found one of their own missing, especially one who had been on a mission to spy on Black Isle's fortifications, they would retaliate.

Teaq followed the procession of soldiers as they led the mermaid to the longship they had arrived on earlier. Broc remained on the sea wall and stared darkly over the choppy waters ahead.

He needed the Elders' help, and quickly. They simply did not have enough soldiers to man all the fortifications. One could never predict where an attack would land.

Black Isle's army consisted of extremely well trained, skilled fighters. He had bears and wolves manning his land defenses, and eagles in the skies above, each fully in control of their human as well as their animal form.

And for all his arrogance, Teaq was an excellent commander and strategist as well.

But the Sea Folk were a formidable enemy. Previous battles had not ended in victory for anyone.

Both sides had simply kept going until they had exhausted themselves.

So many lives lost.

This time, Broc had an added concern. Kelly. An innocent; a newcomer to all of it. The urge to keep her safe seemed all important.

Black Isle would need a lot more than just skill to win this war once and for all.

They needed a true advantage.

Broc once again thought of the prophecy. A stranger with great power, that could win or lose battles. The outcome of the war was not yet decided. The mermaid had shown no great interest in any of them. Put perhaps whatever her power was, it could be utilized somehow.

Perhaps the Elders would learn something from her that could tip the scales in their favor.

"Halt!" Broc called after the soldiers, who had nearly reached the dock. "I'm traveling with you."

———◆———

Broc paced the Great Hall. Back and forth, then back again. He'd wanted to call a meeting with all his advisors to discuss the mermaid's capture, but upon arriving at the castle found that Rhea had something even more pressing to discuss.

In a day, everything had changed. Only hours ago, he had known so clearly what to do. He'd had a definite plan for how things would go with Kelly. It had all been so simple, and now this.

"I don't understand. Are you absolutely certain that's what you saw, Rhea?" he demanded.

Rhea cocked her head to the side. "I would never lie to you, my king. She's a witch."

He shook his head. She had disapproved of Kelly since her arrival, for obvious reasons. But he did not believe her capable of such deceit. Rhea had always taken her role in his court seriously.

She'd always been honest, sometimes a little too honest, especially when she disagreed with him.

"It's really quite obvious that the prophecy is being fulfilled," Teaq remarked. "We can only hope it's not too late to counter this attack!"

Broc glared at him. *Oh he would just love to be right, wouldn't he.* This was the most Teaq had said since they'd left the Eastern Isle.

"This certainly demands further investigation. So we can determine what exactly has happened," Broc said. "And in case you've forgotten, we've just witnessed another incident that could very well be a part of this prophecy of yours."

Teaq's face twisted in anger. He had been unusually

quiet on the way back to the castle, and now he still seemed touchy at any mention of the mermaid.

"It's quite clear what has happened, brother!" Teaq argued. "The witch felt cornered, out there doing combat training with Rhea, and she exposed herself for what she is. An infiltrator. An enemy disguised as an innocent peasant girl from West Hythe. How the humans managed to find a witch after all these years, I cannot say. But she's here, so the hows and whys of it are irrelevant. This Reaping was obviously a trap."

"Now, now… " Broc interjected. "We do not know for sure what the humans intended. Or if they even knew about this. After all, the prophecy speaks of a *secret* power. Perhaps it was a secret to them as well."

Teaq and Rhea shared a dark look. The latter scoffed and shook her head.

"Fine, even if it was all *her* idea and *her* plan," Rhea began. "And the humans had no knowledge of it. We are still at the brink of war. The prophecy—"

Broc lost his calm at that point and stopped at the nearest table, banging his first hard onto its surface.

"I am fed up of everyone's speculations! Sick of it! We *are* at the brink of war, but with the Sea Folk, not with the humans. We'll get to the bottom of this matter with Kelly also, of course. I will speak with her. I must—"

"You will do nothing of the sort!" Teaq's heavy voice echoed against the granite clad walls of the Great Hall.

Broc squared up against him and kept his gaze locked firmly onto Teaq.

"In case you have forgotten. I am King. I do not need your permission to—"

"My king, if you'll hear us out…" Rhea interrupted.

Broc shook his head. No, he would not hear them out.

This was a dark day. Black Isle had gained two prisoners tonight, and potentially lost a queen. It was senseless.

Whose capture would more likely drag them into an armed conflict? An alleged witch, completely isolated from any of the people she grew up with? Or a mermaid, found lurking around the least defended island in their kingdom? Who was more likely to be a spy?

"We do not know for sure if Kelly means us any harm. But we are *certain* that the Sea Folk are our most pressing enemy. Am I wrong?"

Broc looked around for confirmation, but found Teaq merely staring in the distance, and Rhea sulking with her arms crossed in front of her chest.

His logical conclusion did not fit into their narrative. Too bad. He had always aimed to be a just ruler, but he was still king. It was his decision.

"I am going to interrogate our human prisoner now. Personally."

Rhea raised an arm. "My king, I do not think it safe for you to see her unguarded. We do not know enough of her powers."

"That's enough! She's chained up. She even let you carry her down the hillside without attempting to fight back or escape. What is she going to do to me? Blind me with a flash of light?" Broc bellowed.

Teaq shook his head and turned to leave without a word.

"Brother," Broc called after him. "Perhaps you could interrogate the other prisoner. Find out what she knows and whom she's told. And for all our sakes, try to find out if her people are planning an attack."

Rhea scoffed again. "She's not going to just spill everything."

Broc gestured vaguely. "Use your powers of persuasion, brother. Our safety may depend on it."

Teaq, who had paused for just a moment to hear Broc's orders, glanced back once, then started to walk away again without so much as a word of acknowledgement.

"My king," Rhea spoke up again.

Broc shook his head. "No. I've made my decision."

That was that. He also left the Great Hall and headed straight for the dungeons.

CHAPTER THIRTEEN

"Wake up, my child," a voice spoke.

Kelly's eyes were still heavy, but she finally managed to open them. Standing over her was a figure, bathed in white light. It took a moment for her sight to adjust. Kelly tried to stir, but her body was so cold, her muscles refused to cooperate.

That face. That voice. Was she still imagining things?

"Mother," Kelly said. "Is that really you?"

The woman smiled. "Of course. I've been watching all this time."

"Watching and speaking to me."

Mother nodded. "Once you were ready to hear me. You called out for me and I came."

"How can it be? You're dead. I saw them bury your body all those years ago," Kelly whispered.

"Our people do not die as humans do. Our energy lingers in this realm."

Kelly shook her head. *What energy?* "I do not understand."

"You have questions. It is only natural."

Kelly finally managed to get up and approached the figure. But upon raising out her hand attempting to touch her, there was nothing there but air. Kelly looked down and found that her wrist was cuffed; a heavy chain connected it to a ring on the wall.

"How do I know you are real?" Kelly wondered aloud, as she rubbed her sore arms. As soon as she'd moved, all the aches she'd developed in training with Rhea had flared up again.

Mother let out a short laugh. "You know it in your heart."

Did she, though? Kelly wasn't so sure, but she kept her doubts to herself. Her wrist, meanwhile, was on fire. She tried to soothe it by massaging herself. The cuff made it impossible to reach the right spot.

Dejected, she wrapped herself in her woolen cloak and sat down again, resting her back against the stone wall.

"What do you mean 'our people'?" Kelly asked finally.

"Beings of light. Guardians of men."

Kelly frowned. Of course she'd heard of them, but those were just stories. Fairy tales.

"Witches and wizards," Kelly said.

Mother smiled mysteriously.

"What you're saying is you, my mother, are a witch. That's why you didn't truly die all those years ago?" Kelly wasn't sure what she expected the answer to be. Part of her suspected she might soon wake up and find this was all a strange dream. If only the pain wasn't so intense. You weren't supposed to feel pain in your sleep, right?

"You're focusing on the wrong thing, my child."

Kelly took a deep breath in an attempt to collect

herself. It all felt so real. But then, so had the events on the plateau earlier. And none of that could be real either. The lines between truth and fantasy were blurring and she could no longer tell one from the other.

She rubbed her eyes, and upon opening them again found that her mother was still very much there. If it was indeed her mother, and not some apparition pretending to be her.

"Come on. Think it through," Mother said.

Kelly pressed her lips together and tried to focus. Her mind was still so fuzzy. She averted her gaze.

Wait…

Her own hands had taken on a similarly eerie glow, though it was weak in comparison. Kelly's heart skipped a beat.

"You're saying… Oh, Mother, when you said 'our kind' you meant me as well?" She held up her right hand to have a better look. It was flickering, like a candle about to be extinguished, but it was unmistakable. She hadn't imagined it.

Mother smiled and nodded. "You're my blood. You and Ferris."

"I'm a… By God, that can't be true!" Her heart was pounding now. And with it, so was the throbbing pain in her right wrist.

"You saw it. The power we wield." Mother raised her hand, palm upwards. In the center of it, a small ball of blue light developed. Just as quickly as it had appeared, it vanished again.

"That's not… Rhea was tricking me."

Mother shook her head. "She provoked you. But there was no trickery involved."

"How come I never knew?"

"The world is a dangerous place for us. Even before the Great War, our kind was often misunderstood. We were persecuted. Over time, we were all but forgotten, except for the odd mention in ancient tales or songs. That was for the best."

"They'll punish me, Mother. Rhea said I'm an enemy of Black Isle. What do I do?" Kelly's voice cracked.

"She has her own troubles."

Kelly nodded. Her jealousy. She had disliked Kelly since her arrival because of it.

"Do not concern yourself with her. My child, you have to decide which side you're on."

"Side? I'm not on any side," Kelly protested.

Was she, though? Where did her loyalties lie? The villagers, including her father, who sent her off as a human sacrifice? She'd hated them for it. Her initial urge to escape had been equally about her own safety as it had been about revenge on the people who had singled her out all her life. The small-minded inhabitants of West Hythe, who had never made her feel like she belonged.

But now she was mostly indifferent about them.

"I don't side with the people of the mainland," Kelly

mumbled.

What of Black Isle and its people? They were a strange lot, and not all equally friendly. But here, everyone seemed to have a place. Everyone had value.

And up to this point, they had treated her fairly, all things considered.

And then there was Ferris. Only God knew where he was right now.

Mother smiled knowingly. "Think it through. When you find your answer, you'll know what to do."

Kelly looked around for the first time since waking. A cold, dark cell, only lit up by the glow surrounding her present company. The perfect place to put someone you want to forget.

Even if she decided, as Mother insisted she should. How would it help? She was stuck here.

Rhea had locked her up, and once word got out about what happened on the training ground today, everyone else would be equally keen to keep her here.

Witches were something to be feared. Something to be imprisoned and destroyed. *Misunderstood.*

Kelly should hate her for it; Rhea, the reason she was locked up. But she had found a new kind of clarity of mind in all of this confusion. Jealousy would make a person do things they ordinarily wouldn't. Bree had told her the other day that Rhea wasn't a bad person. And so far Kelly had no reason to doubt Bree's word.

And Broc… Why would Broc keep Rhea around; put

her in charge of the Castle Guard even, if she had no redeeming qualities?

Broc…

Did he even know she was down here? Did he condone it?

Kelly's heart grew heavier at the thought. She'd grown so close to him. He was her first. The only man she could imagine giving herself to.

She loved him, strange as it was.

Had he abandoned her down here as well? Cast her off once word of her sorcery reached him? Just the thought was enough to make her lose hope.

"What if it's no use? What if I'm stuck down here?"

Mother shook her head. "All this is only temporary. No chains can hold you. No cell can contain you."

Kelly frowned and looked down at her own hands again. The glow surrounding her skin had grown more intense and the flickering had stopped.

"Time will heal all."

Hopefully.

Kelly glanced up again. It had been a whirlwind of a day and this latest information was a lot to digest. She knew so little still, she didn't even know what to ask next.

Mother's own glow was weakening, though. *Strange.*

"You won't leave me again, will you?" Kelly wondered aloud.

Mother smiled. "I've passed a lot of my remaining

energy to you. I cannot stay like this for much longer. The spirit world is calling."

Kelly's chest tightened as she finally understood.

The light, Mother had transferred it to her. And the change was happening even faster now. She was weakening right before Kelly's eyes.

"No! I'm not ready! Don't leave me now when I need you the most!"

Mother shook her head. "My child. Now that you are self-aware, you'll find your own path."

Kelly's eyes burned with the onset of tears.

"I don't even know how to use this… This energy. I cannot do this alone."

"Oh, but you are not alone. You are of the light. We are one. Once you're ready, you'll know exactly what to do. Soon, you won't be able to see me anymore. But I'll always be in your heart."

Not only was the glow reducing quickly, it was as though Mother's form had become less defined. Her whole being was fading and taking on a translucent quality as she slowly turned away from Kelly.

"No, please!" Kelly begged. "At least tell me what powers we have?"

Mother looked back for a moment. "That's different for everyone. Yours seem to be defensive. It's all instinctive. You'll learn."

Kelly remembered being sucked out of her own body and watching the entire spectacle unfold. She had been able to hear Rhea's thoughts as well, it seemed.

By the time Kelly looked up to ask a follow-up question, she found that she was once again alone.

So much to think about. So much yet to learn. Mother's words still rang in her ears.

Choose a side.

The moment she'd stopped thinking about escaping, she'd made her choice. Her current predicament did not change that. But how would she convince everyone of her loyalties, especially Broc?

Even if she did by some miracle manage to prove herself, she was still a witch. And he was the king. Their love did not stand a chance.

Kelly curled up, burying her face in her hands. It was hopeless. He wouldn't be interested in hearing what she had to say.

She could only hope that sooner or later, when her powers grew, she would find a way out of this black hole. And then? She had no idea.

Minutes, hours went by, while she remained in the corner of her cold, dark cell. Giving up wasn't usually in her nature. But it was hard to remain hopeful when the only person in the whole world who understood you had just vanished into thin air.

Kelly let the entire conversation with Mother run through her mind again and again. She also thought about the events leading up to her incarceration.

She was a witch. It was so obvious now, even though she'd had trouble believing it at first.

When Rhea aimed to strike, Mother had granted her the energy for some kind of protective spell.

But as much as that explained, one thing was still a mystery. If she had defensive and mind reading powers, then why had Rhea's appearance changed, if only for a second?

Did she also have the ability to change people into animals? That seemed like an odd power to have.

Although her mind tried to wander back to Broc and the hopelessness of it all, she forced her thoughts away again and again.

Through the tears, loneliness and despair, she kept on focusing on this one problem: how Rhea had nearly turned into a bear.

Yet she was unable to solve it.

CHAPTER FOURTEEN

roc was still shaking his head to himself when he neared the stone steps leading down into the bowels of the castle. But before he could enter the dungeon, he was intercepted.

"My king," a soft voice spoke.

Bree appeared from the shadows.

How had she found him here? Had she followed him from the Great Hall?

"Yes, Bree."

"I did as you asked," she said, while suspiciously scanning the hallway behind the two of them. "I followed Kelly today. Saw everything."

Broc, who had always banked on his calm and collected demeanor, grew tense. He hoped… he wasn't even sure what he was hoping for.

"Well, what did you see exactly?" Broc demanded, then immediately regretted his tone when

Bree flinched.

"It happened as Rhea said. Mostly." Bree kept her eyes fixed on the ground between them.

The girl was probably just nervous, but Broc felt his impatience at her vague responses grow. This time, he managed to collect himself.

"Mostly?" he asked.

"It was Rhea who instigated it. The battle training was rough. Rhea had an unfair advantage. Upon disarming Kelly, she…" Bree's voice trailed off and she scanned the hallway again.

"I would have intervened. I probably should have done so sooner," she muttered to herself.

"Go on, speak freely!" Broc urged.

"Rhea raised her sword, as if she meant to strike Kelly. Only, she didn't get the chance. A blue light surrounded the two of them and Rhea was thrown over the edge of the plateau."

Broc inhaled sharply. He didn't know what to make of it all. If Kelly indeed had magical powers… She had played the part of defenseless human very well indeed.

She'd tricked him.

And Rhea, she'd sensed it somehow. Even Teaq had had his suspicions.

A sense of dread filled his chest. He'd let her beauty enchant him.

"Thank you for bringing this to my attention," Broc spoke in a curt tone.

Was there any point in going down there anymore? He did still need to get to the bottom of it all, or he wouldn't find any rest.

"That's not all, my king," Bree said.

Broc turned to face the timid servant girl again.

"I've been watching her since. Taking care not to be seen by anyone, including Kelly herself."

"And?"

"I don't think she had any idea what was happening. On the way down the hill she passed out, and when she awoke, I heard her talking to someone. So I peered inside her cell. There was a mysterious figure in there with her. She kept calling her 'Mother'."

Broc frowned. Perhaps Kelly was talking in her sleep, just like she had done that morning, before any of this had happened. Still, his curiosity was sparked.

"But surely, there was no one inside with her?" Broc asked.

Bree pressed her lips together. Her face was full of doubt, and healthy dose of fear.

"By all means, girl. Speak!"

"Oh, but there was someone in her cell. A woman. I've no idea how she could have got in. The guard never left the hallway. I only managed to pass him because I'd changed to my animal form."

Broc was stunned for a moment.

"She was…" Bree finally did look terrified. "She was glowing! It lit up the whole cell."

"So what? You said she'd done that even out on the plateau," Broc mumbled.

"Not Kelly! Her mother. The strange woman was glowing."

That made even less sense.

"So you're saying we have two witches locked up down

below?"

Bree shook her head. "No, that's the thing, the woman vanished into thin air when their conversation was finished. Like she'd never even been there at all. That's what I can't comprehend. How is that even possible?"

The girl was rambling. Understandably, she was deeply affected by everything she had witnessed. Still, Broc had to know the whole story. There was so much he did not yet understand.

"Back to Kelly. You said she didn't know what was happening? What makes you say that?" Broc asked.

"Just, their conversation. Kelly thought Rhea had tricked her and that's why she was imprisoned. I don't think she realized she had powers. Until that woman, her so-called mother, told her about it."

"Ah." Broc scratched his beard.

A glimmer of hope after the darkest of hours. Was it possible that Kelly, his intended, was innocent after all?

Sure, she was still a witch. But if there was no *intent* there…

"Thank you, Bree. Your loyalty will be rewarded."

Bree nodded briefly. "Thank you, my king."

Broc watched her leave in a hurry. Then he quickly continued on his way to the dungeons.

Somewhere in this maze of dark corridors, further down below the mountain, the other prisoner was being held.

Broc did not care to look for her, or to check if Teaq

had indeed followed his orders and started interrogating her. He only had one goal: to speak with Kelly.

Throughout this entire debacle, he'd done his best to remain objective. He'd tried to listen to Rhea's story, and act statesmanlike and fair. But there was a large part of him that was incapable of rational thinking when it came to Kelly.

His inner beast had already chosen her. Claimed her. How could he deny that?

He had to find a way out of this mess. Luckily, what Bree had told him gave him something to cling onto.

"My king!" The guard posted near Kelly's cell jumped to attention.

Broc gestured at him to calm down. "I mean to speak with the prisoner."

He held out his hand, and waited. It took the guard a moment, before he realized Broc wanted the bundle of keys and indeed handed it over.

"Shall I…" He didn't finish his question. The man was obviously new at his job and uncertain about himself. He'd chosen to stand as far away from Kelly's cell as he could manage. No wonder Bree had slipped past easily and watched Kelly unseen.

"You're excused. I will do this alone," Broc said.

The guard hesitated, but then shrugged and left as ordered. Rhea and Teaq had a lot of leeway in how they acted around Broc, but most of the soldiers on this island did not have that luxury. An order was an order, especially when it came directly from the highest of places.

Broc's heart was racing in a way he hadn't felt in a very long time. Faced with the prospect of speaking to Kelly at last made him feel exposed. She held a strange power over him.

Magic?

Probably not, even though Rhea might have wanted to believe so.

Not that it mattered, what Rhea believed. He closed his eyes and focused.

Kelly was just beyond that heavy door. He could hear her heartbeat. Her breaths.

That sweet scent of hers that had enchanted him right from the start tried to draw him nearer even now.

His inner beast reacted almost violently. He had to get inside there. To find out if she was still loyal to him.

If their bond was still true.

He rushed to open the door. It swung wide, with a violent screech. Kelly, who had been lying on the cold floor, flinched backwards in fear.

"Don't be afraid," Broc said, as he stepped in and closed the door behind him. For the conversation he was intending to have, it was best that nobody, especially the novice guard, overheard.

Her perfume overwhelmed her; tore at his insides. He found it near impossible to control himself and not rush over there to comfort her. She'd obviously been miserable;

who wouldn't be, locked up in this cold, damp place. There were no windows; no source of fresh air or light. It was easy to forget all sense of time in here.

It was a terrible injustice to find his intended here, especially if everything Bree had told him was true.

What happened today?

He wanted to know every detail, but he could not bring himself to ask. Every question that entered his mind sounded like an accusation.

"It seems I haven't been honest with you," Kelly whispered.

She looked so small, so vulnerable.

"It seems not," he said.

His voice sounded a lot weaker than he had intended. Such was his relief that she'd spoken first.

"I hope you'll believe me. I don't even fully understand myself what happened out there."

Kelly looked up with those big green eyes of hers. "I'm a witch. This I've learned to be true. But I mean you or your people no harm."

Even though her face and hands were muddy, and her hair tangled and dull, her beauty was still blinding. Those large, red-rimmed eyes… She'd been crying; the dirt on her cheeks was streaked.

Broc was no stranger to physical pain. Nearly everyone on these islands had seen battle at some point or other. To be a warrior of Black Isle meant to be scarred by combat.

But seeing *her* like this was unbearable. It all but tore him in half.

During the few days they had spent together, a connection had formed. A sacred bond between lovers that many a song had been written about. He'd never taken the stories seriously, but now he knew better.

Fate had brought them together.

Their bond was true. How could he deny it now?

"I believe you," he whispered.

Kelly's eyes widened in surprise.

All the doubts that had plagued him since he'd heard the news were gone now that he saw the truth in her face.

But that didn't mean that this matter was resolved. There were still Rhea and Teaq, and a council of Elders that would need convincing

As king, his decision was final in most matters, but pardoning a supposedly dangerous enemy after wounding one of their own, that would go too far. It would open him up to challenge, something which Teaq would be all too happy to take advantage of.

But to have their union broken and their love destroyed by an unjust accusation, that was even worse.

"Choose a side," Kelly mumbled.

"What?" Broc asked.

She shook her head. "Just what someone told me. To choose a side and everything would work itself out."

"Your mother," Broc stated.

Kelly looked up again. "How did you know?"

"Bree. I'd sent her to watch over you. She overheard." Broc had answered mindlessly, without considering the consequences. But it was too late to take it back.

"Bree was *here?*" Kelly asked.

There it was. The inevitable question. Answering her truthfully meant ignoring his promise to Teaq and the others. It would mean exposing Black Isle's secret to a supposed enemy.

Broc nodded.

"I never saw her," Kelly stammered.

"Some of us, we can move almost unseen," Broc said.

Kelly frowned, then closed her eyes and remained perfectly still. A soft glow surrounded her only briefly.

Broc's heart raced as he watched a change overcome her. Her expression became vacant, her body looked almost lifeless.

Show yourself, her voice entered his mind. Then he felt the change in himself. His inner beast, which had been raging to get out ever since he smelled her presence, answered her call and clawed his way to the surface.

It only took the briefest of moments before Broc managed to force him back in.

Kelly gasped in surprise.

"What did I just see?" she stammered.

Broc wasn't sure how to respond. He wasn't quite sure what had happened himself.

"You're…" Kelly stood up and took a hesitant step in his direction. "You're like Rhea? Half bear half man!"

That was impossible. Rhea was always in control of those primal impulses. Had she shown her true self to Kelly in the heat of the moment?

And if she had just seen Broc's inner bear, how come she wasn't terrified like most humans were after their first sighting?

"I… What did you just do?" Broc asked.

Kelly paused. "I'm not entirely sure. When I focus really hard, it seems I can enter people's minds."

Seeing as he'd heard her thoughts too, even if just for a moment, perhaps that wasn't all she could do.

He walked over to her and took her hands. Cold as ice. Seeing the shackles on her wrists filled him with rage as well as regret. He had to get her out of here, and soon.

All he needed was a way to justify it to the others. So that they wouldn't call his judgement into question and challenge his right to the throne.

This power of hers, though she seemed to not have it fully under control, brought with it great opportunity.

"This is how we will convince them," Broc said.

Kelly frowned and shook her head. "I don't understand."

"The Elders. Teaq and Rhea. You'll practice this skill of yours, and we'll use it to our advantage."

"I can try." Kelly looked up at him with large, hesitant eyes.

"Let's get you out of here first," Broc said. "Nobody else knows about what went on today. There's no sense in missing the third night of the feast and raising suspicions where there shouldn't be any."

"You mean to do this tonight?"

He gently rubbed her icy hands between his. "I can't leave you here. But perhaps it's best if we keep you in hiding for a few days before confronting everyone."

A tear formed in the corner of Kelly's eye as she smiled up at him.

Thank you. Her voice entered his mind. *Thank you for believing in me.*

Kelly looked down at her wrists. A blue light enveloped the restraints until they snapped open and fell to the ground.

It should have shocked him, perhaps even frightened him. But watching Kelly's magic, however small, just filled Broc with pride.

"She was right, my mother," Kelly said. "She said I'd know what to do. Once the time came and I'd made my choice."

"And, what have you decided?" Broc asked.

"That I'm on your side. For as long as you'll have me."

CHAPTER FIFTEEN

---◆---

Kelly closed her eyes and inhaled deeply. She was so grateful.

For her mother, who had saved her from Rhea's blinding jealousy, even if her well-meaning intervention had created a whole host of other issues.

And Broc, for believing her when she wasn't even fully sure what to believe herself.

She was also grateful for this hot bath Bree had run for her in preparation for tonight. Despite the two days' rest since being rescued from the dungeon, her body was still bruised and sore.

Their reunion was awkward at first, but Bree quickly relaxed once Kelly confided in her about everything that had happened down in the dungeon.

It was such a relief to have another person to talk to.

Her release had been handled quietly. Rhea and Teaq had not been informed. The only people who knew so far were Broc, obviously, Bree, and the guard outside her cell. Thankfully nobody else had thought to check her chambers, so their secret was still safe.

She'd spent these days in hiding, trying to hone her skills by practicing on either Broc or Bree. But tonight was the night Kelly would reveal herself.

She would attend the final night of the Reaping feast.

The element of surprise would be on their side. Then she'd use her newfound powers to appease everyone.

She'd have to confront Broc's council of advisors, starting with Rhea and Teaq. Just how easily she would be able to convince them to see her not as a treacherous enemy to their way of life, but an innocent bystander in all of this, was hard to say.

There was no conspiracy here. She hadn't been put up as an offering in the Reaping to infiltrate their ranks and destroy them from within. What a ridiculous notion. The villagers of West Hythe were way too set in their ways to come up with such a cunning plan.

A woman spy. Most, her own father included, would spit on the idea.

The mainland was a very different place from the Black Isles. Surely everyone would see that eventually?

Kelly's stomach growled angrily. She hadn't eaten for hours. But until she could change everyone's minds and secure her place here, food was the last thing on her mind.

"Bree," Kelly called out. "If you could hand me that towel… I'd better get ready now."

———— ◆ ————

When Kelly entered the Great Hall, accompanied by Bree, she was once again painfully aware of the eyes fixated on her. Two pairs, in particular.

Teaq and Rhea could not hide their shock at her

presence and jumped up from their seats in protest. It was unnerving to watch their faces twist and morph to reveal their true selves; half bear for Rhea, and Teaq was half wolf.

"My king!" Teaq's voice was so loud, Kelly could hear it over the chatter and commotion created by the ongoing celebrations. "We must talk, immediately!"

Broc gestured at him to sit back down, but it had no effect.

Rhea was even more distraught. Her face reddened with anger.

"This is… My God, this is an insult!"

Some of the other giants looked up, curious at what had sparked her outburst. Their faces also changed briefly, enabling Kelly to finally see the full diversity on the island. Bears and wolves, she'd already known about. Now she also saw foxes, badgers, as well as the occasional eagle.

Oh no. Would they be able to tell now that she was different? That her influence had revealed their secret?

Kelly's heart was pounding.

This was never going to be easy, but Kelly hadn't counted on being put on trial in front of the entire populace of the castle. Her skills were still in their infancy. How would she manage, if she continued to feel so… *watched?*

Broc intervened quickly. "This is not the time or place. We're feasting. Celebrating our survival as a people."

Rhea looked furious as she stared Kelly down. Flared

nostrils, lips curled slightly into a snarl.

Luckily it seemed the rest of the crowd was losing interest and focused once more on the filled plates in front of them. Kelly could breathe a little easier again.

Time to focus. She had one chance to make this right. She could not afford any mistakes now.

Just like she had done with Broc multiple times already, she closed her eyes and concentrated. Like a muscle undergoing regular training, slipping in and out of her own body had become easier with each attempt. She started to float above the crowd unseen, allowing her to look down on her own form as well as Bree, who continued to stand by her side.

Then she diverted her attention to Rhea.

Our king has been compromised. This witch is going to be the end of us all!

Kelly focused again and allowed her thoughts to connect more deeply with Rhea.

Just as she'd done with Broc, earlier, and even Bree, in an attempt to explain herself, she opened her mind. Her thoughts, memories, hopes and dreams. Everything flowed freely. In return, Kelly felt the envy, the hate Rhea had shown her as well as the hopes she'd had for her future.

He was mine. I ought to become queen, not you. The rules be damned.

Kelly responded. *I understand your sorrow. I mean you no harm.*

Rhea's expression softened as she sank back into her seat. Stunned and speechless.

But… you're a witch.

That I am. But I'm not your enemy. She transferred her own emotions, her own memories into Rhea's mind as best she could. Broc had likened their previous connections to a dream. Fragmented at times, but so very real.

Rhea shook her head; her expression was ashen. Their exchange had taken its toll.

Kelly's energy was waning as well, but she knew she had to make a final push.

Teaq.

The general was a difficult case. His mind was a lot more challenging and guarded than Rhea's had been.

Kelly found it hard to penetrate him.

I mean you no harm. Let me in.

He didn't react immediately. His walls were thick and his defenses strong.

When she finally reached him, what she found surprised her. Beyond his harsh exterior, he wasn't hateful or even angry. He wasn't even thinking about Kelly so much as he was preoccupied with someone else.

His thoughts were a confused mass of regret and guilt. Being inside of his thoughts filled Kelly's heart with dread. He knew something he wasn't sharing. Dangerous secrets. Kelly wasn't sure she wanted to know. Teaq was a very troubled man.

Overcome by a guilt no man should have to bear.

She fought through her own tears as she once again tried to share her truth with him.

He wasn't open to her. It was no use.

Kelly's body demanded her return. She had used up all the energy she had. As she entered her own self again, she wasn't quite the same. That sense of dread she'd picked up in Teaq's mind had lodged itself in her heart. Looking at him now, she couldn't hide her sadness.

He did not speak a word as he turned away from the festivities and walked away in silence. A hollow man. With unspeakable secrets even Kelly's growing powers could not decipher.

"We will discuss everything, in time," Broc spoke up again. "But tonight, we celebrate. Our people deserve it. Who knows how long this peace will last."

Rhea nodded; she didn't look happy about it, but she no longer had the will to fight.

"Where's he going," Broc wondered aloud, as he watched Teaq leave the Great Hall.

Kelly shook her head. "I don't know. Your brother… he has a troubled soul."

Broc gave her a questioning look, but she just shook her head instead of answering. The darkness within him had shaken her to her core. Best not to dwell on it now.

They had overcome the first hurdle toward her redemption.

Tonight, they would celebrate this initial victory. Later, they would deal with the Elders the same way.

———•———

They hadn't stayed until the end of the feast.

Beyond the obligatory speech by Broc, and the food Kelly's body so desperately needed, there wasn't much keeping them there. They walked through the long, dark corridors in silence, until they reached the Watch Point.

"It's funny," Kelly spoke up, making her voice just a little louder than the winds whistling around the castle fortifications.

"What is?"

"Just how quickly things change."

Broc nodded then stared darkly at the waters below. It would be so easy to connect with him and find out what he was thinking, but it did not seem fair.

Kelly wrapped herself tighter in her woolen cloak; still the gales tried their best to penetrate the heavy fabric.

"I never liked this tradition, you know," Broc said.

Kelly looked up at him, studying his face. Hardened by the difficult life on these islands, yet also kind.

"The Reaping. It's a necessary evil," Broc elaborated.

"I've wondered about that."

Broc looked down at her and smiled briefly.

"Of course you have." His expression became serious again. "Towards the end of the Great War, our numbers had declined so much it would have been impossible to continue on without outside help. Sisters bearing their brothers' children… It's a recipe for disaster."

"Hence the treaty," Kelly whispered. She'd known as much since the first night of the Feast.

"Yes. But despite the feasting and the celebrations, we don't revel in it. Taking someone away from their family… Their way of life. I don't take it lightly."

Kelly also turned thoughtful as she looked ahead at the dark clouds collecting overhead. "In a way, it's almost a kindness. The mainland is not always a pleasant place for women."

Broc took her hand. Excitement washed over her as it did each time he touched her, though this time the feeling was bittersweet. The heaviness she'd carried with her since infiltrating Teaq's mind had never fully left.

"Dark days are ahead. We're expecting war. Bringing you into this as an innocent, it's not just."

"I already told you, I've made my choice. I don't have anywhere else I'd rather be," Kelly said.

"I still have to ask."

Broc took her other hand as well and got down on one knee in front of her. The sight of this powerful man in a pose of submission took Kelly's breath away.

"Knowing of all the uncertainty and danger ahead, would you still become my queen? The mother of my children?" Broc's voice was almost a whisper.

His concern for her almost broke her heart. To think of how she'd arrived here. How she really hadn't had much of a choice. All that had changed when she found out about her powers. Now she had nothing but choices. And none made more sense than this one.

"Yes. Of course. Always."

"I will protect you. I will try to keep you safe if it's the last thing I do. But this life is not without dangers."

Kelly freed her hands from his grasp and wrapped her arms around his neck, which for a change was conveniently within her reach. She buried her face into his hair and closed her eyes. Even though she wasn't trying to, she could feel his emotions deep within her own heart.

"In barely a week I've learned more about life, and love, than all the years that came before. Suddenly I feel like I don't need much protection after all."

Broc pulled back just enough to look at her. "The prophecy."

"What?"

"The Elders spoke of an outsider whose powers could win or lose wars."

"They meant me?" Kelly didn't need an answer. It made perfect sense. Her defensive powers could be helpful. If only she could develop them further.

Broc gathered Kelly up in his arms and stood up again. Kelly rested her head against his shoulder as he carried her back inside the castle.

She would train. She would do everything she could to

help. Just not tonight.

Tonight they'd celebrate their love. Just as they had done on prior nights. Only this time, there were no more secrets between them. Were there?

She inhaled deeply, closing her eyes again as his masculine scent threatened to overwhelm her. How had he done it? How had he awakened such fire within her, that only his touch could douse?

Magic...

"Do we *have* to wait until marriage?" Kelly wondered aloud.

Broc chuckled as he continued to carry her through the maze of stone hallways, leading inevitably to his quarters. "It *is* tradition."

She knew he was right, of course, prompting her to change course.

"Then how about..." she paused for a moment, uncertain if she should complete her thought.

"What is it, my darling?"

"You show me your true self. Willingly." Kelly's heart started to race. The suggestion had escaped her lips before she could fully think it through.

"I thought... You'd already seen?" Broc asked, taking a step back.

"Yes... Maybe... I can't shake the idea that there's more to it." Kelly waited with bated breath. Had she gone too far? Had she offended him?

Finally, a smile broke through his previously thoughtful expression. "I don't see the harm."

They rushed the rest of the way to Broc's quarters, just as they'd done the previous night. Once he'd secured the door behind them, he cast off his garments, one by one, revealing more of his tan skin.

It was hard to see in the flicker of the torch on the wall, but Kelly found herself once again marveling at the beauty that was him. She'd never seen a man quite like Broc before.

Then again, he *wasn't* like any ordinary man, was he?

He closed his eyes, his face tense with concentration, then within the blink of an eye, a change came over his entire body. Muscle, morphing and twisting into alien shapes. Fur sprouting where there had been none.

Kelly covered her hand with her mouth, though an errant gasp escaped when the transformation was complete.

It wasn't just his face, like before. Within a fraction of a second, the giant man who had just stood before her had turned into a real life bear. Claws, teeth, snout and all.

Then within the blink of an eye, the animal was gone, and Broc was himself again.

"Are you alright?" he asked.

Kelly was speechless. Her heart was still racing.

"I hope I did not scare you?" Broc urged.

She shook her head. "No... No, that was simply..."

"Terrifying?"

"I was going to say, magnificent." She smiled and let out a nervous giggle. "None of what I'd seen earlier could have prepared me for this."

She dropped back onto the bed and breathed deeply. Her man. Her future husband. He was something quite special indeed.

EPILOGUE

How far she had come.

Kelly looked at her reflection in the mirror that had finally arrived for her only this morning. The white dress with gold embroidery wasn't just elegant, it was fit for a queen.

"It's lovely," Bree remarked.

Kelly glanced at the young giant's form, also caught within the mirror, and couldn't suppress a smile.

When she'd first arrived here a couple of weeks ago, she couldn't even have imagined the reason why there wasn't a single reflective surface anywhere in the castle. Mirrors revealed the Black Islanders' animal form. Bree's feathered complexion smiled back at her.

An owl. How fitting.

Of course, at the time of her arrival, nobody, not even Kelly herself, could have predicted how things would turn out. That she'd develop the power to see everyone's inner animal without outside help. How hard they'd tried to keep their secret…

"Are you ready? It's almost time." Bree's question dragged Kelly out of her daydream.

"Yes, of course."

She made sure everything was in place, and readjusted the crown that sparkled from on top of her deep red curls.

Finally, she slipped into a pair of delicate shoes decorated with sparkly stones matching the embroidery on her dress. These people weren't the sort to dress up. But for today—for their new queen—they had gone all out.

It was time.

Kelly's heart was aflutter as she walked slowly and deliberately down the aisle. The Great Hall, elaborately decorated for the occasion, was filled with so many onlookers, there was only a narrow space between them for Kelly to pass. Even those who normally did not reside on the main island had made the trip to see their new queen.

Broc waited at the end, together with the leader of the Elders; a frail man in a long light grey cloak whom Kelly recognized from her meeting with the entire Council some weeks earlier. Uri.

Teaq and Rhea stood by further towards Broc's right. Neither were happy about it, but they'd finally accepted Broc's decision once it turned out that the Elders were onboard too. It was all part of the prophecy. She would use her powers to help them in their time of need. If it ever came to that.

Finally, Kelly stood in front of Broc. Her soon to be husband. Looking into his eyes still made her knees weak, but she tried not to show it. Not in front of all these people.

Uri cleared his throat and slowly raised his right arm.

The crowd grew silent.

"This," he spoke with a thin and shaky voice. "Is a very special day. For today, we celebrate a royal union."

The crowd cheered, then settled again as Uri shot a strict look in their direction.

"It is in front of you all that Broc Bearclaw, King of the Black Isles and ruler of the Northern Sea, accepts as his queen Kelly Chaslain of West Hythe. May their bond remain true forever, and their union fruitful!"

Uri shuffled backward as the crowd erupted again.

Broc took his place in front of Kelly. In his hands was a heavily decorated sheath and sword. It was the most beautiful weapon she had ever seen. Intricately carved designs decorated the shiny metal. The handle was studded with expertly cut precious stones in a multitude of colors. With one palm underneath the handle and the other underneath the sheath, he got down on one knee and held it up in Kelly's direction.

They'd practiced this bit, the night before, but Kelly still felt her throat close up as he started to speak.

"This sword is a symbol of my protection. Accept it and know I and my people will keep you safe for as long as you shall live. As my queen. My wife. My life."

She did her best to swallow her emotions.

Kelly had never wished for marriage. On the mainland it was just this thing everyone did. Like being born and dying, all the girls of a certain age got married. It had nothing to do with love, or passion, as far as Kelly could tell.

But this…It was something else entirely. He'd asked her. She'd said yes. And now he was asking again in front of everyone in terms grander than even the most romantic poem or song.

She looked down at her man, who remained in position at her feet. At those honest eyes she had fallen for. The lips that seemed to beg for her kisses.

Kelly reached out and took the sword. It weighed heavy in her hands as she also supported it from either end with her palms.

"I accept," she whispered. "My king."

"Go on, kiss her already," someone at the back of the crowd shouted.

"Yeah!" More people joined in.

"Oh come on, don't ruin the moment now," Broc retorted, then looked up at her again.

Though her eyes had become a bit moist, she could not suppress a grin. These people… *Her people*, they were a strange lot. But their enthusiasm was contagious.

He got up, slowly, and waited as Kelly fumbled with the leather strap of the sword, fastening it around her waist.

Then he held out his hand, which Kelly gladly accepted.

"May I?" he mouthed.

She nodded.

Broc pulled her into his arms and kissed her, just as the crowd had demanded. Applause erupted. People whistled and shouted.

She ought to be embarrassed, but the excitement that swept over everyone had infected her too. She wrapped her own arms around him too, and forgot herself in the moment.

Music started to play; barrels of wine and beer appeared through the various doors of the Great Hall. The formalities had ended and the party had begun.

But neither Broc nor Kelly were interested in any of that. They stayed but for a moment. Once the well-wishers got distracted, and nobody came up to congratulate them anymore, they quietly slipped away. Free from further scrutiny, away from the well-meaning but crude remarks some of the giants had shouted their way. Nothing stood in their way anymore.

Today was the first day of the rest of their lives.

Man and wife.

King and Queen.

They paused in front of Broc's quarters, giving him the chance to carry her across the threshold. He'd done it before, many times, but it felt different now. There was no more tradition forbidding them from following their hearts. They did not have to hold back anymore. For the very first time, they could follow their desires to the very end.

"It's beautiful," Kelly whispered, as Broc lay her down

on top of his giant bed. In all the time she'd been here, the vegetation she'd taken for granted on the mainland had been sorely missing. But for tonight, Broc's bed had been carefully decorated with flower petals in various colors.

"You like it?" he asked.

It wasn't really a question, because Kelly was certain the way she stared into his eyes now was enough of an answer.

She inhaled deeply of the familiar scent of his room; the leather gear he was so fond of added a spicy tone to the sweet fragrance of the flowers.

The first blooms of early summer. A little part of the home she'd left behind.

Broc got off the bed, just for a moment, before settling on the end. He lifted the skirt of her wedding dress, exposing her shapely thighs and spreading them with both hands.

She had already become familiar with this strong, confident grip. Firm but not painful. A man on a mission she could not refuse.

He leaned down between her legs and tasted her flesh.

It wasn't new to her, and yet each time he worshipped her like this felt unique.

Kelly settled into the pillows and closed her eyes. She focused solely on this most exquisite pleasure which he bestowed upon her most intimate parts.

The tip of his tongue caressed her where it mattered

most, then before the sensation grew too intense, backed away again to give her some relief. Though the room was cool as usual, her skin was on fire. It was a burn only his touch could soothe.

She reached for his hair, gripping it firmly between her fingers.

This was otherworldly. This love they shared. This pleasure they could inspire in each other.

But it was only the beginning.

Kelly's hips bucked, her body aching for a firmer touch. Broc's lips responded.

Then suddenly, he backed away.

"No! Don't stop!" Kelly pleaded.

He smiled and licked his bottom lip as he looked down at her. His eyes were a deep black, yet still managed to simmer. He would not be denied what was his tonight.

Not that Kelly could ever refuse him. Her own desire was much too strong.

Was this how all the girls felt on their wedding night? So special.

She was the luckiest bride in the world.

"I want you. All of you," he whispered.

There was a rawness in his voice that spoke directly to Kelly's most inner urges. Whenever she was with him, a sweet ache developed in her lower abdomen that she could not put into words. Tonight, it had grown more intense than ever.

"You have me," she responded.

"You know what this means," he said.

Kelly shook her head. It was beautiful, insane, unexpected and entirely surreal. But that was all she knew.

"If we become one tonight…" Broc started.

"Yes?"

"Then perhaps, our family will grow."

Kelly bit her bottom lip. *Family.* It was hard not to think of Ferris and what had become of him upon hearing that word. And yet, it also filled her with hope, and excitement about what the future might hold.

"I'm ready."

Broc cast off his clothes. There he was at his most honest.

Glorious. Powerful. Naked.

As he approached, Kelly could see in more detail. His skin, marked by the scars he'd earned in training and battle alike. She traced them all, one by one, with the tip of her finger.

Across his chest, his arms, even his back. How much pain he must have endured over the years.

At the same time he lavished her shoulders and cleavage with kisses. She ought to feel weak and helpless in front of him. Instead, she felt powerful.

She raised herself off the bed, allowing him access to the laces at the back of her dress. Free at last.

His manhood stood proudly, almost teasing her with its presence. This wasn't something nice girls talked about, but Kelly knew what to do. The growing fire in her stomach burnt up any remaining trace of patience.

She ached for him.

She was ready and would no longer be denied this ultimate pleasure.

As her dress fell to the floor, she felt empowered to take this new step with him. She crawled back onto the bed, and reached for his chest, pushing him backward against the pillows. He did not protest.

Then she straddled his hard, muscular thighs and lowered herself down on top of him, supported by his strong grasp. A raw moan escaped her lips as she allowed him inside of her.

His body merged with hers for the very first time. It stung at first, but not in a bad way. Soon, the initial pain was forgotten.

This was the way to soothe the sweet ache within. She started to rock back and forth on top of him, guided by instinct as much as his hands. He reached for her neck, twirling his fingers around stray locks of her hair as she held on tightly to his wrist for balance.

Her other hand found its way down onto his abs.

Though she was on top, he was moving along with her. Where her movement ended, his began.

A perfect rhythm, like waves crashing onto the beach.

Many times she'd imagined what this would be like. Two becoming one.

She closed her eyes, swept up in the magic of the

moment.

Rolling her hips backwards and forwards, she felt her thoughts reach a new plane. Reality mattered no more. The threat Broc had mentioned so many times, the coming war.

It was irrelevant. As long as they had each other, everything would work itself out.

Faster and faster, they moved. Like a dance, only much more intimate.

Their bodies seemed to sense exactly what the other desired. A slight pause to build the tension, or a more feverish pace to try and relieve it.

The ache was growing. Ever sweeter, ever more intense.

She would not last through the night. The anticipation for this moment had been too great.

Kelly opened her eyes again, and found Broc already staring up at her. His face betrayed a change in him too. He wasn't his calm, collected self. He was no longer in control.

Their union had brought out his wild side.

He dug his fingers into her hips, spurring her on. She sped up, more and more, feverishly working towards their mutual release.

It was coming. She knew it.

And with it, she knew something else.

His prediction would come true. She could sense it.

As he reached the pinnacle of his pleasure, he let out a primal groan. A shudder originated in his body, seemingly transferring all his pleasure into her.

She could keep quiet no longer, crying out with tears in her eyes as she tensed up as well. Bearing down hard on top of his still trembling manhood, he exploded into her.

Kelly's mind filled with light. Her eyes, wide open.

Through the blinding white surrounding her, Broc's face appeared in front of her. His eyes, staring into hers.

"I love you, Kelly Chaslain of West Hythe."

"I love you too," Kelly whispered in response.

The words held less meaning than the feeling that passed unrestricted between the two.

Light.

Love.

Life.

Kelly snapped back into reality, and found that she was still where she had been only moments earlier. The blinding light had gone, replaced by the dimly lit room decorated with flowers. Underneath her on the bed, her man, with a satisfied smile on his face.

"What happened," he asked.

Kelly shook her head and returned his smile. "I don't know. A vision. A dream."

"And what did you learn in this vision?"

She reached down and placed his hand on her lower abdomen. It still took her breath away just how much bigger his hand was than hers.

"That you're right. That our family will grow."

He grinned widely. "Well, that's a good vision indeed."

He threaded his fingers through hers and pulled her down into his arms. She rested her head against his chest, but did not stir otherwise. Nothing else mattered anymore. Kelly was content to remain in this embrace, listening to the calming beat of his heart.

If she died right now, it would have been with a smile on her face.

That was how they remained. Time had lost all meaning. They were not in a rush to get up.

Until a distant sound disturbed the peace.

"What was that?" Kelly asked, lifting her head. The noise had sent a shiver down her naked skin.

Broc's expression and tone had grown dark in an instant.

"The war horn. As we've feared. It has begun."

***

The Soldier and the Siren

CHAPTER ONE

————◆————

Liliwen had already lost the argument before even starting, but she had to give it one final try. After all, her entire purpose, her reason for being, was at stake.

"Perhaps if I could learn how to fight. I might be of use. Send me to Siren's Rock to train, please, Father!" she pleaded.

King Weiland merely shook his head and averted his gaze, as Liliwen paced the large coral hall that was the seat of the Merfolk's power. He might be content sitting there on his throne, but Liliwen was unwilling to remain a passive bystander. She wanted to *do* something with her life.

What would it take for him to see sense? Why should she waste her talents by sitting around at home, watching, waiting, as the men of the Deep prepared for a battle they were unlikely to win?

Their bloody conflict with the Others who lived on the islands east of their borders had raged on for so long, nobody alive remembered when or how it had all begun. What were they even fighting for?

Actually, the entire situation was stupid. But convincing her father to end the war was even further outside of the realm of possibilities.

"The battlefield is no place for a woman. Why can you not be content with what you have? Leave the fighting to your brother," King Weiland finally replied.

Liliwen rolled her eyes. Why should Cadfael have all the fun, while she was stuck here in what might as well be a gilded cage?

"But, Father!" she argued.

King Weiland looked up at her, and forcefully banged his three-pointed staff into the ground. Its sound bounced around the hall, making the echoes sound a whole lot louder than the original noise.

"That's enough. I will hear no more of it!" King Weiland roared.

Liliwen had no choice but to retreat. The conversation was over.

She looked back once at the elaborate throne, covered in precious stones and shells of all shapes and sizes polished up to a pearly shimmer. Her father still refused to acknowledge her.

Did he think they could go on as they had and still stand a chance to win? If something did not change, they would surely lose.

And without his approval, there was only one thing she could do: take matters into her own hands.

———◆———

The Soldier and the Siren

Liliwen waited in her chambers, determined to follow through on her earlier decision. No matter what her father, the ruler of the Deep, had said, she had her own plans.

As soon as the change of the guard was complete, and the halls of the royal palace were mostly abandoned, she made her move.

"Lili," a voice whispered as she made her way down the hallway. "Hey, Lili. Where are you going?"

Liliwen froze in her tracks immediately. There were few soldiers around at this time of day, but clearly she still failed to move around unseen.

"Cara." Liliwen sighed as she spotted her closest friend waiting in a doorway several feet away from her own. "I'm just going out for a swim. Clear my head."

"Lovely. I'll join you," Cara said. She blinked a few times and smiled one of her most radiant smiles. They'd grown up together and had been inseparable for most of their lives.

Liliwen's heart sank. She couldn't involve Cara in her plans. At least not directly.

She shook her head. "No, I wanted to go by myself."

Cara frowned and brushed a long lock of her golden hair out of her face. "Did something happen?"

Liliwen scanned the hall. There was nobody else in sight, but one could never be too sure. She gestured at Cara to follow her back to her chambers.

Once inside, with the door securely locked behind

them, she finally spoke up again.

"Have you ever felt like you were... I don't know. *More?*"

"I'm not sure I understand. More than what?" Cara asked.

"More capable. More useful. More than what we're being given credit for."

"We're of noble blood. We don't have to work like the commoners. We wear the best fashions and jewelry. And when the time comes, we'll have our pick of eligible bachelors. How much more do you need?" Cara folded her arms and cocked her head to the side.

Liliwen looked down at herself. The elaborate necklace that hung halfway down her chest. The numerous pearl bracelets and gold rings that adorned her hands.

These feelings she'd been battling, they proved harder to explain than she'd anticipated. And dressed up as she was, as was expected of a princess under the sea, her thoughts seemed out of place, even silly.

"But the war... Don't you ever wonder what will happen if we lose?" Liliwen said.

Cara shrugged. "We're safe here. The war happens out there." She gestured vaguely at the door. "It's nothing to do with us. Even if we do lose, do you think those savages are going to come down here and kill us? They can't even breathe under water like we do."

There was no arguing with that last point. Perhaps the enemy wouldn't come down here even if they won.

The Soldier and the Siren

Perhaps nothing would ever change.

Liliwen wasn't sure whether that was a happy or sad prospect.

"Well, I for one wish to find out what's out there. I want to see what's beyond the Deep."

Cara shook her head. "I don't know why you would. There's nothing there for us. We have all we need right here."

"I'm just curious, alright? These walls are starting to feel like a prison rather than a home. I need space." Liliwen turned her back and faced one of the few windows in her chambers. The view was uninspiring. The same old courtyard of the same old palace she'd lived in all her life. A couple of guards, a few statues of their ancestors, and seaweed.

A whole lot of seaweed in various shades of green, blue and purple.

She'd been stuck here, while Cadfael, her elder brother, was climbing the ranks and making a real difference out there.

What would it be like to go on dry land? Merfolk could do it; that was how they were able to fight effectively even on the enemy's territory. But of course she'd never been outside the Deep. Even Siren's Rock, the Merfolk's land-based training colony, was well out of bounds to her, and that wasn't even far away.

She had tried to run away once when she was younger,

but was quickly recovered by her father's guards. Ever since then, she'd never tried again.

She turned around again.

"You can't tell anyone. Promise me," Liliwen urged.

Cara rolled her eyes. "Just don't do anything stupid."

"I won't." Liliwen hid her lie with a smile. Once she got out there, there was no telling what she would do or how stupid it would turn out to be. But she couldn't sit around in the palace any longer. The outside world was calling, and Liliwen was determined to answer.

———◆———

It was a morning in late spring, stormy, like any other morning in late spring. The clouds hung low, hiding the sun from view. It was only a matter of time before the rains would start.

Overall a gloomy day. Perfect for hunting.

The Reaping was upon them. It had been eight years since the last human had moved onto the Black Isles. And what a long eight years it had been.

Teaq found it hard to think about all the changes his people seen during this time, without feeling bitter about it all. He should have been king. He was the firstborn.

Instead, his younger brother Broc had been crowned seven years ago. And now he intended to take the human as his own, to guarantee himself an heir.

Again, Teaq would be passed over in favor of his

younger sibling.

Not that he was overly interested in taking a bride at this moment, but that was hardly the point. It would have been nice to be considered, at least.

"Sir, the ship is ready. As are the men," someone said, interrupting these dark thoughts of his.

"We'll leave shortly." Teaq gestured to dismiss the soldier, while keeping his gaze fixed on the dark clouds gathering in the distance. One solitary bolt of lightning lit up the sky.

He could have ordered someone else to go on this excursion to the mainland. As General, it was his responsibility to keep the Isles safe from invasion, to command the army in battle and to strategize and strengthen their defenses during times of relative peace. Hunting was not in his job description.

But the truth was, he relished the thought of letting his inner beast loose on the vast plains of the mainland. Hunting had always served as a much needed outlet for Teaq. Nothing cleared the mind like an intense chase. Nothing was as satisfying as returning home with a boatload of wild boar, caught with his own bare hands.

It was a pleasure Teaq and Broc had shared when they were younger, and one of the things the king was forced to sacrificed upon claiming the throne. In a way, Teaq's participation in today's hunt would be all the more enjoyable because of that.

Teaq forced himself into action and made his way down the path leading toward the harbor. A longship was waiting at the furthermost pier, and the hunting party he would lead had already gathered up on the deck.

It was a mixed group; men as well as women, not all of them soldiers, but everyone eager to get their hands dirty. It was a rare pleasure, travelling to the mainland, which had traditionally been their home many generations ago, before the humans had forced them out during the Great War.

The crowd consisted of land animals—predators, as one would expect. Wolves, like Teaq, and bears mostly. The most notable exceptions were the eagles, who would circle the skies as the hunt took place. Lookouts.

Of course, for the moment, everyone was in their human form. But once they got onto the mainland, they couldn't risk being seen. Their truce with the humans forbade them from entering their territory. The islanders were simply too large to be mistaken for fellow humans.

Luckily their animal side would enable them to disguise their presence during the hunt. It also made it unnecessary for them to carry weapons ashore.

"Ready?" Teaq called out as he boarded the ship.

The captain—the only fox on-board—nodded. "Yes, General."

"We'll sail to the White Cliff," Teaq ordered.

"Raise the sail! Rowers, take your positions!" the captain shouted.

The Soldier and the Siren

Teaq closed his eyes and took a deep breath of salty sea air. It smelled of opportunity, but also of a looming threat.

They were not a seafaring people by origin, but by necessity. Still, they had adapted fairly well in the centuries since they'd taken up residence on the Black Isles. The water didn't bother them anymore. Neither did the harsh climate.

Farming was an impossibility on the Isles, but most of its residents preferred meat or fish over vegetables anyway.

Indeed the islanders' biggest struggle wasn't their own, but the continuing conflict with the Sea Folk, who considered the Black Isles part of their own territory. It was this ongoing war that made today's hunting expedition twice as dangerous.

Not only did they risk the truce with the humans on the mainland if they were discovered, they also had to be on the lookout for Sea Folk soldiers who might try to ambush them along the way.

It was these and similar thoughts that occupied Teaq as the longship started to cut through the choppy waters. He studied the expressions of the remaining hunting party, only to find that they were a lot less thoughtful than himself, and a lot more excited.

Obviously they were looking forward to spending a few hours on a land much more vast than their own. He was too. But as General, he didn't have it in him to ignore the dangers that lurked all around.

So he turned to face forward, his hand firmly gripping the butt of his sword, and scanned the waters for any sign of the enemy.

Until finally, two hours into the journey, the stark white cliffs of the mainland came into view.

CHAPTER TWO

Liliwen had swum for miles, further and further away from the palace she'd called home all her life. She had made sure to avoid areas that she knew would be heavily guarded, Siren's Rock especially. So instead she found herself traveling east.

Nothing about her surroundings looked familiar anymore. But getting lost wasn't a risk she needed to concern herself with. She, like all of her people, possessed an immaculate sense of direction. No matter how many times she'd change course, she always knew in the back of her mind where home was. She'd find her way back with ease.

At first, she'd felt anxious, be it for another reason. Had someone noticed her departure? Would she be intercepted and taken back home just like all those years ago?

After her earlier disagreement with her father, the punishment for her act of rebellion would be unpleasant to say the least. The King under the Seas could be harsh when his authority was being challenged. He wouldn't let a small detail like Liliwen being his only daughter discourage him from dishing out justice. Even Cadfael, who'd always had a soft spot for his baby sister, wouldn't be able to shield her from that.

But as the time passed, Liliwen felt calmer and more self-assured. She had been stealthy enough to slip away unseen. For once in her life, she was completely alone.

And the views that accompanied her journey were indescribable.

Schools of colorful fish darting through exotic coral reefs as far as the eye could see.

The water even smelled different here. Fresher, crisper.

She didn't just stay down by the ocean floor either. In her eagerness to discover as much as she could, she swam closer and closer to the surface, hoping to catch a glimpse of the kind of creatures who lived beyond the sea, but which she had only ever heard of in stories and song.

Birds. Seagulls.

There weren't any out in the open sea, at least not on this day.

But Liliwen did not let that discourage her. She kept going, until the landscape changed dramatically once again. A huge black granite landmass came into view. It grew upwards out of the ocean floor and rose steeply, extending up and out of the water. She had never seen anything as imposing in her life.

"An island," Liliwen whispered to herself, as she tried to catch her breath.

Having come so close to the Other World, she could not stop herself from exploring further.

Sure enough, the winged creatures she had wanted to see earlier were plentiful around the shoreline. She approached the island and made her way up to the surface, mesmerized by the way they moved through the skies. Flapping their wings, up and down, diving and soaring effortlessly through the air.

It was the most beautiful thing. How were they able to do that without being in the water, she had no idea.

Liliwen knew she should be careful. The Others would be on the lookout for incoming Merfolk intruders. But her curiosity spurred her on to explore more and more of this foreign land. In any case, it seemed like nobody was watching.

———— ◆ ————

The hunting party had been a success. Teaq felt a great sense of accomplishment and calm as their ship started on its return journey. Although he still wasn't thrilled about the Reaping, at least the feast would be lavish. They had all the supplies they could have hoped for.

Of course, his own efforts had accounted for a fair share of the wild boar caught by the islanders today. And the after effects of letting his inner beast out and running across the vast plains of the mainland were still raging through his body. His heartbeat was still elevated. His senses were heightened as though he was still in his wolf form.

This high which followed any hunt would last for

another hour or so at least. Exactly this feeling made hunting such a satisfying pastime. One which Broc, his little brother, could no longer partake in.

Teaq scanned the boat. His hunting mates were in a similar state of ecstasy. Each one of them looked content with their respective achievements, even the eagles, who had only served as lookouts. Hunting offered all the thrills of battle, with very few of the dangers.

After adjusting his armor and sword, Teaq forced his attention back toward the waters. They had managed to keep their presence on the mainland a secret, but they weren't home safe yet.

Luckily the two hour return journey passed without incident. They made it back to the Eastern Isle with plenty of daylight to spare.

As the unloading began, Teaq decided to take some moments for himself. He went for a walk along the mostly neglected fortifications along the desolate easternmost side of the island.

Dark clouds hung low on the horizon, promising an upcoming storm. Bad weather was common this time of year and not something the islanders ordinarily had to worry about.

The diffused light and dramatic skies gave the entire island a wild and untamed look. Like nobody was meant to be here. They were only living here on borrowed time.

Would the Black Isles survive the next Great War? Only time would tell.

The Soldier and the Siren

A shimmer just under the surface of the waters down below caught Teaq's eye. He grabbed for his sword and took a step forward, when he found himself face to face with the most unusual creature.

Her silver hair floated gently in the water, framing her heart-shaped face. Her eyes widened as she spotted him, but neither he nor she made a move initially.

She was unlike anything he'd ever seen. A Sea Folk female.

Mesmerized, all he could do was stare as time seemed to slow to a crawl.

Teaq tore himself away for just a second and checked his surroundings. There was nobody else within view. The two of them were completely alone, with only a handful of circling seagulls keeping them company overhead.

He climbed over the wall and onto the rocks lining the shore and got onto his haunches just beside the water's edge.

She did not move an inch initially.

But then, within the blink of an eye, she swam all the way up to the surface.

"Well I'll be damned," he mumbled, in awe of her agility and grace.

With her head and shoulders up out of the water, he could get a better look at her. Everything about her was beautiful. From her silver hair, to her shimmery skin and eyes that shone like pure gold. Her slender body was adorned with all sorts of trinkets and jewelry. Pearls, shells and precious stones. These were all unfamiliar sights on one of her kind.

As far as Teaq knew, no one on the Isles had ever seen a Mermaid before.

After countless battles with her male counterparts, Teaq knew very well that she was one of the enemy. The similarities were undeniable. He knew he ought to capture her. After all, she was clearly a spy sent in to distract and confuse. A new tactic to give the other side an edge in a conflict that had raged on for generations.

But she had neither armor nor weaponry. She was completely defenseless.

Teaq did not believe in chivalry as such, but even he couldn't justify attacking an unarmed female, no matter what species she belonged to.

"What is your business here, Mermaid?" Teaq asked. His voice was not as firm as he would have liked it to be.

She blinked a few times and cocked her head to the side as though she was hearing spoken words for the very first time. That did not make any sense, though. Teaq had exchanged enough slurs and threats with soldiers of the same species to know this.

"I know your people speak our language," he said. "Why have you come here?"

She averted her gaze and coyly brushed a lock of her wet hair behind her ear. A hint of a smile was playing on her shapely lips.

How very human she looked, and yet so alien as well.

"I..." she began to speak. The sound of her voice shook Teaq to his core. It was lyrical, as though she wasn't talking, but rather singing her words.

Even she looked shocked when she met his gaze again, but then quickly recovered.

"I just wanted to see the birds," she said.

Her answer was ludicrous, of course. See the birds. Teaq looked up at the seagulls that continued to circle overhead, no doubt looking for their next meal in between the rocks surrounding them.

"And you specifically came to the Black Isles to see them? Why should I believe you?" Teaq demanded.

He wanted to be firm with her, to do his duty as a protector of the Isles. But he was unable.

"It's so beautiful here. Unlike anything I've ever seen," the mermaid said.

Her eyes were still fixed on his. Within them, Teaq thought he could see truth. Not that that made any sense either.

Although the Elders had learned a great deal about the Sea Folk over the years—the way they fought to the death, showing neither remorse or fear—there was precious little known about their females. Ancient songs told of their beauty, which was evident in front of Teaq right now. But that was all.

Every ounce of sense Teaq still possessed told him he

should be suspicious of this creature. That she was trying to trick him. But his heart couldn't accept it.

"If you think this place is beautiful, tell me of your land, so I may judge it for myself," Teaq said.

The mermaid smiled briefly, then raised herself up out of the water and sat on top of a smooth rock just a couple of feet away from Teaq. If he reached out, he would be able to touch her easily. It was as though she wasn't even trying to evade capture.

"It's mostly seaweed, really," she said.

Teaq couldn't suppress a chuckle, which in turn made her giggle as well.

The voice of an angel.

"Well it's mostly rocks, here."

"I like these rocks. They have depth," she said as she patted the smooth, black stone that currently served as her seat.

They shared an intense look that made Teaq's skin hot and cold all at the same time.

"You're a soldier," she said.

Her tone was firm. It wasn't a question, but rather, a statement. As such, Teaq did not feel the need to answer or correct her, though his position as General was one he held with great pride.

"My brother is a soldier too," she continued. "But he doesn't have so many scars."

They remained silent for what felt like forever. So many unspoken truths between them.

THE SOLDIER AND THE SIREN

Teaq knew how Sea Folk soldiers fought. All or nothing. If he met her brother in battle at some point in the future, likely only one of them would survive.

The way she looked at him, he knew that she was thinking the same as well.

Yet somehow, these horrors did not seem to matter. They had connected, no matter how brief this meeting might end up being.

Her presence here today had awoken something in Teaq. A flame that would prove impossible to extinguish.

CHAPTER THREE

Liliwen hadn't planned on getting so far into enemy territory. In all her excitement, she had gotten carried away.

And once she was discovered, that meant there was no turning back at all. She would have been captured if she'd tried to run, so her instincts told her to do the exact opposite. Perhaps she could enchant him, just like the sirens of old.

The man was so different from everyone she knew. Yet it was so easy to turn on her charm for him.

A soldier, like Cadfael, and yet completely and utterly different.

As soon as she'd emerged from the water, her senses became overwhelmed by smells and sights she could not have foreseen. Dry land felt weird. Her skin prickled in the air, making it hard to put up a calm front. There was a current of sorts as well; Liliwen supposed it was called a wind. Much colder than the surrounding air, and very... dry.

And the man. He smelled earthy and spicy and completely incomparable to anything she'd smelled before. Liliwen could not get enough of it.

It was a bit of a chore to hide her excitement and play coy. The latter was especially important if her plan was to work. At least he seemed to want to talk to her, rather than catch her.

"Why have you come here?" he asked.

A fair question. She wasn't quite sure, now that she thought about it. It would be best to keep her answer simple.

The Others had magical powers; legends were told of how they fought. They could shape shift into other beings and often did so in battle. That gave them an edge the Merfolk did not have.

Liliwen knew very well that if this man wanted to, he could transform in an instant and kill her. She knew what he was. A wolf. Every time she closed her eyes, she could see his true form clearly in her thoughts.

"I just wanted to see the birds," Liliwen answered. Although it wasn't the whole truth, it wasn't technically a lie either.

The sound of her own voice was so different out of the water, it startled her at first.

It didn't seem to startle him though. And as silly as her answer sounded, he seemed to be amused by it, which only encouraged her further.

They chatted a little, forgetting for just a moment that they were meant to be sworn enemies.

Finally, after the conversation had died down for a moment, Liliwen felt compelled to take things just a little further.

She raised her arm and reached out for him, brushing her fingertips across his arm. How strange he felt.

Her own skin was flawless, a blank canvas of flexible scales, whereas he was covered in marks. It looked like it would be rough to the touch, but nothing could be further from the truth. So soft, so delicate was his skin.

She quickly pulled her hand back and looked up at him to gauge his reaction. He didn't seem to mind it.

"Your skin is very strange," she observed.

The man grinned and shook his head. "Not from where I'm standing."

Although Liliwen's curiosity was far from satisfied, she knew she'd better quit before she got herself into real trouble.

"I'd better go now." Liliwen smiled briefly, and felt her heart surge when he responded in kind.

It was kind of fun, flirting. She hadn't tried it before, because she'd never found anyone interesting enough to try it with. But his reactions told her that she was more than a little talented at it.

"That's probably for the best," he said.

After one last moment of eye contact, she slid back into the water.

He wasn't coming after her.

She smiled to herself, then swam as fast as she could. What a day. What an adventure!

Cara had made her promise not to do anything stupid. And precisely this promise had been broken in the most grandiose way. 'Stupid' wasn't quite strong enough to describe what had happened today.

And yet…

Her little outing away from the palace couldn't have gone any better. She had truly broken free from her little domain and seen the world.

What would her father say if he found out she'd been talking to one of the Others? A soldier, no less.

———◆———

Liliwen's heart was still pounding when she made it back to the palace. She'd swum at full speed, but the exertion hadn't sent her heart racing. It was the unexpected encounter with the Other. The man-wolf. Or should that be, wolf-man?

She had come so close to being caught. But the threat of capture hadn't really spooked her. It was the man himself.

Tall, broad, more muscular than any Merman warrior. His eyes, an unfamiliar brown that seemed to reveal unspeakable depths and secrets.

He'd made her skin crawl, though not in a bad way.

Every time she blinked, she could still see him in her mind's eye.

The soldier.

A man unlike any other.

The scars on his skin told her he'd seen many a battle.

He had survived, even thrived. How many of her people had he killed? She wasn't sure she really wanted to know.

And yet, he'd let her live. He'd even let her go back home.

A knock on her door startled her.

"Yes?" she called out, trying her best to keep her voice steady. Had her father found out about what she'd done and sent someone to summon her?

Cara burst in. "Lili! You're back. Praise Poseidon."

Liliwen quickly recovered. "I wish you'd stop with those silly superstitions. Yes, I'm back."

Cara grinned. "I'm only teasing you."

Liliwen sat down on her bed and folded her hands in her lap.

"So… where did you go? What did you do?" Cara asked.

There was no way Liliwen could share what had happened. It was too risky.

But how could she keep it all to herself?

She brushed away Cara's question. "Oh… I just swam for a bit. It was very refreshing."

Cara eyed her suspiciously. It was making Liliwen feel uneasy.

"You don't look refreshed. You look like you've seen a ghost," Cara observed finally.

Liliwen looked up at her best friend and pressed her lips together. Should she? Could she risk it?

"You'd never tell on me, if I shared a secret?" Liliwen

asked. Her heart had never quite stopped pounding ever since she'd reached her chambers.

"Of course not. I didn't tell anyone that you left either."

"Promise?" Liliwen cocked her head to the side and studied Cara's features. There was no sign of deceit or ill will in her expression. Not that Liliwen could see, and she'd always been rather good at reading her friend and confidante.

Cara nodded solemnly.

"Fine. I swam all the way to the Black Isles."

Cara's eyes went wide in shock. "No! Why would you do such a thing? What if someone had seen you? They could have taken you prisoner, or worse, just killed you on the spot!"

Liliwen averted her gaze. Someone *did* see her. The reality of just how close to death she had come today was starting to sink in.

And yet... Being in the wolf-man's presence had not made her feel like she was in danger at all. As soon as she realized that he wasn't going to attack her, she had wanted to see just how close she could get to him.

And in doing so, she had *touched* him. She had touched a man other than her brother or father, without first being betrothed to him. That in itself was forbidden. And considering who, or what, the man was...

As Cara had pointed out earlier in the day, she'd never been denied anything in her life. All the treasures of the

Deep were hers for the taking. If she said the word, there would be scores of willing suitors battling each other for the honor of her company.

But that man. That enemy soldier, he was something her father couldn't just give to her. Therein lay the challenge.

If Liliwen wanted him—and she was becoming quite certain did she did—she had to get him for herself. She wasn't a warrior. Her father would make sure she'd never see battle or do anything of note. But *he*… The wolf-man would be her ultimate conquest.

That meant one thing though. Something Cara would not be happy about. Today was only the beginning. She'd have to sneak away more often.

"Hey, are you even listening to me?" Cara demanded.

Liliwen blinked a few times. "Sorry, I was lost in thought. What did you say?"

Cara scoffed. "You're impossible, Lili! I said, promise me you won't go back there. I don't know what I'll do if the Others catch you. I'll die of boredom here on my own!"

Liliwen pressed her lips together. She could promise nothing of the sort.

"But… you don't understand, Cara. Now that I've seen the Islands myself, I have to try and learn all I can about the enemy. I want to help our people, you see…" Of course that last bit was a lie. Liliwen did need to go back. All of her father's guards couldn't keep her away from the

Islands.

Her motives, of course, were entirely selfish.

"You're beyond reason!" Cara complained. "I don't even know what to do with you! Why can't you let things be and let Cadfael and your father worry about the war?"

Liliwen shook her head. "I just feel like I have to do this. Like it's my calling. Does that make sense?"

It was a calling of sorts. The memory of her meeting with the wolf-man was summoning her to go back for more.

Cara shook her head and sat down beside her. "It doesn't. But I suppose I've never had a calling, so what would I know."

Liliwen put her arm around her best friend, rested her head on her shoulder and continued to day dream. It was too bad she couldn't share all she had seen with Cara. Perhaps in time, she'd be ready to speak about *him*.

Silly. He'd had such a huge impact on her after such a short meeting, and she didn't even know his name.

But Liliwen wasn't worried about that. Whenever she'd manage to sneak out of the palace unseen, she'd see him again. She'd go back to the same spot at every possible opportunity, and sooner or later she'd find *him* there. They had an unspoken understanding. She'd seen it in his eyes.

Perhaps he considered her his conquest as well.

Liliwen lay back on the plush pillows that dotted her bed, pulling Cara down with her. There they lay in silence, staring up at the ceiling. Finally, Liliwen's heartbeat began to slow to a more normal pace. And all she could do was smile.

CHAPTER FOUR

————◆————

He should have caught her. Of course he should have.

Teaq knew he'd made a mistake, technically. But then why had it felt so right to let her go?

Their little encounter had stayed with him throughout the evening. After she'd left, he made his way back to the longship and sailed back to Black Mountain and the castle he called home. Even knowing that there was no chance she'd lingered around all these hours, he still caught himself scanning the waters for any sign of her.

What a magical being. Such beauty and grace. And yet such naivety.

She'd come to see the birds.

Teaq, just like the rest of his people, had lived with a constant threat of war all his life. The Sea Folk were a fierce enemy who could strike at any moment.

They considered the seas to be their domain. And of course, the Black Isles were surrounded by vast amounts of water, which the Sea Folk sought to dominate.

And then this young woman had come along, and told him she'd arrived on their shores just to see the birds.

Had she never seen birds before? He'd never seen a Mermaid before, so perhaps not. Perhaps they didn't travel like their male counterparts did.

Perhaps she'd run off from her own people to go on a little expedition of her own.

She'd seemed enterprising enough, as well as surprisingly fearless for an unarmed intruder. When she'd reached for him and grazed his arm with her fingers, Teaq had wondered for a moment if that was it. If she was hiding some secret weapon or spell that would turn him to dust at her touch.

But actually, she'd just been curious. How laughable. Laughable and in equal measures adorable as well.

He never thought he'd think this way about one of the enemy, but this Mermaid had seemed completely innocent. As if there was no war. And their people hadn't murdered each other over these rocks in the sea for generations now.

But the inconvenient truth was that they had. And what had occurred earlier on the shores of the Eastern Isle while nobody had been watching was an act of treason on both their parts.

Of course, nobody needed to know that.

Teaq was a man of few words usually. Keeping a secret, even one this big, would not be a problem for him. Hopefully she'd be equally discreet and her people wouldn't be on the warpath as a result of their interaction.

As soon as the ship arrived at the Harbor of Black Mountain, Teaq left the crew to their own devices and headed straight for his chambers in the castle. He didn't even see Broc to announce their arrival, or the report on the outcome of the hunt.

THE SOLDIER AND THE SIREN

All of that stuff suddenly did not seem important anymore.

Teaq, despite his serious, almost cynical nature, was caught in the Mermaid's spell.

He simply could not forget their meeting, however short.

It wasn't just a passing infatuation either. He knew that he would carry these thoughts with him for the foreseeable future. There would be only one remedy: he had to see her again.

Would he, though?

Would she ever come back?

He himself didn't have any reason to return to the Eastern Isle any time soon, and it wasn't even very far for him. She had travelled all the way from the Deep, where the Sea Folk had made their home.

Unusually, he was feeling optimistic. Something told him that indeed, she would make the effort again. And as long as he made sure he returned to that same spot regularly, and kept any nosy onlookers at bay, they would meet again.

———◆———

Teaq marched into the Great Hall just a bit later than he would have liked. It wasn't in his nature to be tardy.

"Brother, good you are here. Let's begin," Broc said, then turned to face the others who were already present.

The Great Hall was the biggest room within the castle and as such the place where get-togethers, feasts and council meetings were held. Of course, the Islanders never did get very formal, even during official occasions such as audiences with the king. The long benches and tables used for more festive occasions were still placed around the hall in their usual fashion. The Elders sat together on one of the benches, whereas Broc and Teaq preferred to stand. Rhea, their cousin and head of the Royal Guard, along with her second in command, Yorrick, leaned against one of the other tables.

"We have much to discuss," Broc began. "The Reaping. Are we on track?"

Rhea spoke up first. "The castle is as secure as it's ever been. I see no problems."

Her tone was even more gruff than usual. Rhea was obviously unhappy about something. That was nothing new, though. She did not possess what one might call a sunny disposition at the best of times.

"Great. Have someone prepare the chambers near my own for the human's arrival. I intend to keep her close."

"Do you think this is wise, my king?" Rhea asked.

Broc folded his arms. "She might as well get used to my presence from the start, so yes, I do think it is a good idea."

"Might I suggest a guard at her door, at least during the transition?" Rhea asked.

Broc shot her a disapproving look. "She's to be a guest,

not a prisoner. I will not have her treated as one."

"How about you, brother? How did the hunt go?" Broc turned to face Teaq.

"Good," Teaq responded.

Broc continued to look at him, probably expecting some sort of clarification.

What was he hoping for, exactly? A blow-by-blow report?

"We managed to remain unseen by the mainlanders. No problems while sailing either," Teaq added.

"No Sea Folk sightings?"

"No, why?" Teaq responded, then immediately regretted his defensive tone.

"I just want to ensure this Reaping goes smoothly. The last thing we need is for an invasion to hit our shores right in the middle of it all."

Teaq kept quiet this time. It had been an innocuous question. His reaction had been way out of line. This sort of suspicious behavior would get him into real trouble.

"Well, then." Broc turned around and faced the Elders this time. "Uri, do you have anything to add?"

The leader of the Elders stood up and folded his hands in front of his long grey robe. "My king, as you are aware, the last Reaping did not go as planned."

Broc nodded. "I recall that there were problems, yes."

"So we have come up with an idea to minimize these issues going forward," Uri spoke in a thin but commanding voice.

Teaq had no idea how old the man was, but he was certain it was an impressive number. Islanders did not often live to old age. A seat on the Council of Elders was a rare honor only few managed to achieve.

"I'm all ears," Broc said.

"Well, we have decided it would be best if the human is kept in the dark about the true nature of these Isles and their inhabitants, at least during the transition period."

"I'm not sure I understand," Broc said.

"Our powers," another one of the Elders spoke up.

Uri nodded. "Exactly. The human world, although much more vast than our own lands, is also very small in some ways. They do not react well to things they do not understand. As such, we think it is best we introduce any newcomers into our ways gradually. Let's at first make this offering think our ways are much like her own. That way she won't get too spooked."

Broc nodded slowly. "I see. So we pretend to be essentially human."

"That's correct. We advise a ban on transformations in front of the human for the transition period."

Broc remained silent for a moment.

Teaq glanced over at Rhea, who had an even more pronounced scowl on her face now. She was very unhappy about something. It wasn't like her to keep her thoughts to herself.

"Very well. I can see the sense in that," Broc said.

"What if there is an attack though?" Teaq interjected. "I cannot have my men neutered in the face of an enemy invasion."

"Which is also a fair point. Can we agree that there will be no *unnecessary* shifting during the transition period? At least not within the castle, where the human might see? If there's an attack, the ban will be temporarily lifted."

Teaq nodded reluctantly.

Broc turned to get Rhea's input. The latter just shrugged.

"Anything else?" Broc asked.

The Elders shook their heads. Neither Rhea nor Teaq spoke up either. The meeting was over.

Teaq was the first to leave, marching down the hallway toward the stairs. He wanted nothing more than some time alone. After his strange encounter earlier in the day, he had much to think about.

"Teaq," a female voice interrupted. "Teaq, wait up!"

He stopped with a sigh. "What is it, Rhea?"

"This Reaping business. I'm not happy about it," she said.

That much had been obvious throughout the meeting as well. Teaq could only guess what her reasons might be.

"Oh?"

He studied her face. She was visibly tense. The muscles in her jaw were working furiously.

"It's all very well, bringing a human onto our shores for

the survival of our people, but..."

"Our people need the fresh blood." Teaq shrugged. This is how it had been for centuries, whether any of them liked it or not.

"But things are different this time. Broc intends to take her for himself. He's going to have her live in the castle. Unguarded," Rhea complained.

Teaq took a deep breath and folded his arms in front of his chest. "So?"

"So, he's the king. The king's protection is the Royal Guard's main responsibility. *My* main responsibility. It's an unnecessary risk."

"What would you have me do about it?" Teaq asked.

"Speak to him. He's your brother. Make him see the risks involved."

"Do you have any reason to think that this human poses a bigger risk than the previous offerings we've taken?" Teaq asked.

"Call it instinct."

"Could your instinct have something to do with the fact that you wouldn't want to see *any* woman paired up with my brother? Human or otherwise?" Teaq asked.

He didn't care much for gossip or speculation, but even he had noticed that Rhea had developed a liking for Broc. Sadly for her, they were second cousins. The rules forbade any union between partners who were so closely related. There were no exceptions, especially not when the heir of the throne's health was at stake.

Rhea's face darkened even further. If looks could kill…

"I take my job very seriously. And I don't appreciate these kinds of accusations!"

"Fine, fine. I can see how it would be a security risk having a stranger—a human, no less—roam around the castle unguarded. But he's made up his mind already, it seems."

"Just speak with him," Rhea urged.

Teaq sighed. "Fine. But if you want someone to keep an eye on the human once she gets here, you're most likely going to have to arrange for it yourself. Without my brother finding out."

"Right."

She still didn't look happy, but that was as much as Teaq felt like talking about the matter. He had his own problems to think about.

"I'll speak with him," he promised. Then he left Rhea in the corridor and went on his way.

With his younger brother getting ready to take a mate, it was only natural for Teaq himself to consider doing the same. But there was no human girl being shipped in for him. Neither was he interested in one. After today's events, there was only one female he had his eyes on, and she was well out of bounds.

Teaq let out a bitter chuckle as he wondered what the

Council of Elders might say if he sought permission to take a Mermaid as his mate. The rules didn't forbid it. *Technically.*

CHAPTER FIVE

———◆·———

The days passed at a crawl. Liliwen grew more and more restless, the longer she found herself confined to the palace.

She had to slip away again.

Her memories of the brief meeting with the Other stayed with her at every waking moment, and even in her dreams. The longer she stayed away, the less likely it would be that she'd meet him again.

And she really did have to meet him once more. Every fiber in her body screamed for another chance to see him.

Finally, she got her chance a whole four days from her initial excursion. Her father was preoccupied with the upcoming premonition ceremony. As a result even the castle guards had better things to do than keep track of one rebellious princess's whereabouts.

Liliwen told Cara, just because the secret felt too big otherwise. Cara of course tried to discourage her, but Liliwen didn't listen. The urge to see the soldier again was simply too strong.

Once she had slipped out of the palace unseen, she knew exactly where she was going thanks to her impeccable sense of direction. She did not let herself get side tracked by exotic fish or birds flying overhead. Liliwen was heading straight for the island where she had met him the first time.

As soon as the black cliffs came into view, she felt her heartbeat surge again, just like that day.

It was a beautiful kind of thrill. The danger was palpable. How romantic, to risk punishment by her own people, as well as capture by the enemy, just to see a man. If she could catch but a glimpse of him, it would all be worth it, she told herself.

He wasn't there, though. She waited just underneath the surface, in exactly the same spot as last time, for what felt like hours.

The skies were cloudy, though occasionally a ray of sunshine broke through and changed Liliwen's entire outlook. It was only her second outing, so the bright light reminded her that there was still so much for her to discover in this strange land.

She'd never seen sunshine before. It was gorgeous and renewed her hope that today's journey wouldn't be for nothing.

Breaking the surface of the water just for a moment, Liliwen felt the heat of the sun on her skin. It was so warm. The air felt even drier than last time. She quickly went under again, only leaving her head and one raised hand exposed.

"Hey, Mermaid!" a voice interrupted her experiment. "You'd better be careful if you don't want to be discovered."

She turned as quickly as she could.

"You came back!" she exclaimed with a smile.

"As did you." The wolf-man climbed over the fortified wall and sat down on the same rock as the last time.

He stretched out his right arm and dipped his fingers into the water. "Oh, it's nice and fresh today."

"Same old," Liliwen joked.

"You don't have to tell me."

"My name is Liliwen," she blurted out before she had the chance to think whether giving her real name was a good idea or not.

The man paused for a moment. "That's a beautiful name. I'm Teaq."

"Teaq, the soldier," Liliwen repeated.

The man smiled briefly. Even last time he hadn't given the impression he was the sort of guy who laughed or smiled a lot. And yet here, with her…

It made her happy just thinking about it.

A loud noise filled the air, causing Liliwen to cover her ears. "Oh my, what was that?"

"Just the change of the guard. Nothing to worry about."

"Are there many guards here?" she asked.

Teaq squinted as though her question had raised his suspicions just a little. "Just enough so we'll come to know if something—or someone—tries to approach unseen."

"Aha." They shared yet another, more sensual look.

Liliwen thought for a moment, then decided to go with

a shock and awe approach for this second conversation. He would never see it coming.

"I told my friend that I was going to the Black Isles to find out anything I could to help our cause." Liliwen watched carefully for his reaction to her words.

"Did you?" Teaq folded his arms in front of his chest.

"I lied, though." She smiled, then looked away at the distance. "I mean, what am I going to learn here, anyway? If I make sure I remain far away from the guards, then I can't be spying on them either, right?"

"Indeed… So why did you actually come here? To see more birds?" Teaq asked.

"To see you," she said, lowering the pitch of her voice just a little.

His reaction was obvious. The way his expression softened and his gaze grew more intense. He liked her answer.

Should she leave it at that, or take things just a notch further?

"Are you stationed on this island, or did you come here just for me?" she asked. Although she had tried to keep her tone light and innocent, it was a loaded question.

Liliwen knew exactly what she wanted to hear and anything less would be a great disappointment.

"I think you already know the answer to that," he said.

Oh, what a tease!

She let out a soft chuckle. This game, it was getting easier by the minute.

The Soldier and the Siren

"You know, I'm not even allowed to be out here." Liliwen caught a stray lock of her hair with her finger and twisted it round and round. Her hair felt weird out of the water. Sticky. She was certain it looked crap too, though the way he continued to look at her suggested he hadn't noticed that.

"I've been wondering about that. We don't get to see a lot of Mermaids around these parts."

Although it was an obvious truth, the fact that she was the first of her kind that he'd ever seen gave Liliwen a thrill.

"My father would be furious if he found out. In fact, I'm pretty sure he'd punish me for swimming off on my own," she continued.

"You don't seem to be the sort who follows the rules," Teaq observed.

Liliwen smiled. "If I'd followed the rules, I would have never met you. And then where would we be?"

"You'd be at home, safe. And I'd be..." His voice trailed off.

Liliwen pouted and looked down at the water below. "So you'd prefer if we hadn't met at all?"

"You'll admit that this—whatever we're doing here—is rather complicated. The risk we're taking if discovered..." He reached out for her. The back of his fingers gently caressed the side of her face, until they stopped just under her chin, and guided her face upward again.

His touch sent shivers down her whole body and took her breath away all at the same time.

"Easy is just another word for boring," she whispered, as she met his gaze.

Just how long could she continue like this? Putting up a calm front, while Teaq was toying with her emotions so effortlessly?

Within a couple of exchanges between the two of them, Liliwen's state of mind had gone from joyful, to hurt and now… Excited didn't quite explain it. His touch had set her alight, and soothed her all at the same time. And yet there were still those nagging doubts just underneath the surface.

He pulled away his hand again, which nearly made her wince.

Don't stop!

Wait, since when did this game turn to his favor instead of hers? She had already become obsessed with him, but was he perhaps just playing with her? Did he not have a stake in this?

"I doubt you'd ever be boring, Liliwen." The way he spoke her name made her even weaker inside. But she was determined not to let it show.

No, she thought, he's as involved as I am. Otherwise he would have simply taken her prisoner by now.

She reached for his hand, and weaved her fingers in between his. So warm, even more so than the sunshine she had encountered for the very first time before his arrival.

The Soldier and the Siren

Liliwen's thoughts began to wander. What it might be like, to feel more of his touch? How would it feel, to really come together? To connect as man and wife. The ultimate bond. Was he this hot all over?

The same hideous noise from earlier filled the air again. She quickly let go of him and covered her ears for some relief. "Doesn't it hurt your head? This ruckus."

Teaq shook his head. "It's not all that loud. You should hear our war horn."

Liliwen frowned. "I don't think I'd like that very much."

Teaq stood up and scanned their surroundings. "I think it would be best if you went on your way now."

"Is anyone coming?" Liliwen asked.

"It's time for the evening patrol," he explained.

Teaq gestured at her to get into the water, which she did, reluctantly. There was still so much to talk about. There were an infinite number of things she wanted to know about him, which she hardly knew how to ask about.

"I'll see you again," he said.

With a heavy heart, Liliwen nodded. "Soon."

Just how soon she would get another chance to slip out of the castle, she couldn't be sure about. All she knew was that she couldn't bear being away from him for days on end. This little game they were playing had turned very serious, very quickly.

This isn't just a flirtation, Liliwen thought to herself. This... This might be love.

———◆———

"Lili," Cara barged in. "Hey, Lili!"

"What is it?" Liliwen looked up and found Cara in the doorway with wide eyes and an excited grin on her face.

"Cadfael is back!" she squealed. "Just in time for the ceremony, too!"

Liliwen jumped up and took Cara's hands, such was her excitement. "Really? Where is he?"

"He's just entered the throne room to speak with your father. Shouldn't take him too long, I would hope."

"Oh my, I wonder what stories he'll tell this time. Where all he's been. I have much to ask him."

"You cannot!" Cara warned.

"I cannot what?" Liliwen placed her hand on her hip and stared Cara down defiantly.

"You cannot tell him you swam off! You'll be in so much trouble. We both will, since I covered for you."

Liliwen pressed her lips together. "Fine, you're right. But I still have a lot to talk to him about."

Cara smiled. "I'm just glad he's back in one piece."

Liliwen cocked her head to the side and studied her friend's face. "Me too."

"I mean... it's so dangerous out there. I wish he didn't have to go back on patrol."

"Indeed…" Liliwen squeezed Cara's hand.

"Yes?" Cara met her gaze.

"You like him!" Liliwen observed.

Cara instantly looked down at the ground. "I… Well, he's nice and all."

"You *like* like him!"

Cara shook her head. "Don't be silly. Though he is rather handsome."

"Don't be ashamed, Cara. He's a fine soldier, and a kind man as well. You could do a lot worse."

"You mean… Do you think he'd be…?" Cara stammered.

Liliwen shrugged. "Only one way to find out, don't you think? Why don't you talk to your mother, and have her speak with my father about it. See what he thinks?"

"I… Yes. Perhaps I should do that. But I'd like to see *him* first," Cara said.

Liliwen smiled and nodded encouragingly. "Alright. Let's go find him then."

"You don't mind? It's not weird, me with your brother?" Cara whispered.

"We're almost like sisters anyway. What's weird about it?"

"Oh, Lili. Wouldn't it be amazing if this works out?" Cara's voice was heavy with emotion.

Just the thought of the two of them finding love almost at the same time nearly brought tears to Liliwen's eyes. She really ought to say something, share her own story with Cara. But it was too early. Too uncertain. And way too forbidden.

Or could she risk it?

"It would be… Speaking of amazing," Liliwen's voice reduced to a whisper. "Keep another secret?"

"For you, of course!" Cara said.

"Okay, in that case I have something very big to tell you…"

And just like that, Liliwen spilled all. After keeping all these feelings locked inside of her with no one to tell, it felt good to let it out. Even if another person knowing doubled the risk. If Liliwen's father came to know… The repercussions would be huge.

CHAPTER SIX

onight was the night. The Reaping was upon them.

As general of Black Isle's armies, Teaq was onboard the ship sailing to the mainland to collect the newest addition to the islanders' ranks. Broc was also onboard; no matter how hard Teaq had tried to discourage him, his brother certainly had a mind of his own.

This was no place for him though.

And because the king was onboard, Rhea, as his appointed protector and head of the Royal Guard, had accompanied them as well. That meant that on this very ship, the three most important and powerful people of the Black Isles were together at once. An easy target, should anyone wish to attack.

The whole thing was idiotic anyway.

Broc had made up his mind already; he was going to take the human as his queen. And Rhea's concerns, although borne in jealousy, were not completely unfounded. Any newcomer was by their very nature a security risk.

Teaq could have handled the pick-up on his own, along with some hand-picked soldiers and sailors. But instead, Broc was intent on putting himself, and along with it, the stability of the Black Isle's rule, in harm's way.

All for a woman he'd never even seen before.

How he could do such a thing, Teaq couldn't begin to understand.

Teaq and Rhea shared plenty of disapproving looks throughout the journey to the mainland.

Thankfully it was foggy, meaning the humans would not be able to spot them easily.

Sure, the rules of the Reaping forbade anyone from lingering around the shore to watch as the islanders picked up their prize, but humans could be unpredictable. You never knew if this particular one had an unhappy parent or sibling, willing to risk everything for her recovery.

And so, as the ship approached the shore, Teaq kept his eyes fixed on the misty beach for any sign of movement.

"Drop anchor!" Teaq ordered, and braced himself as the ship came to a very sudden halt in the shallows.

He had his hand on his sword as he carefully stood lookout at the bow of the ship.

In the distance, Teaq could just about make out the outline of the post to which the girl had been tied.

"There she is," Teaq grumbled.

"Remember, she will be shown the respect deserving of any citizen of the Black Isles," Broc responded.

Teaq didn't react, only rolled his eyes.

Behind him, Rhea mumbled something unintelligible. She was understandably pissed off as well.

The Reaping only took place once every eight years. One fertile female of marriageable age, picked from one of the villages of the mainland, left alone on this beach for the islanders to claim.

This arrangement was all part of the truce the islanders and the humans had enjoyed for generations, ever since their banishment to the Black Isles at the end of the Great War. So far, nobody had broken it. But one could never be too careful.

For Teaq, this was the second Reaping he had taken an active role in. During the last one, their father, the late king Ryk, had still been around, though he did not come along to pick up the girl herself. He had stayed at the Black Mountain, just as Broc should have done.

"Just remember what we discussed," Teaq grumbled. "These are troubled times. The last thing we need is further complications within our own walls."

Part of Teaq could understand that Broc wanted to be among the first to lay eyes on his new bride, but just why he had taken to the ritual with so much excitement, he couldn't understand. The last time, they'd had a hell of a time getting the girl to adjust to her new life. Teaq, for one, could not stand the kind of drama human females seemed overly fond of. The entire Reaping ritual was an irritating, be it necessary evil.

Mating with humans wasn't by choice. It was a must, to ensure the health of their offspring during times when their numbers had thinned so much that inbreeding became a very serious risk.

Teaq himself couldn't imagine participating anyway. He had his sights set on something much more special than any human. The Mermaid, Liliwen, had made a permanent impression on him. She did not play games like human females. Neither was she blunt like some of the islanders; Rhea included. She was unapologetically and elegantly herself.

"I wish you'd reconsider and at least let me put a watch on her. We do not know of her intentions," Teaq muttered. Some of the things Rhea had said had left a lasting impression on him.

"Alright. That's enough of that," Broc scoffed. "We've laid down the rules already. But I won't have her treated as a prisoner under my rule. Let's get on with what we came here to do."

Teaq shrugged and jumped over the edge of the boat, into the freezing water. The cold didn't bother him. Neither did the harsh winds that swept across the desolate beach.

Broc followed him, as did a few more soldiers.

Once everyone had made it to dry land, they marched straight toward the girl, with Teaq leading the way, his sword at the ready. There was a strange smell in the air; hers, probably.

The small group crossed the distance of the wind swept beach in no time.

"Hold on," Teaq warned Broc, intending for him to stay behind him in relative safety. Of course, his little brother did not listen and stopped right next to Teaq.

"What's your name, girl?" Teaq asked.

The girl, who had obviously not noticed them approaching, let out a shrill squeal, but quickly recovered and spoke her name. Kelly something.

Teaq wasn't even listening anymore.

He undid her ties at Broc's request, but otherwise was preoccupied trying to compare her to Liliwen. The human had striking red hair, but otherwise looked ordinary. She was rather tall for a human, though, so at least she had that going for her. At the very least Broc's heir wouldn't be too short, then.

But she had nothing—absolutely nothing—on Liliwen.

Teaq raised an eyebrow, when, shortly after speaking with Broc, the woman fainted, much to Broc's excitement, who managed to catch her. The guards who had accompanied them weren't much in the way of company. For once, Teaq wished Rhea was here so he could roll his eyes at her and be met with understanding, rather than blank looks.

He breathed a sigh of relief when Broc turned around and led the way back to the ship. There was no use sticking around here any longer than necessary.

As soon as they had climbed aboard with their human cargo, Teaq gave the order to sail back to Black Mountain. They completed the journey almost completely in silence, with a sleeping girl in their midst.

Teaq hoped Rhea would stick to her plan and have the human followed, at least at first. She really had no business wandering the halls of Black Mountain unaccompanied, no matter what Broc thought about it.

————◆————

All through the following day, Teaq walked the halls of the castle in a daze. He hadn't slept, just tossed and turned for most of the night. He hadn't spoken to Rhea to find out what she was doing about the human.

Neither had he done anything about the matter himself.

Never before in his life had Teaq felt so distracted. It was as though Liliwen had cast a spell on him. He might as well go back to the Eastern Isle to wait for her, since that was all he was thinking about anyway.

Of course, sneaking off to the most remote of the Black Isles without rhyme or reason wasn't something a man in Teaq's position could afford.

He was the second most powerful person in the kingdom. The commander of Black Isles' armies and Broc's right hand man. And right now they were in the middle of one of the most significant of the Isles' traditions. They had picked up the human offering from the mainland the preceding night, and as such the Reaping had begun.

It wasn't just a cause for celebration for whoever would claim the human bride; Broc, in this case. It was also an event the entire Isles looked forward to. An excuse for a rare and lavish feast that would last for five entire nights.

This was what Teaq and the others had been preparing for. They had stocked up on meat from the mainland, as well as ale, wine and any other treat the islanders normally wouldn't indulge in so much.

Inhabitants of the surrounding islands had flocked to Black Mountain to take part in the Reaping Feast. If there was ever a worse time for Teaq to shirk his responsibilities as the protector of the Isles, this was it.

He and his men would also feast, of course. But they would also stand by in case of any attacks. The thing about being at war with a formidable and unpredictable enemy was that you could never be sure when the next attack happened.

It had been a quiet winter, but the weather had warmed up. Sea Folk were more likely attack in the summer. So they all had to be on their toes.

But instead of inspecting the defenses of Black Mountain, Teaq had been skulking around the empty hallways of the castle, thinking about Liliwen. Thinking about how her skin had felt when he'd touched her. About how being so close to her had made her feel.

These had been the thoughts that had haunted him throughout the night as well.

Considerations of right and wrong hadn't really come into it. In all his interactions with her, he'd relied on instinct. His instincts hadn't told him to treat her as an enemy, no matter what species she belonged to. In fact, his inner beast was shouting the loudest that he should just forget about everything else, and make her his.

How that realistically would work, he didn't know. His rational mind knew that there was no future for them. That this little fantasy would end in tears.

But his heart wouldn't listen. Hence he found it impossible to get out of this funk.

"Hey, there you are!" Rhea's voice startled him.

"What?"

"What's wrong with you? You look like you've seen a ghost," Rhea said.

Teaq quickly recovered. "Just thinking. Never mind. What do you need?"

"I don't need anything. But, the feast is about to start."

The feast... Teaq rolled his eyes.

"It would be odd not to attend, wouldn't it?" Teaq grumbled.

Rhea shrugged. "I don't feel much like celebrating either. But yes, it would border on being insulting not to."

"Well, then. Let's not keep my dear brother waiting," Teaq said.

He led the way through the zig-zagging corridors of the castle, straight to the Great Hall. The festivities inside were already well underway. Crowds and crowds of people had taken their seats on opposite sides of the long tables, chatting excitedly. The food and drink had not been brought in yet.

Teaq and Rhea were meant to sit on the main table next to Broc. One difference compared to previous feasts was the addition of a carved chair beside Broc's throne.

Teaq sighed. So he was expecting the human to join them as well.

Not only was Broc intent on ignoring Rhea and Teaq's warnings about the new addition in their ranks, he would rub their noses in it by seating her right next to him.

Teaq turned and glanced at his companion. Rhea had spotted the new throne as well. Her already grumpy expression had turned hateful as she glared at it.

CHAPTER SEVEN

———◆———

The throne room was fully decked out. Decorations adorned the walls, the furniture, even the throne itself. King Weiland had on his ceremonial robe, along with a crown made of shark's teeth and precious gems reserved just for this occasion.

Liliwen had slipped inside along with the last guests. Hiding out anonymously in the crowd was not an option, unfortunately. Ordinarily she did not mind taking her seat by her father's side, but today, she would have liked to stay out of view.

She had been carrying her memories of her last meeting with Teaq around with her like a heavy burden. Although she'd told Cara about it— the thrill of a man's touch, experienced for the very first time—hiding the truth from everyone else weighed heavy on her.

It wasn't just the journeys she'd made to see him that were forbidden. If it came to light that anyone had made advances on Liliwen, even touched her, her father would likely cut off his hands. If furthermore it turned out Liliwen had been a willing participant, she would be punished for that as well.

And as she made her way through the visiting dignitaries from all over the Kingdom of the Deep, she felt as though Teaq's fingers had left a lasting mark on her face. Like anyone who looked at her closely could see what she had been up to.

Thankfully though, nobody said anything. Cadfael, who was already seated toward the king's right, winked at her, giving her a little more courage.

She made her way up the raised platform and found her own, slightly smaller seat at her father's left hand. Liliwen straightened her back and met the crowd's looks head on as she sat down. Whatever happened, she couldn't show anymore weakness without attracting suspicion. She was a princess, after all. Her position did not give her much power, but it did garner attention.

Oh, how she wished she could just swim away from it all.

King Weiland banged his three-pointed staff on the ground to attract everyone's attention, then got up from his seat.

"My dear citizens, who have traveled far and wide to be with us today on this auspicious day!"

Liliwen scanned the attendees, looking for Cara. Sure enough, there she was, but she didn't notice her best friend at all. Cara was staring unapologetically in Cadfael's direction. Liliwen glanced over to her right, past her father's throne. Cadfael was looking at Cara as well!

So in the short while he'd been back from Siren's Rock, she had somehow gotten his attention.

Liliwen sighed and sat back. Good for them. Not that it

helped with her predicament, though.

"We are gathered here, as we do every two moons before every summer solstice, to consult the currents and predict our fortunes in battle this fighting season."

Liliwen tried hard not to roll her eyes. Not once had she heard a specific and useful prediction during one of these ceremonies. And still, everyone sat through them religiously every single year.

"Bring in the Seer!"

The large double doors at the end of the throne room swung open, and half a dozen priests in ceremonial gowns floated in. In their midst was the Seer. A Merman just like the rest of them, and also unlike any of them. His scaly skin wasn't greenish like Liliwen's kin, but had a grayer, almost bluish tint. His eyes weren't golden, but a stark white. And he had no hair on his head at all.

Baldness wasn't something Merfolk ever suffered from. Except this particular one.

The last of his kind, Liliwen thought. The ceremony was nonsense, of course, but the Seer did creep her out a little.

They said he was the last survivor of a clan of Merfolk who had ruled the Deep before Liliwen's people had even arrived here. Wiped out by some kind of disease that had claimed all their lives. Perhaps that was why he was bald.

Either way, he was meant to have mystical powers, or so people believed.

"My King." The Seer bowed deeply in front of Liliwen's father, who nodded and gestured at him to get back up.

"Let us begin the Premonition Ceremony!" King Weiland said, as he ran his right hand through his long white beard.

The six priests formed a semi-circle around the Seer, who closed his eyes and raised his arms up toward the ceiling.

Drums started to play, adding to the creepy ambience that was specific to this ceremony.

"Great Currents of the Northern Sea. What truths do you carry? What predictions do you have for all our fortunes?" the Seer asked aloud.

The priests began to dance around him to the rhythm of the drums, moving first in a clockwise direction, and then as they completed a whole revolution around the Seer, they returned counter clockwise, to their original positions.

"Tell us, oh powerful currents! Messengers of Poseidon, speak to me!"

He then reached for the large conch that hung from a gold chain around his neck and held it up to his right ear. He aimed it upward at the ceiling.

Liliwen watched the whole thing with mixed emotions. She didn't really believe in any of it. But what if…

"The Black Isles are in trouble," the Seer spoke.

A whisper passed through the crowd.

Liliwen sat up straighter in her seat. This year's

prediction seemed to be a lot more specific than she was used to.

"A stranger, unlike any of them. A stranger will move onto the Isles, changing their fortunes forever. She will turn brother against brother. Soldier against soldier."

The Seer looked straight ahead, his gaze meeting Liliwen's.

Her heart sank. He'd seen it. He'd figured it all out. She was found out. All was lost.

"A stranger, with great power," he continued. "A human, with a secret."

Finally, Liliwen could breathe.

The Seer closed his eyes again. "Oh Poseidon. Send your messengers to us with more predictions. Will we be victorious, oh mighty Currents?"

Liliwen sat back in her seat, trying hard to catch her breath without anyone noticing.

"The stranger's arrival will have them at their weakest yet," the Seer concluded. "The currents have spoken. This is all."

King Weiland got up from his throne and applauded. "Do you hear this, my friends? Poseidon favors us. The Black Isles will tear themselves apart, and we'll attack to make the most of their weakness. Victory shall be ours!"

The crowd roared as the priests moved into a two by three formation and walked out behind the Seer.

"Long live the Deep!" one of the visitors shouted.

"Long live King Weiland!" the entire audience replied.

The Soldier and the Siren

"This is getting to be a habit," Teaq said with a smile.

Liliwen smiled back at him and slipped her hand into his.

This. This was what she had craved. Despite her scare the other day, during the Premonition Ceremony, she had been unable to stay away.

Although she had confided in Cara, she had been unable to put into words just how he made her feel. These stolen moments, away from the conflict that had raged on between their people. Away from stupid superstitions and predictions.

How she wished she could just stay here forever. But the risks were too great. They were too visible out here.

"Is there somewhere we can go? Somewhere a little less exposed?" she asked, desperate not to have today's meeting cut short like the last time. She had, after all, just swam halfway across the Northern Sea for this. For him.

Teaq turned around and studied the barren countryside.

"There is a place, but it's some way up the hill," he said.

Liliwen followed his gaze. The island looked very different than the ocean floor she had travelled along to get here.

Seaweed provided vast expanses of lush greenery for the fish and many other sea creatures to hide in. This land had none of that. No vegetation. Not even any wildlife. Not another soldier in sight either.

How would she get up there? She'd heard the stories of her people climbing onto dry land to fight, but how it really worked was hard to imagine. She'd never done it before.

It was the only way she'd be able to spend more time here, though…

"Okay, help me up," she said, reaching out for him.

Teaq reluctantly held her by the wrist and gave her a pull. Before she knew it, she was balancing on top of the rock she had only just sat on. He hadn't even broken a sweat getting her out of the water, such was his strength.

It was a challenge staying upright. How did Cadfael and the others do it?

Liliwen looked down at her tail, which was bending awkwardly trying to hold her height. With a bit of practice she might stand on it without any support, but how was one supposed to move around like this?

"Ugh, this is weird." Liliwen smiled awkwardly.

"Where are your legs?" Teaq asked.

Liliwen looked down again. Legs? Had he seriously just asked that?

"What do you mean?" she asked.

"When the Merfolk attack… I mean, your people, when they come here, they can crawl and walk much like what we do. On two legs. Not…"

"Not one flipper," Liliwen mumbled, suddenly very

conscious of her body. "It's useless, isn't it?"

"It's beautiful. You are beautiful," Teaq whispered under his breath, then cleared his throat. "Perhaps it's something only your men can do."

Liliwen frowned. She was just as capable as any man. There had to be a trick to it. She couldn't be handicapped on dry land just because she was a woman. That would be unacceptable.

Unless it was magic. Did her people possess some kind of secret magic she didn't know about? The stories made it sound so natural.

"I can just carry you, if that's acceptable," Teaq suggested.

"Absolutely not. I will go myself," Liliwen argued. *But how?*

With Teaq's hand on her shoulder, keeping her roughly in position, she put all her energy into that all important first step. Or should that be, her first hop?

She gave it her all, and immediately lost balance and fell backwards into the water with a big splash. So much for trying to impress him.

Liliwen was furious when she jumped out of the water again and onto the rock. This time, she was steady.

"Ah, there they are," Teaq observed with a grin on his face.

Liliwen looked down and was shocked to find that her tail had split in two right through the middle. She had legs!

Scaly, like the rest of her, and not quite the same shape as his, but legs nonetheless. And even her tail had come apart and formed two sections to serve as her feet. She shuffled the two halves apart, copying how Teaq was standing, and found that her balance was much improved.

"So this is how it works," she mumbled to herself.

"You know, I never thought about this before. Just how did you do it?" Teaq asked.

Liliwen shrugged, and shook her hair back as a show of confidence. "I'm not sure, but the important thing is, I can go now." His question did play on her mind though. More importantly; how would these two halves merge again for her long swim back? If they didn't, there was no way she could be seen at home without every single person knowing that she'd been up to no good.

She took a deep breath. That was one hurdle she'd have to cross later.

Teaq offered her his hand, which she gladly took as she unsteadily climbed over the rocks toward the boundary wall of the island. He did lift her over the top of it, which she accepted grudgingly. That was better than making a show of herself falling off the damn thing.

The rest of the way up the mountainous island took her a while, but she managed it with Teaq's help. Surely, with a bit of practice, she'd be as comfortable out of the water as any of her male counterparts.

As they made it further up the hill, the place Teaq must have been referring to came into view. A cave, sheltered from the surrounding landscape. The ultimate escape from prying eyes.

Liliwen's heart skipped a few beats as she thought about everything one might get up to in there, without anyone knowing. Had he taken other women there? Or was she the first?

The mystery of not knowing made being here even more exciting.

"Here we are," Teaq said. He stepped aside to let her enter the cave.

It was pitch black, but Liliwen had no trouble seeing inside. In fact it was easier on her eyes than the bright island.

She wandered in, and found herself a suitable place to sit and rest her newly formed legs. Swimming for hours was effortless for her, but this short hike had taken its toll.

Teaq sat down a couple of feet away.

Neither of them said a word initially. The silence between them increased the tension tenfold. It had been her idea to come up here. What were his motives, though? Was he thinking what she was thinking?

"It's nice," she remarked, finally. A meaningless statement, but her nerves wouldn't allow her to stay silent any longer. "Not so dry and windy."

Teaq didn't respond.

She placed her hand on the ground beside her. The entire cave was covered in a soft and springy material. Like a very fine and dense seaweed. Liliwen caressed it, marveling at how the thin sprigs sprung back upright after she'd touched them.

"What do you call this?" she asked and patted the ground, gesturing Teaq to come closer.

"Moss." Teaq got up and joined her. His movements were wooden, as though suddenly he wasn't so sure of himself anymore.

"Moss," Liliwen repeated after him. "Such a cute word."

She looked over at him and wondered what her next move should be. His behavior since they'd arrived in the cave was confusing. Was it all one-sided after all? She had to be sure.

"Why haven't you taken me prisoner yet?" she finally asked, then held her breath as she waited for his answer.

CHAPTER EIGHT

"**W**hy haven't you taken me prisoner yet?" Liliwen asked.

Teaq nearly choked on his own breath. Islanders weren't known for mincing their words. Though Liliwen had been straightforward with him so far, she still continued to surprise him with her candid questions.

"I… Well, that's the question, isn't it?"

"I want to know the answer," she insisted.

He couldn't very well tell her that from their very first meeting, he'd been so fascinated by her that he couldn't bear the thought of missing out on these moments together? That he'd been obsessed with her to the point of not being able to sleep at night. That he'd sat through one too many Council Meeting or discussion with Broc, only listening to half of what was being said, because the image of her, glistening in the diffused light of early summer, had been etched onto his mind permanently.

"I think you're just toying with me," she said, looking down at her hands which were now wrapped around her legs. Or was that her tail? Whatever it was.

"One day when you grow tired of me, I'm going to come visit, and you'll put me in chains."

"Never," he said. His voice sounded more hoarse than normal.

She knew exactly what buttons to press. It was infuriating. And addictive.

"Prove it," she mouthed.

Teaq leaned over, placed his hand on her cheek more firmly than he'd ever touched her before and looked into her eyes. Though the cave was dark, her eyes shimmered golden as usual. It was a beautiful sight to behold.

"I would never."

Liliwen's eyelids fluttered, then shut entirely.

His senses were overwhelmed by her. Her quick shallow breaths sent his own heartbeat into a frenzy. This. This was what he'd been thinking about doing sometime between their first and second meeting. These were the dreams that haunted him at night, no matter how hard he'd tried to fight them.

He leaned in closer, breathing in the scent coming off her lips. Sweet, yet salty. Tempting.

"Kiss me already," she whispered against his lips.

So he did. Gently at first, then when her lips parted, he tasted her more passionately.

She wrapped her arms around his neck, and pulled him against her. It was only now that he realized that despite her petite frame, she really was rather strong for her size.

She tasted of a gentle summer breeze. Fresh, refreshing even, with a hint of sweetness.

Her body felt cold against his, but not unpleasantly so. He cradled her in his arms, marveling at just how small and fragile she seemed to be. But every movement of hers reminded him that she was nothing of the sort.

She might not be a soldier like those of her kin he'd met in battle before, but she was a warrior at heart.

He could respect that, even admire it.

No matter what Broc was planning, Teaq could never settle for a human mate. He'd already known so before, but this first kiss only served to make him more determined. Islander women were strong and fierce as well, but they weren't *her*.

He hadn't been able to confess it to her earlier, but it was clear as day now.

There was only one woman that could make him weak. Her name was Liliwen, and she was in his arms right now. In a simpler world, he'd stay in this cave with her forever. He wouldn't just kiss her lips, but explore her body all over with his mouth. He would do so much more; unspoken things which only husband and wife did with one another.

But there was nothing simple about this world.

Teaq pulled back and studied Liliwen's face.

"What are you doing here with me, when it could get you into so much trouble back home?"

She smiled briefly, as she continued to hang onto him with both her arms crossed behind his neck. "Finding happiness."

How she could be innocent and sweet and fierce and brave all at once, Teaq had no idea.

She was an enigma.

"I was actually found out. Almost," she said, her expression turning serious.

The sudden change in her woke Teaq's protective instincts. "What happened?"

"The Seer, he said something that sounded a lot like me. He was looking right at me as well. I had such a fright."

Teaq shook his head. None of what she had said had made any sense. "What Seer? Said what?"

"Oh, we had our Premonition Ceremony last night. It was the summer solstice, you know," she said.

Teaq didn't understand that either, but didn't ask further questions.

"So when the Seer performed the ceremony, he said that a stranger was coming to the Black Isles which would turn everyone against one another. Brother against brother. Soldier against soldier. That the Isles would be at their weakest yet. The way he'd said it, I thought he was talking about me!"

Teaq's heartbeat sped up again. He didn't much believe in premonitions, but for the Sea Folk to hold a whole ceremony dedicated to it every year... Perhaps their Seer had visionary powers that the Islanders had no access to?

"And he wasn't. Talking about you, I mean?" Teaq asked, still concerned for Liliwen's safety, as much as his own.

She shook her head. "I shouldn't be telling you all this, obviously. But if my people do decide to attack... I don't want you unprepared. I don't want you in danger," she whispered.

Teaq nodded. He wasn't sure what he would have done in her place. His responsibilities to the Isles had always been the only thing he cared about. But with *her* in the picture… His own loyalties were well and truly challenged. It made sense that hers were too.

"So the Seer said that this stranger was human. With great powers."

Teaq's heart skipped another beat. Human. There was only one human the Seer could have been talking about. Broc's intended. And she was already here.

"You're sure he said it's a human?" Teaq asked. But in his heart he already knew the answer. That was why he'd been getting an off feeling about the whole situation.

Those were his instincts trying to tell him something. The human, Kelly, meant trouble.

He had to talk to Rhea. He could play on her jealousy to get her to be vigilant. If anyone could handle a powerful opponent, it was Rhea, anyway. Being a woman, she could get closer to Kelly than Teaq ever could.

Without tipping off his brother.

And if he could somehow convince Broc to be more vigilant as well…

"You look troubled," Liliwen said, as she snuggled her face against his chest.

The sweet girl had no idea.

"Thank you for telling me. You've helped me greatly."

"You're welcome," she whispered. "I aim to please."

Oh, if she kept on saying things like that, Teaq would find it impossible to keep things decent between them. Already his inner beast was screaming for her; desperate to claim her as his own.

She deserved better than this, though. She didn't deserve to be violated in a damp cave up on a hill on the Eastern Isle. She ought to be treated like a queen.

But instead, there was a treacherous human in one of the finest rooms on Black Mountain, scheming, plotting to bring them all down.

He kissed the top of Liliwen's head, marveling at how silky her hair felt. His own was crude and rough in comparison. She was something else entirely.

"Are you comfortable here? Not too dry?" he asked.

"It's perfect."

Teaq knew he had to get back to Black Mountain and speak with Rhea urgently, but he owed it to Liliwen to stay here with her at least a while longer. He owed it to his inner beast also.

And so he remained there, leaning against the mossy wall of the cave, with Liliwen in his arms. Sharing more kisses, caresses, and conversation.

He asked her about her home. What she got up to when she wasn't swimming across the Northern Sea, breaking the rules. She asked him about his achievements in battle.

It was perfect, just like she'd said. Until a good long while later, her demeanor seemed to change a little.

"What's wrong?" he asked.

"I'm okay," she said. The strain in her voice suggested she wasn't, though.

"No, really."

"It's just… a bit dry." Liliwen leaned back and looked at Teaq with large apologetic eyes. "I would have liked to stay a little longer."

Teaq smiled at her. "Come, let's get you back into the water."

Liliwen nodded, with disappointment written all over her face.

"Now, don't be sad. This isn't the last time we'll see each other." Teaq tried to sound upbeat to cheer her up, even if deep down he didn't want this moment to end either.

"Promise?" she asked.

Teaq nodded, and sealed his promise with a kiss.

————— ◆ —————

Back at the castle, it didn't take long for Teaq to find Rhea.

"We must talk," he said.

Rhea nodded darkly. "Our King hasn't heeded my advice."

Obviously the human, and Broc's instant infatuation with her, was the only thing on Rhea's mind these days.

Good. At least he wouldn't have to steer the coming conversation.

"I think we need to tighten up our surveillance on the human," Teaq said. "There's something I don't trust about her."

"Why, has she done something? Because if she has, you must tell your brother!" Rhea urged.

Teaq shook his head. "Nothing concrete, sadly. Call it instinct."

Rhea scoffed. "I've had that instinct from the very start of this whole mess."

"Indeed you have. I trust that in time we'll find proof that even my brother cannot overlook."

Rhea nodded. "How about we approach the Elders? If they look hard enough, they might be able to find something in the old scriptures that could help our cause?"

Teaq thought for a moment. The Elders had a habit of taking any suggestion and twisting it to their own objectives; or perhaps they were just so old that they merely forgot what they were looking for once they started reading. Still, it was the most innocuous way of getting ahead at this point.

"Fine. I will speak with Uri in confidence. Meanwhile, you keep an eye on her yourself."

"How am I supposed to do that?" Rhea complained.

"You're a woman, so you're allowed in her quarters. Find a reason to spend time with the human. Show her around the island for all I care. Or better yet, give her some combat training."

"Okay…" Rhea thought for a moment. "I suppose I can work with that. I'll plan something first thing in the morning. If the human can drag herself out of bed on time."

"Good. I'll find Uri now. We'll convene a Council Meeting once we have something to tell Broc."

Teaq left Rhea in the hallway he'd found her, and made his way straight to the Library, where the Elders spent most of their days. If now he could get Uri on his side, he might be able to act on the information Liliwen had given him without attracting any suspicions himself. He couldn't very well go around telling people he suspected the human because a Mermaid had shared some secrets from her own people. A prediction made by a mystic, no less.

Not only would nobody believe it, Teaq would soon find himself locked up for questioning himself.

And then not only would Kelly be beyond reproach, the entire defense of the Black Isles would be in shambles, just at a time when the Sea Folk planned a large scale invasion.

Teaq barged straight into the library, and found that Uri was sitting by himself at the large study table in the center of it.

He looked up. "Fancy seeing you here, commander. Planning to do some light reading?"

"Uri, I need your help," Teaq said.

Uri's expression turned serious. "Very well. There is something I have been meaning to discuss with you anyway."

Teaq's curiosity was piqued instantly. "What's that?"

"I've been studying these scriptures and I found a passage that concerns me." Uri pointed down at the tattered old scroll in front of him.

Teaq leaned over and was speechless as he read the words Uri had pointed out.

During a time of great change,
Two moons before the summer solstice,
A stranger arrives,
Hiding a terrible secret.
A power that could win or lose wars,
One that could destroy all or be our salvation,
Bringing with it the third great age of war,
As our enemies aim to acquire it for their own gain.

"Serendipity," Teaq whispered.

"Sorry?" Uri cupped his hand behind his ear.

"Thank you for bringing this to me, Uri. We must inform Broc immediately."

"What of the Reaping Feast? It's about to begin," Uri argued.

Teaq muttered a few choice words under his breath. The bloody Reaping Feast was becoming the bane of his life. "Fine. First thing tomorrow, then."

The Soldier and the Siren

Teaq had never been superstitious. Until now he'd often wondered if the random stuff the Elders found in these old writings was 99% nonsense and only 1% useful. But tonight, his mind was changed.

In a twist of fate, everything had worked out exactly in Teaq's favor. Rhea would take Kelly out to keep an eye on her in the morning, and in the meanwhile Teaq and Uri would brief Broc with this latest bit of information. A concrete lead to start being a bit more careful with the human.

Teaq headed for the Great Hall with a spring in his step. Now, he would be unstoppable.

CHAPTER NINE

Just how it had happened, Liliwen wasn't quite sure. But while waiting idly for Teaq to arrive at their designated meeting place, she had found herself swimming off course. At first it had been the birds floating in the sky that caught her eye.

Then a school of fish weaving their way through the pointy rocks that dotted the coastline of the Eastern Isle.

Her heart was light, full of excitement at the prospect of seeing him again. The memory of their first kiss in that magical cave was still vivid in her mind. That, of course, was the reason she'd come back so soon. She wanted more.

He loved her too. She was sure of it. He hadn't said it in so many words, but the way he'd kissed her… Surely that meant something. The way they'd spoken, more intimately than before… It was obvious now. She'd even told Cara about it already.

Still filled with hope and an energy she hadn't felt before, Liliwen swam on. Her mind was filled with a mishmash of idle thoughts. Cara was to marry Cadfael; the looks they'd shared during the Premonition Ceremony were undeniable.

And Liliwen was in love with Teaq.

Further and further she swam, discovering new sights

at each turn, and reliving old memories all at the same time.

Until suddenly, she could go no further. Something constricted her movements, and within moments, a frenzy of activity descended upon her helpless form.

All the excitement, all the joy Liliwen had felt just moments ago vanished.

She'd been caught in a net. And to make matters worse, the net had closed around her and she was being dragged to shore against her will. No matter how hard she fought, it was no use.

When she broke through the surface of the water, she saw not the familiar face she had been waiting for, but a whole lot of new people. Her heart grew heavy as she realized that the worst had happened. The Others had captured her.

Two of them were hauling her onto dry land.

"What is it?" Teaq called out in the distance, filling Liliwen briefly with hope again. Would he rescue her?

Her heart sank when she realized the truth that was written all over his face. The horror. He couldn't acknowledge her; no way.

If she said anything to suggest she knew him, it would only escalate things. For the both of them.

Struggling also seemed to make matters worse. The net was rough, painfully so. It rubbed her skin raw almost to the point of causing real damage. That was nothing compared to what these soldiers would do to her later, though.

"Well, let's see it," another man shouted.

Liliwen was quickly overpowered by the two men who had previously hauled in the net. One had wrapped his arm around her neck to keep her still, while the other took yet more of the hideous rough material from the netting and tied it around her wrists. It stung and burned against her skin, but she didn't let her discomfort show.

Instead, she took a moment to size up her captors.

The two soldiers looked rather unimpressive. One was a wolf, like Teaq, but actually he was nothing like Teaq at all. The other was something else, a bigger, furrier sort of creature. A bear, probably. Two more stood by a little further up the wall, with yet more of them overlooking the entire spectacle from the highest point of the fortifications.

Liliwen could barely stand to look at Teaq anymore, whose expression was one of pure horror, so she quickly skipped past him and looked at his companion. This man had the same animal form as one of the foot soldiers holding her, but he was more sizeable and wore fancier attire.

"Well, you don't see that every day," the stranger beside Teaq said.

From his armor, as well as the tone in which he addressed the others, Liliwen could make out that he was in charge.

"There's your intruder," the same man said, while

turning to face Teaq, who continued to stare at Liliwen. "Seems like the Elders might have been onto something with all their talk of prophecies."

Liliwen frowned. *Intruder*, that obviously referred to her, but what Elders? *What prophecies?*

The soldiers meanwhile tried to drag her up the stone steps to reach the wall level where the others were waiting. Liliwen wasn't sure how to react to all these strangers manhandling her, so she followed her instincts and spat at one of them.

This only enraged him further and earned her a firm hand to the throat.

"Don't lay a hand on me, wolf!" she threatened. Her anger had made her legs come out again, allowing her to stand strong on two feet.

Just exactly what she would do if he didn't let go, she wasn't sure of. But this wasn't a situation she'd ever found herself in, obviously. And the treatment she was receiving so far was unbecoming of how a princess of the Deep deserved to be treated.

If they knew her true identity, matters would undoubtedly get worse, though, so she stopped herself from berating them on royal etiquette and decided to cooperate. For now.

Just for a second, she dared to look into Teaq's eyes again. There was nothing but sadness there.

She couldn't let that affect her, though. She had to be

calm and calculating.

This romance of theirs had been doomed from the start. Just a fantasy.

But this right here, this was the cold, hard reality.

The worst had happened.

It had been a risk from the first moment she'd slipped out of her father's palace and come to these Isles. She had evaded it all this time simply because it was Teaq who had found her initially. And against all odds, they had connected. They had even fallen in love.

Now, all that was over.

She wouldn't be able to charm her way out of this situation.

Princess or not, she was a prisoner of war now.

"Lock her up underneath the deck so she doesn't dry out, then transfer her to a nice, cozy puddle in the castle dungeons at the earliest," the man in charge ordered.

Teaq didn't say a word.

"Brother?" the man spoke up again. "Will you accompany the prisoner transport?"

That last statement activated Teaq, whose one sentence response summed up the entire situation much more succinctly than Liliwen would have been able to.

"Dark days are upon us."

Indeed, they were. *Brother.* Teaq and the other man were siblings. The similarities were there, clear as day. Still, this revelation shocked Liliwen to her core. And although Teaq didn't show it right now, he looked to be higher up in the hierarchy as well. He wasn't just an ordinary soldier, but a commander, much like Cadfael.

Right now, he didn't look in charge of much, least of all himself.

Liliwen wished she could have a moment with him. To tell him that it was alright. That she was ready.

She was a prisoner, to be taken away and locked in the enemy's dungeon. She had known about this risk from the start and taken it anyway, just to steal a few more moments with Teaq.

Now, she would die for her indiscretions.

And once her father and Cadfael found her missing, and got Cara to spill all her secrets, all these people would probably die as well. Her family's vengeance would be swift as well as cruel.

And for what? For a choice she had made. A stupid decision, which had led her here again and again. She didn't even regret any of it, except to see Teaq so distraught. To know that her recklessness had hurt him, and would hurt so many of his people as well.

But she didn't get a moment with him and she could tell him nothing.

She was hauled across the wall, towards a large wooden vessel, where she was roughly deposited in the lowermost compartment, along with the same two guards who were meant to keep an eye on her.

As disorienting as it was, travelling like this, she still

knew roughly where she was. Her sense of direction was still strong. She closed her eyes for the duration of the boat ride, keeping track of each minute change of course.

If she managed to escape, it wouldn't be a problem to find her way home.

Of course, these people had no intention of letting her go, so these were just idle dreams.

She curled up on the floor, and rested her head on a pile of rope and just lay there, staring at the two dark outlines of the soldiers guarding her. The entire ordeal was a shock to her senses. She had been out of the water for all of one hour in her entire life, when she had spent those precious moments with Teaq in the cave only a couple of days ago. This was going to be a lot longer than just an hour. Staying on dry land for long wasn't just going to be unpleasant, it was also potentially dangerous for her.

Teaq's brother's order to prepare a puddle for her in the dungeons had sounded patronizing, but now she was yearning for even just a sip of water to soothe her burning skin.

She hoped beyond hope that they would show her this little kindness, even though she was their enemy, technically. And if not, she hoped that her end would be swift.

The boat rocked back and forth in the choppy waters of the Northern Sea. It was an odd movement, which threatened to turn her stomach upside-down.

Thankfully the journey didn't take too long.

The Soldier and the Siren

Unfortunately it ended with her in a prickly sack of sorts, being hauled unceremoniously to her final destination.

Before long, she found herself deposited in a cold, damp room. The so-called dungeon.

There wasn't much light. Neither was there much water, much to Liliwen's chagrin.

The soldiers who accompanied her said their goodbyes by spitting on her, and slamming the door shut behind them. Finally, she was alone.

As desperate as her situation was, Liliwen couldn't stop thinking about Teaq. Where was he, and what was he doing?

Would she ever see him again? Or would he deny their connection and avoid her until she was eventually put to death. Part of her hoped that he would. She didn't want him to see her this way, covered in mud and filth, withered and mistreated.

It was unbecoming of her position. She didn't want to be remembered this way.

No, it would be best if he steered clear and never came down into this forsaken place.

Soon enough, it would all be over. She'd be dead and he might get on with his life.

Strange, these thoughts whizzing around in her head. How calmly she considered the benefits of her own demise. This was why her people were such formidable fighters. She'd never thought about it before, even during her lengthy conversations with Teaq.

It wasn't that Merfolk didn't consider their own mortality. They did. It was just that they—herself included—did so with a rationale that left little room for emotions and despair.

Death wasn't something to be feared.

After all, everyone was born, and everyone must eventually die.

Liliwen was ready to accept that her time had come.

CHAPTER TEN

———◆———

The entire spectacle was horrific. Teaq could barely watch. None of the gore and violence of war could compare to the moment when his very own underlings hauled his Liliwen out of the water and took her prisoner.

She'd fought back initially, and valiantly so. But she was outnumbered, so it was a lost cause from the start. He had known that she was feisty and impulsive, so he half expected her to scream and shout at her captors, and call on him for help.

But she had done nothing of the sort. They had exchanged a couple of painful looks in silence, and that was that. She showed the sort of quiet resignation Sea Folk soldiers did in the rare occasions they were caught during battle. Like she had given up.

That was the most painful part, seeing the change in her. From defiant and proud to meek and helpless. As though her spirit was already broken, a mere ten minutes after her capture.

Teaq followed the patrol soldiers and Liliwen onto the longship. It felt as though they were taking *him* away with them as a prisoner as well. Or a part of him at least.

Just how she had ended up on this side of the island, and swam right into one of the islanders' nets, was unclear to him. She had been careless, but he could not blame her. She was not as worldly wise as she pretended to be. She did not know any better.

He should have protected her from all this.

Instead, he'd let her down. If only he'd scared her away after the first meeting. Or if he'd been clearer about which areas around these islands to stay away from.

Teaq had not been a stranger to disappointment in his life. Most notably when he lost the chance to become king to his little brother. That crushing defeat paled in comparison to what had happened today. Seeing Liliwen being hauled away in restraints was an image that would haunt him for the rest of his life.

So he remained silent for the entire journey back to Black Mountain, struggling with the ever present question: *how can I help Liliwen?*

He did not have an answer.

It was impossible not to lose hope.

Just what Broc planned to do with her, Teaq had no idea. But it couldn't be good. This was exactly the sort of thing they had been talking about. The next invasion was imminent. Liliwen would be branded a spy.

And Broc was convinced Liliwen was the outsider the Elders' prophecy had talked about.

But he did not know her; Teaq did. How could he possibly convince Broc that Liliwen wasn't a threat?

Meanwhile, there was the human to think about. The Sea Folk Seer had predicted that a human would cause a rift in the Black Isles that the Sea Folk could exploit. The Elders' prophecy had confirmed this, but hadn't pointed toward a human specifically, leaving Broc free to make his own interpretations.

Of course his little brother had been naive to consider the human innocent right from the start. And now that he'd seen her... It was obvious that he wasn't thinking with his head anymore.

———◆———

Teaq had wanted nothing but to retreat to a quiet corner of the castle and drown his sorrows in ale, if that was what it took. But upon returning to the castle, he and his brother were intercepted by Rhea, who insisted that they follow her immediately. Broc was quick to agree, whereas Teaq was hesitant.

But the look Rhea shot in his direction left no room for wavering. Whatever she had to say, it was significant.

So they both joined her in the Great Hall, where she broke the news.

"As you're aware I have been taking the human out for combat training," Rhea started.

She talked faster than normal, as though she was agitated. Or excited. It was hard to tell.

"In the midst of showing her some moves with the practice swords, we were engulfed in a blue light. The human, she curled up into a ball, and I was thrown right across the edge of the plateau."

Teaq frowned. This wasn't what he had expected to hear. He glanced over at Broc, who didn't seem to understand a word Rhea had said to him so far.

"My king," Rhea spoke more firmly now. "The human, she's not what we thought. She cast a spell on me! If I hadn't been so quick on my feet, she might have killed me. I immediately placed her under arrest."

Broc shook his head, then started pacing back and forth through the hall. His footsteps echoed against the granite walls.

Teaq wasn't sure how to react either. Part of him felt like laughing, but he managed to keep himself in check. How bizarre.

At exactly the same time as his own world had fallen apart with Liliwen's capture, Broc's woman had been arrested by Rhea for performing witchcraft. It would be hilarious, if it wasn't so tragic.

Still, Teaq felt vindicated at having his suspicions confirmed. So far Broc had waved his concerns away as paranoia, but now... It was undeniable. The prediction Liliwen had shared with him had come true, as had the prophecy of the Elders.

"I don't understand. Are you absolutely certain that's what you saw, Rhea?" Broc asked.

"I would never lie to you, my king. She's a witch." Rhea put her hands to her hips in a show of confidence. She never did like her authority being questioned.

The Soldier and the Siren

"It's really quite obvious that the prophecy is being fulfilled." Teaq tried very hard not to sound flippant, which he almost failed at. "We can only hope it's not too late to counter this attack!"

His remark earned him a furious look from Broc.

"This certainly demands further investigation, so we can determine what exactly has happened," Broc said. "And in case you've forgotten, we've just witnessed another incident that could very well be a part of this prophecy of yours."

That hit Teaq right where it hurt.

"It's quite clear what has happened, brother!" Teaq argued. "The witch felt cornered, out there doing combat training with Rhea, and she exposed herself for what she is. An infiltrator. An enemy disguised as an innocent peasant girl from West Hythe. Quite how the humans managed to find a witch after all these years, I cannot say. But she's here, so the hows and whys of it are irrelevant. This Reaping was obviously a trap."

"Now, now…" Broc raised his hand in protest. "We do not know for sure what the humans intended. Or if they even knew about this. After all, the prophecy speaks of a *secret* power. Perhaps it was a secret to them as well."

Unbelievable. Teaq was shocked at his brother's reaction. First he had refused to believe Rhea's account of events, and now he was arguing in favor of the mainlanders? What had gotten into him?

Rhea scoffed. "Fine, even if it was all *her* idea and *her* plan, and the humans had no knowledge of it. We are still at the brink of war. The prophecy—"

Broc slammed his fist into one of the tables lining the Great Hall, sending echoes across the room and making both Rhea and Teaq flinch.

"I am fed up of everyone's speculations! Sick of it! We *are* at the brink of war, but with the Sea Folk, not with the humans. We'll get to the bottom of this matter with Kelly also, of course. I will speak with her. I must—"

That sent Teaq over the edge. If he didn't control his anger, he would be tempted to plant a great big fist right into Broc's face.

"You will do nothing of the sort!" Teaq hollered.

Broc immediately swung around and adopted a threatening pose. "In case you have forgotten. I am King. I do not need your permission to—"

"My king, if you'll hear us out..." Rhea tried to defuse the situation.

Neither of the two brothers paid much attention to her.

"We do not know for sure if Kelly means us any harm. But we are *certain* that the Sea Folk are our most pressing enemy. Am I wrong?" Broc asked.

Teaq took a step away from his brother and tried to calm his breathing. His inner beast was a hair's breadth away from clawing his way out and showing his little brother just what he thought.

He was seething. And the worst part was, Broc's

assessment did make a tiny bit of sense. The Sea Folk were the confirmed enemy. And an invasion was imminent.

"I am going to interrogate our human prisoner now. Personally," Broc concluded.

No way! Teaq turned to face him again, but Rhea had already approached Broc.

"My king, I do not think it safe for you to see her unguarded. We do not know enough of her powers," she argued.

"That's enough! She's chained up. She even let you carry her down the hillside without attempting to fight back or escape. What is she going to do to me? Blind me with a flash of light?" Broc barked.

That was enough of that. Teaq could stand it no longer. He turned and marched straight toward the nearest door.

"Brother."

Broc's voice stopped him in his tracks, though he did not turn around.

"Perhaps you could interrogate the other prisoner. Find out what she knows and whom she's told. And for all our sakes, try to find out if her people are planning an attack."

Broc's suggestion got Teaq's mind working overtime.

Interrogate Liliwen. Of course ... As long as nobody knew the truth, he could come and go from her cell as much as he wanted. He could make sure she was well taken care of. That she was fed. Make the entire ordeal just a little less terrifying for her.

"She's not going to just spill everything," Rhea complained in the background. Oh, if only she knew the truth. Liliwen had already told him so much, without asking for anything in return. And all it had earned her was to be chained up and thrown in a dark hole underneath the castle.

"Use your powers of persuasion, brother. Our safety may depend on it," Broc said.

Teaq didn't need any more encouragement. Whatever Broc had meant by 'powers of persuasion', Teaq wasn't sure. But he wouldn't need any tricks to get her to talk.

He would head straight down to her cell and see her. But first, he would make a stop to pick up some food and some water along the way.

CHAPTER ELEVEN

Seconds merged into seconds, minutes into minutes and hours into hours.

Liliwen didn't know if day had turned into night, or even back into day yet. How long she had been locked up here, she had no idea.

No doubt Cara had noticed that she hadn't come home. Had her father found out yet? What about Cadfael?

What would they do once they did find out? Would her father, in a fit of blind rage at her disobedience, and encouraged by the Seer's predictions, order a large scale attack on the Black Isles?

She hoped she would never find out.

If she was in luck, she would be put to death before that.

Her skin was getting very dry; it was starting to ache more and more. Perhaps that was their plan. To leave her here to rot, until she dried up entirely.

It wasn't a nice prospect. A slow, painful death.

They hadn't given her any food either. Would she starve first or dry out?

Footsteps could be heard outside, which wasn't that unusual. There had been a guard outside from the very start, who occasionally wandered back and forth, patrolling the hallway.

This time, the steps were accompanied by an imposing and familiar voice. Liliwen couldn't hear what was being said, but she was pretty sure Teaq was outside. Her heartbeat surged.

He had come for her.

Sure enough, the wooden door of her cell swung open, and her rescuer appeared.

Unsure of who was listening, Liliwen chose not to speak at first.

Teaq entered and pulled the door shut behind him.

Liliwen wrapped her arms around her legs and just looked up at him in silence. She was certain she looked like crap. This was not how she wished to be seen. But he held in his hands the much needed thing that her body was dying for.

A pitcher of water.

"I'm meant to be interrogating you," Teaq whispered as he kneeled beside her.

"Has the guard gone? Can he hear us?" she asked, while reaching for the pitcher.

She dipped her hand in and instantly noticed how her skin soaked up the moisture. Such sweet relief.

"I sent him away," Teaq said.

Liliwen poured little splashes of water over herself, soothing the worst of the aches caused by the net as well as the general dryness in the air that had been getting the better of her. Once she had emptied the jug and looked up, she found that Teaq had been observing her the whole time.

"Stop staring at me, you're making me nervous," she complained. Her objection was only partially meant in jest.

Although she was grateful for the relief the water had brought her, a large part of her still wished Teaq hadn't come. Seeing him made it so much more difficult to accept her fate.

The pain in his eyes that she'd seen earlier was still very much there. Every time she looked at him, it tore at her insides. That was an ache no amount of water could fix.

"I'm so sorry," Teaq whispered.

"Whatever for? You couldn't have done anything. I understand that."

"I shouldn't have let things get this far," he said.

"Don't say that. Don't you tell me that we shouldn't have met. Don't take that away from me too," she threatened.

Teaq pressed his lips together and nodded. "Fair enough."

"How long have I been in here for? I can't tell if it's been an hour or a century," she said.

"Not even an hour."

Liliwen sighed. At this rate, her incarceration would be a lot more difficult to manage than she thought. All the time spent alone in here had passed at a snail's pace. Perhaps it wasn't so bad that he had come. At least his visit offered some distraction.

"Now, what are you supposed to be interrogating me about?" she changed the topic.

Teaq handed her a bowl full of something soft and slimy which she did not recognize. "Have something to eat first."

Liliwen's stomach was growling, but she wasn't too sure about this supposed food he'd brought. "What is this meant to be?"

"Fisherman's pie," he said, as though it was the most normal thing in the world.

"You make pie out of fishermen?" Liliwen frowned, then held it up closer to her face and sniffed it. Perhaps it wasn't so bad.

Teaq burst out laughing. "Not fishermen. It's made with fish!"

His correction made her chuckle as well. "Okay. I suppose I can eat that."

It had been an unintentional joke, but it still lightened the mood significantly. As she started pecking at the food and found that it was indeed better than starving to death, their conversation continued a bit more smoothly.

"You're not the only prisoner down here, you know," Teaq said.

Liliwen looked up from her bowl with great interest. "Do tell. Did you capture any more Merfolk?"

"Not quite. Remember the prediction of your people's Seer that you shared with me? It came true, somewhat. We had a human join our ranks some days ago," Teaq said.

"And you've imprisoned it too?" Liliwen asked.

"Well, not quite. Let me start at the beginning," Teaq began. He then shared the whole story of Kelly, the human offering, the Reaping Ceremony which the Others held, and how his brother had chosen her as his queen.

Liliwen found herself engrossed in his tale, asking for occasional clarifications when she didn't understand something. The strange food, meanwhile, was starting to get cold.

"And so Rhea, our cousin, arrested her and locked her up in a different part of the dungeon. Now it remains to be seen if Broc accepts the truth..." Teaq concluded.

"Love is a strange thing," Liliwen observed.

"What makes you say that?" Teaq said. "I'm telling you the prediction has come true, and you're bringing love into it."

"It's obvious he loves her, though. Your brother. And now both of you have had their women locked up. It's so romantic, isn't it?" Liliwen said.

Teaq frowned. "I wouldn't call it romantic, exactly."

"You ignored our peoples' age old conflict for me. Broc wants to ignore the truth that his woman is a witch."

"That's different."

Liliwen shook her head. *No, it isn't.*

Teaq looked at her in silence for a moment. "Well, romantic or not. I'm not sure I can find a way out of this."

Liliwen shook her head again. "There is no way out of

this. This is the end. It's fine, though. We'll be fine. You cannot expect your brother to accept something you cannot accept yourself."

Again, he was quiet for a little while.

"I'd better go, before word spreads and people start to get suspicious. Remember, I can only bring you food and water for as long as nobody knows about us," Teaq spoke up again.

Liliwen nodded, though part of her was dreading that she'd soon be on her own again. "That's obvious. You be on your way. I'm alright down here. But…"

"Yes?"

"There's a part of the prophecy that hasn't happened yet. My people will soon find me missing. It's only a matter of time before—"

"They'll come for you," Teaq agreed. "We cannot fix everything in one day. It will take them a while to figure out where you went."

Liliwen had to agree. The whole thing was inevitable. Neither he nor she could do a thing about it.

"I'll see you," she said.

He leaned in for a kiss, but she refused. Not here. Not in this filth. "I can't. I hope you understand," she whispered as she averted her gaze.

"I'll come back in the morning." Teaq got up and gathered the pitcher and bowl he'd brought, then he left. It was a relief, as well as a disappointment.

Hopefully morning would come soon.

The Soldier and the Siren

———◆———

Teaq's visits were regular as clockwork. They helped Liliwen break up her days and nights. And now that she was sufficiently hydrated, thanks to the regular supply of water Teaq had arranged for her, her stay in the dungeon had become just a little bit easier.

At least it wasn't painful anymore.

And the stories he continued to tell her, of Kelly, the human; Rhea, his cousin; and Broc, the king, kept her imagination occupied even when he wasn't around. They discussed the challenges that lay ahead. The impending invasion of her people, as well as its repercussions, was something she thought about a lot.

Two nights and days passed. The next time Teaq arrived in her cell he was in a particularly agitated mood. Of course the first thing on her mind was just that; had her people come?

"No, no, nothing like that," Teaq grumbled.

"Then?"

"My brother has freed the human," he said.

Liliwen's eyes widened. "I knew it," she whispered.

Teaq frowned at her, but didn't comment.

From the start, she had wondered if the king would accept Rhea's account of events and stand by as his chosen bride remained locked up. Perhaps love had prevailed, at least for those two.

"What happened? How did Rhea react?" Liliwen asked, eager to get the full story.

This snippet of news was the most exciting thing that had happened in three days. She'd never been much of a gossip before, but being stuck in a dark hole had a way of changing people.

Teaq scoffed. "My brother didn't consult anyone. He just freed her, and had her attend the final night of the feast. I had a taste of her witchcraft myself."

Liliwen noticed herself leaning forward in anticipation for further details. "She performed magic? Right there at the feast?"

Teaq nodded. "She can read minds. Her talents are crude at best, though. I don't know how she managed to overpower Rhea on the hill top initially. She's one of the best fighters on the island."

Liliwen nodded slowly. This Rhea sounded very impressive from the stories Teaq had told so far. A woman after her own heart, not limited by the stupid rules the Merfolk had. Oh, to witness the confrontation between Rhea and the human, Kelly. Liliwen would have loved to have been there.

Teaq's stories had to suffice, though.

"So she read your mind?" Liliwen asked.

Teaq shrugged. "She tried. I heard her voice in my head. She was pleading with me to let her in, but she didn't seem to be successful. Rhea, though. She had Rhea eating out of her hand. It was a sight to see."

Liliwen cocked her head to the side. Indeed, it would have been.

"Did she tell you what happened? Rhea, I mean?"

"She was too shocked to say a word. I could see it in her eyes, though. The human had penetrated her thoughts. An entire conversation went on in silence. And by the end, Rhea was defeated."

"Wow. So the Seer was right. This human does have a power my people might fight over."

"I don't see how." Teaq's expression was still dark.

"Think about it. To see into the minds of your enemy. It's a valuable weapon to have."

Teaq was about to protest.

"Even if it doesn't properly work on everyone. Perhaps she's still learning to use her magic," Liliwen continued.

"Perhaps," he grumbled. "But for my brother to set aside everyone's opinions and free her on a whim… We're family. That should mean something."

Liliwen smiled briefly. How could this man be so stubborn? In the face of everything he was doing down here with her?

"Wouldn't you?" she asked coyly.

"Wouldn't I, what?"

"Wouldn't you free me, if you could?"

Her question remained unanswered, but the look in Teaq's eyes told her everything she needed to know.

CHAPTER TWELVE

One hundred and sixty seven hours. That was how long it had taken for Liliwen's people to track her down and launch their attack.

Teaq happened to be on the View Point when the war horn blew, rocking the castle down to its very foundations. It was a chilling sound.

All the more so because it was all his fault. His people would risk their lives in combat with the Sea Folk, because he had been stupid enough to enter into a relationship with one of theirs. Sure, technically it was her capture that had attracted King Weiland's wrath, but in a way it was only a matter of time before her presence at the Eastern Isle was discovered.

He should have known better.

Teaq forced himself into action. With his hand already tightly gripping his sword, he sprinted down the steps and through the winding corridors of the castle until he reached the drawbridge, shouting orders to any guard he found along the way.

He had started this. And now, he would be there at the frontline, next to his men, aiming to end it.

But what he found as he ran out of the castle and straight toward the fortified walls protecting Black Mountain's harbor, was just a little different than any normal Sea Folk invasion.

There were no hordes of angry soldiers, climbing out of the water and onto their island to confront his fighters.

That wasn't to say that there were no Sea Folk warriors in the water; there were hundreds, perhaps even a thousand of them.

But they were still submerged, just watching the islanders scramble into position.

In their midst, just out of range of the archers lining the castle turrets, was a floating vessel of some kind featuring a throne upon which was seated a Merman with the most impressive looking armor Teaq had ever seen. On his head, a crown of precious metals and stones; in his right hand, a long staff with three points on top. It looked like a ceremonial version of the spears Merfolk soldiers carried to battle.

Beside him stood another, younger Merman, who carried the usual combat gear of their people; a standard-issue long spear and a shield.

This was not an ordinary attack, otherwise the low ranking soldiers would have swarmed the island already.

Meanwhile, Broc was nowhere to be found.

Teaq scoffed to himself. Typical. Their world might be coming to an end, and his little brother was probably still in bed with his witch bride.

This made Teaq the highest ranking islander in present company, meaning that he would handle this however he saw fit. He filtered through the ranks of soldiers, reaching the front of the fortified wall and raised both his arms to attract the invaders' attention.

"I am Teaq, General of Black Isle's armies. I speak for my people. What is your business here?"

The figure on the throne stood up proud and arrogant as Teaq had come to expect from his kind. "I am King Weiland, protector of the Deep and rightful ruler of the Northern Sea. I have come to take back what's mine."

Teaq raised both his eyebrows, then quickly, before anyone got the wrong idea, turned to face his people. "Hold fire."

His order echoed through the ranks. Nobody moved a muscle.

Teaq turned back to face the Merking. "Feel free to clarify what you've come here to take."

As soon as he'd finished his sentence, he was joined by a disheveled looking Broc by his side.

"What have we got here," Broc asked.

Teaq gestured at the sea shell clad float in front of them. "King Weiland himself has graced us with his presence."

"First you will surrender my daughter, then you'll surrender these islands!" King Weiland bellowed.

Teaq was speechless.

"Did he just say his *daughter*?" Broc whispered. "Bloody hell, this is getting better and better."

Teaq was still frozen in place, when his brother stepped

up. "I am Broc Bearclaw, King of the Black Isles and Ruler of the Northern Sea. You'll have to take these islands from my cold, dead hands!"

"That can be arranged, you filthy land dweller!" King Weiland shouted back.

A rough prod in the shoulder brought Teaq back to reality. He exchanged a quick look with Broc. "I have to verify this. I mean, this changes everything."

Broc nodded. "Go. I'll handle this."

Teaq left his brother on the boundary and rushed back toward the castle. Although he didn't want to think of her this way, Liliwen, being the bloody Merking's daughter of all things, gave them leverage they previously did not have.

He had to speak with her, to figure out a way to resolve this mess while keeping bloodshed to an absolute minimum. The Sea Folk had arrived in great numbers. If they decided to strike now, there was no telling how long Teaq's men could defend Black Mountain. And if Black Mountain were to fall…

Teaq shook off these dark thoughts and focused on the task at hand. He had to see Liliwen. Immediately.

Although she was being held in a remote part of the dungeons, Teaq crossed the distance in no time at all. He ordered the guard away as usual, and quickly unlocked the door to her cell.

"We must talk," he said.

Liliwen looked up. "They're here, aren't they? I heard

the war horn. It shook the walls and ceiling. I thought the entire dungeon was going to fall on my head."

"Your father is here," Teaq said, folding his arms in front of his chest.

Her eyes widened. "He must be furious."

Teaq had wanted to be firm. After all, she hadn't been entirely honest with him. But seeing her cowering in the corner of her dirty little cell… He couldn't go through with it.

"He's furious with us for capturing you, yes."

"Oh. I…" Liliwen averted her gaze. "I didn't think he would come himself. He hardly leaves the palace."

"Why did you never mention you're a princess? King Weiland's daughter. Of course he's brought the full might of his army along with him to ensure your release."

"Perhaps for the same reason you never said you're your king's brother. And a general on top of it," Liliwen observed dryly.

Teaq couldn't suppress a smile. As usual, she had managed to cut through all the nonsense. "I think you'll find that I'm not merely *a* general, but rather the only general," Teaq corrected her.

"Fine. *The* general, and *the* princess. What does it matter, though? I'm still a prisoner and you're still under siege."

"They haven't actually attacked. Yet."

Liliwen looked up in surprise. "They haven't… That means…"

"He really wants you back in one piece, I suppose. That means we have all the leverage." It didn't feel right referring to her that way, but she had a practical way of looking at things so Teaq figured she would understand.

She nodded. "He wants me back so he can punish me himself. But yes, leverage."

"So what's left to decide is, do we attack first? What's the way out of this mess?" Teaq wasn't really asking her as much as he was thinking aloud. He was the military strategist after all.

"There's one thing…" Liliwen's voice had thinned to a whisper. "No, I couldn't ask you to do this."

"What is it? I'll do anything, as long as it helps," Teaq urged.

Liliwen's gaze met his, and he could see they were misted up. Ever since her capture, he'd felt close to tears at times, but not once had Liliwen shown this kind of weakness in front of him. Not once had she cracked under the pressure. It nearly broke him.

"Please, tell me."

"If you were to ask for a duel. Your strongest fighter against his." Her voice was cracking as she spoke.

Teaq frowned. This was her grand idea? "What good is that going to do?"

"You have to set the terms in advance. If he wants me, then you promise to set me free if his man wins. My father is many things but he's not dishonorable. He will respect the rules of a duel."

"So we will duel for you," Teaq mumbled, still trying to understand what she was trying to tell him.

"Well, you'll duel for whatever terms you set." Liliwen shrugged. "Demand a truce. Who's your strongest fighter?"

Teaq responded without hesitation. "Well, I am. That's why I hold the position of general."

Sure, Broc had beaten him in hand-to-hand combat seven years ago and won the throne, but that had been a fluke. Destiny, perhaps. Teaq had historically been the stronger fighter. Now, with the additional years of combat experience behind him, he was unchallenged. Undefeated in seven years.

"Who's your father's best fighter?" Teaq asked.

Tears had started running down Liliwen's cheeks. "Shh, it's alright. Have a little faith in me," Teaq whispered.

"I do. I do have faith. It's just... My father's best fighter is Cadfael. My brother." Liliwen turned away from Teaq and curled up into a ball, sobbing softly now.

Finally, Teaq understood. She had reluctantly offered him a way out. And she had foreseen this right from the start of their conversation. The other Merman on King Weiland's float must have been *him*. Liliwen's brother, Cadfael.

Sea Folk did not accept defeat easily. And because of what was at stake, neither would he.

He would fight her brother, possibly to the death. Two men she held dear, battling it out, all because of her. No wonder she was at her wits' end.

Teaq's heart had broken once, on that dark day of her capture. Now, it was threatening to shatter all over again.

"Don't cry. It'll be alright. Whatever happens." Teaq spoke these words because they were expected. But they sounded hollow.

Liliwen's sobs grew louder.

It was torture to stand there and watch as she broke down.

"Just go!" she shouted suddenly, startling Teaq.

He wasn't sure what to say.

"Go and get it over with! You don't have time for this. The enemy is already at your gate, readying for a fight," she cried.

Teaq nodded briefly. She was absolutely right, as always. The enemy *was* right outside. And he had a job, no, a duty to do. This wasn't just about Liliwen and him. It was about his people. About these islands, and everyone who lived on them.

First he would have to get Broc onboard with the idea, then they'd set the terms with King Weiland.

If he could win the duel, he could negotiate a truce for everyone.

"I love you," Teaq whispered, as he left her cell.

As he pulled the heavy wooden door shut behind him, he could still hear Liliwen's cries.

It took all his self-control to pull himself together and

not let his emotions get the better of him. His recklessness had caused all this. Now it was up to him to fix it.

It was time for him to face up to his mistakes and confess everything to Broc.

Teaq rushed back up the many stairs and across the drawbridge back to the spot where he'd left his men and Broc.

King Weiland was still waiting on his elaborate floating throne with Cadfael by his side.

Teaq took his own brother aside.

"I have confirmation." Teaq paused, then added: "And if I could have a moment alone, there's something else I have to tell you."

Broc frowned. "What, now? We're kind of in the middle of something here."

"Trust me. You need to hear this. Alone."

Broc nodded. "Fine. But make it quick. We have a war to fight."

CHAPTER THIRTEEN

The worst had happened. Beyond the initial shock, Liliwen hadn't cared about being imprisoned. She had accepted it. And Teaq's regular visits and stories about what was going on with Broc and the human had been a great help to pass the time.

But this... This was a horror she could not have foreseen.

She and her big mouth.

The two men she cared for. Her brother and her lover, standing on opposite sides of a battlefield. She knew how Cadfael fought. All or nothing. If he had half a chance, Teaq would not make it out alive.

Similarly, she knew Teaq would give his all in the duel. Either way, she would mourn a loved one's death by the end of today. All because of her stupid urge to go on an adventure. If only she'd stayed in the palace like her father had ordered her to...

Then she wouldn't have known this pain.

She wouldn't have known Teaq.

She would have never loved like she had loved him.

That in itself was something to regret as well. If she had known the outcome of her actions, would she have done it anyway?

Liliwen could do nothing but cry. Not for herself;

never for herself. But for the lives she had destroyed.

Cara. She had warned Liliwen. She had told her not to do anything stupid.

If Teaq won the duel... Liliwen would be solely responsible not just for the death of her brother, but her best friend's heartbreak as well. The guilt was overwhelming.

And if Teaq lost... Liliwen dared not think about how that would affect her.

The only thing left to keep her from losing her mind was that she was surrounded by these thick impenetrable walls. She didn't have to see it happen. She wouldn't even hear the fight.

Footsteps echoed down the corridor outside. Liliwen wiped the tears from her eyes and waited with bated breath.

It was impossible to gauge time down here, but that seemed too fast. Teaq couldn't possibly have come back already. Was her brother dead?

The heavy wooden door swung open yet again, only to reveal a stranger.

"Get up," he ordered.

Liliwen was frozen. What was happening? "Why, what's going on?"

"Look, I have my king's orders. That's all. Get up or I'll make you," the man spat.

Liliwen reached for a solid iron hook set into the granite wall of her cell and heaved herself up. She stood uneasily, but the guard didn't care. He dragged her around by her arm and tied her hands behind her back. Then he shoved her out the door and into the dark corridor.

"Where are you taking me?" she asked.

Had Teaq's brother decided against the duel and ordered her execution? Was this the end?

She stumbled through the maze of corridors, up multiple flights of stairs, with the guard continuously poking her in the back with the butt of his sword.

Her outburst from earlier had drained her, and the walk was long and strenuous. She blinked uneasily as she emerged from the final hallway, through a huge wooden drawbridge. Daylight.

The guard had taken her outside.

She could smell the salty sea air and feel the wind on her parched skin. A slow drizzle started, giving her body some much needed relief. Her mind was working overtime though. Why was she being dragged up here?

"There she is," the man she recognized as Teaq's brother, King of the Black Isles, called out loudly while pointing at her. "She's safe and sound, for now."

Liliwen blinked against the light, and finally saw who King Broc was talking to. Her father was waiting out at sea, seated on a replica of the throne he sat on at the palace, mounted on top of a floating wooden deck.

Liliwen's eyes filled with fresh tears as she spotted Cadfael standing beside their father's throne.

"Liliwen, have they treated you with the respect a princess of the Deep deserves?" King Weiland called out.

Through her tears, she nodded. "Yes Father, I'm fine." Liliwen's voice cracked a little as she spoke.

Of course, she was anything but. But the islanders' treatment of her had nothing to do with that. They didn't honestly plan to hold the duel here now, with her watching? She couldn't bear the thought. What a cruel and unusual punishment for her sins.

She looked around and saw Teaq, who was in the process of casting off his armor. So they had agreed on a simple duel, according to Merfolk customs. Only one weapon of choice; no shields or armor.

Whatever the outcome, it would be quick.

"The terms are set. The fighters are ready. Let the fight begin," King Weiland bellowed.

He gestured at Cadfael to make his way forward.

Teaq meanwhile ordered his soldiers back to clear a space on the fortified wall, just thirty or so feet away from Liliwen's current position. She was close enough to smell the blood.

And there was no doubt in her mind that there would be lots of it.

Teaq approached the makeshift arena. Mid-step, his human form warped and shifted. His skin sprouted fur, and his body elongated as she got down on all fours.

The sight took Liliwen's breath away.

For a moment, she forgot who she was watching, and

thought of all the stories Cadfael and the others had told of battles with the Others. Of the animal forms they had encountered and defeated.

Though Teaq wasn't carrying his sword anymore, he looked every bit the formidable opponent Liliwen thought he would be.

Similarly, Cadfael made his way toward dry land. His movements were smooth and powerful as he cut through the choppy waters. In one fluid jump, he emerged from the waves and landed on two feet onshore. The spectacle could not have been any more different from Liliwen's first steps on land.

Despite his smaller frame, Cadfael was imposing in his own right. Liliwen couldn't help but feel proud as well as afraid for both of them.

"Remember the rules," Broc, King of the Others, shouted. "My man wins, you forget you ever had a daughter and withdraw your troops immediately. Your man wins, we release her into your custody."

"What of the Isles?" King Weiland asked. "My man wins, you surrender the Black Isles along with my daughter."

Broc and Teaq exchanged a look. It was obvious that Broc was unhappy with the arrangement. But the prerequisite for a proper duel was that both parties agreed to the stakes in advance.

"Fine. Your man wins, you get your daughter as well as

the Black Isles," Broc said, then turned away in disgust.

Despite their differences, these two brothers, Teaq and Broc, must have had a great amount of trust in one another.

"Don't bloody lose," Broc hissed at Teaq, who nodded briefly.

Liliwen's chest tightened as the two fighters circled one another, waiting for the countdown. She didn't know who to root for, which side to take. Too much was at stake either way.

Whatever the outcome, the duel was already a tragedy.

The counting began, backwards from ten. Liliwen held her breath and turned away, only to be shoved back into position by the guard who had dragged her up here.

"You'll watch," he spat.

Liliwen pressed her lips together and fought further tears as the count hit zero.

Cadfael was the first to attack, leaping forward at Teaq with his spear raised high. Teaq dodged him effortlessly, then flipped back around and went for his arm.

But Cadfael fought him off easily and tried to slam the back of the spear into his head.

Another miss.

Teaq growled; the sound sent shivers down Liliwen's spine. Then he jumped up toward Cadfael, aiming right at his throat. Cadfael got down on his haunches, raising his spear up. It grazed Teaq's flank.

The Merfolk watching from the water cheered.

The Soldier and the Siren

A sharp pain pierced Liliwen's heart, watching the spray of blood emerge from Teaq's wound.

But the injury did not slow him down. He recovered immediately and snapped at Cadfael's leg, taking a small chunk out of it.

Liliwen cried out in horror, then covered her mouth with both hands. The soldiers surrounding her on the fortifications roared in excitement.

Both fighters were now staining the ground with their blood as it dripped slowly but steadily into the dust. And both were completely unfazed by the pain. As if they didn't even notice it.

Evenly matched, they circled each other, attacking and defending in a deadly dance that lasted multiple rounds.

Neither showed any sign of slowing down, no matter how many times they were hit or scraped.

So far no serious injury had been inflicted, but it was only a matter of time.

Sure enough, it was Cadfael who succeeded first, slamming the long end of his spear into Teaq's ribs so hard Liliwen could hear the crack of bone.

Teaq fell and rolled over onto his side, before jumping up again and lunging at Cadfael with his teeth out. He bit down on Cadfael's right forearm, causing him to drop the spear. It clattered to the ground and was quickly pushed away by Teaq's paw.

The rules forbade any fighter from picking up a

weapon that was pushed out of the arena.

But Merfolk did not need spears to fight.

Even with a fractured arm, Cadfael's retaliation was quick. He punched Teaq in the side of his head, throwing him down and onto his back.

It only dazed him for a second, and Teaq was back on his feet and readying himself for another strike.

Both the fighters were limping now. Their skin and fur was getting covered in the same muddy red of the blood soaked ground. If one of them did not succumb to their injuries directly, blood loss would inevitably claim their strength.

Liliwen could bear it no longer.

"Stop," she whimpered. "Please, stop."

But nobody was listening.

The fight continued, on and on, until neither fighter had any unscathed body part left. Sweat, mud, blood and tears had mingled on their skin until they were barely recognizable anymore.

The fight was slowing proportionately to the amount of injuries either party had received. Their movements became clumsy, their dodges ineffective.

Would she mourn not one but both their lives tonight?

The ground was slick now. The water that lapped at the fortifications below was stained by the blood that had dripped down from the arena.

And still. Blow by blow, the two men continued to fight. Slowly. Badly. Giving it their last shred of strength.

Teaq, recovering from a blow to the rib cage, where Cadfael's spear had done its damage earlier, buckled at last.

"No!" she called out. *If you don't live, neither do I!*

Tears ran freely down Liliwen's face. She felt empty. Nothing left to give.

Four feet away, Liliwen's brother sunk to his knees, gasping for air. He looked up at her, mouthing just a single word.

"Sorry."

As both of them collapsed, so did Liliwen's world. A black cloud descended over her, pulling her down along with them. She did not remember anything after that.

CHAPTER FOURTEEN

Teaq tried to open his eyes, but could not see a thing. His lids were swollen shut.

He tried to move, but his limbs did not cooperate.

The pain coursing through his body was blindingly sharp, but that was not what he was most concerned about.

Liliwen!

The first thing on his mind was her. Windswept hair and cheeks streaked with tears. Broc had summoned her on King Weiland's demand. She'd seen the whole thing. How painful it must have been for her.

Where was she? More importantly, *how* was she? Was she safe?

He tried to open his mouth to speak, but his jaw was swollen shut. His throat was so dry, he could barely make a sound.

"Lili—" He coughed, then immediately regretted trying to speak at all. His chest was on fire, his mouth filled with the metallic taste of blood.

Of any of the battles he had been in, the duel had been in a league of its own. Lesser men might have given up sooner. But too much was at stake.

And the worst part was, he couldn't recall the outcome.

He was alive, wasn't he? Had he won? Had he

capitulated?

His head was throbbing so hard, he was certain that he was shaking along with it.

Where was he?

And where was everyone else?

What of his people? Had everyone been slaughtered by King Weiland's men, and he now found himself in hell?

Before he could try to speak again, he was pulled back under. Drowned in darkness, his mind gave way again.

———◆———

There were voices. Female as well as male.

And water. Waves lapped at her body, waking her gently.

Liliwen opened her eyes and could not recognize where she was. This wasn't her dark cell in the dungeon; rather, there was light all around, making it hard for her vision to focus.

Walls lined with shelves of colorful bottles. Her eyelids fell shut again.

Warm water surrounded her, coaxing her body as well as her mind back into reality.

"She's coming to," a female spoke.

"About bloody time," another responded.

Liliwen blinked a few times, and finally saw her present company.

There were two women, one with flowing red hair.

Short. Dressed in the most beautiful gown Liliwen had ever seen.

Another, much harder looking female, wearing an armored bodice, short skirt and not much else.

Kelly, the human newly crowned queen, and Rhea. Teaq had spoken about them so often during his visits to the dungeon, she was certain she recognized them.

Off to the side of the room stood Broc, looking in equal parts hesitant about being here, as well as concerned.

She looked down at herself and found that she was lying in a fancy basin filled with warm water. What was this place?

"Is she in decent shape?" he asked. "We don't want any more trouble."

What was she doing here? Why were they all talking about her as if she wasn't here herself?

"How is he?" she asked, though she was unable to articulate her question as well as she'd wanted to.

"What did she say?" the taller female, Rhea, asked.

"She asked 'how is he'," the human responded.

"Your brother will be fine. He's injured, but he will make it."

Liliwen choked back a sob. Her chest felt hollow, like someone had taken her heart and crushed it.

"She means Teaq," Kelly said.

"Oh."

Broc stepped forward. "Princess Liliwen. The challenge ended in a draw. Neither fighter could finish, so I've negotiated a compromise with your father, King Weiland."

Liliwen tried to process what he had said. *A draw? Did that mean...*

Teaq was still alive.

Again, tears flowed, but this time, they were tears of relief.

"You will be returned to your people as soon as King Weiland has ordered back his armies. This is how it must be."

Liliwen shook her head, then tried to raise herself out of the water, but slipped back down under. This tub was proving more effective in keeping her contained than any prison cell.

"I cannot go back," she protested.

"It's the only way. We break our word and your father invades. And with Teaq out of action, who will lead the troops?" Broc's voice trailed off.

"Will he make it?" she asked.

"Teaq? Oh yes, given a week or two, he'll be good as new."

Finally, some more good news.

But what would happen next? If the outcome of the duel required that she return to the Deep, then she had no choice but to comply.

Strangely, it had been easier for her to accept her fate as a prisoner. Having to return home and face her father... The humiliation would be immense.

And how would she face Cadfael, who had nearly given his life for her? And Cara, who had almost been widowed before ever being wed.

That wasn't even the worst part.

"Can I at least say goodbye?" Liliwen whispered.

Rhea scoffed, as did Broc.

"You seem to have forgotten that you and Teaq caused all this. He's my brother, and nearly gave his life to save these Isles, so I cannot judge him too harshly. But I have no love lost for you, Mermaid!" Broc said.

Liliwen averted her gaze. There was no arguing with his assessment. She was at fault. And now she had to face the consequences.

"I think she's well enough now. Even her color has changed back to normal," Rhea observed.

Liliwen raised her hands and looked at her skin. The warm water had undone all the damage caused by those endlessly long days spent in that dark cell. The only scars she carried now were invisible to anyone who wasn't a mind reader.

Liliwen eyed the human, Kelly, who had been silent during the final couple of exchanges.

So that was what a witch looked like. Had she already performed her magic and learned Liliwen's deepest, darkest secrets?

If she had, her expression did not let on.

"Then let's not waste any more time," Broc said. He turned around and left the room in a hurry. "Kelly, are you coming?" he called out from outside.

Kelly didn't move an inch, though. She kept on staring at Liliwen to the point of making her uncomfortable. *Please don't turn me into a fish or something,* Liliwen thought.

Kelly chuckled.

"What happened?" Rhea asked.

Kelly shook her head. "Just something I was thinking."

Liliwen cocked her head to the side. *You're listening right now, aren't you?*

Kelly turned around to check on Rhea, then made eye contact with Liliwen again and smiled briefly.

I understand, you know. The men ... they're finding it more difficult.

It was the strangest feeling, having this human—a creature Liliwen had never even seen before—infiltrating her mind like this.

Teaq told me your story. So romantic. From prisoner to queen.

What about your story? From princess to prisoner.

Liliwen shrugged. "Perhaps it is all written somewhere," she whispered.

Rhea turned to face the two of them "What?" She studied both their faces, then rolled her eyes. "Up to your usual tricks, I see. Well, I don't see what's keeping me here, then."

She still hates me. Kelly smiled apologetically, then turned and watched as Rhea left the room.

I'm sure she's not too fond of me either.

Will you be alright? You'll be released soon.

Liliwen lowered herself in the basin, wetting her hair. How good it felt to do that after so many days. *I'll have to be. Somehow.* It was still a scary prospect. Her father would be furious. She'd be monitored day and night.

You're not giving up on him, are you? Kelly raised her eyebrows in concern. *He loves you. I know he won't give up on you. I saw it in his thoughts during the fight.*

Alas, a glimmer of hope. Liliwen shook her head. No, she wouldn't give up.

Kelly nodded at her encouragingly. *Don't lose hope now.*
I won't.

They had only just finished their exchange, when Rhea returned, along with a number of guards. "That's enough of that, you two. It is time."

Liliwen bowed her head and surrendered as Rhea picked her up out of the slippery tub and set her down on the ground beside it. Her legs were shaking a bit, but she managed to stand on her own, briefly. Then the guards took her by the arms, and dragged her out of the room, through a maze of hallways, and finally, out of the castle. It all happened in such a blur, Liliwen could hardly find her bearings. Until she found herself in a familiar place, that was.

The fortified sea wall, where the duel had taken place.

Liliwen bit her lip hard as she spotted the makeshift arena. The ground was still soaked. The smell of stale blood hung in the air.

The Soldier and the Siren

Broc, who had already been waiting by the very edge of the wall, cleared his throat. "So, as agreed. One princess, being returned hale and hearty to King Weiland. He would be wise to respect our deal."

Liliwen also hoped that he would. Even though she would not be able to stay in the Deep for long.

———◆———

The next time Teaq awoke, his eyelids opened just enough to let in the flicker of a torch some distance away. His surroundings remained a blur; nothing came into focus.

He did not recognize anything. Even his nose could not pick up any familiar scents. Perhaps he'd broken that too in the battle, along with almost everything else.

Every part of his body ached. But most of all, it was his heart that bothered him.

He had no idea how long he'd been out for.

And still he didn't know how the fight had turned out.

Where was Liliwen? Where was everyone else?

He fought the seething pain in his arms and chest and raised himself up. Now, he could get a better look at his surroundings, though his eyesight still hadn't cleared. He'd obviously received some significant hits to the head during the battle.

No problem, he'd heal. Islanders usually did.

But if Liliwen was still locked up somewhere, and there

was no one looking out for her, then she might not make it that long. He had to make himself noticed. He had to know what was going on.

Teaq inhaled deeply, only to cough violently. After catching his breath, he tried again.

"Hello?" he called out.

His voice sounded pathetic. Weak, just like the rest of him.

Another coughing fit forced him onto his back.

Footsteps approached. Thankfully, his efforts hadn't been in vain.

"Come quick, I think our general has come to," someone called out.

At least he was among his own people. That was a good sign.

More voices could be heard now, approaching his position.

Teaq tried to focus again, but he could not recognize the faces that surrounded him now.

"Sir, can we get anything for you? Water? Food?" someone asked.

Teaq shook his head. "Broc. Get the King."

"What did he say?" another person said.

"The King. He means to speak with King Broc."

"No problem, Sir. We will send someone to find him immediately."

Teaq closed his eyes and just tried to breathe deeply. Ideally he would not be talking right now. He should just surrender to the healing process. There was a reason fighters passed out, often for days, after a particularly rough battle. Islanders healed quickly, much quicker than humans or Sea Folk. But they could only do so while at rest.

The more he fought it, the bigger the risk of permanent damage.

But there was no way Teaq would allow himself to fall asleep again without finding out what had happened. He had to know if Liliwen was safe.

Footsteps could be heard moving back and forth. His attendants had dispersed again.

Perhaps they had more soldiers to look after. More casualties of battle.

Teaq didn't know how long he lay there, with his eyes closed, listening to the sounds in the rooms or halls surrounding him. Where was he, anyway?

He had almost given up, when at last, he heard a commanding voice in the vicinity. "Where is my brother? Take me to him!"

Teaq forced his eyes open just in time to see the outline of Broc's person standing in front of him. At last, he would find out the truth.

CHAPTER FIFTEEN

The swim back to the Deep was long and arduous. Not because she was physically struggling, but rather, because she dreaded it. Liliwen was accompanied by a handful of guards from the palace, not the sort of people one could have a proper conversation with.

No, she was basically on her own with her thoughts.

When the palace came into view, her heart sank even lower. She'd expected to be executed by the Others, but she'd never planned for this. Death would have been simpler. Less messy.

Liliwen and the guards had barely made it inside the strong walls, when she was almost assaulted by Cara.

"I told you! I told you not to go. Not to do anything stupid. And you had to go off anyway! How dare you!"

Liliwen froze.

Cara had obviously been crying. And why wouldn't she be? Liliwen's recklessness had affected everyone back home, especially Cara, who had no doubt been caring for an injured Cadfael since his return from the duel.

"Sorry," Liliwen whispered. "I'm so sorry."

Cara pressed her lips together and looked at her for a moment. It was the most awkward of silences. Liliwen did not know what to do with herself.

"Oh, Lili! I thought I'd never see you again!" Cara cried out at last.

Liliwen still didn't know whether to stay or run, when Cara wrapped both her arms around her and hugged her tightly.

Liliwen hid her face in her best friend's hair and her eyes filled with tears as well. This part, at least, had not gone so badly after all.

"How is he?" she asked. "How is Cadfael?"

Cara pulled back. "He fought bravely for you."

Guilt filled Liliwen's heart, threatening to overwhelm her all over again. He *had* fought bravely. Both of them had. Her two heroes. If only they knew she had been rooting for both teams.

"Come with me. We'll go see him."

The guards had stood by in silence so far, but now one of them made his presence known with a cough. "Princess Liliwen, we are to bring you to your father immediately."

Oh dear.

"In time. Allow her to see her brother at least, who came so close to giving his life to ensure her safety! It's the least you can do!" Cara argued.

The guards exchanged a few awkward looks.

"I'm afraid we must insist," the same one spoke again. "Orders, you see."

Time to face the music. Liliwen took Cara's hand and squeezed it.

"I'll come find you soon," she said.

Cara nodded. "You'd better."

Lord, give me strength.

———◆———

"**B**rother, you cannot be serious!" Broc complained.

Teaq just stared at him. He was. Deadly serious.

"You of all people ought to understand. Your own woman was a guest at our fine dungeons not so very long ago. After attacking one of our own, no less! And it took you all of two hours to get her released in secret."

"But… She's a Mermaid! She's the enemy! You've been harping on and on about the next invasion. Well, in case you forgot, it arrived already. To get *her* back!"

Teaq sighed. His head was pounding and he was fighting shooting pains in his chest, but this was a conversation he could not put off any longer. He'd had a lot of time to think while in recovery, and it was the only thing that made sense to him.

"Brother, she will not stay in the Deep. She will come back. And when she does, wouldn't it be wiser if I made sure she wasn't here for the Sea Folk to come and retrieve?"

That was the story Teaq told Broc, anyway. In truth, even if she did not come back, he was prepared to venture out there and find her for himself.

The Soldier and the Siren

As he'd drifted around the edges of consciousness these past few days, she had been on his mind the whole time. He would not give her up so easily. Life wasn't worth living if it wasn't with his Liliwen.

"How can you be so sure? What if all this time she was a spy, and she was just toying with you. What if she's back home now, telling them all about our weaknesses, so their next attack will really hit us where it hurts?"

"How could you be so sure about Kelly?" Teaq retorted.

Broc paced the room, as he usually did when he was struggling with something.

There really was nothing more Teaq could say to convince him. He hadn't seen it that way at first, but Liliwen's comparisons between their own situation and what Broc and Kelly had gone through were starting to ring true now.

They were both slaves to their emotions. Nothing any outsider could say or do would get in between either couple.

Teaq and Liliwen were meant to be. Whether Broc chose to accept this fact or not.

"And what of your duties here?" Broc asked at last. "We need you. *I* need you here!"

That was the one weak spot in Teaq's plan. He didn't have a proper answer. But he knew he had given all he could to Broc and the Isles. Now it was time for Teaq to do something for himself.

"You could promote Rhea to general. She's been a formidable head of the Royal Guard. A fearsome fighter in her own right. She's proven herself worthy many times over," Teaq suggested.

Broc stopped pacing. "She's a good candidate. But I still don't like it."

"Have I ever asked you for anything before?" Teaq said. "Plus, you have an advantage over the Sea Folk now. One that we never had before. Kelly's powers will only grow as time goes on."

"Kelly," Broc mumbled. "As much as I'd hate to involve her in the ugly business of war, it may be inevitable going forward."

As painful as it was, letting down his little brother, he could not help it. From the moment Broc had taken the throne, this moment had been inevitable, whether either of them realized it or not. Sooner or later, their relationship would change again.

It was just ironic that it happened because of a woman. Teaq had never thought himself capable of changing his entire outlook in life for love.

But it was too late for second thoughts now.

"Then you know what to do. As do I," Teaq concluded.

"Her people will come for her. Again." Broc's expression darkened further.

"They will. But this time, you and Kelly will be ready."

"I hope so."

"And if not, there's always Saras…" Teaq said.

Broc looked up in horror. "No, I couldn't. He's been asleep for so long… Don't you remember the stories Father told us of what happened before he went to ground?"

Teaq nodded. "I remember. But between a witch and a dragon, there's no way the Sea Folk can compete with that."

Broc sighed. "There will be challenging times ahead."

Truer words had never been spoken.

"Where will you go, anyway?" Broc asked.

Teaq shrugged. "Wherever Liliwen's people won't find us."

"I hope you know what you're doing."

As do I. Teaq closed his eyes, giving them much needed relief. It would still be a few days before his body regained enough of its former strength to put his plan into action. Until then, he'd have a lot to think about.

"I'll see you, brother," Broc mumbled as he made his exit.

Teaq would have liked to be able to help. But Broc was king. In the end, the safety of these Isles was his responsibility.

———— ✦ ————

"You have returned." King Weiland's statement almost sounded like an accusation.

Liliwen kept her head bowed, careful not to make any move to enrage him. "Father, I apologize for all the trouble I have caused."

"Mhmm."

She waited, but there was deadly silence all around. It was enough to drive a person mad.

This couldn't be it. The hammer would drop any second now. Yet, minutes passed without a word being said between them.

Liliwen dared not move.

"I had ordered you to leave the fighting to Cadfael, had I not? Or had I just imagined that? Are my orders not good enough for you?" There it was.

"I'm sorry, Father. I did not mean-"

"Silence!" King Weiland roared.

Liliwen flinched.

"You will speak once I am finished! Do you understand me?"

She nodded.

"What was that?"

"Yes, Father."

"It seems you felt the rules do not apply to you, because you are my daughter. You'll address me as your king from now on. So you do not forget that my orders stand, regardless of what our relation is!"

"Yes, my king," Liliwen whispered.

Of course he was furious. She had ignored a direct order; something nobody else would have dared to do.

"I ought to lock you up and throw away the key. But it seems the Others beat me to it."

"Yes, my king. Punish me any way you see fit."

"How could you be so stupid? After the premonition ceremony promised us good fortune this season. We weren't ready. The element of surprise; ruined!"

"I am ashamed of my actions, my king."

"As you should be! You have set us back months, if not years. And your brother, he's been severely injured because of you!"

Liliwen's chest tightened. That was the worst part. She did not give two hoots about the invasion or the war effort. But people she loved had been hurt. All because of her.

"I wish to see him. To thank him for his courage," Liliwen mumbled.

King Weiland got up from his throne and towered over her. He was tall for a Merman, but not compared to the Others.

"You will see him, and you will beg him for his forgiveness."

"Yes, my king." She intended to.

"And once you do, you will return here at once, and await your punishment."

"Yes, my king. I deserve punishment."

With her head still hanging low, Liliwen slinked out of the coral hall, leaving her father alone with his anger.

If he wished to imprison her, fine. He couldn't keep her—his only daughter—locked up forever. She would bide her time, and make one final journey away from here.

After everything, this place no longer felt like home.

CHAPTER SIXTEEN

Liliwen turned around to face the guard who had been shadowing her since her return. "Where are they keeping Cadfael? Take me to him," she said.

The guard led the way as they crossed into the residential wing of the palace.

This part would be the most painful. The guard opened the door to the infirmary and showed her in. Liliwen held her breath as she stepped inside.

Nothing could have prepared her for the sight that awaited her. Cadfael, laid up on blood stained sheets. His wounds were still seeping, even though they had been covered in medicinal tinctures and seaweed. He was in bad shape.

Cara sat on a stool beside him, tending to his many bandages.

"Oh, Cadfael, I'm so sorry," Liliwen cried out as she approached.

He opened his eyes, and smiled awkwardly. His formerly handsome features were disfigured by bruises and cuts.

"What does the healer say?" Liliwen turned to ask Cara.

"It'll take time, but nothing permanent," Cara responded.

"I'm sorry I couldn't win for you," Cadfael said.

Liliwen burst into tears and buried her face in her hands. "Oh, brother. I have been so unfair to you. This is all my fault."

"Shhh, little sister. I'll be fine. It's a soldier's duty to fight for his princess after all."

Liliwen looked up through her tears. "I must tell you something which might change your mind."

"Yes?"

"The Other you fought... he..."

Cara gasped and covered her mouth. "It was *him*, wasn't it! I don't believe it."

Cadfael frowned as he looked first at Cara, then back at Liliwen. " *Him*? Him, who?"

"Brother, while you have been courting Cara, I'm afraid I had an ulterior motive to visit the Black Isles again and again too..."

"She's been hanging around one of them. One of the Others," Cara added. "I did not tell your father this, but..."

Cadfael closed his eyes and breathed in deeply. "Things are falling into place."

Liliwen sank onto the other chair beside Cadfael's bed and lowered her head into her hands. "I'm so sorry for everything. For putting you in harm's way. For dragging you into a fight you could not win," Liliwen said.

"Oh, I could have won!" Cadfael protested. "It was not a totally fair duel, though."

"How so?" Cara asked.

"I did not mention it to anyone, but when *he* entered the ring, he spoke to me. He said he wished not to kill me. For your sake. That he was fighting for your safety as well."

Liliwen looked up in shock. "He said what, now?"

"I did not know what to believe, but something in his tone gave me pause. I tried not to kill him either. Did I?"

Liliwen shook her head. "No, he's alive."

"Well then. Everyone got what they wanted. The Black Isles got a truce of sorts, and we got our princess back."

Liliwen's fragile heart could take it no longer. She had to confide in them fully. Her secrecy had brought everyone nothing but trouble. No more.

"I intend to go back."

"What? You cannot! As your best friend, I forbid it!" Cara exclaimed.

Liliwen got up and took her friend's hands. "Don't you understand? What you have here with Cadfael, I have with him. He walked into the duel knowing Cadfael would try to kill him, and yet he sought to spare his life for me. I love him, Cara. I cannot be without him."

Now it was Cara's turn to cry. Cadfael, meanwhile, was stoic as ever.

"I wish it could be any other way, but it can't," Liliwen added.

"Oh, Lili… I don't know what to say," Cara sobbed.

There was nothing she could have said. Liliwen had

made up her mind.

"Father will not be happy," Cadfael observed. "He'll break the truce in retaliation."

"Then I'll have to make sure I'm not on the Isles for him to find."

"Where will you go?" Cara asked.

Liliwen shrugged. "Far away. Beyond Father's reach."

Cadfael opened his eyes again and reached for Liliwen's hand. She closed her fingers around his. Despite his injuries, he still had a firm grip.

"Little sister, I hope you know what you're doing. And you're not walking into another trap."

"My heart is already with him. And a person cannot live without a heart."

Their moment was interrupted by the guard, who first knocked, then opened the door.

"My princess, it is time. Your father means to deliver his punishment."

Liliwen shared a long look first with Cadfael, and then Cara. "I'm so glad I could tell you both the truth."

"Be safe, little sister," Cadfael said.

"Be safe, brother."

As she returned to the coral hall, accompanied now not by one guard, but half a dozen of them, Liliwen felt like an offering being brought to slaughter. She wasn't sure what to expect, but when she saw the hooded soldier, already holding his whip at the ready, she realized that she hadn't expected *that*.

The Soldier and the Siren

King Weiland looked on from his throne, not a word said between them.

The first crack of the whip shocked her in its harshness. Then, Liliwen braced herself and prepared to endure the rest.

Two good men were laid up with severe injuries because of her. It was only right that she received her fair share.

For Teaq, she told herself as the whip came down hard on her back again.

For Cadfael. Blood started to flow soon thereafter, as her skin gave way.

Four lashes done, seventeen left to go.

No longer would she possess flawlessly beautiful skin. After this, her sins would be etched into her back forever, for all to see.

When she looked up, after it was all done, she noticed that her father was no longer present. Just how long ago he had left, she did not know.

———•◆•———

"You came," Liliwen spoke first. Night had come and gone once since her arrival. Still, she hadn't moved an inch from her position to avoid detection and capture. She wouldn't make the same mistake again.

"Was there any doubt in your mind?" Teaq asked.

Liliwen shook her head. "And anyway, I would have

waited for you, for as long as it takes. Forever."

"I wouldn't have," Teaq said.

Liliwen's chest tightened. Although it had happened days ago, the lashes on her back still stung. A painful reminder of what she had endured, and would endure again for her transgressions. "You wouldn't have?"

"If I hadn't found you here, I would have sailed all the way to the Deep to get you."

Her heart softened and she smiled. "Just how exactly would you have done that? A one-man assault on the palace, without being able to breathe underwater?"

Teaq shrugged. "I would have found a way."

"Aha." Liliwen cocked her head to the side. "*Sailed* to the Deep, you say?"

"I have a vessel. It's moored not too far from here. It's small but seaworthy."

Liliwen followed Teaq's hand as he pointed at a wooden structure visible in the distance.

"We cannot stay here," Liliwen observed.

Teaq shook his head. "Indeed, we cannot. Your father—"

"He'll come looking for me again. This time he won't be content with a duel."

"We just have to decide where to go," Teaq said. "The mainland is not an option. The humans would kill either of us on sight. And if we go west, our route would lead us right to the Deep."

Liliwen breathed in deeply. She wanted to remember

this place in as much detail as possible. Where everything began.

"I know of a place," she said. "I mean, I've heard stories."

"Where?"

"It's off to the north-east. At the edge of the world. If it exists, we'll find it." Liliwen looked up at Teaq, studying his face. When she had left, Cadfael had still been covered in cuts and welts. Teaq looked in better condition, but there was still something off about him. "How are you doing? I heard you were badly injured."

He shrugged. "I'm fine enough. A few more scars to add to the collection."

Liliwen nodded. Her punishment had earned her a fair number of scars of her own.

She reached for Teaq, who took her hand and helped her out of the water. This time, she did not protest when he lifted her up in his strong arms, though his touch on her injured back made her whimper slightly.

He carried her across the pathway to his boat, and finally Liliwen felt like she could relax. She had left in the dead of night, from the infirmary where she was meant to recover from her punishment, straight into the vastness of the Northern Sea. Her journey was not yet over, but at least she did not have to go it alone anymore.

In Teaq's arms, she felt safe. Like nothing and no one could hurt her ever again.

But things had changed from the last time they'd met each other here.

They were no longer innocent. No longer carefree.

Both had suffered for their love.

Liliwen knew it would take time for them to find their way back to each other.

As she watched him prepare the sail and haul up the anchor of his boat, she had to smile despite everything.

It would take time, but now that they were together, sailing away into their new life. They would have nothing but time.

As the boat started to move, and Teaq set its course to northwest had Liliwen had said, they both stood side by side, watching the Eastern Isle get smaller as they moved further and further away from it.

Bye bye, Black Isles, Liliwen thought.

"It's strange. I'm leaving everything I've ever known," Teaq observed.

Liliwen turned to face him. She had to strain her neck to get a good look at his face, that was how tall he was. "I have everything I need to know right here," she said.

Teaq looked down at her and smiled.

She realized then that he hadn't changed at all. He'd been a battle-hardened soldier all along. That was part of his appeal.

She wrapped her arms around his neck, and he lifted her up again so their faces were at the same level.

"And I wouldn't have it any other way," she added.

"Me neither." He glanced back at the island for a moment, then looked at her again. "The course is set. As long as the winds don't change, there is nothing for me to do right now. What do you say we retreat below deck for a while?"

Liliwen's eyes widened as her heart started to beat a little faster. "I would like that very much."

Since the first time they'd met, right up to the time he took her up into that secluded cave, so many questions had been on her mind. So many fantasies left unexplored.

She would find her answers now that they were finally completely alone.

EPILOGUE

Teaq lay Liliwen down onto her back, admiring her beauty, which shone brightly despite the dim conditions below deck.

The simple cot was not fit for a princess.

None of this situation right now was as she deserved.

But in all its imperfection, this moment still felt completely right.

He kneeled beside the bed, fighting stiffness in his legs as he went down.

As she ran her hands up and down his aching body, all the pain started to melt away. He had not come out of this unscathed. The wounds would take time to fade. The fractured ribs, especially, would keep on bothering him for a while. That was fine, though. He was used to it.

But as he looked her up and down, he found that she also, had been changed. She was not as free in her movements, not as deliberate and in control as she had been previously.

She turned onto her side to make room for him, and he saw a glimpse of something different.

Her skin, which had previously been a flawless expanse of greenish flesh, had blemishes now. Red, and angry looking.

He leaned over to get a better look at her back. What he saw shook him to his core.

"My god, did my brother have you caned while you were locked up? Why didn't you tell me, I would have stopped it. I would have—"

"Shh," she said. "It's alright. Your brother did not do this."

He took her face gently into his hands. "No, it's not alright. I made a vow to myself to keep you from harm."

"It is the punishment my father chose. Considering what I put you through. And my brother, as well, it's only fair."

Teaq looked deeply into her eyes. They had both sacrificed. Fate demanded its pound of flesh from everyone, without exception.

He leaned in for the first kiss in ages. How parched his lips had been without feeling the softness of hers. How hungry was his flesh, now that they were free.

She responded instantly. The passion he'd felt earlier, when they had shared their first intimacies, was back with a vengeance. Their bodies were desperate, aching to become one.

Liliwen grabbed him by the back of his neck and guided him closer, onto the small bed with her. It barely fit them both, but it would suffice.

Through the grazes and cuts that still lingered on his skin, pain mixed with pleasure, until he could no longer distinguish one from the other. She seemed to feel the same.

The awkwardness from before vanished, and she took on a more active role with him.

Every touch of his, she answered with one of her own. Every exploration, she seemed to savor just as he did.

"You're so warm," she whispered.

Yes. Yes, he was. And she was not. Her cool skin was pleasantly soothing. Despite the fresh scarring on her back, her skin still had a smooth quality to it that he had not known before touching her.

It was addictive. Tempting. Seductive.

"We don't traditionally do this. Not without a formal union," Teaq said.

He wasn't sure what he meant by that, because he certainly did not intend to stop now.

"You mean, a wedding?"

"Yes." Teaq leaned down and kissed the dip underneath Liliwen's collarbone.

How beautiful she was. The greatest artist in the world could not have sculpted perfection like her.

"So marry me, then," she said.

Teaq pulled away from her to look her in the eyes. Golden, with a depth not unlike the seas they currently sailed on. The seas that were her home.

"There's a whole ceremony. It doesn't just happen."

"It doesn't just happen for us either. You'd have to ask my father for my hand. We both know that's not going to happen," Liliwen said. "But we're not like our people anymore. Perhaps we can make our own way."

Teaq smiled. "I like that. We'll do it our own way."

"So. What happens in your ceremony that we can do?" she asked.

Teaq thought for a moment, and looked down at the many items of jewelry that still adorned her gorgeous body. "We exchange rings."

She did not hesitate for a moment, and took off one of her rings and presented it to him.

"We have to say our vows first," Teaq said, while weighing the gold ring in his hand.

"Sure. How do they go?"

"I ought to know this, but then, I've never been married before," Teaq joked. This wasn't a joking matter, though. He'd never planned this for himself, but that didn't make it any less special or important.

He slipped off the bed and kneeled down again, with the ring in the palm of his outstretched hand. "With this ring, I promise to keep you safe, to love you and care for you, until death takes me."

Liliwen took the ring and placed it back on her finger. Then she removed another, as well as one of the multiple chains around her neck.

"With this ring, I promise to keep you safe, to love you and care for you, until death takes me." She leaned down and reached around his neck, fastening the chain on him.

He reached for it, feeling the little gold ring that hung from its lowest point.

"That was beautiful. The vows, they're so romantic," Liliwen swooned.

"I'm not sure those were the actual words," Teaq said.

She shook her head. "They are now. For us. I'll never forget them."

He wouldn't either.

Liliwen smiled and gestured at him to get back onto the bed. "Now nothing stands in our way. Neither tradition nor law."

"We're free to do as we like. Until death takes us."

"Until death takes us," Liliwen repeated after him.

She wrapped his arms around him again and coaxed him on top of her.

All this time he hadn't been sure how this part would work with her, and of course berated himself for thinking such crude thoughts about a woman so pure. He needn't have worried, though.

As more and more of his armor and clothing came off, to be discarded on the floor, their bodies knew exactly what to do. Instinct took over.

Liliwen's body had already adjusted to being on dry land; her transformation had become easier each time she had come out of the water.

Two legs, much like his own anatomically, which spread to reveal very human, or islander-like features. Her hands continued to explore him. His chest, with its chiseled muscles and bit of hair that she seemed utterly fascinated by.

His back and buttocks, along with the fresh scars that still occasionally stung. It was a sweet pain, one he could not get enough of so long as it had been caused by her touch.

Finally, her hand reached down, where his manhood was already standing proud. Her grip sent shivers down his entire body.

She was firm, with him. Self-assured, just like a lover should be.

Their love knew no shyness. No shame.

"I've been wondering what this would be like, right from the start."

She had said exactly what had been on his mind all along.

He reached down between her legs, and found that indeed there was one spot where she wasn't cool to the touch. She was red hot, and wet for him already.

"Ohhh, that feels so good," Liliwen moaned.

Her words were superfluous. Her entire body had told him already.

As her hands gripped him tighter, his inner beast was raring to get out and take over. His most base instincts were clawing their way to the surface.

"I'll pleasure you the way you deserve to be pleasured," Teaq spoke in a low growl. "My princess."

Liliwen moaned again; her voice was musical. It enchanted him, spurring him on to do better.

He positioned himself between her legs, and sought to enter her.

"Please me, my husband," she said.

That last statement sent him over the edge of control. He pushed his way into her, and felt her body close around him.

If this was somehow wrong, if it was against the rules, even against nature, their bodies had no idea. Everything about it felt absolutely right.

She bucked her hips upward, drawing him in closer.

He responded with a kiss to the side of her neck.

So beautiful. So fragile and yet so strong.

His wife. His Liliwen.

He thrust into her, again and again. Deeper and deeper. Her hands found their way to his hips, guiding his movements. They were in perfect harmony. Two bodies, one soul.

Like waves on the ocean's surface, they rocked back and forth, breaking into one another, both of them drowning in ecstasy. They both gave it all they could. Whatever their bodies had left to give; working toward the ultimate aim: supreme pleasure.

Teaq felt it creep up on him. Like a growing tension, simmering underneath the surface of his skin, until finally he could ignore it no longer.

Liliwen also was in the throes of desire, moaning with

each of his strokes, louder and louder, until she screamed out and dug her fingernails into his ass. "Oh yes! Oh yes, take me!"

He did.

With one final push, he claimed her. His inner wolf rejoiced.

Liliwen gasped for air, as did he.

Drained as he was, he sunk down on top of her and rested his head on her shoulder.

"You know I love you, right?" he whispered.

"As you should. I am your wife," she replied.

"That you are. And I am your man."

"Forever."

***

A Dragon's Treasure

Down below the mountain, in a cell deeper than deep,
A creature, fierce and powerful, blissfully asleep.
He must not be awoken, unless the need is dire,
For if he is roused, he will blanket the Isles in fire.

CHAPTER ONE

I t had come as somewhat of a surprise to Rhea to be summoned by King Broc at this time. It was a quiet morning, and there was no Council meeting planned that she knew of.

The Sea Folk invasion had been foiled thanks to General Teaq's valiant efforts in hand to hand combat. He had even won them a truce.

So what was there to discuss?

Unless it was a personal matter… But Broc had already made his choice weeks ago. He had even married his human bride, Kelly, already.

What could he possibly want with Rhea, then?

Spurred on equally by curiosity and her ever-present sense of duty, Rhea rushed through the corridors of the castle until she reached the agreed meeting point.

The Great Hall was mostly reserved for official meetings as well as feasts. With just Broc in there waiting for her, it looked unceremoniously barren. An appropriate seat of power for these equally barren Isles they called home.

"My king," Rhea greeted him. Her king indeed, but he was so much more than that.

Unfortunately he had never seen it that way.

"Rhea. We have much to discuss." His expression was different somehow. He wasn't his usual self. Whatever it was, it was big.

She raised an eyebrow.

"What's wrong?"

"It's about Teaq."

Rhea's gaze was briefly attracted by Broc's right hand, which had found the butt of his sword and grasped it instinctively. She swallowed hard. Bad news.

"Is the General alright?"

Last she had visited him, he was well on his way to recovery. The duel he had fought with the Sea Folk warrior who had challenged him had taken its toll, but it was nothing the seasoned fighter couldn't manage. Wolves like Teaq healed particularly quickly. Another week at the most and he would be back to his old self.

"Teaq is fine, yes." Broc all but dismissed her question. So it wasn't Teaq's wellbeing he was worried about. There was something else going on.

"Well, what is it then?" Rhea urged. Patience wasn't one of her strong points. If there was something she needed to know, then why didn't he just come right out with it?

"My brother will be leaving us." Broc looked down at the stone floor between them.

Rhea didn't know what to say. *Teaq, leaving?* She had never seen Broc quite like this, except when she'd arrested Kelly, maybe. So despondent, he did not even make eye contact anymore.

"Why? Some kind of mission?" Rhea asked softly.

It was difficult to watch him like this.

Broc shook his head. "He has chosen a mate."

Rhea frowned. "That's good news, surely?"

"It's the bloody mermaid, Rhea. There's nothing good about it!"

Broc's outburst startled her, but she quickly recovered as the meaning of his words hit her.

It shouldn't have been a surprise, of course. She had known for a while now that there was something going on between Teaq and the mermaid they'd captured on the Eastern Isle. Initially it was just guesswork, but after the duel when they had returned her to her people, the mermaid had all but confirmed it herself.

It was in the way she'd asked about Teaq's wellbeing. The shocking part was that the feelings were apparently mutual.

And now, Teaq was leaving. To be with her.

Rhea sunk down onto one of the long wooden tables that lined the Great Hall and shook her head.

Never had she seen anyone who took their role in the court so seriously. Teaq had been a great general. And he was giving it up for one of the enemy.

You think you know someone, she thought.

"That's insane," she mumbled.

Broc scoffed. "That's what I said."

Rhea looked up at him. He was hurting, it was so clear

to see. Abandoned by his own brother.

"I will speak with him. I won't stand for it," Rhea said.

Broc shook his head. "What's the point? He's made up his mind. In any case, it's too late now. He is leaving as we speak."

"Then I'll go after him. I'll gather some of our best men and bring him back by force," Rhea suggested. "He cannot turn his back on us like this. Not now."

Broc let out a soft laugh. "I appreciate the sentiment, Rhea, but you'll stand down. That's an order."

Rhea pressed her lips together. Tears of anger stung her eyes.

It was a betrayal against everything she believed in. To turn his back on his home. On his people. And for what? A stupid infatuation.

She had loved Broc for years and he had chosen someone else. Sure, the rules specifically forbade their union, but still. His rejection had hurt her deeply. But that was no reason to abandon everything she stood for. The job was more important. Apparently not to Teaq.

"You can count on my loyalty no matter what," Rhea mumbled.

"I appreciate that, Rhea. Which leads me to the next thing I was going to talk to you about."

Rhea looked up.

Broc turned around and picked something up from the table behind him. Then he turned around and presented it to her.

"I would like you to take over from Teaq."

She looked down at the object in his hands. It wasn't hard to recognize. The General's Sword.

Teaq had carried it, as had every general before him. Rhea's own father had worn it with pride when he'd served as general to Broc's father, the late king Ryk. Funny, that it should find its way to her now.

The elaborate carvings on the leather sheath had worn faint with age. The metal on the grip had smoothed over time as well. But it was a good sword. Forged in dragon fire many generations ago.

Rhea bowed her head and held out her hands. She could barely breathe as Broc handed her the precious object.

"I appoint thee General of the Black Isles. Will you serve with honor, fight valiantly, and protect these lands with your life if your duty requires it?" Broc's voice grew thin as he completed the ceremonial question.

Rhea nodded and took a deep breath.

"It would be an honor, my king."

"I will announce your appointment at the next Council meeting."

She was still somewhat in shock, staring at the sword in her hands, and barely noticed Broc leaving. Just how long she stood there, alone in the Great Hall, trying to process what had just happened, she could not be sure.

B roc had been right, of course. By the time she emerged from the meeting, it was too late to stop Teaq. Plus, an order was an order.

Rhea sighed deeply as she watched the small sailboat set off from the harbor below. She never had been particularly close to anyone, but she'd considered Teaq a friend. He'd never even said goodbye.

The events of the past week or so should have been enough of a warning, but she still hadn't seen it coming. His departure felt like a betrayal.

Teaq, former General of the Black Isles, had fallen for one of the enemy. A Mermaid of the Deep, who just happened to be King Weiland's only daughter. The entire situation was bordering on ridiculous and she would have laughed it off if she hadn't seen it happen firsthand.

And now he was leaving, probably forever, because he had chosen her over his job and his brother, the king. As well as the rest of his people. He had forsaken them in favor of his scaled temptress. It was nearly impossible for Rhea not to feel bitter about it.

Crazy, the things people did for love…

Rhea pressed her lips together as the silhouette of the boat grew smaller and smaller, and eventually became obscured by the mist that hung heavily on the water. That was it then. The last she would see of her distant cousin,

A Dragon's Treasure

Teaq. Going forward, her only connection to him would be the fact that she had been appointed as his replacement.

Rhea, General of Black Isles' armies. It had a nice ring to it, but the promotion was not earned. She had only been given the job because he had decided to run away.

Rhea shook her head and averted her gaze from the grey waters below.

The worst part was, she could empathize somewhat now that she had been able to let the news sink in. She could understand Teaq's motivations, at least in part.

She too knew what it was like to love someone with all your heart. Only in her case, that someone didn't love her back. No grand gesture, no ultimate sacrifice would ever change that.

The object of her affection, Broc, King of the Black Isles, had already taken a mate. He had married her in front of his entire court, sparing little thought as to what Rhea thought about it. And worse still, Broc's new bride was a witch. With one brother marrying a sorceress, and the other running away with a mermaid, she had to wonder if she was the only sane person left on this godforsaken rock in the sea.

Her chest felt tight, like she was due a good scream. Or a fight. She had carried this anger and frustration around with her for weeks now, and if she did not find some release for it, she might explode.

What was the point of it all? What was the point of

love itself? All it brought with it was pain, at least for her.

Best to steer clear of it. After all, with Teaq gone, she had his job to do. She was now single-handedly responsible for the defenses of these lands. Whether she liked it or not.

And if Teaq indeed managed to get away with his cold-blooded girlfriend, her father, King of the Sea Folk, would come knocking at these gates again looking for vengeance.

And who would be there to stop him? Rhea, apparently. With an under-equipped army that simply did not have the manpower to thwart a full scale Sea Folk invasion.

The first time King Weiland had arrived on their shores, they had seen but a taste of what the enemy could direct their way. They had lived to fight another day mostly by chance.

And because Weiland wanted his daughter back.

The next time, they would not have any such advantage. The mermaid and Teaq would be long gone and with them, Black Isles' only leverage was reduced to ashes.

If Rhea was going to prevent her people from being overrun, she needed a strategic advantage, and quick.

But she was getting ahead of herself. Her promotion wasn't even official yet.

CHAPTER TWO

———◆———

The Great Hall was abuzz with conversation and rumor. By the time Rhea arrived, the Elders were already there, talking irately amongst themselves. Yorrick, as well as representatives of the Eastern, Northern and Western Isles, stood in a small semi-circle together, deep in argument.

Nobody even noticed her arrival.

She folded her arms and just observed. Obviously everyone was upset.

And why wouldn't they be? The Isles were in crisis.

Only last week they had nearly been conquered by Sea Folk, and now their general had run away with his enemy girlfriend. It was a disaster.

Rhea did not interact with anyone. There was nothing to talk about as far as she was concerned. Not unless someone had thought of a solution to their troubles.

She looked up briefly when Broc arrived. Nobody else took notice.

It was still difficult for her to look at him. Her king. The only man she'd ever had eyes for, but who saw her as nothing more than another member of the court. He had shown weakness in front of her when he told her about Teaq, which had made things even more difficult. She couldn't even hate him for rejecting her if she also felt sorry for him.

She averted her gaze and waited. Still, the mood in the room had not changed.

Broc cleared his throat, in a hopeless attempt to attract attention. It did not work.

Rhea wondered for a moment if she should step in.

Nah, let him sort out this mess. She wasn't even officially appointed yet. Presumably that was why he'd called this Council meeting in the first place.

"Order!" Broc called out. "I understand emotions are running high, but I must demand order!"

Emotions, running high. What an understatement.

A murmur passed through the Great Hall, but finally all attendees, including Rhea, focused their attention on their king.

"My king, these are dark days!" Uri, the leader of the Elders called out.

Broc nodded. "They are indeed."

"Is it true that the General has sailed off to the Deep?" Yorrick spoke up.

Rhea raised an eyebrow.

It was unusual for Yorrick to say much at any of these meetings. Perhaps his pending promotion within the Royal Guard would be just what he needed to step up more.

Broc frowned and shook his head. "That's insane. My brother is not travelling to the Deep."

"Then where has he gone?" Uri asked. "Because he is no longer in the infirmary. I happened to find out about his absence when I tried to visit him there."

"And what of the boat that's missing from the harbor? That's no coincidence," another Elder said.

The remaining Elders shuffled in closer. They were obviously eager to hear Broc's explanation.

Rhea kept quiet. She couldn't wait to hear what Broc would tell everyone.

"My brother has departed these lands, this is true," Broc said.

Another murmur travelled the room.

Though she was still hurt by his choice of mate, Rhea couldn't help herself from staring at him once he started to speak. So nearby, and yet so out of reach.

"I cannot tell you with certainty where he has sailed off to. He thought it best that nobody knew."

"Why did he leave his post? Why did he leave us?" Yorrick asked.

"His reasons are his own," Broc said. His tone was firm.

Rhea sighed. So he wasn't intending to give the Council an explanation after all.

She had never had much use for diplomacy, as some people called it. Dishonesty was a more appropriate term for it in her mind.

Surely the Elders needed to know. Even Yorrick. Teaq's actions would affect them all. It was a safety issue. And safety was her responsibility now.

"My king," Rhea spoke for the first time.

Broc met her gaze with a stern expression on his face. He wouldn't like what she had to say, but she did not let that faze her. Yet.

"We should not pretend Teaq's departure is some kind of random coincidence!" she said.

Broc's face grew even tenser. Perhaps she should tread lightly, at least until her new position was announced. Lest he change his mind.

"We should not," he said. "At the same time, we should not speak out of turn."

Five minutes into the first meeting since her promotion, and she had already angered him. Well, that was nothing unusual. She had always seen herself as a voice of reason and truth. She could not stand politics. And not even her feelings for Broc would stand in the way of her keeping his rule honest.

"Very well. Please continue, my king." Rhea bowed slightly. She herself wasn't even sure if she was being sarcastic in her gesture.

Broc sighed and folded his hands together.

"As Rhea has correctly pointed out, it is *not* a coincidence." He shot her a disapproving glance.

She simply watched, unfazed, as he continued his explanation.

"The mermaid that was captured off the Eastern Isle… and Teaq… None of it was a coincidence."

The elders started chatting excitedly amongst

themselves. They presented themselves as serious scholars, but Rhea had already noticed that they loved nothing more than a bit of juicy gossip.

"My king, it was written!" Uri exclaimed. "One of our own, and one of theirs—"

Broc shook his head. "Oh no, you don't. Mention another prophecy to me at your own peril. We have hardly recovered from the last one you brought up in this very hall."

Uri stepped back, his lips pressed together tightly.

Rhea couldn't suppress a smile. Poor man. He was only doing his duty.

"So there it is. Teaq's choice obviously puts us in a difficult position. We cannot provide sanctuary to a mermaid on these lands. That is why he has left. To take the target off our backs."

That was a nice spin.

Rhea cleared her throat. "My king. His intention may be to draw King Weiland away from us, but that's only going to work if the Sea Folk *know* where their princess has gone. They'd have to be certain that she's not here."

The Great Hall grew silent. Even Broc had nothing to say, at least for a painful few seconds.

"An astute observation, Rhea. One I am sure he has planned for," Broc said.

Rhea could tell he was still annoyed with her. But it was the truth. You could not hide from the truth.

"We will also plan for the same," Broc continued. "And in light of these preparations I felt it important to that we get back to life as normal. At the earliest. So I have already chosen Teaq's successor."

Everyone in attendance nodded in agreement.

"Yes, my king," Uri said. "We cannot afford a disruption in our defenses."

Rhea straightened herself. This was it. She may not have earned the job, yet, but she was going to make damn sure that she would do her absolute best.

"I present to you, Rhea, our new general," Broc said.

Yorrick shot her a smile and appreciative nod.

"This, of course, means her old position in the Royal Guard now goes to Yorrick."

Broc waved the two of them closer. They took position to the left and right of the king and stood with their heads bowed as the remaining Council members applauded. Whatever led up to the events of today, it was still an honor for the both of them.

"Now that this is out of the way, what's next on the agenda for today?" Broc asked.

Uri and the Elders spoke amongst themselves for a moment. Their voices were too hushed for Rhea to make out what they were saying. Then Uri raised his head and ran his hand through his long white beard.

"My king, in light of the sheer strength shown by the Sea Folk during their recent excursion into our territory, I feel it will be imperative to strengthen our own defenses significantly."

Broc nodded, as did Rhea.

Everyone was silent for a few moments, before Rhea realized this was her moment. Her role as general would take some getting used to.

"Uri, what have you in mind?" she asked.

"We do not have the weapons. Our walls cannot keep them out should they invade in earnest."

Rhea nodded again. She didn't want to hear it, but he was right.

"Our hand-to-hand combat skills are good enough. The duel Teaq fought proved that beyond any doubt. We're well matched. But they vastly outnumber us. We must look at better weaponry to gain an advantage," Rhea concluded.

"We do not have the materials or even skills to develop such weapons. Even that sword you now carry, Rhea, was made during different times. We do not have the technology anymore. All that was lost in the Great War all those centuries ago," Uri said.

Rhea placed her hand protectively over the sword on her hip. He was right. The Elders usually were.

"So if we cannot develop better weapons with what we have, what do you suggest we do?"

"We have but one weapon. One secret weapon nobody else, including the Sea Folk, has."

Rhea frowned. "The witch," she said.

Broc looked at her disapprovingly. Again.

"Queen Kelly, and her magic," Rhea repeated, choosing more diplomatic words this time.

Uri nodded. "We have her, too. But she's not who I was talking about. Her skills require more training to be effective in battle. This is something I have been meaning to discuss with our king anyway."

Broc sighed. "Very well, Uri, you are right to bring this up."

"Do I have your permission to work with the Queen to see what powers she might yet unlock?" Uri asked.

Broc nodded. "You do."

"Good. Now, the weapon we have, which is already at the peak of its power…"

Rhea leaned forward, eager to hear what he had to say.

"Perhaps you remember the old song, you would have learned it as a child," Uri said.

Rhea frowned and looked at Broc. Did he have any idea what Uri was talking about?

His expression was dark, as it had often been lately. He knew.

Uri cleared his throat, then with a thin, crackling voice, he started to sing.

"Down below the mountain, in a cell deeper than deep,"

Rhea gasped as the remaining words came to her. He could *not* be serious!

A Dragon's Treasure

Down below the mountain, in a cell deeper than deep,
A creature, fierce and powerful, blissfully asleep.
He must not be awoken, unless the need is dire,
For if he is roused, he will blanket the Isles in fire.

"You speak of the dragon, Saras!" Rhea exclaimed.

Uri nodded slowly. His expression had turned equally serious.

"We can't. Broc, we can't," she stammered.

Broc shook his head as well. "This is a last resort, Uri. The risks are simply too great."

"I do not disagree the risks are very grave indeed. I can assure you it's not easy to bargain with a dragon. If you wish to gain his cooperation, you'll need enough time to convince him of your cause." Uri paused for a moment, and studied the room. "But if there's one thing beings of water are particularly sensitive to, it's heat. Fire."

Rhea frowned. How did he know so much about the dragon? Saras had been asleep for generations, and with good reason. Nobody in living memory had ever interacted with the dragon. The story of what had earned him his confinement in the dungeon was the greatest tragedy their people had lived through since the Great War.

Dragons were only loyal to themselves. The old stories made that very clear. On a whim, he could turn on them and kill them all. It wouldn't be the first time.

"My King, General Rhea. While your concerns are very

valid, I have been reading up on the matter. There is plenty of information available in the old archives."

"Feel free to share your findings, then," Broc said.

"Dragons are fickle creatures. But if we can figure out something he *wants*, he'll do anything to get it."

"In theory. How can you be so sure?" Rhea asked.

Uri's normally pale skin turned pinkish. Apparently her questions were starting to infuriate him too.

"This is the collective knowledge of our people we're talking about here. They're not fairy stories!"

Rhea sighed and shook her head.

"This is not a decision that should be made lightly." Broc folded his arms. "I'll consider your advice carefully, Uri."

"Of course, my king. Just don't think for too long. Once the Sea Folk arrive, it might already be too late."

Broc nodded.

Rhea could only hope that he wasn't seriously thinking about letting him out. Dragons were a double-edged sword. He could very easily harm them more than the Sea Folk would. She needed another strategy. Something she'd already been thinking about in her old job.

Knowledge was power. They needed a warning system so the enemy could no longer surprise them.

Rhea cleared her throat, attracting everyone's eyes back onto her.

"My first act as general will reflect these troubling times. We cannot afford to be overrun without warning.

So I would like to draft all those capable of flight to scour our borders for any sign of enemy activity."

Broc's expression softened slightly. At last she'd said something he did not object to.

"Good idea, Rhea. We must be vigilant."

CHAPTER THREE

⸻ ◆ ⸻

ire! Fire!

The calls echoed against the stone walls of the castle.

Black Mountain was on fire.

Saras turned around to see where the screams were coming from, but he could not see anything through the smoke.

What had happened?

Where was Gillian?

In his human form again, he looked down at himself. His clothes were hanging off him in charred rags.

His skin was blackened by soot.

His hands…

He turned them over to inspect his palms.

The dimmed light could not obscure it. He knew exactly what he was looking at. In fact, he could smell it.

Blood.

He had blood on his hands.

The screams grew fainter. Were people fleeing?

He ran to follow them, but then a memory—a flash—stopped him in his tracks.

His Gillian, lying in bed with her eyes closed. Flames licking at the sheets.

Blood.

A Dragon's Treasure

Rage coursed through him, prompting his body to change form again. Scales covered his once smooth skin. His fingers extended into talons, and sharp spikes emerged all the way down his spine.

The beast had taken over and he was furious.

His Gillian, dead! Whoever responsible had to be punished.

He would tear this place apart, killing all in his path until he found the culprit.

Soundless, like a phantom, he rushed through the corridors, heading right toward the heat.

"Gillian! Your death will be avenged!" he roared.

Another memory found its way into his clouded mind.

He had already found the murderer.

The realization hit him like a knife being thrust right through his heart.

The fire. The death and destruction.

It was him.

It was all his fault. Her rejection had hurt him so deeply that he'd lost all control.

For but a moment, Saras opened his eyes. But they would not stay open. His dark surroundings barely registered before he was drawn back into the world of shadows.

A loud sigh escaped his lips and he turned over onto his other side.

Part of him knew that none of this was really

happening. At least not right now. It had happened, a long time ago.

The tragic fire of Black Mountain had killed many. Saras had accepted his punishment without argument.

The outside world was no place for him. Indeed, there was nothing out there to keep him. He'd given his heart to the wrong woman, and everyone had paid the price.

Down here, he was contained.

His fire could not harm anyone else.

But the isolation and the time passed since Gillian's death hadn't taken away its sting.

His fragmented memories continued to haunt him in his sleep.

———◆———

Rhea did not waste any time. Soon after leaving her first Council meeting as General, she set her plan into action. She started with those on Black Mountain itself.

Even though they were a mixed people, flight was a rare talent to have. Mostly bears, wolves and other land animals hid behind their human-like features.

But there were a few eagles she knew about; they were an important part of any hunting party that headed for the mainland. They kept an eye on their surroundings so they could travel unseen by the humans they'd hidden from for all these generations.

A Dragon's Treasure

Their skills were about to be more in demand than ever.

It was easy to enlist them in her latest surveillance strategy. But if she was going to make this work, she needed more. Way more.

So she mobilized the senior members of her army to do the same. They set sail to the other isles and gathered up anyone of use. Whatever their current job or background, they would belong to Rhea's army now.

Within a couple of days, she stood face to face with a group of about a dozen islanders who had little to no idea why they had been summoned to Black Mountain. They suspiciously eyed the armory they found themselves in.

Some were too old to bear arms. Some too young. But none of that mattered, as long as they could fly.

Rhea straightened herself as she faced her reluctant new recruits.

"You must be wondering why you were called here," Rhea started.

One woman with long, greying hair stepped forward with her hands on her hip. "I do, yeah! My work's pilin' up higher and higher the longer I'm away from home."

"Someone else will have to do your work from now on. You have a new job now."

The woman scoffed. "Says who?"

Rhea did not hesitate for a moment to put her back in her place. "Your king does! I don't know if you noticed the enemy knocking at these very gates only last week!"

The crowd shuffled uncomfortably at her outburst.

"We are in crisis. Every man, woman and even child can be called on to help out. That's just the way things are," Rhea said.

Many exchanged fearful looks. Others mumbled hushed words of disbelief.

Nobody challenged her openly, so she continued.

"We cannot hope to fend off the next attack if we do not know they are coming. We need a warning system. This is where you come in."

"General Rhea, if I may," a young woman wearing nothing but a simple dress spoke up.

She nodded sternly.

"We are not soldiers. We don't have the training."

She raised her hand. "You misunderstand. I don't need you to be soldiers. I need you to be our eyes and ears. You'll observe only."

"What good will that do?" a man questioned from the back of the crowd.

"You have skills we do not have. You can fly high above these lands and surrounding seas. You'll be well out of reach from the enemy, but nothing will escape your notice," Rhea explained.

Finally, Rhea could tell from the changing expressions in front of her that her new recruits had understood their purpose at last.

"You chose us for our animal forms," that same

woman in the dress said.

Rhea nodded. "You're a fast learner. Trust me when I say, without you all, we cannot win this war."

"Do we at least get some body armor to protect us?" the woman asked.

Rhea smiled. She had convinced at least one of them, even if her idea was ludicrous.

"What's your name?" she asked.

"Eryn."

"Fine, Eryn. I'll see what I can do."

The crowd grew restless once more as they started to discuss what they had learned amongst themselves.

That was probably enough for one day. Time to draw up a schedule for regular patrols. Rhea turned on her heel and marched straight toward the exit leading to the drawbridge. A familiar face stopped her in her tracks.

"Kelly," she mumbled, unable to hide her displeasure.

The witch smiled and nodded. "Nice speech. Even if it almost went wrong."

Rhea squinted. "Can I help you with something, my queen?"

"I hope so. Broc likes to keep me out of the business of war, but we all know it's going to be a reality sooner or later."

"Right. Did you want to pick up your combat training again?" Rhea asked. Oh, how she hated her. The only reason their last session had turned out so badly for Rhea was because Kelly had cheated. With magic.

Kelly let out a short laugh. "No, it's probably best if I leave the fighting up to you and your soldiers."

Rhea waited, lips pressed together, and wondered if this witch was ever going to get to the point.

Finally, Kelly's face turned serious as well. "I just wanted to know if I could help in other ways, you know. I live here now, for better or for worse. And I have no interest in seeing these Isles fall before my first winter here."

Rhea wanted so badly to tell her to go away. That she had it under control, and that Kelly should just focus on her fancy clothes and her new husband, and leave these serious matters alone. But what was the saying? Keep your friends close, and enemies closer.

Perhaps it could be useful, having a witch by her side. A mind reader, no less.

"What did you mean, my speech almost went wrong?" Rhea asked, finally.

Kelly nodded briefly. "Well, your leadership style…"

Rhea regretted asking for Kelly's input already. "My leadership style is *what*?"

Kelly pursed her lips. "It's a bit… combative. That may work fine with soldiers, but these people, they're not used to that. I think they'll respond better to a lighter touch."

Rhea rolled her eyes. All she had done, all she ever did, was tell the truth. If that was too much for people, then it was their problem, not hers.

"You think you can handle them, be my guest. But the harsh reality is that we could lose this place in a heartbeat if King Weiland hits us with all he has."

Kelly nodded. "I didn't realize it before last week, but I do now. I saw the thousands of soldiers crowding the waters, same as you did. That's why I want to help."

Rhea sighed. "Fine. I won't stand in your way. But don't expect me to hold your hand either."

"Fair enough." Kelly smiled and stretched out her right hand.

Rhea just looked at it for a moment, before forcing herself into action and shaking it.

I guess that's it then. Along with a dozen or so clueless eagles, I also now have a witch in my army.

Would that prove useful? Only time could tell.

———◆———

As he sank deeper into another dream, Saras returned to a better time. He dreamt of a morning in early spring. Of when he first saw her.

He sat atop the highest tower of the castle, as he often did, surveying all of Black Mountain and the seas surrounding it. Although she was far away, he had never seen anyone so clearly.

Her long brown hair swayed with every step as she walked down the path leading to the harbor. A gust of wind stopped her momentarily, and she turned around for the briefest of moments.

A vision of beauty.

Gillian, daughter of the king's most senior advisor.

But in this version of events, something had changed. Her walk was different. Even her face was that of another woman.

No… That's not…

Saras frowned. He spread his wings and dove down, hoping for a better look.

But by the time he reached closer to the ground, there was no sign of her anymore. As though she had been swallowed up by the ground.

The scene had changed yet again. Nothing was as it had been.

Scorched earth. Blackened stone. The smell of burning flesh stinging the inside of his nostrils.

He had lost *her*. He had lost everything.

Again, Saras was close to waking. It would just take a little resolve on his part.

Open your eyes! It was a female voice that spoke to him. Not his Gillian, but someone else.

But he didn't. He turned over again, grumbling under his breath.

What was the point, anyway? These memories of a distant past had punished him for so long. He could neither change it nor make up for his transgressions. All he could do was stay down here, alone, until the world crumbled around him once and for all.

A Dragon's Treasure

We need you! You're our only hope!

Again, that voice!

"Lies!" Saras roared into the darkness. "I'm not the bearer of hope! I bring only death and destruction."

The mind played strange tricks, especially on those who found themselves stuck between consciousness and sleep. But he wasn't going to be so easily misled by his own delusions. He had learned his lesson all those years ago, and every day and night since.

CHAPTER FOUR

Rhea did not fear a great many things. As a warrior, she was no stranger to pain. Neither did she fear death itself.

It was failure that she worried most about.

Previously, as head of the Royal Guard, her biggest concern had been the king's safety. And now, the safety of everyone on these Isles had become her responsibility. It was a lot to bear.

It had been all of three days since the Council meeting. Her newly appointed squad of lookouts had patrolled the skies for only a day when the news came.

An enemy sighting. Despite sending out a boat to hunt them down, they did not manage to capture the intruders. It would have been too good to be true, anyway. Sea Folk did not allow themselves to be caught easily, or at all.

Confirmation, in Rhea's mind, that King Weiland was on the lookout once again for his daughter. The threat was imminent now. The next time his armies arrived, they would show the Isles no mercy. Truce or no truce.

She should not have rejected Uri's idea so quickly. The old tales had scared her too much to consider things logically. A dragon would be a formidable ally. That might be the only thing causing King Weiland to think twice about ordering an attack. The state Teaq's mermaid had been in after mere days in a dry dungeon… heat would be devastating to these beings.

But if Uri was right, it would take some convincing on her part to get the dragon to cooperate.

Was it too late already? Was this war already lost before it even began?

Still, Rhea had no other choice. As she saw it, the Sea Folk's next attack would leave them in ruins. At least with a dragon on their side, they had a chance.

A chance was all they could hope for at this point.

She brought her case to the king, who agreed with her assessment. It was worth a shot. He even sent along one civilian companion, Queen Kelly. In case the dragon proved hostile, her protective magic would keep both of them safe.

And so on this damp summer's day, she found herself travelling down the spiral staircase deep down into the belly of the castle. Deep beneath the part of the dungeon reserved for regular prisoners was a special cell nobody ever visited. There was just one narrow shaft hewn straight into the mountainside that led to this place.

Rhea felt like she was marching toward her doom. Only, she was not alone. Kelly remained right by her side. She had grudgingly agreed to her presence here, but Rhea's inherent dislike for the witch still weighed on her mind. She could only hope that bringing her along wouldn't prove a mistake.

A heavy gate secured by numerous chains blocked their way at first. Rhea ordered the guard stationed down here to open the locks. Beyond it was another door, covered in brass, which was also unlocked for them. And finally, one made of solid iron, with only a small window from which Rhea could see inside the dark cell.

What a godforsaken place. Even the light from Rhea's torch could not illuminate all of it. There was no sign of movement. Not even a shadow or silhouette to tell Rhea where the prisoner was. Unusual. Rhea's eyesight was ordinarily very keen. To not be able to see something in the dark was unheard of.

"Anything?" Kelly whispered.

Rhea raised her hand in a gesture to silence her.

"It's too dark. We're too far underground."

One might almost be led to believe that it was all just a myth after all. That there was nobody down here. But Rhea wasn't so easily fooled. She could hear faint breaths, even a heartbeat. There was something down here. Something which had survived for centuries without food, water or company.

Stuck in a place so terrible, no doubt he'd beg, borrow and steal his way out. That was the thing she'd tempt him with: his freedom. Of course he'd jump on the idea. Who in their right mind would want to be stuck down here any longer?

She nodded at the guard, whose face had turned ashen with fear.

"Open it. And lock it again once we're inside."

"But, General! There's no knowing what he'll do once it's open," the man stammered under his breath.

She could not blame him for being afraid. Hell, she was afraid herself.

"That was an order, soldier! I'm not going to tell you again."

He finally did as he was told, then cowered behind the two women. *What a hero,* Rhea thought to herself.

It took considerable force to push the door open. These hinges hadn't been used for so long, the door groaned in protest.

Rhea held her breath and raised her torch up high, which finally earned her a better look of the cell. Still, no dragon.

She was about to turn and question the guard, when a voice echoed loudly against the granite walls of the cell.

"I've been expecting you."

Rhea had already been holding her breath, or else it would have been taken away by the sheer majesty of the dragon's voice. Behind her and Kelly, the door creaked yet again as the fearful guard secured it behind them.

"I am General Rhea, commander of the armies of Black Isle. I'm here to offer you your freedom, in exchange for your help in defeating our common enemy, King Weiland of the Deep."

The voice laughed. "I have but one enemy, and he's

already in here with me inside this cell."

Rhea's heart started to pound and grabbed for the sword on her hip. *Oh hell, he thinks we're a threat.*

Kelly, on the other hand, did not flinch at all. She took a step forward, even.

"This is your queen speaking. Why don't you come into the light so we can speak properly?"

Rhea shot a surprised look in her direction. She had some guts, this witch.

"Be careful, Broc will never forgive me if you get burned to a crisp on my watch," Rhea warned.

Kelly turned and smiled briefly as her presence entered Rhea's mind. *I'm not sensing any hostility. Treating him as an enemy will only make this negotiation harder.*

Rhea grudgingly remembered the discussion they'd had about her so-called leadership style. She wasn't about to let Kelly's opinions change how she dealt with her soldiers, but this was uncharted territory. Nobody alive today had ever interacted with a dragon before, and Kelly's powers did provide certain insights Rhea did not have.

"Please come out." Rhea rephrased Kelly's earlier request. "We mean you no harm."

Laughter erupted from the darkness. "Well, that's a relief."

Rhea's fears turned to frustration. Kelly might not have sensed hostility, but Rhea did not need mind reading skills to pick up on the arrogance in the dragon's words.

Still, they'd made progress. There was movement in the

shadows.

Rhea held her breath as she waited for the dragon to reveal himself.

What she saw shocked her greatly. She had expected scales and talons and a pair of great big wings. But she saw none of that. In front of the two women stood an ordinary man.

Well, perhaps not entirely ordinary.

He had been down here in this dark hole, asleep, for hundreds of years; even the Elders could not be sure exactly how long. Without reprise, without even nourishment. And yet, before them stood a young man in excellent physical shape.

His features were flawless, even boyish. His body… it rivalled even the fittest fighters on the Isles, with one major difference. There was not a single mark, not even a smudge of dirt on him.

He was perfect.

Rhea couldn't stop staring at him, until she realized he was smirking at her.

"I must have been asleep a long time," Saras spoke. "I see they have girl soldiers now. Interesting."

The mockery in his tone pissed Rhea off immediately.

"A little respect would be nice. After all, we're offering to let you out of here," she hissed.

Saras laughed again. He was even more gorgeous now, infuriatingly so.

"If I wanted out of here, I would have left a long time ago, dear."

Rhea stepped forward, her hand still gripping the General's Sword. "You'll address me as General Rhea. Not *dear, darling, sweetheart,* or any other such nonsense."

Kelly's mind infiltrated Rhea's again for a moment.

It might be best to play along with his game, Kelly suggested.

Rhea frowned. *What game is that?*

He's been down here on his own a long time. Plus, he's from a different time. We can't expect him to know the rules as they are now. If he wants to play, let him.

Rhea folded her arms and sighed. So her esteemed queen wanted her to allow him to treat her as a mere piece of meat. Charming. She preferred to try a different tactic. "Here's the thing. We're at war and our weapons alone cannot defeat the enemy."

Saras took a couple of steps forward, until he was standing right in front of Rhea. He gazed down into her eyes for a moment.

"So? What does that have to do with me?"

She didn't want it to, but his presence shook her. He was within her reach. She would just need to reach out for him. Smooth, sculpted flesh, a feast for the eyes, and so much more.

And his eyes… For a body so young in appearance, his eyes reflected the sorrow of a thousand lifetimes. She couldn't stand looking at them for too long.

"Your powers could turn the tide for us. If you'll help

us," Rhea spoke. Her voice sounded just a bit thinner and breathier than she would have wanted it to.

"And what's in it for me?" he asked. The corner of his mouth rose in a subtle grin as he glanced down at her lips.

"Your freedom. A full pardon from the king," Rhea said.

Saras shook his head. "You said that already. Plus, the king isn't here. Why should I trust a word you speak?"

"I speak for my husband, the king," Kelly spoke up. "What is it you want?"

Saras glanced over at the queen, then back at Rhea, his expression thoughtful. Then he abruptly turned away and slowly walked back toward the darkest part of the cell again. "I'm not interested. This isn't my war."

Rhea couldn't believe his reaction. "Like it or not, you live on these Isles just as we do. If Black Mountain falls…" Rhea couldn't bring herself to complete that thought. It wasn't a matter of *if* but rather, *when*.

When Black Mountain falls…

Saras paused with his back turned. "Let them come. It makes no difference to me. Their weapons couldn't even scratch me if they tried."

Just like that, Rhea was furious again. "There must be something. Something that'll change your mind?" Rhea called after him.

"Now that you mention it." He looked over his shoulder back at her. "I might do it for a kiss from you, beautiful."

Rhea was aghast. "How dare you speak to me like that! I've fought men bigger and stronger than you for less!"

Saras chuckled, then vanished into the darkness. "I very much doubt that. Good luck, General Rhea. With the war, and everything."

Rhea shook with anger. She ought to go after him, teach him a lesson. Kelly placed her hand on Rhea's arm, which infuriated her further, so she shook it off.

Uri said it wouldn't be easy, didn't he? Let's give him some time to think it over. Another day in the hole might make him see the benefits of what we're offering, Kelly suggested.

Rhea scowled. "Guard, open the door! We're leaving."

"Farewell, Rhea and Kelly of Black Mountain," Saras spoke.

Rhea shook her head in frustration as the two of them left in silence. Through the iron door and the brass covered door, as well as the gate.

"That went relatively well," Kelly mumbled.

Rhea shot her a furious look. "How on earth did *that* go well?"

Kelly shrugged. "At least he didn't attack us. It was a discourse, not a fight."

Rhea scoffed. "If you say so."

"So what are you going to do?" Kelly asked. "Will you consider his demand?"

Rhea just stared at her blankly. How presumptuous of Kelly to assume that she'd discuss her strategy with a witch. Especially when it concerned something so personal and intimate.

"That's none of your business."

CHAPTER FIVE

urious… When the door to his cell opened, Saras had not been sure if he was waking or dreaming. He wasn't even sure what had woken him up, except a persistent feeling that it was time.

And boy, had he been rewarded for his efforts.

Not one beauty, but two of them. Women of nobility, even. A queen, with radiant red hair, outdone only by the fine clothes she wore. She was pretty in her own right, but it wasn't she who had enchanted him.

No, it was the other one. Rhea. She'd said she was the General of Black Isles' armies. Whether he believed that, he wasn't sure. Maybe things had changed a lot since he had gone underground.

Back in the day, females were not enlisted in the army.

Why any man would stand by and watch the fairer sex get slain in battle, he did not know. He wasn't noble or chivalrous, but even he would lay down his own life in her stead.

Rhea. Dressed in a tight armored bodice and knee high boots. Her outfit was clearly designed to allow for maximum movement and flexibility. It left little to the imagination; still, his imagination was working harder than ever.

She would fuel many a dream. In fact, ever since she

had unexpectedly stumbled into his cell, Saras couldn't think of anyone else. Not even his love, Gillian. Was Rhea to be his new love? Was this finally a sign from the Gods that his crimes had been forgiven and he was offered a second chance?

Of course he hadn't accepted her terms. He was least interested in fighting a war.

Perhaps it was a mistake to dismiss her so quickly. If she was going to be his redemption, he couldn't make use of it down here. All he could do here was drift in and out of consciousness, dreaming now of a new woman.

The trouble with dreams was that they had a pesky habit of returning to the same events that had haunted him for so long. Fire and smoke sullied the image of beautiful Rhea. He had to keep on reminding himself that that hadn't happened yet.

But it so very easily could, though. If he wasn't careful, he could hurt her, even kill her too.

And then what? Dream of the event for eons to come, full of regret over yet another senseless death? Like he had been doing all this time for Gillian?

Perhaps it was better to stay here. The dreams would come and torment him, of course. But they were just dreams in this case. She would be safe from him as long as he was here.

Saras reasoned and argued with himself on this. Round and round in circles, his mind went. And it kept on arriving at the same two conclusions: as long as he was locked up, she was safe from him. And yet, he wanted her. He yearned for her so badly it made his bones hurt.

What was a lonely dragon to do?

As the hours passed, the latter of the two realizations started to overshadow the first. He was first and foremost a creature of instinct. As an immortal he had but one instinct to guide him on his journey through life. It was the same one that had led him astray with Gillian all those years ago…

Above all else there was one thing Saras desired. One thing his inner beast needed.

And that was a mate. One companion to share eternity with.

Perhaps if he answered this call, he could prevent any further madness from taking hold.

The next time anyone visited, he'd act accordingly. He would agree to their terms and leave this cell. And then he would work tirelessly, day and night, to make Rhea his.

If she put up a fight, he'd take it as a challenge. He'd been waiting for a thousand years for a second chance. This time, he wouldn't give up so easily.

This war she kept harping on about was but an obstacle getting in the way of what was really important. She would be his, and he would be hers, and everything else could go to hell.

Why else would the Gods send her his way, if it wasn't meant to be?

A Dragon's Treasure

———— ✦ ————

Rhea could not get over the man's arrogance. She had offered him everything within her power, a way out of the hopeless conditions he found himself in. A chance to redeem himself. And he had laughed at her.

She did what she usually did when faced with an impossible dilemma. After leaving Kelly behind on the lower level, Rhea wandered aimlessly around the castle. Through the maze-like hallways, up and down the various steps. Once she reached the Viewpoint and breathed in the refreshing sea air, she paused for a moment. She couldn't believe Kelly had suggested she take the dragon up on his offer. Who was she to advise her, anyway?

The witch was the last person Rhea would turn to for such advice. She needed someone she could trust. Teaq would have been the obvious choice, but since he wasn't here…

Broc… Maybe he would know what to do.

Rhea turned on her heel and marched back down the hallway she had just come from, heading for Broc's quarters. She didn't even stop to think about whether it would be inappropriate to visit him at this hour. These were   desperate times.

Rhea paused in front of the door and knocked twice.

"Yes?" he answered.

Rhea pushed the door open and entered without hesitation, only to be faced yet again by an extremely attractive topless man.

She glanced down at the armor lying on the chair next to him. Perhaps this was a mistake.

"I caught you at a bad time, I apologize," Rhea mumbled.

He shook his head. "What is it? How did it go with the dragon?"

Rhea wasn't sure what to say anymore. At any other time, faced with Broc in this state, she would have found it impossible to focus. And yet, right at this moment, she had become strangely indifferent.

She shook off these idle thoughts and considered how to answer his question.

"Well, he did not attack us," Rhea said, remembering Kelly's assessment of the negotiation.

"Good. Is he open to helping us?"

He'll do it for a kiss, Rhea thought, once again growing angry at the dragon's disrespectful comments and Kelly's insinuations.

"As Uri warned already, it's not easy negotiating with a dragon. I offered him his freedom. A pardon from you. He seemed unimpressed."

Rhea bit her lip. Were this any other man, and had Saras asked for any other thing... Rhea had always been truthful, even blunt. Why hide the truth of their meeting with Saras, when Broc would no doubt find out about the whole thing from Kelly, anyway?

A strange feeling burned inside her, preventing her from telling the truth in this case. Her voice had no strength to. The words simply would not pass her lips.

"Perhaps he is playing a game. To see what else he can get out of the deal," Broc suggested.

Rhea nodded. "That's probably it."

A game indeed. He was playing a game of seduction at her expense. And the prize he wanted would cost Rhea her dignity.

"Well, keep at it. We cannot give up on the idea so easily. Not when enemy scouts are lurking around our borders already."

"I will, my king."

"Speak with Uri, will you? Perhaps he has learned something else that can help."

Rhea nodded. Talk to Uri, and tell him the dragon wished for a kiss? Yeah, that would go down very well.

"Yes, my king," she mumbled, and turned to leave again.

She had done her duty, and informed the king. Now she was once again alone with her thoughts, or at least she wished to be. The castle was too busy, with too many people walking up and down. Any quiet corner could be disturbed at any moment by a passing guard or worker. She needed a better place to think, because she certainly did not intend to bring Uri into this.

Rhea ordered the drawbridge open, and made her way outside. The cold winds stung pleasantly against the bare skin of her arms and legs. This feeling that she carried with her ever since her encounter with Saras, she'd only felt it once before. When Kelly had thrown her over the side of the plateau when she first found out about her magic. It was the feeling of failure. Of humiliation and shame.

Her feet carried her back to the same place automatically. Now that she saw the flat hilltop up in the distance, it all made sense. She sped up the rest of the way.

Here, she would be able to reflect properly. Hopefully it would lead her to a solution.

So she sat down on one of the flat rocks that lined the plateau and rested her head in her hands.

This was all new to her.

Her entire life had been entirely action oriented. The harder she worked, the more effort she put into her training, the more successful she became as a fighter. Smarts had very little to do with it.

But this new job brought with it new challenges. And the matter with Saras, the dragon, in a way perfectly represented the entire problem. She had found herself in an impossible situation.

She couldn't use brute force on Saras to bend him to her will. Just as she could not single-handedly defeat King Weiland's army. She needed a strategy for both these things.

And if she managed to solve one of the two problems,

the other would solve itself.

So she continued to analyze the day's events.

Why had she hidden the truth from Broc?

Shame . Perhaps a misplaced sense that she owed him something, when he had never shown interest in her like that.

But why feel shame when she had done nothing wrong? She hadn't even yielded to Saras' demands.

Why not?

Rhea lifted her head and stared out across the barren landscape that surrounded her.

She wasn't spoken for. Broc couldn't care less, so why should she? If it solved the problem...

Rhea nodded to herself. "If that's what he wants, that's what he'll get."

If Saras was willing to trade his cooperation for some affection from her, feigned or otherwise... Then who was she to deny it? Could she not sacrifice something as small as a kiss for the good of her people?

Rhea closed her eyes and breathed in deeply. The tightness in her chest had reduced, but it hadn't gone completely. On top of it, her heartbeat continued to be elevated. Yet another feeling she unfamiliar with. Nerves...

Her mind was made up now. Rhea rushed back to the

castle just after twilight. First thing in the morning, she'd head down into the dungeons. Nothing would stop her from securing the dragon's help now.

CHAPTER SIX

He could hear them coming from quite a distance. The footsteps echoed against the narrow shaft that led to his cell. The three doors were being unlocked, creaking and groaning as they were pushed open.

His heart was aflutter already. He'd made up his mind and was ready to leave this place. Here arrived his way out.

"You returned," he said, as his visitor appeared inside the dark cell.

Rhea looked every bit as appealing as she had the first time around. He approached her with a smile on his face.

"We have unfinished business," she said.

Saras nodded. "Where is your charming companion? The queen was not in the mood for another trip down into the bowels of the castle?"

Rhea shook her head. Her expression was so serious, so stern. "She isn't needed for this."

"Oh?" Saras asked as he reached for a lock of her dark brown hair and twisted it around his index finger. Wild, it was. Untamed.

Even her scent reminded him of windswept mountainsides and choppy seas. Fresh, yet charmingly sweet. She smelled of vast open spaces, of freedom.

Basically of everything he had been missing down here.

She put up such a brave front, but she could not hide those involuntary reactions her body had when being touched. The slight dilation of her pupils, the flush in her cheeks.

As though he was the conductor, and she was the instrument.

He'd always reveled in the dance of love. It truly made the world turn. Too bad it was so difficult to find a willing partner.

"I've given your proposal some thought," she said.

"Have you?" Saras couldn't hide the amusement in his voice. The more serious her tone, the more he felt like laughing. He wasn't even quite sure why. "What proposal is that?"

"Don't make me repeat it," Rhea warned.

Her breath tickled as it hit his face. He breathed in deeply, then slowly opened his eyes again.

"Forgive me, I have been alone for a long time. I'm afraid I may have gotten carried away and said whatever rubbish came to mind. Doesn't mean I remember it all." Saras grinned. "I remember you very well, though. You've been on my mind constantly since then."

Rhea frowned. How adorable she looked when she was annoyed.

"When I asked for your assistance. To help us win this war."

Saras nodded. "Yes, yes. Not my war."

"I was going to release you, your freedom in exchange for your help," Rhea continued.

Saras waited. "And?"

"You said you'd do it for a kiss."

Saras laughed again. "That does sound like something I'd say."

"Well, did you mean it?" Rhea asked. Her face was now bright red.

"You mean you came back for a kiss? Well, this is unexpected." So far, their second meeting was going a lot better than he could have hoped.

"For you this might be a joke, but I'm deadly serious." Rhea folded her arms and tapped her foot impatiently.

"I can see that," Saras said. "You're a very serious woman, aren't you, madam General? All work and no play."

She opened her mouth in protest, then closed it again. Her heartbeat had sped up significantly, as had her breathing. She was getting angry now, which wasn't Saras' intention, but it amused him greatly anyway.

There was something about her that egged him on to keep poking and prodding, just to see how she'd react. Probably the fact that he did indeed get a reaction so easily. What were her limits? How long before she'd lose her cool completely?

Anger and passion were two sides of the same coin. She had some fire within, it was so clear to see. And he would love to see it exposed.

"So you weren't serious. You don't want to get out of here and help us fight the Sea Folk," Rhea said.

Saras cocked his head to the side. "That's not what I said."

"So what will it take?"

He reached for her, and although she flinched initially, she did not shake his hand off as it touched the side of her neck.

"Why? Why should I help you?" he whispered as he guided her face closer to his.

She had offered him a kiss. What a tempting prize. Why shouldn't he take it right now?

Her eyes fluttered shut and she just stood there. Passive. Helpless.

All their interactions so far suggested that she was the sort of woman who made sure she was always in control. This was completely out of character.

He shook his head. "No. This isn't right." Saras let go of Rhea's face and took a step back. "I won't do it."

"Why not?" she called out. He could see now that her eyes were moist. She was obviously disappointed. But it was all about the favor she wanted from him. General Rhea hadn't come back to surrender, she had come to buy his involvement in her war.

"There's no joy in it," he said and shrugged his shoulders. Her offer was empty. Soulless.

"Is that all you seek? Joy? What about duty? Do you

never do anything just because it's the proper thing to do? We had an agreement!" Rhea argued.

"Duty is an entirely human construct. I have no use for it. You don't know very much about dragons, do you?" he asked.

She was still red in the face, but it was different now. This wasn't the blush of arousal, but rather of shame. He'd gone too far and embarrassed her.

That hadn't been his intention, but there was little he could do about it now.

"No, I don't. There are no dragons anymore," Rhea spoke dryly. "You're the last one."

Saras was stunned for a moment. No clever comeback or teasing comment came to him.

"That's probably for the best," he mumbled.

"Probably," Rhea agreed. "If there's nothing else I can offer you to change your mind, then there's no point in staying here and talking to you."

Saras still didn't know what to say. So he just watched as she turned around and knocked on the door.

This wasn't how this meeting should have gone. He'd gotten too excited and wanted to toy with her a bit. He wanted to test the boundaries, to uncover the real Rhea. But what he got was a shocking dose of reality he had no use for.

His second chance was about to fall apart.

"Wait," he called out.

Rhea stopped, though she kept her back turned toward him.

"Look, I'm sorry if I insulted you. I'm a bit out of practice," he said.

"A *bit?*" she asked.

Saras shrugged. "Fair point. A lot. For that I apologize."

"And?" she asked.

Her question puzzled him. He'd gone too far, and he'd apologized. "And, what?"

She shook her head and reached for the door again. "Sorry I asked."

He could do nothing but watch as she left him.

Alone once again. Dejected, he returned to the corner of his cell, farthest from the door. He'd been awake for a while now and all it had brought was false hope and disappointment. Best to leave this world to these new inhabitants and retreat into his dreams. At least he knew what to expect there.

It did not take him long to drift off.

———◆———

By the time Rhea left Saras, her embarrassment had made way for anger. Other responsibilities filled the rest of her day, but at night in bed, everything came back to her.

She was shaking with rage thinking back to it.

A Dragon's Treasure

From the start, he'd just been toying with her. Whenever she thought she knew what he wanted and was prepared to give it to him, he changed his mind and they were no closer to reaching an agreement.

He was so full of lies, he probably didn't even know the truth himself.

Never had she felt so small and meaningless as she did in front of him. Not that he was particularly tall or imposing. For all his beauty and supposed strength, he was of average stature.

But at the same time, she was in awe of him. Not that she would ever admit it. Oh, he'd have a grand time laughing at her if he ever found out. She hadn't even thought of Broc lately; her mind did not have the capacity to concern herself with two men at once.

That was the worst part.

She wanted to hate him with all her being, but part of her was so intrigued, so enchanted, that the thought of him never left her mind. Not when she woke up in the morning, or went to bed at night, or at any point in between.

And now there was the other thing she felt. Pity.

When she'd told him he was the last dragon, she thought she'd finally seen a glimpse of the real Saras. Unless that was all part of his game of deception; though it had seemed completely genuine to her. For but a moment, the mask had fallen off.

Saras was a creature of opposites. Immense power, yet he refused to leave the confines of his cell. He had mercilessly flirted with her, yet he'd refused to kiss her once she yielded. Always grinning and joking, but intensely lonely in this world.

Perhaps the many years underground had taken their toll on his mind. Was it possible that the dragon was beyond reach now? That there was nothing anymore in this world that he wanted enough to come to an agreement with her?

This was not something she could solve by herself, no matter how much she tossed and turned in bed.

It was time for outside counsel.

Come dawn, she headed straight for the library in search of the Elders. If anyone could help, it was them. They were the custodians of the collected wisdom of their people, after all.

With no time to waste, Rhea burst through the door of the library.

"Uri!" she called out.

The Elders who sat at the long study tables, poring over ancient scrolls and bound volumes alike, jumped up in their seats at the sudden and loud interruption.

"General, what an unexpected surprise," Uri spoke up as he appeared from behind an overloaded book case.

He didn't like her much, his tone made that very clear. Rhea didn't care. She didn't have time to.

"I need your counsel," Rhea said.

All heads in the library were still turned in her direction.

"I see. How can I be of help?"

Rhea gestured at a couple of empty chairs further away from where the remaining Elders were conducting their studies. "I'm having some trouble," Rhea started.

"The dragon." Uri folded his hands in his lap. "It's not easy bargaining with a dragon, as I said."

"You mentioned during the Council meeting that we need to find out what he wants above all."

Uri nodded. It was hard to tell with his substantial beard covering most of his face, but Rhea thought she could detect a hint of smugness. He enjoyed being right.

"What is it that you have tried so far?"

"I offered him his freedom, obviously," Rhea said. Her heart was pounding again. She hadn't been able to tell Broc the whole truth about what went on with Saras because she'd felt ashamed. Would she be willing to expose all this ugliness in front of Uri?

Uri nodded and ran his right hand mindlessly through his long beard. "If that had worked, you wouldn't be here."

"Indeed." Rhea chewed on her bottom lip for a moment, before gathering the courage. The greater good demanded her honesty. "He seemed to show some interest. In me."

Uri looked up at her and smiled briefly. "He has been alone for a very, very long time."

Rhea nodded. "Well, that's what I thought. I thought it would be a small sacrifice. For the safety of these lands."

Uri did not ask for any clarification, he simply waited for her to continue.

"That also did not work," Rhea said, then waited for a response.

He took his time, stroking his beard slowly, looking thoughtful.

"I can only conclude one thing," Uri said finally.

"What's that?"

"That you did not give him what he *really* wants."

Rhea frowned. That wasn't very helpful. "If I cannot trust what he tells me, how will I ever find out what he desires?"

Uri gestured at the vast collection of books surrounding them. "In all these books and papers is the recorded history and knowledge of our people. A great many things are written. But nowhere does it say what Saras, the dragon, wants above all. Believe me, I've checked."

Rhea sighed. What a waste of time. She got up out of her chair, preparing to leave.

"But," Uri said.

Rhea turned to face him again.

"Think about this: deep down, what is it that every living, sentient being really wants? That might give you a starting point."

Rhea scowled. How she wanted to give him a piece of

her mind. What good was a Council of Elders if they had nothing useful to share and only spoke in riddles? She didn't, though. She said the most diplomatic thing that came to her mind.

"I'll give it some thought."

"Wonderful. Now if you don't mind, I'll get back to my work." Uri heaved himself out of the chair and shuffled back to the huge bookcase.

As Rhea left, nobody paid her any attention anymore. The novelty of having the Black Isles' newly appointed female general in their midst had worn off quickly.

Once outside, she could hear some commotion further down the hallway. Rhea sped up and nearly bumped into one of her men.

"My General!" The soldier looked like he'd seen a ghost.

Rhea's chest tightened. Had the invasion begun already?

"What is it?" Rhea asked.

"It's about the dragon…"

CHAPTER SEVEN

he dreams; they were an endless source of pain. After watching Black Mountain engulfed in a fiery blaze for perhaps the billionth time, Saras forced his eyes open again.

He let out a desperate roar that shook the walls of his cells.

That last image his subconscious had served up to him was the final straw. No longer did his dreams end with the memory of Gillian's death, they now predicted a different tragedy. Different and yet all the same.

Rhea.

He looked down to check for *her* blood on his hands, but his palms and fingers were clean. Of course they were. He had only dreamed it, after all.

Saras shook his head and started to pace his cell. If he stayed here for another moment, he'd lose whatever was left of his mind.

He had been consigned to his fate for so long, the idea seemed ludicrous. But she was his chance at redemption, wasn't she? What good was another chance if he didn't take it?

And after he'd insulted her the last time she was down here, there was no way she'd come back any time soon. Or perhaps at all.

A Dragon's Treasure

He wouldn't wait for her. This was the time to act. A dragon did not need to bargain for his freedom; he simply took it. The only reason he'd been locked up all this time was because it had been his own choice.

Saras focused for a moment, waiting for the beast to take over. His human body was too feeble; this transformation was his last hope of breaking through the heavy doors that stood between him and freedom.

But he was out of practice. His skin tingled and itched, but nothing happened. The laser focus he needed to succeed was beyond reach for a mind as cloudy as his. Still, he did not give up. Surely a thousand years of sleep didn't override his basic nature. Back in the day, he had often transformed accidentally, out of excitement. And now...

The more he tried, the more frustrated he grew. His body ached, but not as much as his heart did.

Finally, Saras could take no more. He charged at the heavy door of his cell, punching it with his bare firsts until his knuckles bled.

He was no stranger to pain, though what he'd endured all these years in his sleep had been pain of a different nature. The sharp sting of the fresh wounds on his hands provided a new kind of clarity.

Encouraged, he started to kick at the door as well. Finally, he decided to do a run up and throw his whole body weight against it.

That was when the switch finally flipped. His body

changed in a split second. No more smooth skin and long, flowing hair.

Scales and talons, wings and a long, pointy tail made way from his unimpressive human form. He grew to three times his original size, and more than ten times his human strength.

The door could not hold him back, and neither could the two that lay behind. Like a snake, he wormed his way through the narrow shaft connecting his prison to the rest of the castle.

From the corner of his eye, guards scurried back and forth. One tried to attack him with a spear, but its tip simply broke off against his scaly body.

Saras ignored them. They couldn't harm him if they tried.

Before long, he had made his way up to ground level. Nothing, not a single thing about the castle, looked familiar.

Of course, in his present state, he did not need to concern himself with the layout of it. The first window he saw, the first whiff of outside air, and he smashed his way through the heavy wall. Rock and mortar crumbled around him.

Once free, he could do the thing he had only done in his dreams all this time. He could stretch his wings.

He closed his eyes and shook off the dust from the broken wall. This was it. This he knew.

The great outdoors smelled the same as it had done the

last time he'd been out here. Nothing had changed.

Saras flapped his wings a couple of times, just to get used to the movement again.

Then he jumped as high as he could, launching his body into the sky. He made it to the tallest tower of the castle in just a couple of thrusts of his wings, then he circled around, surveying the land below.

The air was crisp, the winds were strong. Although his muscles ached still, Saras wasn't about to give up on his journey.

After a thousand years, he was back. This was where he belonged. Nothing and no one would convince him to go back into hiding. Never again.

Just what he was going to do with his newfound freedom, he did not know. His first priority was basic. He needed a good meal above all.

So he set his sights on the lands south of the Isles. The mainland was where all the good hunting grounds were. Surely time had not changed that.

———— ✦ ————

When the war horn roared, it shook the castle of Black Mountain to its very foundations. There was not a man, woman or child who could ignore it.

It was a terrible sound, one that filled your heart with dread the second you heard it.

Rhea, for all her bravery, was no different in that respect. The last time she'd still felt hopeful, and riled up for the fight that she knew was coming.

This time, everything was different.

This time, she knew they couldn't win with what they had.

She had only just found out about Saras' escape when the enemy was spotted. There hadn't been time to send anyone after him, to catch him and drag him back to his cell. Rhea did not even know where he was or why he had left, when her offers of freedom had fallen on deaf ears.

She'd tried everything to convince him, hadn't she? She'd even been willing to trade her body for his help, and he'd just laughed it off. Now he was totally out of her reach. They definitely could not count on his help.

Rhea ran up to the armory where her soldiers had already collected, awaiting their orders.

"This is the moment of truth. We knew it would come sooner or later," Rhea began, addressing her army.

"King Weiland is a formidable enemy, but he isn't all-powerful. He lives and bleeds just as we do. The Sea Folk can and will be defeated." Rhea swallowed hard. Lying was not one of her strengths, but these men were going to go out there and give their lives for this land. The least she could do was try to instill hope in them.

"Where are my eagles?" she asked and scanned the crowd.

One familiar face stepped forward. It was the farm girl

she had come to know as Eryn in their previous interactions. "My General. We are here."

"Fly high, take turns to send someone down to report back to me. I want to know exactly how many of the enemy we're facing. Sea Folk don't have archers, so you're not in any danger. Be my eyes. Go on!" she ordered.

Although they looked fearful, their self-appointed leader, Eryn, whipped them into shape with a few more choice words.

That left Rhea with her experienced fighters. They knew exactly what they were facing, and their expressions reflected it. Some—perhaps a lot—of these men and women would not see the sun come up tomorrow.

Such was life on the Isles. You lived and died at the mercy of not just the forces of nature, but the whim of their fiercest enemy as well.

"Don't do it for me. Don't even do it for your king. Go out there and fight for your wives and children. For your mothers and fathers, and those that came before. Fight with honor and courage. Fight so valiantly your children's children will sing songs in remembrance of this day! Go win us a war!"

Rhea had never been one for speeches, but looking at the faces before her, her words had struck a nerve and inspired even the most reluctant among her soldiers.

"Yes, General!" they responded. A roar erupted among them. Some picked up the weapons of their choice, while others simply limbered up and allowed nature to take over.

The armory was no longer filled with just humans, but a frenzied mass of wolves and bears, each preparing for the fight of their lives in their own way. Shouts of encouragement made way for roars and growls.

Rhea felt strange watching the spectacle in front of her. Ordinarily she would join the fray without a second thought.

But she had a strategic responsibility to stay alive for as long as possible today.

She'd fight, of course, but she'd also have to lead and strategize.

With her hand on the ceremonial sword on her hip, she exited the armory first and made her way to the boundary wall with her fighters right on her tail.

There, Broc was already waiting, as were Yorrick, Uri and Kelly.

"Is he here himself?" Rhea asked. "Or has he just sent soldiers?"

Broc nodded at the troubled waters below. "If he is, he hasn't shown himself."

Rhea stared darkly at the sea. There was not much movement, but her trained eye could see many bodies in the water, all seemingly waiting for the right time to strike. The calm before the storm.

Broc cleared his throat and stepped up to the wall.

"Why are you here? We have a truce with your king. Explain yourselves!"

A Dragon's Treasure

A couple of hundred feet away, a figure emerged from the water. Rhea recognized him as the fighter who had challenged Teaq during their last encounter. He had fought the duel that had given them a truce in the first place.

"Lies! King Weiland demands the return of his daughter, as agreed in the truce!"

Rhea shook her head. There it was; exactly what she'd been afraid of when she first heard about Teaq's departure.

"You," Broc pointed at the enemy fighter. "I know you. She's your sister, isn't she?"

The Merman remained quiet. Perhaps he hadn't expected anyone on this side of the fight to recognize him.

"She's not here. Tell your father," Broc bellowed. "We cannot return what we do not have. You'd do well to think about where else your sister might run off to before coming to us again."

After just a few seconds of silence between the two sides, the enemy asked perhaps the most pertinent question of them all. "Your general. Where is he?"

Rhea's chest filled with anger again at how irresponsibly Teaq had handled things. This mess was entirely his fault. The enemy was a great many things, but he wasn't stupid. Just as Rhea's side knew the truth between the two star crossed lovers, so did King Weiland's men.

Broc exchanged a look first with Kelly, then Rhea.

Don't you tell him the truth! she thought, subtly shaking her head at him.

For once, the truth would not set anyone free. It would just earn them more trouble.

"General Teaq is indisposed. Your fight took a toll on him," Broc said.

Relieved, Rhea studied the enemy prince again.

"Produce him right this moment! I wish to ask him about the whereabouts of my sister myself."

Rhea sighed and shook her head. They might as well give the order now. All this talk was just delaying the inevitable. Nothing they could do or say would convince King Weiland's men that the mermaid was long gone. Before long, their precious truce would be broken.

Just at this moment, Eryn appeared in the crowd surrounding Rhea.

"The eagles have scoured the seas and come up with a number," she whispered in her ear.

"Go on then," Rhea said, bracing herself for bad news.

"They have us surrounded with at least two thousand men, and more yet waiting in the waters outside our boundaries."

CHAPTER EIGHT

What a relief. What a thrill.

Saras flew high, surveying his domain. The land below was lush and green as he remembered. Trees and shrubs sheltered his most precious prey from view. But obviously that wouldn't stop him. He breathed in deeply, then dove straight for a particularly thick cluster of vegetation.

His breath reduced it all to ashes within seconds. The mere sight of it filled him with joy.

What a pleasure fire could be, when nothing more than some trees were at stake.

He hadn't caught anything yet, though. So he repeated the process again and again, choosing any hiding spot that looked promising enough.

Eventually, he did catch his desired prey. Charred like their surroundings.

"Nothing like a well cooked meal. Not like the crap they started to leave for me once I woke up," Saras muttered to himself.

Indeed, it had been a very long time since he had fed the way he deserved. And so he kept going, pushing for just one more, until he was completely sated.

He landed in the midst of the destruction and allowed his aching body some rest.

That was when he realized he wasn't alone. Frantic voices shouted at each other some distance away. Luckily he was still out of sight.

It might have been a very long time since he was last here, but he hadn't forgotten the old rules completely. The mainland was a different place altogether. They were unaware of what went on the Isles. They did not know about all the creatures that existed there, and certainly they did not know about his kind.

The last thing he needed was to be spotted by some superstitious mainland farm folk. They'd attack in fear, and he'd have to retaliate. Keeping his hands clean of blood was his main priority now.

Within seconds, he let go of his majestic form, and transformed. Becoming human was a lot easier. Almost effortless. Now he was small enough to hide.

The only downside was this vulnerable skin. His transformation had lost him what little clothes he had.

Heat rose up from the ground he stood on, burning into the bare soles of his feet. All around, the fire had done a lot of damage and the resulting heat was immense.

It didn't take long for his body to become covered in sweat, and his head to feel faint as a result.

The voices who had disturbed him earlier were circling around his position, no doubt trying to work out what or who had had caused the fire. If he wanted out of here, he had to be quick.

Saras listened for footsteps and chatter alike, and

walked, then ran in the opposite direction. It would be best for everyone involved if he got out of here quickly.

They were no match for him, of course, even in his current state. But he could think of little worse than being forced to fight and kill these people. He had so much weighing on his conscience already…

If he added even one more face to those who already haunted his dreams, he'd never be truly free.

It hadn't taken long for talk to turn into action. As long as they had no mermaid princess to turn over, the enemy would not stand down.

Broc had given the go-ahead at pretty much the same time as the Sea Folk commander had done so. Rhea watched with a heavy heart as the first hundreds of fighters started to emerge from the water and climb up the rocky shore of the island. She waited until they had almost reached halfway up the boundary wall.

"Attack at will! Make every blow count!" she shouted, as she unsheathed the General's Sword.

With feet shoulder width apart, and both hands on the handle, she took on an offensive stance herself.

"If we ever needed a dragon…" Broc mumbled.

Rhea ignored him. In all the confusion, she hadn't even had the chance to brief him about Saras' escape, and this certainly wasn't the right time.

"It would be best for the queen to retreat," she shouted.

From the corner of her eye, she could see two guards ushering Kelly and Uri away from the danger zone. Broc and Yorrick remained by Rhea's side, their own swords raised in preparation for the incoming assault as well.

Although they were all formidable fighters, they weren't at the first point of contact. As the three most prominent people on the boundary wall today, they had multiple layers of soldiers guarding them.

Just how long these defenses would hold was impossible to predict. But she wasn't prepared to hide herself away behind the guards anyway. Today, every soldier—every sword—would count.

Two thousand enemy combatants, at least. Rhea pressed her lips together in determination. The Isles had an army of not even a thousand, spread over the whole territory. Black Mountain itself housed maybe five hundred trained fighters at any time.

The islanders were taller, and in animal form perhaps even stronger than the enemy they faced, but what they lacked in sheer strength, the Sea Folk made up for in determination and grit. They fought to the death. The only way they'd stand a chance was to do the same.

If this was their last stand, she would make sure to take as many Sea Folk with her as possible.

Broc was right, Rhea thought bitterly. A dragon would change everything, most of all morale. But Saras was long gone. He had let them down, had let *her* down.

The first Sea Folk spears clashed against the weapons of her men. Those who chose to fight in animal form charged and used their natural defenses as best they could.

All around was the sound of metal clanging and bones and flesh breaking and tearing.

Her senses became overwhelmed with the smell of blood, enemy and ally alike. They had fought the Sea Folk before, but this battle was on another scale.

Beside her, Yorrick had found his first opponent. Rhea did not get the chance to watch more than the first thrust of his sword, because right at that moment an enemy fighter slipped through the chaos all around and went for her with his spear.

She dodged him with ease, then brought down her sword on his shoulder. The damage was substantial, still it did not discourage him.

The merman simply switched sides and started to wield the spear with his left hand. They were fighting machines. His expression barely betrayed that he was in pain. It had to be considerable too, looking at the deep gash her sword had made. She'd cut all the way down to the bone.

What drive these soldiers had. Was it King Weiland's ruthless rule that kept them in line? Or was it something else?

Rhea was still fresh, meaning she could effortlessly avoid the continuing assault of the Sea Folk soldier's spear.

She had quickly found her rhythm and pushed her doubts about their capabilities and lower numbers aside.

All she had focus for was the fight. This dance of death. Suddenly, with a swift stab of her sword, it was over. She had slain the enemy, but this respite only lasted for a moment, before her dead opponent had been replaced by two more.

Eyes filled with hate sized her up, then they attacked simultaneously. This was more of a challenge. Still, she was quick enough on her feet, and sufficiently skilled with the blade.

There was no time to think or strategize. She could not lead until she had defeated these new challengers as well, and any others who would follow behind.

Spear tips grazed and cut her arms, but never enough to cause permanent damage. She took a few blows from the blunt end too. The enemy was almost acrobatic in his use of the weapon, twirling and waving it around effortlessly like it was yet another limb.

She crouched down to avoid one attack, and used her weapon as a bat to knock the spear out of her attacker's hands. He simply lunged at her, hands extended forward, aiming straight for her neck.

A quick intervention from the left saw Broc join her and even the playing field. With two against two, it did not take long for these enemy fighters to be neutralized.

That was when things got confusing. So many had climbed over the wall, that every one of her men was simply hacking away blindly, hoping to hit someone on the other side. They were outnumbered. They were being overwhelmed.

There was no time to think or even breathe. Before she knew it, her instincts had taken over.

As her inner beast emerged in a rage, she caught one of the enemy in her powerful jaws, and slammed another to the ground with her paw. The General's Sword fell unceremoniously to the ground. She had no more use for it in her current state.

This was the last advantage. The last line of defense.

Blinded by the smell of blood, she went on a rampage, clawing, biting and smashing her way through the many invaders up on the wall.

She did not even know how long this went on for, or how many she had taken out in the process. All she knew was that she was making a difference.

Suddenly, it all changed. Rhea could no longer move freely. She had been caught in something, a net of some kind, and immediately a number of mermen jumped on top of her back and tried to pin her down. Spear tips and blunt objects assaulted her entire body.

She roared in anger. *You won't keep me down so easily!*

But her movements were severely restricted and her strength was waning. They had tied up her limbs, and even covered her head in a hood of some kind.

Was this it? The end of a valiant fight.

As much as she tried, there was nothing she could do. The blood loss was starting to affect her mind. She could only listen as the battle raged on all around. The strange musty hood on her face made it hard to breathe. Disoriented, she sank to her knees. She did not even know which of the footsteps and other noises around her was made by one of her own or one of them.

Not that it mattered. Right now, she was as helpless as she'd ever been. She'd only ever lost a fight once before, when Kelly's powers first emerged, and at least she'd been up on her feet immediately after. This was something else.

Defenseless, she lay down, taking any impact that came her way without making so much as a sound.

Hopefully at least Broc had managed to get away. A general was relatively expendable. But if the Isles were to live another day, they needed their king. She and Yorrick should have protected him better. The sheer numbers King Weiland had sent their way had overwhelmed her.

Rhea closed her eyes with a painful last thought on her mind. It was her worst fear come true.

Their side was losing. She had failed her people and her king.

CHAPTER NINE

What greeted Saras upon his return to Black Mountain was a vision straight from one of his nightmares. Was this even really happening or had he drifted off to sleep somewhere without realizing and found himself trapped in his morbid imagination again?

Circling overhead was a group of frazzled eagles who fled as soon as they spotted him.

Down below there was utter chaos.

Sea Folk and islanders, embroiled in bloody battle. Weapons threw sparks as they clashed together. Bodies, bruised and bleeding, continued to give everything they had to the fight, until they could give no more.

The intruders from the sea swarmed up the steep rock face like vermin, aiming to overwhelm the troops of Black Mountain.

Not my war, Saras thought, but suddenly it had become hard to convince himself of that anymore. Flashes of Rhea's face, bloodstained like in his most recent nightmares, appeared before him. *No, it cannot be!*

He ought to fly higher, and ignore the battle from afar. Much like a human who happened upon an army of ants overpowering and killing anything intruding upon their domain. But he couldn't bring himself to do it.

These weren't nameless, faceless insects. They were *his* people too, weren't they?

He knew at least two of them by name. Rhea and Kelly. Weren't they down there too, fighting for their lives?

How he wished to stay out of it. The smell of it reminded of everything he yearned to forget.

"Have we not suffered enough?" Saras mumbled as he dove nearer the ground.

He scanned the mass of warriors. Roughly half were easily dismissed; they were the wrong color. Scaly, much like he was, and yet nothing like him at all. Small, puny little things. How easy it would be to take them out. All it would take was a deep breath before they'd be burned to a crisp.

But wherever there were any of *them*, they were surrounded by islanders of all shapes, shades and sizes. Wolves, bears, humans in full or partial armor. Some with weapons, some without, most covered in some measure in blood.

Where was Rhea? Was he too late?

Saras tried not to think of it, as dread threatened to paralyze. If he did nothing, it would all be his fault again. Another death to add to his already overloaded conscience.

Don't be a coward, he berated himself.

Some had already succumbed, though; casualties were growing on both sides from the looks of it. Surely, general was not just a ceremonial position. If she held the title, she would have earned it. She would be leading by example, and she wouldn't have gone down so easily in a fight.

He circled the castle, then focused his attention on the southern boundary wall where most of the fighting was going on. She was a bear; he'd picked up on the distinctive scent when they first met. But what exactly her animal form looked like—what color her fur was—he did not know.

He'd have to find her entirely by smell. Sure enough, the more he focused, the easier it became for him to distinguish the various fighters down below. The Sea Folk with their salty, almost fish-like smell were easily identified and ignored.

Where are you? he thought, as he continued to scan the battleground. *Rhea, where have you gone?*

Saras, help us! another voice spoke to him. A female, familiar, as though he'd heard her before... He shook it off. This was yet another unwanted dream, infiltrating his reality.

Saras! Listen to me! There it was again.

His frustration grew.

No, you're just trying to trick me. To distract from what I mean to do.

Down there! Help us defeat them, Saras. Save Rhea!

His eyes fixated on a brown shape cowering against the fortifications. The presence in his head, whether real or imagined, urged him in that direction. He couldn't see her properly, but he instinctively knew it was her. Once he got closer, he even thought he picked up on a whiff of her scent.

A group of the sea people surrounded Rhea, ready to fight off anyone who came close.

It didn't matter to him. Now that he was certain, he sprang into action without further thought.

One deep breath, and fire rained down on everything and everyone in his path. The smell of burnt flesh and blood surrounded him. Those creatures closest to him had simply petrified and turned to ash where they stood. Others yet were cooked like an overdone roast. You could barely even recognize them as anything other than meat. A few of them had survived his attack and screamed in agony as they tried to flee.

Saras looked down. Blood on his hands.

No, it cannot be. It's only a dream.

Sure enough, his talons were still clean. His conscience, however, was not.

He had no choice, surely? This destruction, it was necessary to ensure her rescue, wasn't it? And these were enemy soldiers, so things were different this time.

His chest ached and burned as though the fire had hurt him too, which was impossible, of course. This was his guilt tearing at him, just as it had done for a millennium. It all but paralyzed him. Supposedly different, and yet the same.

"Dragon!" voices from both sides erupted all around.

A Dragon's Treasure

"Dragon! Retreat!"

He paid them no more attention as they scurried away. Forcing himself back into action, Saras gathered up Rhea's still body and hurtled himself back into the sky.

She was still alive, wasn't she? How badly had she been hurt that she'd given up the fight? If he'd done all that damage for nothing… No, his intervention had to mean something. It couldn't be too late!

Saras tried not to dwell on it, and instead flew as swiftly as his wings would take him up to the highest tower of the castle. His favorite place from all those centuries ago. There, he lay her down on an empty stone balcony and crouched beside her.

"Rhea," he said. "Are you alright?"

The wings and scales had faded and made way for his human disguise. Cold gusts of wind stung against his bare skin.

He fumbled with the ropes that held her, releasing her from the netting the enemy had caught her in, and pulled the mask off her face.

There she lay, eyes closed, vulnerable as any human. But she wasn't the same as before. She was a vision straight from one of his night terrors. Blood soaked hair clung to the side of her face. Her entire body was covered in cuts and grazes, each deeper and more serious than the next. She had fought hard before they'd captured her. Every inch of her skin told him so.

"Oh, Rhea," he whispered again as he reached for her shoulder. No movement.

Overwhelmed with grief, he held her gently in his arms. If she did not wake, that meant the damage was grave. The only glimmer of hope he had was the weak sound of her heartbeat.

Would it endure?

The islanders had always been strong and fast to heal, but they weren't immortal like he was. Inflict too much pain, and their bodies gave out.

He lay her down again on the stone floor and simply watched her chest rise and fall. Regular breaths. Surely, that was a good sign?

What was his plan, anyway? He'd brought her here to safety, but there was no one to attend to her wounds. What was he thinking?

He leaned down and as softly as he could, kissed her forehead.

His lips had barely touched her grazed skin when she flinched and awoke. Guided by instinct, she stumbled up into a clumsy defensive stance.

Relief washed over him. He did not know whether to laugh or cry.

He raised his arms in a calming motion and slowly approached her. "It's alright, Rhea, you're safe now."

Her eyes darted back and forth between him and random points surrounding them. For a moment her appearance almost changed over into animal form, but it was just a momentary glimpse which did not take. A defense mechanism; she was primed to attack still.

"Where am I? What happened?" Her voice was hoarse and so very weak.

"I got you out. They can't get to you now."

Rhea's bottom lip shook for a moment. She shuffled over to the edge of the balcony and looked down. A muffled sob escaped her lips.

"What about the others?" she whispered. "What about Broc and Yorrick?"

Saras shrugged. He hadn't paid them any attention. His focus was solely on finding her. Shouldn't she be grateful to be out of there? Confused, he took a step back.

"You were surrounded. I got you out," he repeated.

There was a moment of silence between them.

"You don't seem happy about it," Saras observed. What was she looking at down there? A terrible realization dawned on him.

He joined her by the edge and also peered down at the aftermath of the battle. Despite being so high up, he could clearly see the destruction. His heart started to race and mind grew cloudy. It had happened again. Despite his best efforts.

"Oh, God," he mumbled.

He immediately saw the spot from where he had recovered her. Charred remains served as his marker. They hadn't just been enemy soldiers, had they? Were either of the men Rhea had asked about—Broc or Yorrick—among those who had been caught in his fire? Had he made everything worse yet again?

Only this morning he'd gone out of his way to save two mainlanders who had inadvertently stumbled upon the forest fire he'd caused. But death followed him wherever he went, like a shadow he could not shake.

He'd only tried to help. Which in fact was exactly what she had tried to persuade him to do from the first moment she'd come into his cell. He had refused for a reason.

Because he knew better than to get involved in anything like this.

He should never have left that place.

Imprisonment was his only option. What he thought was his redemption, turned out to be a confirmation that he was beyond hope.

His heart grew cold at the sight of her, continuing to stare down at what was left of the battleground. He'd had this moment. A little glimmer of something that was not to be. Everything good in his life always ended up burned. His first love, Gillian, should have taught him that. But he'd learned nothing.

Just as well that he was the only one of his kind left. He was an aberration. One which should have never existed in the first place.

These people, and especially this woman, would be better off without him.

Saras turned around in silence toward the opposite side

of the balcony. Without looking back even once at Rhea, he closed his eyes and threw himself over the edge.

His wings didn't emerge until about halfway down. Just in time to prevent him from falling to his death. Not that it would have been a great loss to the world.

Saras found the hole he had smashed through the castle wall on his way out, and kept on travelling downward into the deepest part of the dungeon. Once inside his cell, he transformed back and pulled the broken door shut behind him. The locks were still open, but he didn't need them anyway. This was where he would stay, until the world around him crumbled and death finally came to claim him.

CHAPTER TEN

S o much had happened in a fog. It took Rhea a moment to comprehend how she had ended up here on this balcony on one of the highest towers of the castle, while everyone else was down below. She knew their losses had been substantial; she'd seen it before they'd caught her.

So, why had the enemy fled? It wouldn't have taken much for them to win the battle and with it, the war.

Saras… Saras had intervened and brought her here.

Rhea turned to look for him, but she was all alone.

Dull pain throbbed in her chest. She'd been stabbed, beaten, bruised and very nearly completely broken.

But not quite yet.

If Saras had rescued her from certain capture and probably death, then there was hope yet.

She braved the pain and started to walk. Down the spiral stairs leading down to the main part of the castle.

First of all, she'd take stock of the situation. She had to find Broc.

"Rhea, wait for me." Kelly's voice stopped her.

Although she was in no mood to chat, Rhea paused. The queen was in quite a state. Red eyes pleaded with her through tear-stained lashes.

All this while she had been up on the Viewpoint. Too

far for her weak human eyesight to see what was going on down below. Too far to know what had happened to the king.

The two women continued through the maze of hallways in silence. There was nothing to say. Rhea did not know much more than Kelly did at this point. Only that the situation was grave.

It was very possible that down among the bodies they'd find both their worst nightmare come true. Even Saras hadn't seen Broc. He would have said something if he had.

Just why he'd left her up there by herself, Rhea could not yet understand. Maybe he was trying to do exactly the same thing she was. To locate the king and see how much of their army was left standing. With some luck they might even be able to determine how much of the enemy's army was left.

They ran as fast as their feet would carry them until they made it out of the drawbridge and onto the fortified boundary wall. This was where most of the fighting had happened.

This was where Rhea herself had very nearly met her end.

Although the battle was over, the place was abuzz with activity. Soldiers and ordinary citizens helped the injured and gathering up the dead. The stench of blood was enough to turn one's stomach.

Kelly suppressed a sob.

Rhea glanced over at the woman. She would have never seen anything like this. She wasn't battle hardened like the rest of them.

Please, please, please! Please let him be alive! Rhea couldn't bear the idea of losing Broc today. For the sake of the Isles. For Kelly's sake.

"Rhea, where have you been?" Broc's voice called out over the commotion.

Rhea breathed a sigh of relief and waved at him. "Here!"

She waited as Kelly ran toward him, threw her arms around his neck and started to sob uncontrollably. She'd always known that the witch wasn't like them. In the past she would have judged her for it, looked down on her.

Today, Rhea felt for her. Despite their differences. Despite her innate distrust of the witch.

"Kelly, why don't you head back inside? This is no place for a queen," Broc spoke softly.

She shook her head. "I couldn't help during the battle, but I'll help now."

Rhea smiled briefly. Kelly was stronger than she appeared. For the first time since her arrival here, Rhea felt a kind of kinship with the woman. Perhaps Broc hadn't made such a bad choice after all.

Rhea still loved Broc, though. That would never change. But her love for him had transformed, and opened up a little space in her heart to perhaps accept Kelly, too. And all it had taken for Rhea's perception to change was a terrible battle.

Broc nodded, then diverted his attention to Rhea.

"I need you to take stock of where we stand."

"Yes, my king."

"How many have we got left? The Sea Folk retreated in such a hurry they did not carry their fallen. Have them counted so we can have an estimate of how many losses they've had too."

Rhea nodded. She had already thought of that. "Of course."

So she went to work, determined to do the best job she could.

Rather than simply give orders, she got her hands dirty as well. The infirmary was filling quickly, and those were the lucky ones. Many had not been so lucky.

Rhea's heart ached as she watched body upon body being lined up along the seashore. They hadn't seen losses this grave in generations and it would take years upon years for their numbers to recover. The enemy, too, had lost many. So senseless. Over a stupid barren rock in the sea which was hardly a prize for anyone.

The islanders lived here out of necessity, because the mainlanders had sought to stamp them out so long ago, but what motivated the Sea Folk? They had their kingdom in the Deep. What did they need these lands for when they mostly dwelled under water?

Rhea would never understand the point of this war

they'd become embroiled in. For them, survival was on the line. But the enemy seemed to act without reason.

They worked late into the night, trying to make sense of it all. Rhea and those men she had left, along with the civilians of Black Mountain. Nobody paused for food or rest, not even Queen Kelly, who continued to help just as she had promised.

Long after the sun had gone down, and the boundary wall was starting to look clearer, Rhea stumbled across an object in the blood-soaked mud. It was unassuming, but something made Rhea kneel down to inspect it. After brushing away the dirt, she finally recognized what she had found.

Her sword. The symbol of her power and responsibility, discarded in the dirt. It was the perfect image for this battle's outcome. Nothing and no one had been spared. Her father would have been ashamed to see his old weapon lie abandoned on the ground like this.

Rhea carefully picked it up and cleaned it with her bare hands. Tears stung her eyes again as she held it tightly against her body. How would they come back from this?

"General Rhea." Eryn, her main lookout approached.

She took a deep breath and wiped her face with the back of her hand. "Yes?"

"We've completed the count. For every one of ours, we took out three of theirs," Eryn said.

The numbers *sounded* good, but she did not look too excited about it. What was the catch?

A Dragon's Treasure

"How many? How many of ours?" Rhea asked.

Eryn shuffled from one foot to the other, staring at the ground. The woman had tried to spin it initially, but it wasn't good news.

"Well?" Rhea urged.

"We've lost two hundred, General Rhea," Eryn whispered.

From an estimated five hundred present on Black Mountain this morning, Rhea's army had almost been halved. Rhea didn't know what to say. She had sent them out here with a speech consisting only of empty words. She'd given them only idle hope. And now so many were no more.

It had been only a few days since her appointment, so Rhea hadn't known many by name yet. But she knew going forward she'd find faces missing in her ranks. So this was what it felt like to command. To be directly responsible for these lost lives.

"Thank you, Eryn. You've been a great help," Rhea mumbled.

The woman nodded and was about to leave, when Rhea remembered something.

"Oh, have you seen the dragon?"

Eryn's eyes went wide for a moment. "The dragon… Until he appeared I thought those old tales were just that, stories."

Rhea frowned and shook her head. "No, I mean have

you seen him recently? After the battle."

Eryn looked down at the ground between them. "I have not, no. I know it's none of my business…"

"Speak freely."

"He's on our side, isn't he? We could really use a dragon on our side." The woman's voice trailed off as her eyes rested on the blackened stone surrounding them.

This was the spot. Where Saras had joined the fight but for a moment, and changed the outcome in their favor.

Remembering Kelly's words about her supposedly harsh leadership style, she rested her hand on the woman's shoulder. "I assure you that he is. He'll protect us."

At least he had done. Despite his repeated refusals.

Eryn's eyes lit up. "That's wonderful news! Then perhaps there is hope for us yet."

For once, Rhea had to agree. As long as Saras was on their side, there was a hope, however bleak, in light of all this death.

She nodded at the woman and left her there on the wall. It was time to brief Broc on the number of casualties. Would he feel the weight of their loss as keenly as she did? Or had the eight years he'd spent as king already hardened him to these realities of life?

———◆———

A Dragon's Treasure

Back in his cell, Saras tossed and turned. So many faces haunting him. So many lives lost.

Sure, he'd rescued Rhea, but at what cost?

He'd seen it in her eyes once she'd come to: the guilt of surviving such a terror. She was a warrior, who lived and died by the sword. She might have preferred death over being spared when so many of her comrades had fallen.

This was why he hadn't wanted to get involved in the first place. His powers were not like the point of a sword which could be aimed precisely. In the fog of battle, his fire burned everyone indiscriminately. Friend or foe alike.

And that was exactly what had happened. He'd have to live with that.

A thousand years had passed, and nothing had changed. He was still a danger to everyone around him. He could not be trusted outside in the real world.

Best to leave it behind once and for all.

She'd come to see him, Rhea had. She'd pushed open the door even, and made her way inside. But he'd hidden himself in the farthest corner of his cell and sent her away.

Saras couldn't face her. To see the disappointment in her face all over again. At the same time he knew that if he saw her, he'd yearn for her even more. His inner beast had claimed her already, even though in his mind he knew he did not deserve her.

For that very reason he'd raged until finally she left him alone.

It would be best for everyone to forget he even existed. For so long these people had done just fine on their own. It made no sense for him to get involved any longer.

In any case, the enemy had left. The threat was over. They could ask no more of him.

Despite knowing all this, and continuing to repeat it in his head, part of him couldn't accept this fate.

He should have fallen asleep by now, to let the years pass unbeknownst to him, until everyone he'd hurt today had long since died and their offspring had forgotten about him. But instead of years passing him by, he suffered through every second. Awake, haunted by memories rather than dreams.

And in among all the pain and suffering there was the vision of her. Rhea, lying in a pool of her own blood. If it wasn't for his intervention, she would have been killed.

But she was fragile. A mortal, unlike him. If his aim had been off just a little, he could have burned her alive without even knowing it.

An ill-timed sneeze could have done it.

This was why his kind had died out many years ago. It was a dangerous business, being a dragon's mate. He wouldn't wish it on his worst enemy, so how could he subject the woman he loved to such a fate?

For he had come to love her. His heart reminded him at any and every opportunity.

The way she carried herself; her confidence and beauty were unrivalled. And despite his reservations early on, he respected her job now too. To fight among men as their equal, that took a lot of strength.

But she wasn't *his* equal. Therein lay the problem. No amount of talent or skill with the blade could keep her safe from him.

That was why he had to give her up.

CHAPTER ELEVEN

When Rhea was summoned to the Great Hall, she could already guess what it was about. After the battle, Broc had ordered her to fetch Saras and launch an attack on the Deep with him at the forefront. To strike King Weiland where it would hurt him the most and prove once and for all that the islanders were not to be messed with.

Only, she had failed to secure Saras' help. He had refused to see her or speak with her, even.

Just what had changed his behavior, she did not know. And so, she'd have no sensible explanation to present to Broc either. The Sea Folk had retreated, but for how long? Once they figured out that the dragon was no longer fighting with them, they'd try to attack again. The job of general hadn't become any easier for her.

When she made her way through the heavy doors inside the Hall, Rhea was surprised to not just find the Elders waiting by Broc's side, but Kelly as well. Apparently the battle had made the royal couple inseparable.

Rhea waited with her eyes fixed on the ground. She did not know how to explain herself.

"I hear your dragon is being difficult," Broc began.

Rhea frowned at his choice of words. *Her* dragon? Had Kelly told him more than she should have?

"He won't leave his cell," Rhea responded.

"Presumably you've explained to him that we need to strike the enemy now, when they're still hurting? We really have no other choice," Broc argued.

Rhea had nothing useful to say. Saras wouldn't even speak with her. "I did try to explain that," she mumbled.

Broc got up from his seat and threw his arms up in frustration.

"First he escapes, something which you failed to inform me of." His tone was unusually harsh, making her flinch involuntarily. "And then he happens upon a battle between us and the enemy, and burns a half a dozen of our own men nearly to death."

"Now, that's not fair," Rhea objected.

Broc slammed his fist onto the table beside him. "Not fair? What's not fair is that I promoted you to the job of general and you haven't shown me you deserve it yet. You came to me, remember? You convinced me that you could go down there and secure his cooperation. Instead we've had an escape, resulting in a broken wall, which will require materials and manpower to fix which we cannot spare at the moment. And he won't even help us win the war! This dragon of yours has been nothing but trouble!"

Rhea was speechless. For Broc to berate her like this in front of the Elders, and Kelly… They had clashed in the past, but things had never gotten this ugly.

Don't take it to heart, he's just frustrated. Kelly's voice penetrated Rhea's mind.

The two women shared a look. Still, Broc's words had hurt her deeply.

Hard not to, when I have indeed failed.

"Uri. You said the only way to convince the dragon is to offer him something he wants desperately," Kelly spoke aloud.

"That's right." Uri cleared his throat.

Broc turned to face his bride and shook his head impatiently. There was some communication going on between husband and wife which the other people in the room were excluded from.

"I've already offered him everything I could think of." Rhea sighed.

"Do share," Broc urged.

"His freedom, first of all," Rhea said, her face turning a deep shade of crimson. It wasn't enough that she'd told Kelly and Uri about the other thing already, now she'd finally have to admit it to Broc too?

"And he wasn't interested in that, because he knew he could break through the locks and chains at any moment of his choosing," Broc said.

Rhea nodded in defeat. Yes, in hindsight she'd been stupid to think that he was an unwilling prisoner. Clearly he'd had the power to escape all along.

"What else?" Broc asked.

Rhea pressed her lips together. How could she share something so personal, so humiliating?

Yourself, Kelly's voice spoke.

Rhea nodded again and stared at the ground in front of her.

"I thought he might be lonely, after all those years…" she mumbled.

Of all the people to admit this to. The very same man who had possessed her heart for so long. That was the thing, though. Her feelings for Broc were evolving, and perhaps it was time to admit that to herself as well as him.

"If you're unable to secure his help, perhaps appointing you as General was a mistake," Broc said.

Rhea's heart broke yet again. *A mistake?* She had always given her all, in any task. To hear him denounce her like this was the final straw. She fought the sting of tears, determined not to show weakness now. If he had challenged her in any other way, she would have fought back. She would have stood her ground.

Just what she had seen in the man all these years? They'd often argued about what would be best for this land and its inhabitants. This wasn't an ordinary argument, this was just cruelty. Since her first meeting with Saras, her feelings for Broc had started to fade. Right at this moment, they vanished completely. She was free of him.

He's only frustrated because he doesn't understand. Kelly's presence was back inside Rhea's head.

Rhea looked up, at the two of them. Broc refused to look her in the eye. Rhea's hurt made way for anger.

Kelly's eyes, meanwhile, were full of compassion. Or pity. Rhea could not be sure.

How ironic, that Kelly of all people was reaching out to her. After the very rocky start they'd had. How Rhea had hated the newcomer for taking everything she'd ever wanted for herself. And having magical powers on top of it all.

"Yes, my king," Rhea said in a choked voice. "I will try harder."

She did not wait to be dismissed, but simply walked out of the meeting. Broc said nothing to stop her.

Outside, she leaned against the cold stone wall to catch her breath. This tightness in her chest, it had never fully left her since her promotion a week ago. This constant pressure to achieve the impossible was getting to her.

"Rhea." Kelly's voice forced her to open her eyes. "I apologize on Broc's behalf. Hopefully the upcoming feast will improve his mood and he'll see reason. It's not fair to place this burden just on your shoulders."

Rhea shook her head. "He wasn't wrong. I failed. I see that now. We have lost so much in one battle, we cannot survive another."

They stood in silence for a moment, before Kelly spoke again.

"I'd like to share with you something that happened at the end of the battle."

Rhea blinked a few times, but her mind was a blank. What could Kelly possibly say to her now that would change anything?

But Kelly either didn't notice her apathy, or she simply ignored it.

"When Saras came for you, I entered his mind," she said.

Rhea wasn't sure what the woman was trying to say. "So?"

"It provided some insights. Perhaps it'll help figure out what he wants."

Now she tells me.

Rhea scoffed. "He's not sure what he wants himself."

"That's actually… Yes, you're quite right." Kelly smiled briefly. "But there's a chance you can change things yet. You see, he was adamant he wouldn't join the fight. No more death. He wanted nothing more than to fly in the other direction. But he changed his mind anyway. Because of you."

"I didn't do anything. I wasn't even conscious at the time!" Rhea protested.

Kelly nodded. "I told him where you were. He would have done anything to get you out of there."

Rhea didn't know why, but hearing Kelly say that warmed her heart a little. She knew that he'd saved her, of course. But she hadn't thought about what that meant. Neither had she thanked him for his efforts.

"So why refuse to see me now?" Rhea wondered.

Kelly shrugged. "I think that has less to do with the

events that occurred the other day, and more with whatever past he's already lived through all those years ago. His mind was a confusing place to be. Full of sorrow and guilt. I couldn't make sense of it."

Rhea thought back to the tales she'd been told as a child. Of everything that happened which led to the dragon's imprisonment. Fires that burned for days, destroying most of the castle and killing many of Black Mountain's inhabitants in the process.

Just why he had turned on his people, the stories did not explain. Could it be that he was remorseful of that day?

"When I went to Uri for advice the other day, you know what he told me?" Rhea thought aloud. "To think about what every sentient being wants."

"Must he always speak in riddles?" Kelly said.

Rhea smiled through her tears at last. "That's what I thought. So frustrating."

"Well, perhaps my insights will help you figure it out."

Rhea nodded. "I hope so, though it's a work in progress." She looked at the woman who had largely been her rival until this point. "I must confess, I've been unfair to you in the past."

Kelly smiled. "It's fine. I didn't mean to come here and step on any toes, though I'm afraid that's exactly how it turned out."

Rhea let out a short laugh, remembering the circumstances of Kelly's arrival as a human offering. "No, you didn't mean to come here at all, as I remember."

They shared a smile.

"But this is home now," said Kelly. "For better or for worse. Let's hope we can keep it safe together."

Rhea held out her hand. A peace offering, after so much grief and jealousy.

"Thank you, my queen." For once, Rhea spoke those last two words without bitterness or sarcasm and she felt a little lighter for it.

Kelly smiled warmly as she shook Rhea's hand.

———— ◆ ————

*W*hat every sentient being craves above all... these words echoed through Rhea's mind over and over.

That was what Uri had said. But what did it mean, exactly? Saras had retreated to his cell after the battle.

He had isolated himself. After scaring off the enemy and helping the Isles live another day. There had been casualties, but without his intervention, who knew how high the body count would have been? They owed him so much.

From the start, he had the power to give them peace. But he saw only death.

How much had changed in just a couple of days, and yet so much had remained the same. His behavior still puzzled and frustrated her. She still could not get through to him and make him see things her way.

What could she offer him now that she hadn't already attempted to give before?

But one thing was certain, she had to try again. Now that she'd peeked behind the mask and seen the real him, she had to try not just for her people's sake, but also for his. Perhaps Kelly was right in saying he was working through his ancient history. The battle had brought those old memories back into the forefront for him.

Broc was correct, if harsh in his judgment. What good was she as a general, if she let Black Mountain's most precious inhabitant wither away in the darkness of his prison cell? For he was precious. As the last of his species, he was unique, of course. And he was precious to her too.

She'd known it from the moment she'd first laid eyes on him that he was something special. Different than other men. Beautiful, yet infuriating. Unimaginatively strong and also more vulnerable than anyone else she'd ever met.

Rhea realized that she did not just need to save him because it was her duty, but because her heart would not survive if she failed this time. Somewhere in between the arguments and the flirtations, she had come to develop feelings for him. And his actions on the battlefield had proven to her beyond any doubt that he cared for her too. Kelly's insights into his mind had only confirmed it.

Love... Was that what Uri had referred to?

It made sense. Love and companionship. All sentient beings craved it, didn't they? Loneliness was a killer, and

A Dragon's Treasure

Saras had been alone during his many lifetimes in the dungeons. She could relate; despite being surrounded by people, she herself had never found that connection.

How desperate she'd been.

And how bitter it had made her. How dismissive of other people's quest for love and happiness. She'd hated Teaq for choosing his mate over his job. And she'd rejected Kelly simply because Broc had chosen her as his bride.

Meanwhile Saras had flirted with her right from the start. And her heart had been too cold to respond truthfully. By the time she'd decided to trade a kiss for his help, he'd sensed that the gesture was an empty one. Perhaps he'd felt that her heart belonged to someone else.

But this time, everything would be different. This time, she'd go to him and prove that she was changed. She was no longer shackled by the dream of a life with another man.

If that did not convince him to come back into the world, then neither would she. As it was, Broc had begun to question his decision of her appointment.

With a renewed determination in her step, Rhea made her way through the winding hallways of the castle and down the steps leading into the dungeon, perhaps for the last time ever.

She'd do everything she could to reach Saras. And if she failed, or she had misread the situation, she was prepared to pay the price.

CHAPTER TWELVE

Two whole days and nights without sleep, and Saras was even more of a nervous wreck than before. More confused than ever, his mind kept on serving up images he had no use for.

Rhea, bathed in sunlight one moment, covered in bloody burns a moment later.

Shivers ran down his entire body. For the first time in his life he felt cold, as ludicrous as it seemed for a being of fire.

Perhaps this was the end. Perhaps the guilt for all he had done would finally break him in two and the world would be better for it.

Footsteps approached. Saras wasn't certain if they were real or imagined, but just in case, he withdrew as far as he could into the darkness.

"Saras?" Rhea called out for him.

He turned away. "I told you I'm not interested. There is nothing more to say."

"I've only come to talk to you. I promise that's all."

He shook his head, though he knew she was unable to see. "Just leave. If you don't, you'll get hurt."

It would have worked better if he had made it sound like a threat, but he did not have the energy to sound menacing anymore. He did not have the energy for much of anything, such was his level of exhaustion.

"Well, I'm not giving up this easily. Just hear me out."

His head throbbed and his heart pounded in his throat. *No, no, no. Leave now!*

But there was also a conflicting voice that spoke from within. His heart grew curious.

Why not spend a little time with her? One last goodbye before he left her world forever.

No! She ought to leave right now! For her own safety as well as his sanity.

Then again, what would be the worst that would happen? He'd regret talking to her? So what, he already regretted so much, this would make little difference.

She approached the corner where he'd been hiding, finding her footing solely by touch.

The wounds all over her body looked like they'd started to heal, but she was still damaged, and even walked with a slight limp. Every instinct, every fiber in his body told him to get up and help her, but he knew that would only make their farewell more difficult. He needed to keep the distance.

"That's far enough," he said when she was five or so feet away from him.

She stopped and fumbled with something on her hip. Once she was done, she threw an object in his direction. It landed heavily on the ground.

Saras leaned forward to see what it was. A sword, sheathed in leather. It was easy to recognize, because it was one of the few things on these Isles that was older than even he was. And yet she'd discarded it on the floor of his cell like it was nothing.

The General's Sword.

"You can't, Rhea! Pick it back up!"

She shook her head. "It's of no use to me anymore. You keep it."

"It's yours. It was given to you by the king. Nobody else has a right to it."

"I'm not fit for the job. Under my watch, these Isles will be lost to the Sea Folk."

Saras sighed. "I see what you're trying to do. It won't work. Pick up your sword."

Rhea didn't. Instead, she sat down on the cold floor of Saras' cell and wrapped her arms around her legs.

"What on earth are you doing?" Saras asked. "Don't! You should be resting, healing!"

This was no place for her, especially in her current condition.

But she did not move.

"Do you know my father carried this sword once, under the previous king's rule," Rhea spoke softly.

Saras wanted to argue, to make her see sense, but something in her voice gave him pause. This wasn't the Rhea he'd met before. Something had changed. She was no longer hiding behind a wall of pretense and toughness.

"So your appointment must mean a lot to him," Saras said.

"I wouldn't know. He fell in battle a long time ago."

More talk of loss and death. Saras shook his head. Why did it always come down to the same old crap?

"Saras, I haven't been honest with you. I only sought to use you for my own gain. To further my career."

He leaned forward and picked up the sword, weighing it in his hands before brushing the dust off its sheath.

"Everyone has secrets," he said. Most of all him. "You do know why I was imprisoned here, don't you?"

"There was a fire all those years ago. Many got hurt."

Saras nodded. His dreams had told and retold the same tale over and over. But he had long since blocked out the underlying cause for that tragedy. It was difficult to admit it now.

"There was a woman who had caught my eye. The daughter of the king's senior most advisor. Her name was Gillian."

Rhea did not respond, but he could see her looking up in his direction.

"I was convinced she was the one. The true mate to tame my dragon. Instead, her rejection drove me wild. I was no longer in control of my senses. In a burning rage, I..."

"You killed her," Rhea whispered. "I've heard the old stories."

"I don't know why I did it. I no longer remember..."

Oh, how it hurt, admitting his deepest, darkest shame to her.

Rhea stirred. That was it, she was going to leave. Saras would finally get what he'd asked for: his solitude.

But once she was up, she didn't head for the door; instead she came closer and lowered herself back onto the ground right beside him.

"I loved someone once," she said. "It brought me only pain and jealousy."

Afraid he'd ruin this moment of honesty, Saras hardly dared to breathe, never mind move. How was it that she was still here? How was it that her voice did not carry fear or disdain for his actions, but only compassion?

"You saved many lives out there, during the battle. I did not deserve your help, least of all because I tried to trick you to get it. But I'm thankful for your actions anyway."

Saras frowned and shook his head. "But so many were hurt. I hardly knew who I was aiming at!"

"Many always get hurt in war. That's just the nature of it. You sent the enemy running that day. We would not have made it through the night without you."

But... the shock he'd seen on her face after. Had he simply imagined it?

"How many," Saras mumbled. "How many on our side?"

Rhea brushed his question away. "That's not important now."

"It's important to me."

"Five were injured, two were burned beyond recognition. There is no way of knowing whether they'd succumbed to the fight already, though."

"Two lives…" Saras took a moment to let the information sink in.

Rhea looked in his direction. Her eyes were glistening with tears. "Saras, we lost *two-hundred* in total. Almost half of our fighters going in. That's why I can't do this anymore. It's too much of a burden knowing that I sent them into their last fight that day. I failed to keep my soldiers safe."

His heart broke for her. Finally, he understood. The guilt he'd seen in her face after he'd rescued her had nothing to do with him. She was being haunted by her own demons.

Forgetting his earlier reservations, he wrapped his arms around her. This was no longer a game. He wasn't trying to score points, or provoke a reaction like during their earlier meetings.

"I'm sorry, Rhea. For everything."

"So am I." She sighed. "The king sent me in here to get you to fight. To attack the Sea Folk in their own territory and scare them off once and for all."

"Rhea, I can't," Saras protested.

"I know, I know," Rhea interrupted. "I'm not even

going to try. He's wrong to ask this of you."

She rested her head against his shoulder, prompting Saras to run his fingers through her hair. Addictive, seductive…

He closed his eyes and inhaled deeply. Despite the change in her, her sweet scent had remained the same. Still as fresh, as tempting, with rich undertones betraying her arousal. Why had she fought him so hard before?

"Who was it?" Saras wondered aloud. "You said you loved someone once."

Rhea let out a sad chuckle. "Don't laugh. Promise me."

Saras tightened his arms around her just a little. This closeness, this physical and emotional bond, was something he could get used to. "Fine, I promise."

"The King… Broc."

"No way, *that guy?*" Saras said.

"You promised!" she exclaimed. She didn't sound angry, though. Not like the last time he'd teased her.

"I'm sorry, I simply had to…"

"In any case, that's over and done with," she said. "I only have so much to give. Not wasting it any longer on a man who isn't interested. Life's too short."

Saras let out a laugh. "Oh, my dear. I promise, life is anything but short."

"Not everyone can be immortal."

Despite everything, Saras smiled briefly. This was the calmest he had been in as long as he could remember. The fear was still there though, deep in his heart. That somehow, all of this would come undone and it would be all his fault.

"I don't know how to come back from this," Saras said, speaking mostly to himself.

Rhea lifted her head. "There's a door right there. All you have to do is walk through it."

It sounded very simple, though it hadn't been when he'd tried it.

She's the one.

What he felt for her made his memories of Gillian pale in comparison. How naive he'd been in the past. To mistake simple lust for what he felt now.

His heart lightened a little. The voices of protest faded into the background, as his dragon took over from within.

She's the one, and we must have her.

He looked down at her face. Their eyes met in the darkness. His mind had been a battleground of conflicting voices for as long as he could remember. The knowledge that he was no good for anyone versus the hope that the myths were true. That his inner dragon with his violent urges could be tamed by the right woman.

In her eyes now, he saw the truth. His instincts had been right from the start. She *was* his redemption. Where he'd gone wrong was that he'd tried to leave this place alone.

She hadn't known it yet. She wasn't by his side.

But after this shared moment, everything had changed.

Hope had returned.

"How will I redeem myself?" he wondered again.

Rhea reached up and held his face in her hands. "By confessing your sins and sharing your guilt."

Such wise words from someone so young.

"I'm a murderer," he whispered.

"I forgive you."

Had he not seen the look in her eyes, and felt her lips touch his ever so gently, he would not have believed it. But she left no room for doubt. There was no fakery in this moment.

Ancient tales described true love's first kiss as a magical moment that could heal any ailment and right every wrong. He'd often rejected that idea as nonsense, cynical as he had become. But perhaps there was some truth in it.

She felt he was worth her forgiveness. Perhaps that knowledge was enough for him to start to forgive himself.

That was a miracle in itself.

CHAPTER THIRTEEN

I t felt so good, sharing her true self with Saras. At the same time, it hurt so deeply. For the first time ever, she'd bared her deepest fears and pain to another. Just as he had done. Was this what it meant to love?

To feel so naked, so vulnerable, but not judged for it.

The terrible things he'd done obviously had to have been an accident. A young dragon's misguided reaction to heartache. But Saras wasn't young anymore. Someone so remorseful could not be a bad person. He'd bled for what he did.

Did he not deserve a second chance?

If there was one true match for everyone out there, was it so far-fetched that he could be hers? She felt a connection to him that words could not explain.

Their first kiss might have happened days ago, if it wasn't for his refusal. She'd felt humiliated, but now she was grateful for his rejection. It might have been exciting to kiss him then. Like a novelty or a crazy game, but it would have *meant* nothing.

Now it meant everything.

"You know, I've been wondering if you just tried to seduce me because I happened to be the first woman who walked in here," Rhea joked, although it had indeed crossed her mind before.

Saras laughed. "Now that you mention it, that Queen Kelly wasn't bad either."

Up to his old tricks already.

Rhea smacked him playfully on the shoulder. "Watch it, or I'll have you locked up again. This time for disrespecting our queen."

"Yes, ma'am."

His lips found hers for a repeat of their earlier union. This time it wasn't so emotionally charged, but still special in its own way. Like two carefree young lovers, exploring for the first time what it meant to be alive. Only neither of them was particularly carefree, and despite his appearance he wasn't all that young either.

"Funny," she mumbled, in between kisses.

"What is?" His breath tickled her face when he spoke.

"I tried to trade my body for your cooperation, and failed. All I needed to do was give you my soul too." Rhea smiled.

"I'm a great many things, but I'm not cheap."

If his lips felt so amazing against hers, she had to find out what the rest of him was like. Her hands started their own journey of exploration. Slowly at first, fingertips against the bare skin of his arms. It was almost more exciting in the dark. Her other senses intensified to make up for the lack of sight.

He sighed and shivered slightly under her touch.

"You're warm," she noted.

"I *can* breathe fire, you know."

Rhea rolled her eyes.

She turned to face him properly, and wrapped her arms around his neck. "You think you're so clever, don't you?"

He silenced her with yet another kiss.

All of this affection, all of these sensations were so new to her. She'd only felt a fraction of them in her dreams in the past. Nothing of what she'd fantasized about came even close to what she felt with Saras now. Despite the teases and little jabs, or perhaps because of them.

They weren't like other people, saccharine and innocent. They had both looked upon the face of death. They knew life was fleeting and fragile. Perhaps that was why they were suddenly so desperate to claim a moment of happiness for themselves.

This would have never worked with anyone else. Rhea knew in her heart, Saras was the one for her.

Suddenly, Saras pulled away from her, if only slightly.

"What?" she asked.

"Not here. We shouldn't do this here."

She still couldn't see, but apparently he could. He got up and took her by the hand, leading her out of the forgotten corner of this cell, and into the light.

He was handsome as ever, and Rhea's heart skipped a beat as she looked upon her new lover for the first time in days.

"Where are we going?" she asked.

Saras simply put his index finger softly against her lips

and shook his head. "You'll see. No more questions."

Rhea gave in, probably for the first time in her life.

He was in charge.

From high up on the balcony of the tallest tower on Black Mountain, Rhea could see for miles. Vast seas, currently unsullied by enemy movement. A jagged coastline below that acted as their only barrier from the water.

She'd never been too fond of these lands, much preferring the lush hunting grounds of the mainland to these barren islands they lived on. But even she couldn't deny their stark beauty in the receding light of day. The skies were lit up in reds and oranges that showered the landscape below. It was spectacular.

"I see why you brought me here," Rhea said.

Saras smiled at her. "This was always my favorite spot. Though by now, it's about the only part of the castle left that I recognize."

"Things have changed a lot, haven't they?"

"More than you can imagine."

Rhea forced her gaze away from the fabulous sunset and instead turned toward a masterpiece of natural beauty of a different kind. Saras was an enigma to look at. His age had provided him a certain wisdom and depth not found in Rhea's peers. And at the same time his features were so young and unspoiled. You'd never guess the truth from looking at him casually.

Unlike her own, Saras' scars were invisible, hidden deep beneath that flawless skin.

She craved him. As though their affections were the only way to uncover the truth.

He placed his hand on her shoulder, then let it travel upwards. Slow, but determined, he guided her face towards his.

Ordinarily she might have taken the lead. She was so used to being in control.

But in his hands, she was weak. And she didn't even mind it.

His lips touched hers and fogged her mind. Perfection, perhaps more so because they weren't perfect themselves. The only difference was that Rhea's wounds were visible for all the world to see.

Saras' touch burned into her skin. She felt it more keenly on the grazes and cuts hadn't yet fully healed. Bittersweet pain. She wished it would never stop.

"Love me," she begged.

Saras grabbed her neck and pushed her firmly against the wall.

"Trust me?" he asked.

She nodded, though her knees grew weak.

"I asked if you trust me," he repeated himself.

"Yes," Rhea whispered, confirming her submission to him.

His grip on her tightened, but not enough to hurt her. He kissed her helpless lips and pressed his hard body up against hers. She got the message loud and clear. This was what he had brought her here for. To take her in a place of beauty.

He moved with confidence and purpose as he diverted his kisses away from her lips and down the side of her neck.

This was a different side of him. There was no more doubt in his actions, no more hesitation in his voice. She'd seen glimpses of him like this when he'd flirted with her in the beginning. This wasn't Saras, the human. The dragon was in control now and he wanted just one thing.

Rhea.

Her body as well as her soul.

A fire awoke within her, which extinguished any reluctance of her own.

What they were about to do, out here in the cold of the highest balcony of Black Mountain, wasn't just unorthodox, it was forbidden.

That made it all the better.

In the face of this creature from another world, Rhea laughed at the concepts of decorum and propriety. Human constructs, as Saras might say. They did not have any use for either of them.

What their bodies needed was release. They deserved it.

His hands fumbled with her bodice, as hers undid his

belt. The cold winds that whistled around the tower just heightened Rhea's arousal.

Her nipples grew hard against his chest.

She was ready.

"Rhea, I need to know," Saras asked.

"Yes?"

"Will you be by my side, always?"

This wasn't a flirtation, his tone was dead serious.

Rhea could hardly breathe, such was the intensity of the moment. "I'm already yours," she spoke at last.

"Are you sure? There's no coming back from this," he said.

Rhea swallowed hard and nodded. She was ready for whatever he had in mind.

He found a sharp edged stone in the wall beside her, and in one smooth move swiped his hand across it to make a cut.

She'd seen too much blood lately, but this was different. A single drop emerged, so rich, almost luminescent in the fading light.

"Now you," he encouraged her.

Rhea followed his example, and made a cut in her own palm. Rhea flinched when Saras' hand first touched his. Blood against blood. Fingers intertwined. She expected not to feel anything much, but she did. His blood was hot, almost painfully so. An incredible power emanated from it.

A power that her body absorbed, sending her into a fresh high.

A Dragon's Treasure

Overwhelmed and incapacitated, Rhea was a mere spectator as Saras showered her with further affections. He kept a tight grip on her hand, raising her arm above her head as he covered her upper body with kisses. But he didn't intend to stop at just that.

With his left hand, he started to explore her further. Rhea gasped with pleasure as he touched her most intimate parts.

Her head was spinning and her knees buckled underneath her. But that did neither discourage nor disturb her lover.

He simply lifted her up and guided her legs around his waist. When he entered her, Rhea all but lost her senses in the fog of desire.

There was nothing to say, nothing to do, except to act on instinct.

To allow their most primal impulses to take the lead and simply enjoy the ride.

He took her on the balcony, thrusting into her as the last rays of light vanished behind the horizon.

But he was not easily sated, and neither was she. Their bodies craved more.

Faster and faster he moved, feverishly so.

Rhea's body was taken over by even more sensations she'd never experienced before. Pleasure, bordering on pain. Like an itch impossible to scratch. Every thrust of his came closer and closer.

It felt so good, and yet so inadequate.

"More," she gasped.

The rough stone wall scraped against her backside with every movement, which only intensified her pleasure. With her arm tightly clinging to his shoulder, she angled her hips upward to receive him better.

That made all the difference, to her as well as him.

They were one now. Two bodies, one soul.

Deeper and deeper he penetrated her, finally able to reach that spot that had felt so elusive before. Harder and faster, building up to a manic pace.

It had felt so good before already, but now it blew her mind. Every little scratch added up to all those that came before, her body filling with sweet energy, desperate to burst free.

From her lower abdomen to her fingertips, the top of her head down to her toes. Rhea could no longer contain it, and cried out loudly into the darkness.

Saras joined in, his primal roar echoed against the castle walls like thunder.

They had reached their destination. Their love made flesh.

Tears ran down Rhea's face, but in between failed attempts to catch her breath, she couldn't stop smiling.

She shook and quivered with the aftershocks of her release. Steam rose from both their sweaty bodies.

Saras finally let go of her hand as he caught his breath too.

A Dragon's Treasure

Rhea instinctively checked her palm. She was accustomed to fast healing, but what she saw still shocked her. The cut had entirely vanished. It hadn't even left the slightest mark.

"Interesting," she mumbled.

Saras smiled knowingly and wrapped both his arms around her to carry her inside.

The room inside the tower was basic, but that didn't matter. The most important thing was there: a bed.

Saras lay her down on top of the sheets and just looked at her for a moment.

"You know you saved me, right?" he said.

Rhea sighed and closed her eyes. "Come lie with me."

He positioned himself beside her and placed one arm protectively across her chest. Then he rested his head against her shoulder.

They had broken the rules together. Their bodily union should have only taken place after marriage. But it hadn't *felt* wrong. In fact, it felt like the only right thing in the whole world right now.

Partners in crime.

The formalities would follow. They were only a confirmation of everything they already knew.

She couldn't explain why, but somehow Rhea felt powerful, almost invincible now. The fog had lifted. What had seemed so very important earlier in the day no longer mattered.

Her job, Broc's approval—all those things had faded into the background.

Rhea was overcome with a clarity she hadn't felt before. Like all the pieces of the puzzle were finally matching up.

Together, they'd figure out everything. How to defeat the Sea Folk, and keep the Black Isles safe once and for all.

It seemed so easy now.

CHAPTER FOURTEEN

heir love had reached its peak. No longer were they two separate entities, floating through life alone.

She'd given herself to him, as he had given himself to her.

This proud woman, who had never played second fiddle to any man, had submitted to him. He didn't take it lightly, old-fashioned as he was.

That was why he had taken the Blood Bond with her, before crossing any boundaries. Only once their union was formalized had he taken the next step. And what a step it had been.

To come together with a singular focus of pleasure, it truly was magic. As he'd already suspected before, love made the world turn. And now he no longer had to walk this earth alone.

Unfortunately for him, that had unintended implications.

They couldn't stay up there in the tower forever. Despite Rhea's outburst in his cell, she was still general. She had responsibilities that stretched beyond just keeping him company. He did not begrudge her that. Now that they had bonded, there was no need to rush anymore.

When Rhea first mentioned it, Saras had no intention of attending the festivities. But after she left, his mind hadn't allowed him any rest.

In her presence, he'd felt a calm he hadn't known all his life. As they lay on that bed together, in between the pillow talk, he'd even enjoyed a peaceful, dreamless nap.

But once she was gone, he was as lost as ever.

He craved her company so much he had no other choice but to go down there. His vow to stay in the dungeons by himself forever was but a distant memory. Everything had changed the moment she had given herself to him.

The consummation of their love had sealed their bond forever. He was no longer Saras, the tragic lone dragon, but part of a new order. His darker side had been pacified, his madness somewhat cured. He would follow her to the end of the earth if he had to.

Tonight, he only had to follow her to the feast. That was hardly as grand a sacrifice as it had initially felt like to him. Still, he struggled with doubts on his way down from the tower. But the closer he got, the faster and more determined his steps became.

The feast had already begun when Saras entered the Great Hall. It was a lavish spread, especially considering the hardships the people of Black Isle had been through these last few days. Still, they did not miss the opportunity for a party. Something to learn from, perhaps?

Saras found an empty seat near the doors from where he could see her. His Rhea sat next to the king. She was every bit as glorious here, surrounded by all these people as she had been naked in his arms.

In human form, he did not attract attention, for which he was grateful. In his true form, he was accustomed to people staring at him in horror, perhaps even fleeing from him. Luckily this was not the case now.

But his anonymity was short-lived.

"Saras!" Rhea called out from across the crowd.

He flinched instinctively as people turned to look at him.

How pitiful. He was a dragon. More powerful than anyone in this room. Older than the oldest of them, including the Elders. He had lived so many lifetimes, and he would live countless more. Why fear these creatures? Why shy away from them?

Flashes of fire filled his mind's eye. Glimpses of death and destruction. *No, stop it!*

He stood up, his heart beating so hard he could feel it in his throat. The smile on Rhea's face gave him strength. She was genuinely pleased to find him here.

"I am here," he spoke.

The Great Hall was quiet. Not even a whisper filled the air.

"I am Saras, the dragon."

Saras opened his eyes to look at his captive audience.

Scarred, weather-beaten faces stared back at him. Every one of them appeared older than he did, funnily enough.

The silence continued. Saras was unsure if it lasted only

seconds or even hours.

Finally one man stood, his chalice raised high in the air.

"I was facing off against two of the enemy. They had me cornered. My weapon had blunted, and my arms were aching with exhaustion. If they hadn't retreated, I would not be among you today."

Saras blinked and cocked his head to the side. Not the welcome he had expected from this particular crowd.

"I raise a toast to you, my friend. Saras, the dragon. For saving my life."

The crowd roared.

Another man stood up. His right shoulder and arm were bright red and inflamed. Burn wounds. Saras could hardly bear to look at him.

"I lost my brother in the battle. Your fire burned the Sea Folk scum that took his life. To Saras, the dragon!"

Tears stung the corner of his eye, but Saras did not turn away from them. He had to take it all in, every moment of it. The tide was turning.

At the far end of the hall, Rhea raised her chalice too. "The enemy had me tied up. They would have taken me prisoner and I would have never seen these isles again if it wasn't for you. To Saras, the dragon!"

Beside her, King Broc stood too, with his drink in the air. "What use is a toast if his glass is empty? Someone, get our guest of honor some wine!" he demanded, then he turned solemn. "You may be from another time, one which even the oldest among us only know of through myth and legend. But we are all of these Isles, same as you. We are your brothers and sisters. And we welcome you into our midst."

Hearing these words and seeing them reflected in the faces of so many present here for this feast inspired a strange sensation in Saras' chest. Pride, perhaps? Or more likely, relief.

He never wanted to face these people; he'd feared their judgment.

All this time, he'd judged himself much more harshly than they felt the need to.

Rhea had been right, though he hadn't wanted to hear it at the time. They had lost so much during the battle that they were now eager to embrace a new face in their midst.

Indeed there was hope for him here, among these people.

Rhea gestured at him to join her at the main table. He did so, gladly accepting the full chalice of wine someone offered him along the way. Some others thanked him directly as he walked past them. Yet others greeted him with a pat on the back.

How trusting these people were. His terrible powers seemed to leave them unfazed. Perhaps it was the wine they had imbibed already, adding to their courage.

As he took his seat, almost everyone was once again focused on the feast itself rather than his presence here. Saras took a moment to scan his new surroundings. Seated beside Rhea, who in turn sat next to the king, he truly was in the middle of the action now.

Another familiar face smiled at him from across the table. Queen Kelly, who had visited him with Rhea at the moment he'd woken up for the first time.

Welcome, Saras. Her voice filled his head.

You... Rhea said you're a witch, so this is your power? He wondered.

Kelly grinned wider, but still did not speak aloud.

I might not be a fighter like everyone else here, but it's not a bad talent to have.

Saras smiled back at her. The last time this had happened, he'd thought he'd lost his mind.

So it was you who guided me during the battle?

Couldn't let our general get captured by the enemy, could I?

That was something the two of them could easily agree on.

I never realized the two of you were friends, Saras wondered.

It's a work in progress. She's starting to grow on me. Kelly raised her cup in his direction, a gesture which he reciprocated.

"You're very quiet. What's on your mind?" Rhea asked.

Saras stopped looking in Kelly's direction and instead focused again on the only reason he was here today. He would have still been hiding in his cell if it wasn't for Rhea. "Oh, nothing. Just glad to be here."

"Told you so."

Outspoken as ever. Saras had to chuckle. As much as

he'd dreaded this moment, now he *was* happy to have emerged. Feasts in the Great Hall, like the olden days. The Great Hall might look different after the renovation his actions had inspired all those years ago, but the ritual was much the same.

What about the stories, and songs? Would he know any of them, or had those changed too?

Sure enough, a gruff looking man emerged from the crowd and started tapping his hand rhythmically on the table. Others joined in, stomping their boots on the ground, and banging cutlery against their cups.

"Don't know many songs 'bout dragons, but I dedicate this one to you, Saras!" the man said.

He hummed the starting notes of a tune Saras had never heard before. Then, he began to sing.

"Down below the mountain, in a cell deeper than deep,

A creature, fierce and powerful, blissfully asleep.

He must not be awoken, unless the need is dire,

For if he is roused, he will blanket the Isles in fire."

Saras glanced at Rhea, who looked horrified, making the entire situation even more comical. A song, dedicated to him? It was enough to wake his morbid sense of humor.

"Oh calm down," Saras whispered. "I think it's rather sweet."

Encouraged by the first singer, more of the crowd joined in, and soon everyone was singing and humming along as they repeated the same words over and over.

"I think it needs more verses," Saras remarked under his breath, as even he was tapping along with his foot. "I'd better start work on that. Now that I'm back in this world, I'll have plenty of time for it."

Rhea smiled back at him. "That's an excellent idea. It's not exactly accurate anymore."

"And I could use your help."

Rhea studied his face for a moment, before turning serious. "First I'd like your help with something."

Saras nodded. It was obvious what she was going to say. "The war. I know it's still hanging over all our heads."

"I've come up with a solution that doesn't involve fighting. A diplomatic approach. Would you be open to that?" Rhea asked.

Saras stared into her eyes. "I know it means a lot to you."

"It's my legacy."

How could he refuse? These people had opened their arms to him, and accepted him as one of their own. And from the start he took issue with having to fight. If her idea prevented a future invasion, it meant neither he nor anyone else on these isles would ever fight again.

"Yes. Of course," he said, then added in a lighter tone, "The good news is, now we have all the time in the world to do both!"

Rhea frowned. "What do you mean, all the time in the world?"

"That's how it works. A blood bond made in the heat

of passion has bound us together, for all eternity," Saras explained.

Her eyes widened as the meaning of his words sunk in. "You learn something new every day."

"Can't get rid of me that easily now," Saras remarked.

She let out a laugh; the sound made his heart sing with joy. He'd make it his mission to hear her laughter every day going forward.

Saras sunk back into his seat, watching and listening with a smile on his face as the citizens of Black Mountain continued to sing and even dance. Some tunes he knew, others were unfamiliar, but it was still a pleasure to behold.

No longer was he hiding. After a thousand years of torment, he was back at last. With a woman by his side who accepted him for what he was.

This truly would be the age of the dragon.

In her moment of clarity before the feast, Rhea had formulated a plan. A way to secure a peace with the Sea Folk that would last.

Broc had grudgingly agreed, and even Saras was ready to play along.

Rather than attack the Sea Folk in their own homeland, they would negotiate a new truce.

The enemy had retreated after Saras joined the fight, so they clearly did not think they could beat a dragon in combat. Not without suffering terrible losses.

The answer was so simple, so obvious, Rhea couldn't believe she hadn't thought of it before.

Saras' presence was needed. Not to attack, but only to threaten.

They would travel deep into enemy territory, just to show that they could. And then they would show mercy—something the Sea Folk themselves seemed incapable of.

Then, Rhea would tell them the truth about Teaq and their princess. This was the part of her plan that Broc had been most skeptical about. But the enemy knew already, or at least suspected it, and that was why her approach would help pacify them.

She had a simple offer for them. Stop using the princess' disappearance as an excuse to attack her people, or feel the dragon's wrath.

It was a bluff, of course, but the enemy didn't know that.

More than brute force, it was this sort of diplomacy that would help their people. This was what a general was supposed to do, rather than blindly lead people to their deaths against an unbeatable enemy.

She had learned so much over the past couple of days. She had experienced loss, regret, and guilt, as well as hope and of course, love.

She had learned that in one moment with Saras, her entire reality had changed.

No longer was she mortal, but as his consort, she was like him now. That truth had not yet fully sunk in, even though she'd felt the change in herself after they'd bonded. That sense of invincibility and power, it was unmistakable.

Time would take on a different meaning going forward. But she was still sufficiently attached to her old life to know that the Isles did not have that much time unless something was done soon.

And so, Rhea and Saras were up early the next day.

"Ready?" she asked, looking over at Saras, who was already standing by the window looking over the east.

"It's been a thousand years since I've seen a sunrise, do you know that?" he asked.

Rhea joined him and took in the view. This was the best spot in the entire castle, she had to give him that.

"Both of us will see a thousand more, apparently." She took in the beauty of it all. How long would it take for her to get used to the idea of eternity? Probably, a very, very long time.

Saras turned and smiled at her. "True. But first, there's a job to do."

Rhea nodded. "Yes, the sooner it's finished…"

"…the sooner we can truly start our life together," Saras said.

Rhea smiled and took his hand. She had no idea what exactly that meant, or what he had planned, but that was fine.

It was going to be a great adventure either way. And if she had learned one life lesson along the way, it was that she didn't always need to be in control of everything in order to enjoy it.

***

The Warlocks Conquest

PROLOGUE

---◆---

Once in every eight springs, a girl will be put forth by one of the

coastal regions. A peace offering, a condition of the truce between the

Giant Warriors of Black Isle and the men of the mainland.

1. No one shall remain with the offering when the time comes.

2. None shall attempt to lay eyes on or follow the giants.

3. No girl shall ever come home, or her village shall feel the giants'

wrath.

By this ritual we are bound, so long as our truce may last.

Ferris was free, at least for the moment. After a long nine months at sea, the solid ground underneath his feet gave him a spring in his step he hadn't had in a while.

How he had looked forward to this moment. He'd held onto the fantasy of his return through every storm. Or whenever the work threatened to overwhelm him.

Home at last.

Ferris whistled a cheerful tune as he walked through the village where he had grown up. Of course, his home was still a little distance away on the outskirts of the main settlement, but he could have crossed entire mountain ranges if he had to. Such was his excitement.

"Afternoon," he greeted some of the villagers gathered in the square. These faces had just been a distant memory to him while he'd been away…. The butcher and his wife, the tanner and some younger boys who worked as farm hands stood by in silence as he passed them.

Ferris shrugged and carried on. The villagers had never been too friendly with him or his sister, Kelly, especially since their mother had passed. Things hadn't changed much upon his return, it seemed.

Though *he* had changed a bit; his time at sea had hardened him. Whereas a younger him would have been hurt by their rejection, it no longer mattered to him now. They weren't who he had come back to meet.

As he continued up the path that snaked along the dunes surrounding his family home, he took one final look back. More people had gathered in the square. The news of his arrival was spreading fast.

Ferris chuckled. No matter how quickly gossip spread in this small hamlet, his arrival would still come as a surprise to Kelly. And hers was the face he was most excited to see.

There it was in the distance; the modest home he and Kelly had grown up in. It was smaller than he remembered. Just a little more battered by the elements. Just a little shabbier than it used to be.

But it was still miles better than the accommodation on the merchant ships. Deckhands slept in any space they could find. In between cargo, on the floor. With the cats they'd brought onboard to control the mice and rats. They didn't even have enough blankets between them to keep warm on some nights.

But that was all over for now.

Ferris could hardly contain himself as he reached the front door. He didn't even announce himself as he pushed it open.

But there was nobody inside. He turned around and scanned the fields. Perhaps Kelly was busy out there somewhere, though he hadn't seen her on his way up to the house.

"Kelly?" he called out.

No response.

He checked the inside again. There was something different about the place. The changes were subtle. It was much emptier than he remembered, almost desolate.

No pot of stew bubbling away. The fireplace was cold, as though it hadn't been lit in a while. The baskets where Kelly normally stored the family's supply of potatoes and onions were empty.

"Kelly!" Ferris shouted again. "Father?"

Nobody replied.

It was as though no one lived here anymore. Now, he noticed the dust. The table, the chairs; every last surface was covered under a layer of the stuff.

Ferris dropped the small bundle of his belongings on the floor and ran all the way back down the path. The villagers might not like him, or his family, but they owed him some answers.

What on earth had happened during these nine months he'd been away?

Where was his family?

Slumped on one of the chairs of the local tavern, Ferris couldn't do much more than shake his head.

It had taken some time, as well as of threats of violence, to get some of the villagers to open up. The news was worse than he could have imagined.

Kelly had been taken away to the Black Isles by the giants.

He'd been aware of the lottery, of course. Every eight years a village girl had to go. But he never imagined Kelly would get chosen.

What were the chances? He didn't even know this past spring it had been West Hythe's turn to provide an offering.

"How could he let this happen?" Ferris muttered to himself. "And where the hell has *he* gone?"

"Your what?" the bar girl quipped. "Oh, your old man. Don't let it bother ya too much. Mine's run off somewhere too. They get to a certain age and lose their minds. Drinking and gambling is all they can think about. Another?"

She held up the pitcher of ale in Ferris' direction.

He shook his head. "I don't think so."

He picked up the crude stoneware mug and emptied it with one final swig.

As he tried to get up from his seat, he could feel the buzz of the ale starting to hit him, forcing him back down.

But it had done nothing to numb the shock. Kelly was gone. More than one of the people he'd spoken to had tried to hint that she was probably dead by now. Apparently, he shouldn't dwell on the past. Easy for them to say. Kelly wasn't their family, she was his.

And she couldn't be dead.

He wouldn't accept it.

"I won't have it. I won't stand for this."

Ferris balled his fist and slammed it down onto the table. A dull ache pierced his arm all the way up to his elbow. He flexed his fingers a few times, but the pain still remained.

"Now, now. You break the furniture, you pay for it," the girl said.

Ferris shook his head. *Whatever.*

But what was he going to *do* about all this? Would he sail to the Black Isles himself and bring Kelly back? How ridiculous. He was barely eighteen, and although he was tall, he did not have the muscle to match. Plus, they were giants. He would be no match for them.

Nobody in living memory had ever laid eyes on one of them. It wasn't worth the risk, as staying and watching them take away their offering every eight years was punishable by death. But the legends had to be based in truth.

Warriors, they were.

Whereas he was a deckhand.

There was no way he could take the fight to them, at least not now and not on his own.

But he'd-

"In fact, you'd better pay for that ale now as well," the girl interrupted his thoughts.

"What?" Ferris asked.

She pointed down at his empty mug. "How do I know you're good for it, huh?"

Ferris made a face and clumsily checked his pockets for a few coins. He threw them on the table.

"Will that do?" he snapped.

"Thank you very much indeed, sir." The girl smiled as she gathered up the money.

There went a significant portion of his earnings from his time at sea.

But Ferris was least concerned.

He had to think of a way to get Kelly back. Because no matter what anyone said, she was still alive. He could feel it, right there in his chest.

He would have his revenge. This he vowed to himself. Ferris would work day and night to acquire the necessary skills to be able to fight for her honor and her life. If it was the last and only thing he did with his life.

Everyone and everything else could go to hell.

The Warlock's Conquest

Kelly, hang in there. I'm coming for you.

This was the one and only thing on his mind as he stumbled through the village, back to his now empty home.

CHAPTER ONE

*** Almost seven years later ***

A morning like any other, Eryn was readying herself for her shift. She strapped the rigid leather armor across her chest and tightened a pair of matching cuffs around her wrists. Of course, she'd have to discard these items and more, if she took to the skies in her eagle form. But for time spent on ground, she had come to enjoy dressing like this.

Like a uniform, these items gave her a certain confidence, an air of authority.

For seven years she had performed her duties on Black Mountain under General Rhea's leadership. Ever since Rhea had first enlisted her and the other eagles following the first Sea Folk invasion, she had barely spent a day away from her post.

Luckily the Isles had been at peace for the majority of this period, thanks to the truce that had been negotiated with the enemy under the seas. As a result, these Isles had become a different place than the one she had grown up in. Their peace wasn't so fragile anymore.

The people of Black Isle were flourishing now that they did not have to spend every waking hour preparing for a fight. But while some of the other eagles had gone back home, Eryn had stayed on Black Mountain. She hadn't allowed herself to become complacent.

She'd learned to fight, especially with bow and arrow.

She'd learned to read under Uri the Elder's tutelage, and loved nothing more than to spend time in the library, studying up on strategy and science alike.

No longer the simple farm girl she had grown up as, Eryn was now a fully-fledged member of Rhea's army and often acted as Rhea's right-hand woman. And there was no point in wasting these hard-earned talents by tending her parents' land. Plenty of people could do that in her stead.

Eryn had come to enjoy her duties, so it was with a spring in her step that she joined Yorrick, head of the Castle Guard on the fortifications surrounding the castle.

"Morning. Anything to report?" Eryn asked.

"All quiet. Just as quiet as yesterday and the day before."

Eryn stole a glance in his direction. She couldn't tell if he thought that was a good or a bad thing.

"Better than the alternative," Eryn remarked.

"Sure."

Eryn shrugged. He was a man of few words, and seemingly even fewer emotions, which was fine by her. These qualities made him easy company while on duty.

She made her way back down the fortified wall and headed toward the armory. The lookout squad was already assembled inside. All of them were eagles like her, but in many ways they were not alike at all.

There was a reason she had emerged as their leader.

"Ready?" she asked.

They shrugged and grumbled words of reluctant agreement. This was just a chore to them, a job like any other. Like cogs in a machine, they seemed unaware of the bigger picture. Of just how important their role was in the overall defense of these lands.

Still, they turned up every day and did as they were told, so there was no real reason to complain.

"You know the drill. Immediately let me know if you see anything out of the ordinary."

"What's the point? Nothing ever happens," one of the younger males complained.

"Be grateful for that, as long as it lasts. If you don't remember for yourself, ask your elders what happened the last time we were attacked," Eryn snapped.

The boy responded with nothing but a silent stare.

He was somewhat right, of course. Nothing had happened in all these years. Eryn could only hope their peace would remain.

She watched them leave in clusters of two or three, and followed the last group. Eryn was still on their heels as the lookouts made their way through the winding corridors of the castle toward the View Point, a high plateau that could be accessed from one of the turrets. High above the crashing waves surrounding the island, it was the ideal place for them to set off.

The Warlock's Conquest

One by one, each of the men and women threw themselves over the edge and transformed. Deafened by the high winds, Eryn could barely make out the sound of their feathered wings, flapping overhead as they circled once or twice before making off in opposing directions.

They all knew the drill. Where to patrol, how long for, and when to report back. She had trained them well, all things considered.

She paused for a moment, watching them get smaller and smaller before disappearing on the horizon, then she headed back inside.

On days such as these, with neither a hunting party nor Council meeting in the works, there was very little for her to do until her squad of lookouts returned. Yet she wasn't planning to stay idle. Instead she would spend this morning in the library with the Elders, as she had done so many times before.

No matter how much she read, she hungered for more. There was still a wealth of knowledge out there, if you were willing enough to seek it out.

———◆———

Ferris stood at the helm of his ship, with his hands planted squarely on his hips. The Black Isles were within view, though at this distance they were hardly more than a dark outline against the light gray skies. This was the closest he had been to Kelly in all these years.

After more than six years of preparation, the moment of reckoning was upon him. With King Harrold's support, he'd been able to mount his campaign. A ship and a group of men of his own were part of the deal.

On this very ship, he would bring Kelly back home.

For the rest of the fight, there was the full might of the King's navy to count on, which should not be far behind them.

Ferris had fought, cheated and stolen his way out of the simple circumstances he was born into. He'd understood quickly all those years ago that nothing in this world ever came easily.

A deckhand no longer, Ferris had chosen a different path for himself. One of blood and vengeance.

Getting ahead meant taking matters into his own hands. There were no handouts, especially not for outcasts like him. He wasn't proud of some of the things he'd done to get here. But his motivation was noble, and that was all that mattered now.

He'd done it all for Kelly.

Before long, he would fulfill his aim, and then he'd have all the time in the world to consider the rights and wrongs of it all.

"So, what's the plan then?" Duncan, the self-styled leader of Ferris' troupe of warriors asked. The scars across his face told of a life lived by the sword. He wouldn't have given Ferris even one shred of respect, if it wasn't for the coin he'd been paid, and even then, he had a mind of his own.

Money could buy anything nowadays, especially a small army. Every single one of the men on board this ship had a few things in common: They were all battle-hardened, and they would do almost anything for the right price.

But that wasn't to say that they were easy to deal with.

"We must assume they guard their territory. Therefore, we'll hide in plain sight, pretending to be fishermen," Ferris said. "Once the rest of the ships get here, that's when we'll make our move."

"We look like fishermen to you?" one of the other mercenaries quipped, exposing a toothless grin.

A roar of laughter erupted among the rest of the group, who had so far just stood by in silence.

Ferris straightened himself. He wasn't going to let any one of these men ruin this moment. They hadn't seen the worst of him yet.

He closed his eyes and focused his energy.

For but a moment, the skies darkened above the ship, and the low rumble of thunder could be heard. Most of the fighters shuffled around uncomfortably.

Ferris calmed himself before speaking. Suspicions and rumor were all well and good, but magic was one of the few things these men did fear. If he took things too far, they'd bolt and there would be nobody left to fight alongside him.

"You'd better be convincing, or we'll fail before we

even get close enough. And guess what, failure won't get you paid," Ferris warned. "Hide your weapons and armor, then cast nets out into the water!"

"Alright," Duncan grumbled, and nodded at the rest of the group.

Some muttered words of protest, but eventually everyone fell in line. Again, these were men who would do nearly anything for money.

Ferris watched them in silence as they got to work.

He had a plan, of course, but he wasn't going to share it with any of them, even Duncan. Over the years he had discovered talents that went far beyond summoning a few clouds up in the sky.

He had learned to separate his mind and body. If he found a suitable vessel to transport into, a flying animal perhaps, he could travel great distances seemingly without having moved at all.

If this ship could get him near enough, he would easily be able to reach the Black Isles, at least in spirit.

All he needed was another life form within view, ideally a bird, for his spirit to latch onto.

While he and his animal host gathered information about the enemy, his body would remain where it was on this ship, waiting for his return. And then….

He rubbed his hands together. He could already picture it. King Harrold would claim the victory as his own, but that hardly mattered to Ferris. It wasn't glory he was after.

It wasn't even the riches he had promised his men.

The Warlock's Conquest

Sweet revenge.

He would see the Isles reduced to mere ruins and take his sister home with him where she belonged. The giant warriors of Black Isle would not be allowed to tear apart another human family. He would make sure of it.

At the end of this fight, the treaty between the men of the mainland and the giants of Black Isle would end. The coming summer would mark a new era where no lottery would take place. No unsuspecting girl would be abandoned on the beaches of West Hythe, awaiting a fate worse than death as a human sacrifice to these barbarians.

Once the deck was cleared of any weaponry and other suspicious items, and the nets had been cast, Ferris retreated into his cabin and peered out of the porthole.

From there he would bide his time and wait for the right opportunity.

And sure enough, only a short while later, a small speck appeared on the horizon.

A bird.

Ferris squinted at it to get a better look. *Come closer!*

His spirit could not travel long distances from his body, so he still had to wait. Unfortunately, the animal did not approach the ship at all, but instead turned away.

Curious.

No matter, there were still many hours left in the day. Ferris was certain he'd get another chance. He had waited a long time to get here, what were a few hours more? The other ships weren't even within sight yet. He'd have plenty of time to infiltrate the Isles, locate Kelly, and get back, before anyone even found his empty body.

CHAPTER TWO

———◆———

"**E**ryn! Mistress Eryn!" a frantic voice called out to her.

She looked up from the large leather-bound volume in front of her. There stood the same new recruit whom she had reprimanded before shift. His shoulder-length hair was in a mess and his eyes wide as they darted back and forth between her and the Elders also present in the library. His breathing was labored, as though he'd been running before he got here.

"Yes?" she asked.

"Silence in the library," one of Eryn's white-haired reading companions snapped.

The boy hadn't even had the chance to answer her yet.

She made a calming gesture with her hand and got up from her seat. Eryn guided the boy out of the library and into the corridor, where Yorrick just happened to be passing by.

The latter stopped in his tracks when he spotted the two eagles.

"What's happened?" she asked the boy again.

"There's a ship, a human ship I reckon," he said.

Yorrick turned to face Eryn with a questioning look on his face. She shook her head and gestured at him to keep quiet.

"A human ship, where?" Eryn asked.

The young eagle tried to explain the directions, out of breath as he was.

"What were they doing?" Yorrick jumped in.

Eryn shot him a look of disapproval. The boy was already so confused, the last thing he needed was to be interrogated by two superiors instead of just one.

"I dunno, I mean there were nets and things. Perhaps they're fishing. But you don't see humans around these waters, do you? I mean, I've never seen any on previous shifts."

Eryn nodded. He was as yet inexperienced. He'd never accompanied a hunting party to the mainland even. Perhaps it was just the shock of seeing people other than their own kind that had gotten him so riled up.

"Thank you for letting me know. I'll take it from here," Eryn said as she turned toward Yorrick.

"Do we attack them? What do we do?" the boy asked.

She turned back momentarily.

"I said, I'll take it from here. If they're just fishermen, there is no need to panic."

He did not look convinced.

Neither did Yorrick, who slowly shook his head at her.

Eryn waited for a moment, but the boy did not move from her side.

"That will be all," she added in a firmer tone.

The young eagle nodded and hesitated for a moment before turning away. She had often wished for certain members of her squad to show more interest in their jobs, but right now she desired the opposite. This matter was not his concern.

"We need to call a Council meeting," Yorrick spoke under his breath.

"My thoughts exactly, but first I'm going to take a look for myself. Assess the threat."

Yorrick nodded.

"Don't be long. In the meantime, I'll get everyone assembled in the Great Hall," he said.

"Be careful."

"Of course." Eryn left him with a nod and raced to the View Point.

She leapt off the edge and closed her eyes as the wind started to carry her. She dove down the side of the castle wall to collect more speed, then straightened her path in the direction where the boy had supposedly seen the ship.

She was fast. It wouldn't take her long.

Indeed, she had only been flying for ten minutes or so when she saw the vessel bobbing in the waves ahead. The ship did not look typical for what she'd seen of human fishing boats during her excursions onto the mainland. But then again, the local villagers did not venture into these waters. They knew better.

Perhaps these were travelers from further away.

Nothing she saw down below alarmed her too much. The boy who first spotted them had clearly overreacted, inexperienced as he was.

She'd head back soon to report on this sighting, and get a couple of more senior members of her squad to keep an eye on things in the meantime. There seemed to be no immediate reason to panic. Planning an intervention didn't even occur to her.

Until....

The shock nearly threw Eryn out of the sky. Only thanks to her quick reflexes was she able to recover her trajectory. The pull on her from below was immense, and her thoughts became garbled for a moment. She was able to fight the strange sensation that had threatened to overcome her, but with great difficulty.

Something, or more precisely, someone was trying to affect Eryn.

Witchcraft.

Eryn was familiar with the feeling of having someone rummage around in your thoughts. Her training with Rhea had included several sessions with Queen Kelly, practicing her own magic on her.

This was something similar, and yet there were two very striking differences: She hadn't expected it and thus was unprepared. And this wasn't Queen Kelly, but a total stranger. A potential threat.

It was the violation more than anything that had panicked her so.

Helpless, vulnerable. No amount of combat training could help her in the face of such sorcery.

Still, she managed to collect herself somewhat and focus on her duty.

Who are you? Eryn thought.

She circled the sky above the human ship once more and peered down.

The men at work appeared to be fishermen indeed. Half a dozen or so were pulling in a net onto the deck. Others were sitting around just watching the goings on while enjoying a leisurely smoke.

Humans or islanders, some things were not so different after all. A fair number of them seemed to not take their jobs too seriously.

None paid her any attention. Why would they? The only way for her to take flight was to fully transform, so they had no way of knowing she wasn't just an ordinary bird.

Still, she was missing something. These simple-looking men hadn't caused the bizarre sensation she'd felt only moments ago.

But as she circled around once more, she felt a surge of energy and immediately peered down at the source.

Witch!

If she hadn't been looking specifically for it, she would have never noticed the pair of steely blue eyes staring up at her from a small porthole below deck. There he was, her intruder. But what was he trying to achieve?

The longer she looked at him, the more uneasy she

became. Her heart raced ever faster. Every instinct she had told her to run and let someone else deal with the problem.

But she didn't. She kept on staring into those mysterious eyes locked onto hers, trying to read their intent. Hidden behind his beauty was an unmistakable darkness. He was on his own mission, just as she was.

Danger.

Anger welled up inside her. These were no ordinary fishermen after all. There was a reason these humans had ventured so far into their territory, bringing their witchcraft with them.

Remembering her duty to her people, Eryn broke eye contact with the strange man and raced straight toward Black Mountain. Broc, Rhea, the Elders, everyone had to be informed immediately. They needed to mobilize the army.

For the first time in many years, they would have to gear up for a fight.

———— ✦ ————

Ferris' earlier assumption had been correct. After the first bird's sudden departure, another appeared relatively quickly.

It was a type of eagle and rather large too. Brown with white accents on its wings. You saw them sometimes on the mainland, especially around the White Cliff, though this was a particularly majestic specimen. He focused his energy again and readied himself for his bodily departure.

Although he'd left his physical form behind, his mind wasn't getting anywhere. No matter how hard he tried, he could not enter the animal. He looked down at himself and saw he was somewhere halfway between the ship and where he'd first seen the animal.

The eagle, meanwhile, had circled around the ship and came into view once more, then paused in his line of sight. It hovered high above the surface of the water, as though it was looking for something.

Ferris withdrew into his body again and realized what was going on. The eagle was staring down right into his eyes. A shiver traveled down the back of his neck.

How ridiculous. It was just an animal, after all.

Ferris shook off his unease and tried again as hard he could, this time with his eyes closed for extra focus. Usually the transition happened so quickly, he'd slip into his target within a split second. But not today.

His heart started pounding and the veins on the side of his head began to throb. The exertion was immense, and yet he was getting nowhere. Any more and his head might explode.

He exhaled and opened his eyes just in time to see the bird turn away and make a quick escape. It looked like it was fleeing something. As if it had noticed the attempted intrusion and become spooked.

Again, that was ridiculous.

Ferris looked down, trying to catch his breath. His knuckles had turned white; that was how hard he'd been holding on to the ledge of his cabin window.

He'd mastered this talent years ago, so why had he been unable to take over the eagle's body this time? This had never happened to him before.

He couldn't recall the last time he'd messed up a bodily departure. Sure, in the beginning he'd had trouble focusing. He'd sometimes ended up in the wrong animal, especially when practicing on a group of them at once. Birds in particular were one of the easier species, not like dogs or cats, which were much harder to control.

Still, he'd never been entirely unsuccessful. *Except*....

After mastering his skills on various birds and other creatures, he'd once attempted to take over a human body. The resistance he'd felt was immense. It had nearly knocked him out, as well as the villager on whom he had tried his magic. Afterwards, he was fatigued for days.

And so he had never attempted it again.

This failure reminded him of that old experiment gone wrong.

Ferris took a step back and sat down on his cot. It couldn't be, surely. Unless someone else, another warlock, had already transported themselves into that eagle.

Could it be that he was not alone? That there were others out there who possessed similar powers, perhaps on the Black Isles themselves?

For so long he'd assumed he was the only one of his kind. But it *was* possible that others possessed similar powers, wasn't it?

And if this assumption was correct, he had much more to worry about. The animal had turned around rather abruptly. Ferris had to assume that he wasn't the only one who felt something was off.

If another warlock had occupied that bird, he had to consider that his presence in these waters was no longer a secret. As convincing as their fishermen act had been, now the game was up.

The element of surprise he had banked on to make their incursion a success was gone.

Ferris startled into action and hurried onto the upper deck.

"Gather your weapons and gear up!" he shouted. "We are about to be discovered!"

As he watched his men jump into action and gather their swords and armor, Ferris could only hope for two things.

That King Harrold had kept his promise, and secondly, that his navy would reach these waters in time for the first battle.

CHAPTER THREE

E ryn burst through the doors of the Great Hall and found the Council already assembled, ready for the meeting to begin. Yorrick had kept his word.

"My King, we have a big problem," Eryn blurted out.

Broc, King of the Black Isles, waited in silence, while the Elders and Yorrick were engaged in hushed conversation.

Rhea rushed ahead and took Eryn aside.

"I wish you'd informed me before storming in here like this," she whispered.

Eryn averted her gaze. "I apologize, General Rhea, but there is no time to waste. We are under threat."

Yorrick looked up from his discussion and joined the two women.

"All this unfolded moments before I called the meeting," he said.

Rhea let her gaze pause on Yorrick for a moment, but then turned back to Eryn and gave her a nod. She was not pleased; the tense expression on her face made that very clear. Perhaps this was in part because Yorrick had been involved from the start, whereas she had so far been unaware.

But whether or not Rhea was happy about it did not matter. This *was* an emergency.

"Very well then," Rhea spoke more loudly this time. "Please tell us your findings."

Eryn cleared her throat.

"I don't know what, if anything, Yorrick has told you already. This morning one of my squad of lookouts spotted what appeared to be a human fishing boat in our waters."

"Well, that's something new," Saras, Rhea's mate spoke up.

Eryn frowned at him. This wasn't something to be smiling about. And what was he doing in this meeting? Saras was not a member of the Council as far as she knew.

"If only it were a fishing boat. Things are not how they appear. There's a witch on board. He tried to infiltrate my mind as I was circling the vessel to gather information about them, but I think I managed to fight him off, so he wouldn't have learned anything of value from me."

"A male witch is called a warlock, dear," Saras interrupted. He was still smiling, and Eryn was getting more and more annoyed with his casual attitude.

"Thank you, Saras. A warlock, then," Eryn snapped.

Just how Rhea could stand the dragon, she did not know. Love clearly made you stupid.

Broc stepped up and raised his hands. "This is no time for petty arguments. We need to take this seriously. A human vessel with a warlock on board is trying to get close to our territory. This has to be interpreted as a threat against us, and we should take action. Rhea?"

Finally, someone who understood the gravity of the situation.

Rhea gave Eryn a disapproving look. She hated to be out of the loop on this one. Again, Eryn did not let it bother her. She had done what she thought was right for the good of their people.

"My King, I think we should take action immediately," Rhea said. "I'll send a group of our best fighters out to capture the ship and all its occupants. We'll sort out if they're fishermen or not, once they're safely tucked away in our dungeons."

Eryn nodded. This was the best course of action, she had to agree.

"Anything to add, Uri?" Broc turned to face the leader of the Elders. "A prophecy to fit, perhaps?"

Uri turned a darker shade of red. "My King, I have nothing of that sort to report. But of course we'll study the matter as soon as this meeting is over."

Eryn looked around the room. Everyone, except for Saras, appeared to be taking the matter seriously. But there was someone missing in today's meeting, the one person whose input she would have loved to hear the most.

"Where's our Queen today?" Eryn asked.

Rhea shot her another disapproving look.

Broc turned to face her and folded his arms in front of his chest. "The queen's presence is not compulsory at every one of these meetings."

"Obviously not, my King, it's just that she is the only one on this island with firsthand experience of magic," Eryn spoke in a more apologetic tone. "It would have been good to get her input on this."

"I will inform her accordingly," Broc said. "But I think Rhea's men can manage to deal with a handful of fishermen and a rather untalented mind reader, without disturbing the queen at this time."

Eryn bit her lip and nodded, though she disagreed. She'd been able to resist the warlock's influence so far, but who knew what other magic he was capable of. Perhaps they ought to minimize the risk altogether. Perhaps....

"That will be all then. Rhea, I want your best men on board our fastest ship at the earliest. Capture the humans alive, if you can. And don't transform unless it's absolutely inevitable. Best we don't reveal all our secrets just yet."

Rhea nodded and turned on her heel, heading for the door. Eryn did her best to keep up.

"I really wish I'd known about this," Rhea grumbled as the two women marched through the hallway leading towards the armory.

"There wasn't any time."

"And what is it with Yorrick turning up everywhere, getting involved?" Rhea complained. "You steer clear of him, you hear me? It's obvious what he's trying to do."

"Oh?" Eryn frowned.

"He's trying to recruit you to the Castle Guard. It's so

obvious. But I need your full attention on our work here. We've had a good few years of peace, but it looks like those days are behind us now."

Eryn did not respond, just kept on walking half a step behind Rhea.

Just as they arrived in front of the armory, Rhea paused and turned around.

"Eryn, do you trust me?" she asked.

Eryn swallowed hard. "Yes. Yes, of course, General Rhea."

"Our King has given his orders, but I could tell you weren't satisfied."

Eryn pressed her lips together. Where was Rhea going with this?

"I'm going to send you along on this mission. But I want you to do something for me. Promise you won't speak a word of it to anyone."

"Anything you need, my General," Eryn's voice had turned into a whisper.

"You'll focus solely on the warlock. If you think he's a bigger threat than Broc assumes, you'll eliminate him, you hear me?"

Eryn was stunned to silence for a moment. Sure, she had thought the same during the Council Meeting. But to hear Rhea say it out loud....

"We can't risk bringing him onto Black Mountain," Eryn mumbled.

Rhea reached for Eryn's arm and gave it a squeeze. "So,

I can trust you with this?"

Eryn nodded. "You have my word."

"Right. Let's do this." Rhea turned and opened the armory door.

Inside, a handful of soldiers had already gathered for their afternoon shift. Poor bastards. Little did they know that today wasn't the quiet day they had been looking forward to.

Eryn took a deep breath as she followed Rhea inside.

"Guys, we have a development," Rhea started. "Moments earlier a human ship has been spotted in our waters. They appear to be fishermen, but that could be an act. We have orders to capture them."

Everyone present perked up immediately upon Rhea's announcement. There was not a whisper to be heard.

Eryn, meanwhile, shuffled restlessly from one foot to the other.

Rhea glanced at her for a moment, then focused once more on her men.

"We must assume they're a threat," Rhea said. "You'll go in fully geared up and ready for anything. But in *human* form, alright? Do not reveal your true nature!"

Eryn continued to hold her breath. Rhea had confided in her, but she hadn't told these soldiers what awaited them on that ship.

Rhea turned to face Eryn, her eyes softening slightly. "Eryn will be in charge of the humans' capture. These are your King's orders; capture them alive unless there's no other way. I'll be waiting here for your return."

"Let's go get us some humans," one of the more experienced soldiers spoke with glee.

"Remember, we want them alive," Rhea urged, then let her gaze settle on Eryn's before continuing. "Unless there's no other way."

Eryn nodded slowly. She couldn't fault Rhea's orders. They needed the humans alive, to figure out if more trouble was brewing. But the warlock…. He was a liability no matter what.

Still, the thought of what she had to do weighed heavily on Eryn's conscience. Sure, she was well trained and confident of her combat skills.

But she'd never taken a life before.

All Eryn could hope for was that the warlock would put up a fight and provoke her. In the heat of the moment, instinct took over. Only then would she not hesitate to do what had to be done.

Ferris stood at the helm of his ship once more.

But it wasn't an easy victory he was anticipating this time. If his predictions were correct, he had led them right into a trap. And their backup was nowhere within view yet.

"Up ahead!" one of his fighters shouted as they pointed

at something in the distance.

Ferris followed his line of sight and indeed spotted something on the horizon. It was hard to make out against the dark backdrop of the rocky Isles, but the closer it came, the more obvious it was.

An enemy ship. Sails flapped in the firm gusts battering this inhospitable sea.

Ferris breathed in deeply and tightened his grip on the butt of his sword until his knuckles showed white.

He'd proved himself a skilled fighter over the years, but would he be good enough when pitched against the giants? He would soon find out. Of course, he still had his hidden talents to help him if all else failed.

"Your orders?" Duncan's gruff voice interrupted his thoughts.

Ferris glanced at the man. "You're not scared, are you?"

Duncan scoffed and spat on the deck. "You forget, this isn't my first battle. If you're not sure how to handle it, I'll take over command."

How to handle it?

Duncan was right, Ferris had to step up be a leader now. It wasn't just their life at stake here, it was Kelly's as well. Her safety trumped everything. And he would be no good to her if he perished so early in the game.

"The royal navy cannot be far behind us. Best we save our strength for the next battle. You'll put up enough of a fight as to not make them suspicious, but our aim is to buy time," Ferris said.

Duncan frowned. "You mean for us to let ourselves be captured?"

"If it comes to that. By all means, if you're capable of an easy victory, go for it. But it's early days yet in this war. Don't fight to the death. We must live to win another day."

"They catch us, we'll be dead anyway!" another fighter complained. "I heard the giants eat children for breakfast!"

"You're not a child, are you?" Ferris snapped. "You're fighters, all of you. Survivors! If we make sure they don't kill us on the spot, they'll want to keep us and question us. That's what I would do if I found a foreign ship within my borders."

Duncan and Ferris shared a long, silent stare. In the end, the mercenary looked away to address his men. Ferris had won this leadership challenge at least.

"You heard the man," Duncan said. "Fight, but let them win without too much bloodshed. We'll be resting on the Black Isles tonight."

"Once the King's ships get here, we'll take advantage of the confusion and make our escape," Ferris added. "We'll attack them from the inside. We'll outnumber them! Our victory is inevitable!"

A reluctant whisper traveled the crowd. Most of the fighters looked skeptical. Still, nobody had the balls to argue aloud, neither with Ferris nor with Duncan.

"Your sacrifice will be handsomely rewarded!" Ferris said.

The Warlock's Conquest

The promise of money generally worked. Today was no different.

Most of the men visibly perked up and their earlier complaints were drowned out by the clanging of armor and weapons as they started to spread around the deck.

"Take cover, they might have archers," Duncan added.

Sure enough, by the time every last one of them had found a suitable hiding place, the first couple of arrows started to fly past. Warning shots.

Ferris tried to control his emotions and keep his mind clear. Accidentally summoning a thunderstorm would only draw unnecessary attention to himself. If an enemy warlock was indeed out there somewhere, he'd be wise not to expose himself too soon.

As the enemy ship stopped alongside his starboard side, he emerged from his cover, sword held high, and charged forward. He was determined put up a good show, just as he had ordered his soldiers-for-hire to do.

And he would have, if only the first enemy fighter to jump on board hadn't distracted him so.

CHAPTER FOUR

t was unmistakably him. Eryn was instantly mesmerized by the man's eyes.

This was the one who had attempted to read her mind as she had flown past the ship earlier, staring up at her from his cabin, assuming she wouldn't notice.

Only, she *had* noticed.

Now here he stood, his sword held high, circling her in a bid to evade the aim of her bow and arrow. He wouldn't be able to, of course. She was faster than any human. More accurate.

And she had orders to kill. All it took was one swift flick of her finger. The arrow would hit any body part of her choosing instantly.

Time seemed to stand still for her, as soldiers rushed past and clashed with the other humans. The latter were no match, of course. Every single one of her fighters had at least a foot or two on the feeble humans. But *her* opponent was different.

The warlock was unique.

He stood taller than his companions, with broad, muscular shoulders to match. They were about equally matched as far as height went. And he looked younger than the others, probably closer to her own age.

His blue eyes hid all sorts of sins.

But these superficial observations hadn't shaken Eryn. As physically impressive as he was for one of his breed, Eryn had been affected by a much deeper power.

It must be his magic, she thought. And yet she felt no sign of his presence in her own mind.

Strange.

All she could do was observe him, as though she was not truly in control of her body.

Then, the spell was broken by his first move. He charged ahead and swung at her with his sword, and instantly she snapped out of her trance.

She defended herself with her bow, whipping it around to break the impact of his weapon, then swiftly flung it over her shoulder and unsheathed a blade of her own.

They danced around each other, eyes locked on, taking turns to attack and defend. But his impact lacked strength. Were humans really that much weaker? Or was he as reluctant as she was to do real damage?

Where had her hesitation come from? She didn't have time for this!

Eryn bit her bottom lip as she swung around again. In this carefully orchestrated charade of a fight, it was her turn to strike. She'd had enough of the pretense and more importantly, she had orders to follow.

She raised her sword and aimed. He stepped aside to evade her attack, just as she suspected he'd do. In response, she changed direction mid-swing, found an opening, and brought the tip of her blade to a halt right at his throat.

It would be so easy to push a little harder and draw blood. So easy, and yet impossibly difficult. With a heavy heart she realized she couldn't finish it. She couldn't bring herself to kill him.

"You'd better drop that sword," she hissed.

The man did as he was told, but his expression was as calm as it had been all along. Like this wasn't a real fight, and he hadn't really been defeated.

"I surrender." As he spoke, the corner of his mouth curled up just slightly.

Was he smiling?

Eryn could not be sure. All she knew was that the longer she looked at his boyishly handsome face, the deeper she would sink. He'd given up so quickly, she couldn't even justify carrying out Rhea's demand here. Not in full view of her soldiers, who had been given clear orders to keep the prisoners alive.

So in a way, it was she who had lost this fight after all.

Rhea would be furious and rightly so. She was angry with herself.

A quick glance around revealed that most of the other humans had surrendered as well. If this was the sum total of the threat against the Isles, then they had nothing to worry about. As she looked back at her own prisoner, something shook Eryn to her core. His expression was so relaxed, it almost looked smug. There was something more coming.

She might regret capturing him alive before the day was over.

"Tie them up and stash them below deck, then we'll tow the entire ship back to Black Mountain," Eryn ordered. "Good fight, everyone!"

Her soldiers let out a loud cheer before getting to work and doing what she'd ordered. Eryn stood back and let someone else secure the ropes around the warlock's wrists.

There was something about him that she could not understand. She wasn't just apprehensive of his powers; it wasn't fear she felt.

Yet she dare not touch him. Or look him in the eye for too long.

Her heart was beating just a little too fast. Her breaths had become too shallow. If she didn't know any better, she thought it might be nerves. A funny tickle in the depths of her stomach made it hard for her to remain focused.

If she was in fact nervous, there was another, heavier feeling making things worse. A deep sadness had crept into her chest. It tore at her, and dragged her down.

It was only once he was completely out of sight that she could breathe a little more freely.

———◆———

ack on shore, everyone had a job to do. Every one of her fighters had one or two prisoners of their own to attend to, so Eryn couldn't palm the warlock off on anyone else.

She was stuck with him.

That same sick feeling she'd felt earlier on the human ship had crept over her again.

She kept him walking just slightly ahead of her, all the while scanning her surroundings. It had taken them a while to travel back to the harbor with the enemy ship in tow. The barren, windswept landscape looked almost ominous in the fading daylight.

It wasn't just his sight that had her confused. Even the scent of him had an effect on her. Like a kind of musk, it tried to conjure up feelings she had no use for. Eryn tried to keep her breaths shallow to avoid the worst of it.

Was this what failure felt like? She'd never disappointed Rhea before….

As much as she dreaded facing the General's judgment, it was nothing compared to the prospect of making eye contact with her prisoner again.

The journey up to Black Mountain from the harbor below felt a thousand times as long. Thankfully, he hadn't uttered a word since his capture. Not like the other prisoners, who had cursed and spat at their captors.

"Lower the Drawbridge. Prisoners coming through," she ordered in a firm voice. If only she felt as confident as she sounded.

The bridge shuddered and creaked into action. A dozen pairs of eyes were upon them.

She felt a thin layer of sweat collect on her brow.

Let them not notice!

As Rhea's right-hand woman, she couldn't afford a humiliation like this. *Do not show weakness in front of the outsider!*

Once inside, they were surrounded by guards. The familiar smells of home mingled with the invasive scent of the warlock. But that did nothing to lessen its effect, instead it made it worse.

Eryn and the others marched the prisoners down the cold stone steps into the dungeon. There were few cells, so they had to accommodate multiple humans in each one. But she'd lock up her prisoner alone in the farthest, darkest corner. Not that these precautions would help settle her nerves.

Earlier today, he'd tried to invade her mind. Now he had invaded her home.

She watched as the guards locked up. A number of rusty metal doors creaked in place, each secured with heavy bolts and padlocks.

Eryn turned on her heel and started to walk away. It took all the self-discipline she could muster not to break into a run, or better yet, simply fly off as fast as she could.

And still, with each passing step, she did not feel relief as expected. Instead, the burden of his presence weighed on her heavier as the distance between them grew.

Like a shroud of sadness, taking away the last spot of light in her heart.

No matter what happened with Rhea now, she knew she wouldn't find rest tonight. Not with *him* down here.

The confidence she'd felt only this morning had been wiped away. In its place, a crushing sense of doom.

She ought to extinguish it. Kill him, where he stood. The guards wouldn't even notice if she did it right; not until it was too late. But not without talking to Rhea first.

———◆———

So that was interesting. Interesting, and completely inexplicable.

Not only had Ferris allowed himself to be captured by a woman—and what a woman she was—there was something familiar about her. The look in her eyes suggested she'd recognized him too.

But for all his certainty, he could not place her at all. He'd traveled extensively over the years, but she was from the Black Isles. A so-called giant, though she wasn't any taller than he was. Still, she was formidable for a woman.

And her physique was unlike anything he'd seen before. Not like the girls he'd grown up with. Raw muscle, without any hint of softness or femininity that he could see.

Her lack of vulnerability did not make her any less appealing, though. Quite the opposite.

THE WARLOCK'S CONQUEST

She had locked him up all alone, without any of his men for company. He couldn't fault her for that. He would have done the same thing in her shoes. The last thing his captors needed was for him to orchestrate a revolt down here.

The cell was cold, inhospitable, and utterly dark. They'd taken everyone underground, so there were no windows. The air smelled musty and damp. Probably this place hadn't been in regular use.

His current situation complicated his escape plans. If only there was some animal around for him to take over. He'd at least be able to start looking for Kelly….

Still, there were upsides to being imprisoned alone. He would hear no complaints from his men. Ferris had only his own thoughts to keep himself company.

And by God, he had a lot to think about.

During their capture, he hadn't seen any sign of magic. The islanders hadn't needed it; with their superior strength and imposing physiques, they would have defeated his men with ease, even if they hadn't surrendered.

But there had to be another warlock around these lands somewhere. It was the only thing that could explain his baffling experience with the eagle.

And then there was the woman… She alone could occupy his thoughts for the rest of his natural life.

Ferris explored his cell by touch, running his hands along the smooth, cold walls. It wasn't very large; it didn't take him long to feel his way along the irregular shaped walls back to the rough metal door.

Locked . Of course it was.

The only hope of getting out of here was if someone opened it from the outside.

Ferris felt his way to the deepest part of his cell and lowered himself onto the ground. There was a rough cloth-like item on the ground, probably a jute sack of some sort. He sat on top of it and rested his back against the wall.

The cold started to creep into his skin. His fingertips and toes already started to numb. There was no point in fighting it. He'd conserve his energy and wait.

Until someone or something got him out of here.

CHAPTER FIVE

"I thought I could trust you to do the right thing," Rhea hissed.

Eryn kept her eyes fixed on the ground between the two of them. She'd messed up, and she knew it.

"He just surrendered. What was I going to do? Slit his throat in plain view of all the other soldiers?"

Rhea paced the room, as she often did when she was upset.

"Perhaps that would have been better than the mess we're in now. Now he's *here*, in our very home!"

Eryn sighed and shook her head. Rhea was right, of course. Nothing she said was anything Eryn hadn't already thought about. "It's not ideal. I also would have preferred if we hadn't brought him here. But the King's orders—"

"As you know I have great respect for our King, but in this instance, he's wrong. We mustn't underestimate the warlock's powers. We mustn't allow ourselves to become easy targets."

"Right." Eryn shuffled from one foot to the other.

"And the longer we leave him in the dungeon, the more chances he'll get to outwit us with his magic. So tonight, after the feast is over, you'll finish it. When I wake up in the morning, I want some good news."

"You mean…." Eryn bit her lip.

"Do I have to spell it out? You'll go down there at night. The guards will have had their fill of food and wine by then, so they'll have inevitably fallen asleep. And you kill him."

Eryn nodded and closed her eyes. It was the right call. To finish what she had been unable to on the ship earlier. "Yes, General Rhea."

Just how she was meant to fulfill Rhea's demands without drawing suspicions on herself, she had no idea.

"Good. Our fate lies quite literally in your hands."

"I won't let you down," Eryn whispered, even if she already had her doubts.

If she was entirely honest with herself, she knew that she could have killed him during their fight. But she hadn't the will, or perhaps even the courage.

Possibly he'd put a spell on her. And if that was the case, then nothing would stop him from doing it again tonight.

Still, Rhea wasn't in the mood for arguments, so Eryn kept her doubts to herself. With a bit of hope, the prisoner would be asleep and it would all be over soon.

She excused herself and made her way along the endless corridors of the castle towards the Great Hall, where many of the men had already assembled.

King Broc had arranged a hearty meal for all his fighters and everyone in the castle was invited. They were to celebrate the successful capture of the enemy ship.

The Warlock's Conquest

Wine and ale were flowing freely already. Morale was at an all-time high.

However, Eryn had nothing much to feel joyous about. All she could think about was the warlock, and what she had to do come nightfall.

The more she mulled it over, the sadder she felt. Either about the idea of killing him, or the possibility that she'd fail again.

Ferris had no idea how long he'd been locked up. He'd drifted in and out of sleep multiple times. Without any connection to the outside world, it was impossible to judge how much time had passed.

His eyes could not adjust to the darkness, so he didn't even know what his cell really looked like. All he knew was that he was alone.

Or he had been until a moment ago.

Ferris breathed in deeply, letting his other senses take over where his sight was failing him.

She was here. Her scent clung to the cold, damp air. Floral and fresh, like a flowering meadow in early summer.

He opened his eyes, still saw only darkness.

Should he say something? But what?

What could she possibly want?

Presumably he was about to find out.

A soft breath tickled his face, as ice cold steel pressed

up against his throat.

There it was. She had come for his life.

He didn't fear death, he simply regretted having failed Kelly. Still, there was a certain comfort in knowing how it all would end.

He waited with bated breath, but nothing happened. The blade started to warm up against his skin. Her shallow breaths continued to brush against his cheek.

It was a bittersweet sensation, feeling her presence so close. It hardly mattered if her aim was to end him, or perhaps that made it even sweeter.

Was that why she was dragging things out? Had she sensed his attraction and did she feel the same way?

Or was she waiting for his last words, perhaps? Maybe he was dreaming the whole thing.

"What...." Ferris' voice cracked. His throat had become dry. "What's the meaning of this?"

The pressure on the blade reduced, and suddenly, she lifted it off his throat.

"I have orders to kill you," the woman whispered.

Ferris nodded. "I understand. I deserve as much."

They were mortal enemies. He ought to want to kill her too, though he didn't, not really.

"But...."

"But?" he asked, then smiled briefly when he realized what she was trying to say. "You can't do it."

There was a soft shuffle nearby, as though the woman had sat down on the ground beside him.

"I can't do it," she said.

Although he hadn't been afraid to die, it was still a relief to hear her say that. He might complete his mission here yet. Had he found an unexpected ally in this woman, who had come to kill him and failed?

"That's awkward," he said.

"How so?" she asked.

"Well, it will be when you have to face whoever gave you the order."

"Right. Awkward." The woman sighed.

Encouraged by their unusual interaction so far, Ferris decided to ask her just what had been on his mind all along.

"Tell me, where have I seen you before?"

"What makes you think you have?" she asked.

Ferris smiled and shook his head. Of course she didn't make it easy. They never did. But he had to unravel this mystery, one way or another.

"I saw the way you looked at me. There was recognition in your eyes," he said.

Muffled voices on the other side of his cell door interrupted their conversation.

"Why is this unlocked?" another female voice spoke. "Open it! Show me who's in there!"

"Shit," his female companion cursed under her breath, then shuffled away from him.

The door creaked open, letting in a dim ray of light

which finally allowed Ferris to see the inside of his cell. There was nothing much to see. A dirty stone floor, the jute sack he'd been sitting on all this time, and solid walls made out of hewn granite.

There was no sign of the woman who'd kept him company so far, then again, the shadowy corner beside the door was still obscured in darkness.

But as soon as his new visitor appeared, Ferris forgot all about that, and rushed onto his feet.

"Kelly!" His voice cracked again as he called out to his sister.

The past six or so years had changed her. It wasn't just the strange clothes she was wearing, or the way she now kept her hair. He'd remembered her as a girl, and now she was unmistakably a woman. Still, he'd know her anywhere.

She was the motivation for everything he had done all these years. His sole reason for coming here.

"Oh, Ferris!" Kelly rushed toward him and threw her arms around his neck.

Ferris wrapped his arms tightly around Kelly's shoulders. To be reunited, after such a long time.

Had he lost his mind? Had all the events in his cell so far been part of an elaborate hallucination? Perhaps it was the enemy warlock, trying to break him. First with an attractive woman, now with a vision of his sister.

But it felt so real. If this was just an illusion, he couldn't resist its charm. Even her scent was as he remembered. As he buried his nose in Kelly's hair, he felt as though he'd come home.

"When they said they'd captured some mainlanders, I had no idea…. If I had known it was you, I would have come down here sooner!" Kelly said.

Tears were streaming down her face.

Ferris was overwhelmed by his own emotions. He'd dreamed about it for so long, about how their reunion would go. Never once did he consider a scenario quite like this.

It didn't matter, though. All that mattered was that they were together again.

"Ever since I found out you'd been picked in the lottery…. I've been working to get you back. But what was I going to do? I was a scrawny seventeen-year old with no combat skills. I'm so sorry I couldn't come look for you sooner!"

Kelly pulled back and looked at him with a smile on her face. "It's quite alright. I've been well taken care of here."

Ferris frowned. Was this the aim of the deception? To convince him she was happy here?

"What are you talking about? You were taken against your will, and made to live on this barren rock in the sea," he said.

Kelly let out a chuckle. "Yes, that's what it seemed like at the start, but really, it's not so bad. I'll have you know, I'm queen, now!"

Ferris opened his mouth in protest, but didn't get any words out. He stepped aside and peered at the as yet open door of his cell. A giant—roughly seven feet tall—stood guard. His impressive figure was somewhat marred by the sheepish expression on his face.

"Is that right?" Ferris wondered aloud.

"It's true. She's our queen," the guard mumbled, then turned away again and suppressed a yawn.

Just how this particular brand of magic worked, Ferris did not know. But assuming it was an illusion somehow made more sense than considering the alternative. That everything Kelly had told him so far was the truth.

———◆———

Eryn had listened in utter shock.

She never expected anyone to disturb her as she carried out Rhea's orders. The guards had all been asleep at their posts, just as predicted. Nobody had stirred even as Eryn unlocked the creaky door to the warlock's cell.

She'd waited for her eagle eyes to adjust to the darkness inside, and approached him directly with her weapon drawn. But at the last moment she faltered.

Another failure. Messing up was starting to become a habit of hers.

But to be caught unawares by the Queen, of all people?

Eryn did not know how to feel about it all. Brother and

sister. Two humans with magical powers, reunited on Black Mountain. That was a big coincidence, now that she thought about it. It actually made sense.

In hindsight, her failure was for the best. She would have been caught standing over his body, the Queen's brother's blood on her hands. Rhea's anger would pale in comparison to Kelly's, as well as Broc's wrath.

Perhaps her instincts had tried to tell her something when she faltered. Perhaps her subconscious had known somehow that he was off limits to her blade.

Eryn held her breath and silently slid her weapon back into its sheath. It was easy to slip past the two humans; they could barely see in this light anyway.

The guard, meanwhile was too busy rubbing the last remnants of sleep and booze out of his eyes, so he was easy to get by as well.

But coming up the narrow corridor leading to the other prisoners, there was yet another unexpected sight for Eryn to contend with.

"My King," she said, and averted her gaze as she hurried past him. A handful of frazzled guards waited further up the corridor. Their awakening had been rude, no doubt.

"What's the meaning of all this? Wait a moment, Eryn, you're not going anywhere!"

"Yes, my King," Eryn mumbled and stopped in her tracks.

She slowly turned around to face King Broc, but avoided direct eye contact with him.

"First, I find my dungeons unguarded, on the one night when they are fully occupied with enemy fighters. And then I find you sneaking around these corridors? What business did you have down here?"

Eryn bit her lip. She had to come up with something, quickly.

"General Rhea…. She thought the prisoners might have some insights to share," Eryn whispered.

"What's that? You came down here reeking of ale, in an effort to interrogate these men? At this hour?"

"I…. I'm only following orders," Eryn said. It sounded more pathetic now that she'd said it aloud, even if it was technically true.

That Rhea had ordered her to kill the prisoner, rather than interrogate him, was only a minor twist of the truth.

"Broc!" another voice called out.

"Now what in the world?" Broc said. "Kelly, what are *you* doing here, in your condition?"

Eryn's heart was hammering in her throat now.

"Stop bothering Eryn, dear. She was only here to accompany me. You'll never guess who I found!"

"There's someone *else* here?" Broc exclaimed. "Next you'll tell me the entire council of Elders has decided to spend the night in the dungeons as well!"

Kelly smiled brightly, then nodded at Eryn. "You're excused."

"Thank you, my Queen," Eryn mumbled. She breathed a sigh of relief as she rushed away, leaving the royal couple alone. This discussion was one they needed to have in private. Although grateful that the queen had covered for her, Eryn wanted no part of whatever came next.

Instead, she rushed straight up to Rhea's quarters to give her the latest.

CHAPTER SIX

erris couldn't believe what he had learned, even upon coming face to face with the man Kelly introduced as her husband of six years.

Broc Bearclaw, King of the Black Isles.

He could do little else but shake his head in disbelief.

And looking at the man, if you could call him that, it seemed he was as skeptical as Ferris himself.

"This is grand, isn't it? Reunited after all these years," Kelly said.

"Yes, it's wonderful," Ferris said, but his tone couldn't quite match her excitement.

"I can't wait for you to meet little Finlay," Kelly chatted on. "I'm sure he'll be thrilled to meet his human uncle."

"Wait, what?" Ferris and Broc spoke almost in unison.

"I don't think it would be wise bringing Finlay down here," Broc added.

Kelly shot him a disapproving look. "You're not seriously suggesting we leave my brother to rot in the dungeons?"

Ferris opened his mouth, then closed it again when he realized he had nothing useful to add.

"A strange and powerful magic," he mumbled to himself.

Broc turned to face him now, his arms folded across

his chest. "Indeed, let's talk about magic. So, you're a warlock, are you?"

Ferris met his stern gaze, which despite the giant's intentions did nothing to intimidate him. Since the topic was already broached, he'd better try to find out what he could. "I gather you have one of your own? A warlock, I mean?"

"What makes you think that?" Broc retorted.

The two men stared at each other in silence for a moment, their expressions as neutral as could be.

"Not a warlock, per se," Kelly interrupted.

Ferris cocked his head to the side and frowned. "*You?*"

She smiled knowingly. "I found out shortly after I reached here. Not too far from this cell, actually. It's a long story."

Broc cleared his throat. "I'm not sure this is the right time and place for this particular conversation."

"You're probably right," Kelly sighed, and placed her right hand on her lower abdomen. "In fact, why don't we retreat to more comfortable quarters?"

Broc stepped forward and placed his hand protectively on Kelly's shoulder. "Are you alright? Getting tired?"

She smiled up at him as they shared a look which made Ferris feel awkwardly out of place. Which, of course, he was. A third wheel, an unnecessary rescuer, invading what seemed to be a marriage unlike any he'd ever seen on the mainland.

He'd been wary of all he'd found here, and with good reason. But the revelation that Kelly also possessed magical powers had soothed his suspicions somewhat. They were of the same blood. It made sense.

And she'd have no reason to deceive him.

"I'm fine," Kelly said. "But let's get my brother settled in a slightly better room now. We have much to catch up on."

Perhaps she really *was* happy here. Queen of the Black Isles, mother to a royal heir. With a husband who might look like a scary brute, but seemed to truly care for her wellbeing.

Ferris' mind was already spinning with all he had learned, when a sudden realization nearly made his heart stop. The royal navy…. it was still on its way!

"There's something you should know." Ferris briefly glanced at Broc, then settled his gaze on Kelly instead.

"Yes?"

"I had no way of knowing before speaking to you, but I'm afraid I've made a huge mistake," Ferris said. If all he had seen here was correct, even that was an understatement.

"Just what are you saying?" Broc interjected.

"We surrendered easily, let ourselves get captured by your men," Ferris began. "Because this was just the beginning. King Harrold of the mainland has sent a whole fleet of ships. Once they arrive in these waters, that's when the fight for the Black Isles will truly begin."

"Oh no," Kelly mumbled. "How many men are we talking about?"

Broc's face turned a few shades darker, and his eyes narrowed. "An invasion. How far out?"

That's where Ferris' answers ran out. "I cannot be sure how far out. We saw no sign of them when your ship found us. And I don't have exact numbers, but he assured me before I set off that he'd send sufficient troops. Perhaps a thousand. The villagers of the mainland are sick of the lottery. They don't want to send anymore daughters off to their deaths."

Realizing what he'd just said, Ferris quickly corrected himself. "I mean, in their minds, that's what happens. Although the reality seems slightly more complex, looking at Kelly's position here. The point is, they want out of the treaty, and they'll fight tooth and nail to get their way."

"We must wake the Council," Kelly stammered.

Broc did not say a word, though his eyes spoke a thousand words, none of them kind or gentle.

Ferris was overcome with regret. He had no way of knowing what he would find here. Naturally he'd assumed the worst. In informing them, at least Broc could prepare his men, but things would get ugly, as they always did in war.

Just how many lives Ferris' mistake would claim, he could not predict.

"What if I try to call things off?" Ferris wondered

aloud. "If you release my men and me, and we return to the mainland and convince the King that an invasion is no longer necessary? Or perhaps I'll tell him he'll never win?"

"Do you think he'll be so easily convinced?" Kelly asked.

Broc shook his head. "No king worth his salt would give up so easily. He did not send out his navy on your word. He is doing it because he sees a chance at victory. And winning a battle against us will be worth more to him than your assurances, one way or another."

Ferris pressed his lips together. He hadn't made up his mind about whether he liked Broc yet. But he had to agree with his assessment.

"Let's talk to the Elders," Kelly said. "Perhaps they can come up with something better. Something that will actually help us."

Judging from his expression, Broc didn't like her suggestion either, but he chose not to argue. Most men Ferris knew wouldn't think twice about putting their wives in their place, no matter who was listening.

"At the very least we have to involve Rhea," Kelly urged.

"I'll call a Council meeting right now," Broc agreed.

Ferris stood by as Broc all but left the cell.

Kelly cleared her throat. "Darling, aren't you forgetting something?"

Broc stopped in his tracks and turned around slowly to study Ferris for a few silent moments.

"Very well...." Broc grumbled. "Guards!"

The same giant from before peeked inside again. "Yes, my King?"

"This prisoner is coming with us. And please, keep it quiet! I don't want the whole castle gossiping about it before I get a chance to inform the Council."

"As you wish, my King."

Ferris acknowledged the gesture with a nod.

"Do me a favor and take some rest, my dear? Now that everything is taken care of?" Broc addressed Kelly again.

"Yes, dear. Don't you worry about me. Not when you have a Council meeting coming up."

Ferris looked at her more carefully now, as much as the dim torch light allowed. Could he detect a slight flush in her cheeks? A curvier figure than he remembered? Perhaps the changes he'd first noticed in her weren't due to the years that had passed but for a more specific reason. And the remarks Broc had made.... Of course! She was with child!

A fresh wave of guilt welled up in his chest. An invasion couldn't come at a worse time. If Kelly, or her unborn child were harmed in any way.... How would he live with himself?

After Broc had left the two of them, Ferris failed to keep track of where Kelly was taking him.

She kept on talking to him, asking him things, but he could barely answer. His mind was working on just one problem right now: how to prevent the worst from happening.

How to keep Kelly and her new world safe from the harm he had unleashed upon them.

It killed him that he had no solution to that particular problem.

———◆———

As Eryn reached Rhea's quarters, she hesitated just for a moment. In the end, logic won out. Rhea needed to know what had happened, without any delay. Whether or not she'd be happy about it was secondary.

She knocked on the door and waited for any answer. Nothing.

Again, Eryn knocked louder, and called out as well. "General Rhea, I have news."

Finally, someone stirred inside.

"What could it possibly be, at this time of night?" a male voice complained.

"Shit," Eryn cursed under her breath.

Of course, Rhea wasn't alone. Her mate, Saras, was with her.

As awkward as that made things, there was no turning back for Eryn. Rhea had chided her once for being kept out of the loop. She wouldn't make the same mistake again.

No, but I keep on failing to follow through on Rhea's orders to kill the warlock, Eryn thought bitterly.

Even if it had turned out for the best under these current circumstances.

"I have important news for General Rhea. It cannot wait."

"Very well," Saras said, as he opened the door to reveal his immortality in full glory.

Eryn tried her best to keep her eyes to herself, but the dragon shifter had made that nearly impossible. Naked, save for a towel of sorts wrapped tightly around his most pertinent bits, Eryn began to understand just a little bit why Rhea accepted a lot of the dragon's nonsense.

He was something else. But as good-looking as he was, he had nothing on the warlock. Shit, had she actually just meant that?

"Uhm." Eryn cleared her throat. "Where is she? I mean, where's the General?"

Saras grinned at her and stepped aside. "Why don't you enter our humble quarters, my dear. And you'll find out for yourself."

"Eryn, it's quite alright. You can come in," Rhea called out from further inside the room. She looked much more respectable, standing beside the bed in her simple linen nightgown. No frills or lace for the General, Eryn observed.

Again, she tried not to stare, but her curiosity got the

better of her. The furnishings inside the room were an eclectic mix of old and new. Antique weaponry adorned the walls, which stood out starkly against the heavy, lavish drapes that surrounded the luxurious poster bed. It was obvious that the weapons had been Rhea's choice. And it was likely Saras who enjoyed a bit more opulence....

After a thousand years spent in the castle dungeons for whatever reason, Eryn couldn't fault him for that.

"Tell me you have good news?" Rhea's tone was gruff; it made Eryn flinch.

"Right. So, I went down into the dungeons," Eryn started, then shot a sideways look toward Saras.

"I know.... You were supposed to kill the warlock in his sleep. Just pretend I'm not here," Saras said.

Eryn glanced at Rhea again, who nodded and gestured at her to carry on.

Kind of hard to do, when you're so damn.... naked!

Not that Eryn was a prude. Transforming in and out of their human forms required the islanders to take off their clothing quite regularly. That much she was used to. But he was Rhea's mate, which made things awkward now.

Wonder what the warlock would look like. How different would he be?

Focus, Eryn!

"So, did you kill the bastard or not?" Rhea said.

Eryn averted her gaze. "No, but please hear me out."

From the corner of her eye, Eryn saw Rhea folding her arms across her chest.

Eryn took a deep breath. *Best get to the point!*

"I overheard a conversation between Kelly and him."

"What? Our lovely mortal queen, conspiring with the enemy?" Saras exclaimed. "Now things are getting *really* exciting."

"And what exactly was this conversation about?" Rhea asked.

"It turns out, she had a brother, back on the mainland. He came here to find her. They're siblings!" Eryn explained.

"The warlock and the witch." Saras rubbed his hands together. "Of course! It makes perfect sense. So, what were they talking about? Are they going to try and destroy us from within?"

Eryn rolled her eyes and shot him a nasty look. He might be the General's consort, but she didn't care anymore. He was starting to get on her nerves again, just like he had during the Council meeting earlier.

"Excuse him and his rather unusual sense of humor," Rhea remarked wryly.

"Well, sorry, but when you get to be over a thousand years old, very few things tend to excite you anymore," Saras said with a smile.

Eryn shook her head. "All I know is, the warlock is the queen's brother. The king arrived just as I was leaving, so he's aware of the situation. I don't know for sure what any of it means yet."

"Probably a good thing you didn't kill him, huh? That would have been awkward. *Oh, sorry, Queen Kelly, I didn't realize he was your brother!*" Saras' laughter echoed against the walls of the room.

For all the ridiculous things that had come out of his mouth so far, this was the first thing Eryn could agree with.

"And you, too, my dear. I'm pretty sure you'd have been sent to the dungeons for that. But don't worry. I would have waited for you," Saras said in a much gentler tone as the couple shared a look of understanding.

Just what it was they shared beyond sex, Eryn had no idea.

Maybe one day…. With the right man…. How I wish it could be the queen's brother.

This was hardly the time to think about all of that.

"So, how do we proceed?" Eryn interrupted her own illicit thoughts.

CHAPTER SEVEN

Although still plagued by guilt, Ferris was glad to spend a little time alone with Kelly before the inevitable Council meeting.

He followed her through the endless corridors of the castle. Even when he had managed to get an audience with King Harrold in *his* castle, he hadn't seen a structure as large and confusing as this one.

"How do you find your way around?" he wondered.

Kelly laughed. "That's what I thought when I first got here. You get used to it. And…. here we are!"

She gestured at him to be quiet and carefully opened the door. Ferris took a moment to let his eyes adjust. The light inside was dim, with only a small candle lit on a small table at the far side of the room.

There was a huge, empty bed toward the right of it, presumably for Kelly and her husband, and a much smaller cot toward the left. If Ferris held his breath, he could hear the deep breaths of a child, sleeping.

Kelly stepped inside to check on him. It was a beautiful sight. Her expression was full of love as she gazed down on the boy.

Ferris wanted nothing more than to see him too. Would he have her eyes? Her fiery red hair? But to disturb such careless bliss would be too cruel.

He joined his sister at the child's bedside. Kelly leaned over and was just about to touch the boy when Ferris stopped her, shaking his head.

"Don't wake him yet."

He was beautiful. Curly hair—Ferris couldn't make out the color in this light. Perfectly symmetrical features and a cute button nose. Like a little angel.

"Little Finlay," Ferris whispered.

Never in his wildest dreams had he expected anything like this. Not only was his sister happy with her supposed captors, she had a beautiful son now too, and another child on the way. And to think that he had worked for years to try to destroy these lands, when what they really needed was his protection.

He breathed in deeply, but a tear still stung in his eye. Regret. How familiar he was starting to become with that feeling.

Ferris balled his fists and tried to control his breathing to keep calm. He couldn't let anything bad happen to this little man. Not on his watch.

They continued to stand in the darkened room in silence, watching as the boy slept.

Would he ever know how it felt to have a son of his own? If these Isles by some miracle survived the threat from the mainland, only then would he have the chance to make that dream a reality.

Strange, how quickly things could change. For so many years his sole focus had been to get Kelly back. Only now that they were reunited and he'd met her family, as unconventional as it was, had the thought even crossed his mind. A family of his own. With a woman he could care for, just as Kelly's husband seemed to care for her.

A distant dream indeed.

A careful knock on the door interrupted their little moment with Finlay.

Kelly turned to him and whispered. "It must be time for the meeting. Will you join us?"

Ferris nodded.

———— ♦ ————

Ferris was still in turmoil when he was led into a great big hall, filled with impossibly large wooden benches and tables. Remnants of a feast adorned the tables. Empty plates and pitchers galore, with a couple of sleeping soldiers to boot.

He could only guess it was time for the so-called Council meeting. And apparently he had gone from prisoner to guest of honor in under an hour.

Kelly and he waited in silence as Broc ordered some men to clear out the drunken soldiers. What was about to be discussed wasn't meant for everyone. Only select eyes and ears would be allowed inside.

"Where is everyone else?" Broc demanded.

A few guards scurried about, then whispered something in response.

"Well, wake them up, then! Your King commands it!" Broc ordered.

Kelly walked up to him and rested her hand on his arm, which seemed to calm him down only slightly. These two had a very unusual dynamic indeed.

Once again, Ferris didn't just feel like he wasn't needed here, he was overcome with the same deep, dark regret he had felt watching Finlay sleep.

If only he had accepted Kelly's fate, like the villagers had tried to tell him all those years ago. If only he hadn't tried to mess with things he didn't understand. Then they wouldn't be in this situation now.

Calm down. Beating yourself up isn't going to do anyone any good, Kelly's voice said.

Ferris flinched and looked at her, then at Broc, and at her again. She hadn't said that aloud, had she? Nobody else seemed to have heard her.

Oh, is that not how your magic works? Kelly asked.

It was her, right there in his mind. The look in her eye confirmed as much.

No…. no it is not, Ferris thought. *You can read minds?*

Kelly smiled in response.

I wish I could read minds sometimes…. Ferris momentarily glanced at Broc again. *Can you read all their minds too? Anyone of your choosing?*

Kelly nodded briefly. *That's how it started out. By now, I can do a lot more than just that.*

Ferris couldn't believe it. He'd never met anyone else

with magical powers. So naturally, he'd assumed that his unique skills were the norm. To find out that different people could possess different ones.... Well it strangely made sense now that he thought about it.

What can you do? Kelly seemed to ask.

Ferris scanned the room for any sign of an animal so he could demonstrate. A cat, or perhaps a rodent, scurrying about in the scraps of food left behind on the floor. There were none.

I can leave my body for short periods of time and control animals.

Kelly frowned briefly. *What a curious power to have.*

It can be useful.

Their silent conversation was interrupted by the arrival of what Ferris presumed to be the rest of the Council. A handful of haggard-looking old men entered. They were still unnaturally tall like their younger counterparts, although their advanced age had shrunk them somewhat. Their long beards and thinning hair matched the gray of their ankle length cloaks.

Behind them, some more people arrived, men as well as women. Not a familiar face among them, until finally, the last to enter the hall and close the doors behind her.

That same woman. The one who had come to kill him in his cell.

They shared a quick stare of recognition, but neither said a word.

Instead, the woman tried to ignore him and joined

another, much sterner-looking female in leather armor and not much else in terms of clothing, toward the left of the King. The latter gave him a foul look. Presumably he had finally come face-to-face with the person who'd wanted him dead. His captor's commander.

What a strange society this was. Where his sister was queen, and women fought and led in battle alongside their male counterparts, seemingly as equals. Most mainlanders would scoff at the mere thought, but Ferris found it strangely enchanting.

"Finally! Let us begin," Broc said. "I've called you back so soon because we've had a new development. And you will have noticed that there's a new face amongst us."

Everyone's eyes were on him immediately, the woman he'd met already included. And for a moment, it was her gaze which made him forget why he was even here.

What the hell is he *doing here?* Eryn had a hard time keeping her eyes off the warlock.

Sure, he had turned out to be the queen's brother, but to see him here apparently attending a Council Meeting was still unexpected. Presence at these meetings was an honor bestowed on only select inhabitants of Black Mountain. Only the king's closest and most trusted men and women were chosen to attend.

Hell, it had taken Eryn years by Rhea's side to earn

herself a spot.

Royal privilege, she thought.

And worse still, he was looking at her. Still no sign of his presence in her mind, but what if he was just waiting for the right time to strike? His loyalties might have shifted now that he was reunited with his long-lost sister, but Eryn still feared what he might find in her thoughts.

Unspeakable things she couldn't even admit to herself.

Inappropriate glimpses that had entered her imagination since their first meeting, which had never truly gone away.

In a way it had been more bearable when she thought he was the enemy. She could've held onto the idea that sooner or later he'd be dead or banished, and she wouldn't have to deal with these feelings anymore.

If he was now their ally, that made things a million times worse.

He was gorgeous, though. And the way he looked at her made her weak in the knees.

How could she justify thinking that way of the queen's brother? She'd been born into simple circumstances. That she'd worked her way up under Rhea's guidance hardly mattered. She would never be worthy of him.

She only half listened to the King explain certain details she'd already overheard down in the dungeons, distracted as she was by her ever more complicated feelings towards Queen Kelly's brother.

"No offense to our Queen's judgment, but I would advise caution," Rhea's voice echoed around the room.

Eryn forced herself to listen now. If only she could stop *thinking* so much.

"I for one am not convinced we should be having this discussion…. openly." Rhea was once again displeased with how the King was handling things and she wasn't mincing her words this time.

"Hear, hear." Yorrick jumped to Rhea's support, which was unusual. The man rarely spoke much during these meetings.

Eryn stole a glance at Queen Kelly, who had placed her hands squarely on her hip in clear defiance of Rhea's remarks. Finally, some much needed distraction.

"Say what you will, but I know I can trust my own brother!"

"Sure, once upon a time. But how much has changed since the last time you saw one another?" Rhea argued.

"Time can change a person," Yorrick added.

Eryn glanced at him and noticed he was eying the warlock suspiciously.

Meanwhile, the two women stared each other down. This wasn't going to turn out into an altercation, was it? And just who would win such a fight? Rhea was physically superior, but magic trumped all.

"You seem to forget that I can read minds," the queen spoke defiantly.

"And you seem to forget that he has some powers of

his own. Perhaps he's been using them on us all already."

"Enough!" King Broc intervened. "I'll accept no more of this bickering. Whether or not he's trustworthy is secondary to the real issue at hand. He had nothing to gain from informing us about the incoming ships; all it does is help us. And we're unprepared!"

Eryn's heart skipped a beat. There was an attack brewing? Just how much of the king's earlier announcement had she missed while obsessing over the newcomer?

"Fine," Rhea said. "Let's assume the information is accurate for a moment."

"Thank you!" the king said.

"Can't he just call them off? He's their supposed leader, yes?" Rhea asked.

Eryn looked at the warlock again, and then back at the king and Rhea.

"He's simply an envoy to King Harrold of the Mainland," the queen explained.

"Does he not speak for himself?" Rhea asked. "What's your name, anyway?"

"Ferris. My name is Ferris," the warlock spoke up for the first time.

Eryn found herself mesmerized again. Such a strange name.

"My sister is right. I'm here under orders. Sure, I had a hand in organizing this excursion. But the King of the

Mainland would have never given me his blessings, or his support, if he didn't believe in the cause himself. The lottery is a sore point for many of our people and that's why they're willing to fight."

"Lottery?" Rhea frowned and turned to face King Broc.

"He means the Reaping. The mainlanders aren't happy giving up their daughters anymore," Kelly spoke up instead.

Everyone was quiet for a moment.

Eryn looked at them all one by one. Rhea, Yorrick, even the king; they all remained silent. Was no one going to voice the obvious?

"My King, my Queen, General Rhea," Eryn interrupted the silence.

"Yes?" Rhea snapped.

"Well, do we strictly *need* the Reaping ritual anymore?" Eryn asked. "If that's what's standing between our safety and a war we can't possibly win?"

"Nobody said we couldn't possibly win it," the King said.

Rhea looked at him sideways, as did Eryn. Perhaps not, but everyone was thinking exactly that.

Uri banged his staff onto the ground, attracting everyone's attention, and ran his hand through his long, thinning beard. "The Reaping exists for a reason. It was only through fresh stock that our people came back from the brink of extinction!"

Eryn nodded. "Right. Back in the day when our

numbers had dwindled so much, we were but a handful of families left. I've read the history. But our circumstances have changed since then. And if we lose this war, there will be no Reapings to help us recover. We'll be done for."

Again, everyone was silent. Even Uri did not argue further. Her logic was sound, wasn't it?

Eryn noticed Yorrick staring at her. Perhaps she could count on his support at least?

"Do you suggest we sit down with these mainlanders and offer them a deal right away? They'll sense our weakness and strike anyway," Rhea spoke up first.

Eryn opened her mouth to respond, but didn't get the chance.

Everyone assembled started talking over each other; the Elders in one corner, King Broc and Rhea in another, with Yorrick trying and failing to get a word in between.

The only people who didn't speak aloud were Kelly and her brother. But from the looks they were giving each other, Eryn was certain even they were having an animated exchange of their own.

She sunk down against one of the tables and stared at her feet. These arguments weren't going to get them anywhere. They had no way of knowing how much time they had left.

Eryn gave it one minute, even two, all the while shaking her head as she got angrier and angrier. Etiquette was all fine and well, but this ruckus was getting to her.

She couldn't take it any longer, picked up one of the empty earthenware pitchers from the table, and threw it with all her might into the floor, where it shattered into hundreds of pieces.

"Enough already!" she roared.

Everyone stopped talking. *Shit. Do I apologize?*

Eryn straightened herself. To hell with it. She didn't normally have a temper, but this was justified.

"While we're standing here debating about what not to do, our enemy is gearing up for battle!" she said. "Am I right?" she addressed only Ferris this time.

He nodded his head. "They're already on the way."

Eryn pointed at him and nodded as well. "There. So rather than get in our own way, we must prepare ourselves as well. If my idea was dumb, by all means let's come up with something better."

From the corner of her eye, Eryn thought she could detect the hint of a smile on Ferris' lips. It caused a flutter in her chest, which made her nervous all over again.

At least someone was pleased. Most of the others just looked frustrated.

She'd get to hear all about authority and respect from Rhea later. In all her years attending these meetings, never once had she even thought about doing something like this.

Perhaps she was just tired of being ordered around. Or perhaps she needed a proper crisis to come into her own.

"Eryn has a point," Rhea said after a long pause.

The rest of the Council seemed to slowly come around too. Or they were too stunned to argue.

"But we cannot capitulate from the outset," Rhea added. "One must always try to negotiate from a position of power, not one of weakness."

King Broc turned to her and nodded. "True, but how do you suggest we achieve that? If we engage them...." It seemed he didn't want to finish that sentence.

Silence, again. Until the most unlikely person in the room started to speak as well.

"That might be something I can help with," Ferris said.

Eryn swallowed hard upon looking at him again. How could he have such a profound effect on her? If it wasn't magic, then what was it?

CHAPTER EIGHT

erris hadn't doubted it when he first saw her, but this meeting had confirmed it. The woman, Eryn, had some guts. Almost everyone in attendance, except maybe the old men in cloaks, were her superiors. But rather than stand by in silence, she'd made her voice heard.

He was in awe.

But now that he'd come out in her support, he had to follow through and convince the others that he *could* be trusted.

"I don't know if you know this, but the mainlanders are a superstitious lot. Most fear the unknown more than anything," Ferris said.

The islanders nodded, with some hesitation.

"Kelly and I have powers that will send grown men running."

Kelly smiled at him. *Not just grown* men, *actually.*

Ferris frowned. *Tell me that story another time, sis.*

"Right, so you think the two of you alone can hold off a whole fleet of ships?" King Broc asked.

Not quite, it was actually a lot simpler than that. And so obvious, now that he thought about it.

"I can command the weather," Ferris announced.

A whisper traveled the room, but most of the giants

still looked confused at what he was trying to tell them.

"Well, that is to say, I can summon clouds, thunder, mist, that kind of thing," he added.

"Exactly how much cloud and such can you summon?" Rhea asked.

"Enough to hide Black Mountain from view?" Eryn interjected.

Ferris smiled and nodded. "Give me a few minutes and you won't see each other through the dense fog I'll conjure."

"We'll manage just fine," Rhea remarked. "But the humans won't see a thing!"

How's that? Ferris thought and glanced over at Kelly.

It's a long story. One for another day. She smiled. *Nice skill. Can you command lightning, too?*

How did you guess?

She smiled even wider now. *Let's just say perhaps that's where our powers overlap a little.*

Ferris looked around the room and found Eryn already staring at him. Earlier she had impressed him, and now it seemed he had gotten her attention too.

Oh, you like her! Kelly's voice echoed in his mind.

Stop it! Get out of my head!

When he looked at her again, he noticed Eryn was now embroiled in an animated discussion with Rhea. Their voices were hushed, so he could not make out what they were talking about.

"Very well," King Broc spoke up again. "It sounds like we have a plan."

For the first time since realizing his mistake, Ferris also felt a glimmer of hope. If he had brought this danger upon them all, it was only right that his powers should help their cause. It would take a significant amount of energy and focus to hide an entire island, but he was up for the challenge.

Failure was not an option.

"Rhea, you'll get our troops ready. We'll have archers positioned on the fortifications. Eryn's lookouts will start patrolling on overlapping shifts starting right now. Uri, if there's anything in the scriptures, anything that could help dealing with the mainlanders going forward.... But we won't negotiate just yet. Perhaps we can achieve victory without having to give up on the Reaping after all."

"Yes, my King," one of the old men replied.

The two women simply nodded in agreement.

"Get to work, everyone!" the king said.

Everyone moved into action.

That's it? Ferris had to wonder just how they were going to prepare for such a large threat with so little instruction on the king's part. And just how were they planning to fight effectively in zero visibility?

Ferris had all these questions and more, when he noticed Rhea taking the king aside for more hushed conversation. Perhaps a lot of the actual planning would take place behind closed doors. Away from him, just in case.

Fair enough. Just because he'd turned out to be Kelly's brother didn't mean they had to trust him immediately. He wouldn't, were the tables turned.

No matter how much he offered to help, this whole mess was still his fault.

The cloaked old men were starting to leave, as were most of the other attendees of the meeting. He positioned himself further away from Rhea and the king, leaving them to their secret conversation, while Kelly remained by her husband's side.

With nowhere to be and nothing to do, Ferris simply watched the activity around him, until Eryn tried to slip past him.

So much left unsaid between them.

He caught her by the arm. "Not so fast."

She gave him a stern look, then stared down at his hand on her arm.

"I have to get my lookout squad ready. You heard the king's orders. We're about to enter our first war in years, thanks to you," Eryn said.

Although her tone was flat and emotionless, her words still stung. She had voiced exactly what he'd been thinking all along.

Ferris looked away briefly, but he did not release his grip. They were about equally matched in height, but she was strong. A formidable fighter, as their first meeting had proved beyond a doubt. If she wanted to, she'd already have freed herself.

Still, there she stood, with her gaze fixed now on the empty space between them.

"I need to explain my actions. I need you to know that my intentions were pure," Ferris said. Just why he was telling her this, he wasn't sure.

What would she care about his motivations? If she paid him no attention at all, he could not blame her. Still, he cared what she thought of him.

And she seemed willing to listen. So, he continued.

"It was all for her, you see. Growing up, it was the two of us, ever since our mother passed away. Kelly and I. She took care of me when I was little. And when I came home from my first job at sea, she was gone. Just like that. I couldn't accept it. I owed it to her to get her home safely. It's all I've been thinking about all these years."

Eryn pressed her lips together and glanced up at him for the briefest of moments.

"You were trying to do the right thing for her."

"Yes."

"How could you know the truth? That she had made a place for herself here. A family."

"How indeed. On the mainland we know very little of these Isles and the people on them. Nothing but scary stories told around campfires. Rumors in the dark."

Eryn shrugged. "Sounds like we both have a lot to learn about each other."

Ferris nodded. "And yet we have no time to learn it."

Their eyes met, and an eerie feeling overcame him. That same familiarity he'd felt the first time he laid eyes on her.

"Will you tell me now where I've seen you before? Unless it's a secret?"

A smile played briefly on her lips. Finally, some sign of humanity. Perhaps he was getting through to her now.

"Funnily, it *is* a secret, actually."

Ferris shook his head in feigned frustration. If she wanted to toy with him, fine. It was better than the alternative; having her ignore him, or hate him for putting them all in danger.

The last Council members passed them by, and just like that, her expression turned serious again.

"And I *really* do have to go now," she said.

Ferris relented. He'd said what needed to be said. Now it was up to her what she wanted to believe.

"Good luck," he said.

Eryn nodded, and just like that, she was gone.

Ferris checked the Hall and found that only Kelly and her husband were left inside.

"Can you really do what you told everyone?" King Broc asked.

Kelly frowned at him. "Of course he can! Why would he lie about that?"

Ferris raised his hand in a calming motion. "It's fine. I

wouldn't trust me either. But yes. I'll be able to disguise us. Your men have the home advantage. The incoming ships will be drifting around blindly."

"That's all I wanted to know. You'll be informed when we spot the ships," the king said.

Ferris nodded, then turned to his sister.

"Kelly," he said.

"Yes, Ferris?"

"This is going to sound like an odd request. But do you suppose I could go somewhere to rest until it is time?" He turned to face Broc again. "If it's alright with you, of course."

Broc shrugged and turned away from the two of them.

Kelly nodded. "You need rest to conserve your powers. As do I."

A very old and yet familiar warmth overcame him. He hadn't felt like this for years. For the first time in his adult life, he knew someone understood him inside and out.

"I've missed you, sis."

She smiled and placed her hand on his cheek. Like she used to do when he was just a boy. For a moment he was back in a simpler time. Back in West Hythe, in the little house they grew up in.

"I missed you too…. Now let's find you somewhere to stay," she said.

They left the hall and found themselves in yet another corridor, where Kelly turned around and called out for someone.

"Bree, are you around?"

A woman quite a bit taller than Kelly appeared. Her simple wardrobe and timid body language suggested she was a maidservant or worker here at the castle.

"Yes, my Queen?" The woman kept her head bowed as she spoke.

"This is my brother, Ferris. Can you prepare a room for him somewhere to rest? And, Bree?" Kelly paused.

"Yes?"

"No need to be so formal. We're only human."

The joke worked, judging from the little smile that appeared on Bree's lips.

Although he was starting to get used to the idea that Kelly was an actual monarch here, it was still odd to see her interacting with the other islanders, especially her underlings.

He thought *he'd* come a long way in his quest for revenge. She had come a whole lot further, almost entirely by chance.

"Follow me, Sir," Bree addressed him.

"Have a good rest," Kelly called after him.

He waved at her and followed Kelly's maidservant through the maze of corridors that was Black Mountain.

Although he had little idea just where she'd taken him, it wasn't a very long walk. Still, he was relieved when the door closed behind him, and he was alone again.

He did need rest, if he wanted to make sure his powers

were at their peak for the upcoming fight. But he also needed something else. Clarity.

Ferris sat down on the center of the large bed that dominated the sparsely furnished room. Although simple, it was a thousand times more comfortable than most quarters he'd had the misfortune of living in all these years. Having a queen for a sister clearly had many benefits.

After folding his legs, he rested his hands on top of his knees, palms downward, and closed his eyes.

Breathe in. Hold. Breathe out.

Repeat.

Ferris cleared his mind of all the confusion and doubts that had haunted him since his capture.

Focus.

Magic was a funny thing. It had taken him years—and a lot of trial and error—to control it.

The main thing he'd learned during all that time was that mindset was everything. If he could imagine it, he could most likely do it, so long as it was something within his powers.

Controlling the weather was definitely something he could do. He'd used this trick so many times before. All he had to do was alter the scale.

Ferris breathed deeply again, and concentrated on his goal.

What did he want most in this world?

No longer did he meditate on revenge. He'd been so sure of himself all these years. His motivation had been set in stone, and yet it had taken only an hour or so for everything to change.

Now he had to find a new motivation. A new goal.

Safety. For Kelly and little Finlay.

He inhaled deeply and kept these two in his mind's eye, when very suddenly, a third person appeared in his vision.

Eryn.

Ferris opened his eyes and stared right into the flicker of the one candle that lit up this room.

"Eryn," he said to himself.

He had come here with a solitary aim.

That he wanted Kelly and Finlay to be safe was obvious. But if he was truly honest with himself, the thing he wanted most in this world….

Forgiveness.

It was only Eryn who could give that to him. It wouldn't matter if it came from anyone else.

And in time, if he was good enough, perhaps she could offer him more than that. Perhaps she could accept him the way Kelly had accepted Broc.

That was his new ultimate aim.

Ferris closed his eyes again and let his subconscious run free. The change was immediate. A rush of energy collected in his core. Now that he had found his ultimate desire, he felt more powerful than ever.

Perhaps love truly could conquer all.

CHAPTER NINE

Eryn's little encounter with Ferris had sent her thoughts and emotions into turmoil all over again. Just when she had begun to get a grip on herself.

She had no idea why he'd wanted to talk to her of all people. She'd given him no reason to. Unless he had sensed how he made her feel. Could it be that the feeling was mutual?

Her heart jumped a few beats before she got herself under control. It didn't change anything. He was still related to the queen. And she was still unworthy.

Eryn forced herself back into action and all but ran out of the Great Hall. She'd barely made it out the door when she bumped into Yorrick.

"What was *that* all about?" Yorrick's stare made Eryn uncomfortable.

Now what did *he* want?

"What are you talking about?" she countered.

"The warlock. What did he want with you? Or rather, what did you want with him?"

Yorrick didn't seem his usual, calm self. Of course, they were all on edge, but she'd never known him to be the suspicious type.

"Oh, you know…. Unfinished business from the battle," Eryn said. Lying wasn't one of her strengths. "I was the one who captured him, if you remember."

"How about earlier tonight? Did you go see him in the dungeons to discuss this so-called unfinished business then too?"

"What in the world?" Eryn's heart sank. How did *he* know about that?

Her initial shock was quickly replaced with anger. "Have you been following me around, Yorrick?"

Now it was his turn to take a step back. His face turned ashen, and then bright red.

"I'm head of the Castle Guard. I ought to know what goes on in these walls!" His tone was defensive now.

She'd struck a nerve. In any case, there was no point denying she'd visited the warlock in his cell. Even the king and queen knew about that already.

"And I'm second in command to Rhea, our General. If I'm down in the dungeons, you can bet on it that I'm there with her blessing," Eryn snapped.

Yorrick took a step forward and loomed over her, but she didn't flinch or back down. How quickly things changed in these walls.

"I thought we were friends. Now you treat me as the enemy?" Eryn hissed.

Yorrick exhaled and broke eye contact. "Eryn…. That's not what I meant."

She continued to glare at him. What the hell was he thinking? Had he been following her around earlier also?

All those little conversations out on the sea wall, the random encounters outside the library…. Had it all been an elaborate plan of his, rather than mere coincidence?

Rhea had noticed it and warned her. She had taken it as something else, professional rivalry between the Army and Castle Guard. But the truth had become apparent tonight.

"I'm only worried for your safety, Eryn!" Yorrick pleaded.

Eryn shook her head; she was having none of it. "You have a funny way of showing your concern."

"We *are* friends, though. Aren't we?" he asked.

She looked up again into his eyes, but made sure there was no warmth in her gaze. "Sure. Whatever you say. But that's *all* we'll ever be."

Eryn was still shaking with anger. If it was up to these menfolk, she'd *never* get the chance to carry out the King's orders tonight! She left Yorrick standing there in the corridor outside the Great Hall, and rushed off like she should have done immediately after the meeting.

She didn't have time for any of this nonsense. First Ferris tried to distract her with his apologies, and now Yorrick with…. She didn't even know what this was.

Between the king and queen letting an outsider attend the Council meeting, and everyone's apparent reluctance to try diplomacy on the enemy rather than fight them outright…. Had everyone on this rock gone insane, save for her?

By the time she reached her destination halfway across

the castle, she was still annoyed.

Eryn burst into the dormitory of her squad with little patience or compassion. Dawn would break shortly. There was no more time to lose.

"Wake up! All of you!"

Some of her people stirred quicker than others. The room stank of ale; her men had feasted heavily before going to bed.

"This isn't a joke. Get up. Your services are required immediately!" Eryn shouted.

Finally, everyone was up in their cots and rubbing their eyes.

"Mistress Eryn, what's going on?" The same young eagle who had initially found the human ship was first on his feet.

Very well, Eryn would brief him first, then. The others would fall in line soon enough.

"We are under immediate threat. The ship you spotted yesterday wasn't the only one coming," Eryn said.

The young man's eyes widened; she couldn't be sure whether with shock or excitement.

Some of the more senior members of her squad joined the two of them.

"We'll need to patrol day and night," one of them said.

Eryn nodded. "Overlapping shifts. We cannot afford to let the enemy slip past unseen."

It didn't take long for even the laziest of the lot to jump

into action.

Only then could Eryn breathe easy. She had done her part. Her squad would be in the air imminently. Nobody could escape their gaze now.

———•◆•———

After whipping her squad into shape, Eryn was intercepted right outside the dorm room.

"Oh, here you are." Rhea pulled her aside by her arm.

"Now that the *humans* are busy, it's time to have a real conversation."

Eryn blinked a few times. This was it. She was going to get an earful about her conduct during the Council Meeting. Unless Rhea wanted to interrogate her about her little chat with Ferris earlier?

"About?" Eryn asked with a heart full of trepidation.

"We discussed what we could in front of everyone, but I can't trust the warlock, no matter whose brother he is. The king agreed that we cover some things in private. The newcomer doesn't need to know everything. At least not yet."

Rhea was probably being a bit paranoid, but that wasn't any of Eryn's business. She was just glad the woman wasn't shouting at her. Yet. "Right."

"Come along."

Rhea marched off, and Eryn did her best to keep up.

THE WARLOCK'S CONQUEST

"Where are we going?"

"View Point."

Away from prying eyes and sensitive ears, and with the best views of the surrounding seas possible. Good choice.

When they got there, the king was already waiting, his hands on the railing as he peered out over the sea. Although his expression didn't show it, Eryn could almost sense his tension.

"We're here," Rhea said.

King Broc turned abruptly. Had they startled him?

"Good. Let's begin."

Eryn listened in silence as Rhea and Broc laid out their plans for the battle. They would be outnumbered for sure. And although the islanders were much stronger than their human counterparts in hand-to-hand combat, superior weaponry from the mainland could tip the scales even further in their favor.

If they couldn't be stronger, they had to be smarter.

"We will use the fog to our advantage and set sail to join the battle from the other side. Fight them on two fronts," Rhea said.

Eryn thought about it for a moment. "We have one of their ships. They won't come to know it's us until it's too late."

Rhea nodded. "That's exactly what I thought."

I knew that captured ship was going to come in handy.

"For this reason, I will need you to lead the troops on

ground," Rhea said.

Eryn glanced up at the general, then at the king, then back again. "You don't want me on the ship?"

Rhea shook her head. "The men need someone to look up to. You're my most senior officer on the ground."

It made sense, logically. Still Eryn could not deny her disappointment. This was exactly the sort of task *she* should have been given. As general, Rhea should be with the rest of her troops, commanding them, motivating them.

Her failure to carry out Rhea's orders had brought this on her. Eryn was being left behind.

"Any objections?" Rhea asked. Her tone betrayed that there was only one correct answer.

"No. that's fine."

Broc took a step in her direction and placed his hand on her shoulder. This was probably the first time the king had ever touched her, so there was no missing the significance in his gesture.

"I will be up here, overseeing the battle. If you need anything, you need only signal me."

Eryn averted her gaze. "Thank you, my King."

"That's enough now. She's become arrogant enough as it is," Rhea grumbled. "Unless you've forgotten what happened at the meeting."

Broc smiled bitterly. "It was rather hard to forget or ignore. But the girl has sense."

"We can trust you with this, can't we?"

Trust her with keeping up morale at the front line and lead the clash onshore? If he put it like that, perhaps it wasn't a punishment after all.

Eryn took a deep breath. "Absolutely, my King. I will not disappoint you."

"Once the fog sets, all bets are off. We won't hide behind these human faces if the humans reach our shores, understand? They won't know what hit them," King Broc said.

Eryn nodded. "Yes, I understand."

"Now run along and get yourself ready. I'll collect a handful of experienced fighters to join me on my mission at sea," Rhea said.

Eryn still felt a little sore for being left out. Or perhaps she was nervous about acting the leader? It was easy enough to boss around a bunch of inexperienced scouts.... She'd have a harder time with the senior soldiers.

But, as she had proved during the meeting, she wouldn't let anyone push her around anymore.

"Thank you for placing this trust in me," Eryn said.

"Yes, yes. Enough already," Rhea brushed her off.

Eryn nodded and left. As the door leading to the View Point closed slowly behind her, she could faintly overhear Rhea and Broc over the howling winds outside.

"I hope that warlock delivers," Rhea grumbled. "And Eryn, too."

"And if not, can we count on his help?" Broc asked.

"I'll talk to him, but I can't make any promises."

Eryn frowned. What on earth were they talking about now? Still, none of her business. She carried on down the stairs and headed straight for the armory.

With nothing better to do, and nowhere else to be, she would spend the last moments of peace there. Surrounded by the smell of worn leather and polished iron, she would make sure her weapons and armor were in order.

But once the door closed behind her and she was alone amongst all these trappings of war, it wasn't her equipment she was thinking about.

She still made sure to check everything, but once that was done, and she sat idle, with her hands folded in her lap.

There was only one thing on her mind.

It wasn't the immense responsibility that rested on her now. It wasn't even the very real danger that many islanders, herself included, might not make it to the end of the upcoming fight.

Her thoughts were much simpler, and completely inappropriate. Like an unwanted guest, *he* had made himself at home in her mind from the moment he'd set foot on this island.

No matter how hard she tried. Eryn couldn't stop thinking of Ferris.

Perhaps deep down, she knew that he was thinking about her too.

CHAPTER TEN

———◆———

The rumble of the war horn shook Black Mountain to its foundations. A little trickle of dust made its way down from the ceiling and onto the floor.

Eryn was ready, but the sound still made her skin crawl. She'd only heard it once before, when she had been freshly enlisted by Rhea. Years ago, during the first great battle with the Sea Folk; that was the last time the horn had sounded in these walls.

This time she wasn't a novice any longer. She would be in charge of the fighters stationed on the lower sea wall. That was the first point of contact between Black Isle's army and the enemy.

Over the years she hadn't just become a little more mature, but hopefully wiser and more experienced as well. All of these, and more. She would need to do a proper job today.

But just because she was in charge didn't mean she wouldn't pick up a weapon herself. That's not how things worked here. The human ships were coming, and on them, at least a thousand men, all armed to the teeth.

Eryn would fight just like any other soldier.

With the help of Ferris' magic, they would strike the enemy hard in an attempt to scare them off. To quash this invasion before it even got started.

There was no talk of compromise or diplomacy any longer. Rhea had gotten her way and convinced the king that brute force was the way forward. The general herself would flank the enemy using one of their own ships and try to take out as many as possible before they even reached the shore.

Eryn didn't like it, but could do nothing about it now but follow her orders.

All she knew was by the end of it, she'd be a battle virgin no longer. She'd take a life—many lives—before the day was done.

So be it.

For her people, for these Isles, she could do anything.

If she failed, she didn't just let Rhea and the King down, after all. She'd let herself down more than anything. It was her moment to shine and to prove to everyone including herself that she was worthy of her rank.

She ran down the corridors leading to the Drawbridge and almost bumped into Saras.

"Hey. Ready to fight?" she asked in passing.

"What? Oh, I'm not going out there."

Eryn stopped in her tracks and looked back at the man, who continued to leisurely walk in the wrong direction. It looked almost like he was going for an afternoon stroll around the castle. Surely, he had heard the war horn just like everyone else?

"What do you mean you're not going? We're all going into battle. Our future is at stake!"

"I'll be waiting this one out, my dear. I'm sure between Rhea and you, the Isles are in capable hands."

Did he even know what Rhea was up against? How she was putting her life at risk by jumping head first into the fight?

Eryn wanted to berate him. To release all her frustration right now, call him arrogant and short-sighted and all the rest of it.

But she swallowed it.

This anger would come in handy later.

What on earth did Rhea see in him? Or rather, how did she not see all the selfishness hidden beneath that flawless exterior? This man seemed to be Rhea's only weakness.

Speaking of weaknesses, at least *Ferris* was trying to help.... Even if he was an outsider and worse still, the Queen's brother.... But his intentions were pure and he wasn't running away from this fight like Saras was doing.

Eryn shook it off and proceeded through the Drawbridge and down to the sea wall.

They'd have to survive this fight with or without a dragon by their side.

Some archers had already assembled and spread out to their positions. And most of them did not look as fresh or as ready as she would want them to. They had waited for Rhea to join their side, not Eryn. She could almost sense their disappointment.

But Rhea wasn't coming.

This was the best they were going to get.

Not one for rousing speeches normally, Eryn straightened herself and took a deep breath. It was the moment of truth.

"Guys!" she called out to the archers who had already assembled. "Some of you are seeing all-out war for the first time, and some of you already know the horrors that lie in our not so distant future. But our people have survived every challenge, every conflict we were thrust into in the past. And we will survive today!"

Now that she'd started, Eryn was surprised how easily the words came to her.

"With magic on our side, we will prevail. We will crush the opposition. We'll make heads roll. We'll live to fight another day! What say you?" she called out.

"I say death to the enemy!" the senior-most soldier of the group responded. Their eyes met and she could see a glimmer of hope in him. Morale was everything. They might just get away with this. Despite being outnumbered, the Isles could be victorious after all.

Where was Ferris, anyway? From where would he perform his magic?

More importantly, would he make good on his promises at all?

Eryn shook off her own doubts and continued to play the crowd. "That's right! Now the rest of you. What say you?"

"Victory!" the soldiers roared.

The Warlock's Conquest

"Very good! Back to your posts! We attack as soon as the fog sets in."

It felt good to be listened to. To be respected. She held on tight to her bow, determined to do these men and women proud. No guts, no glory.

But for now, they could only wait. Eryn kept her eyes fixed on the horizon, where the mainlander's ships had already appeared. It wouldn't be long now. There was none of the normal chatter amongst the soldiers. Everyone was focusing on the same thing. Waiting, anticipating, until the enemy would arrive.

It was the calm before the storm.

———◆———

On the eve of the battle, Ferris felt fully charged.

He knew he'd need every last reserve, every bit of untapped energy, to fulfill his promise to Kelly's new family.

And to prove his loyalty to Eryn.

But he was ready for it.

There was some arrogance to his excitement. After years of using his powers for selfish means, now he'd be able to help someone other than himself. And perhaps impress Eryn in the process? It was her reaction he was looking   forward to especially.

From motivating all his actions solely on Kelly, he was now doing it equally for the three people most important to him: Kelly, Finlay and Eryn.

As soon as the horn sounded the arrival of the invading ships, a guard had fetched him from his new quarters and brought him down to the Drawbridge, where he waited for further instructions.

But in the coming and going of armed soldiers, nobody took note. No one so much as approached him.

Luckily, he spotted Eryn in the distance. She had already made her way down toward the sea wall that surrounded the whole island. There she stood, completely still, with her back turned toward the castle. As he followed her path, he scanned his surroundings. Archers dotted the entire coastline. Their spread was thin, but perhaps these were all the fighters they had. The only protection for all these fighters were the fortifications of the wall they stood on.

There wasn't a bit of vegetation within sight. The entire island was practically barren, with the castle serving as a great big target for the incoming ships' cannons. The sort of weaponry he'd seen so far on this side of the fight wasn't nearly as advanced. Swords, axes and bows. Unless they were hiding a secret weapon somewhere, he wasn't particularly impressed. Physical strength was only part of the equation in combat.

Good thing he was on their team. Without his help, they wouldn't stand a chance against the military might of the mainland.

He looked up and saw eagles circling overhead. They

bore an eerie resemblance to the one he'd spotted above his ship barely a day earlier. Funny. Had they trained these animals to help in their defense, as an early warning system perhaps?

Clearly there was a lot about these Isles and its people that he did not yet know. They kept their secrets closely guarded, even or especially from him.

No matter, he'd figure it out in time.

"How far out are they?" Ferris asked Eryn as he reached her side.

She looked at him for just a moment longer than necessary before pointing at the horizon. "There."

Ferris squinted, but he couldn't see anything.

"You have extraordinary vision," Ferris mumbled.

"I know," Eryn spoke in a matter-of-fact tone, but then stole another glance in his direction. "What's your plan?"

She was trying to hide it, but Ferris was picking up on the subtle signs now. She was as eager to see him in action as he was.

"Wait for them to just about get into view—*my view*—then blanket the enemy and the island in fog. The rest is up to you and your fighters."

"Sounds good to me."

Ferris continued to observe her, but she did not face him anymore. Her sole focus was now on the enemy. Here she stood, waiting to fight an opponent that outnumbered the islanders probably three or four to one.

Yet there wasn't a hint of fear or hesitation about her. What a formidable woman she was.

Ferris felt it best not to make further conversation. If all went according to plan, there would be plenty of time for that later.

If not…. then it didn't really matter, did it?

He did, however, make a promise to himself.

If they got out of this fight alive, and his loyalties were no longer in question, he would proposition her.

Returning to his homeland was no longer an option. Not when Kelly and his nephew were here, and he'd actively fought against King Harrold.

If the islanders would have him, he would try to make a life here for himself. He could only hope that Eryn was willing to share his future with him.

Because it was obvious to him now that he would never meet another woman like her. Her bravery impressed him greatly. In her, he saw qualities he wished for himself but which perhaps he had not yet managed to attain.

Eryn could be an opponent most dangerous, ruthless and willing to do what had to be done no matter how difficult. That's as far as their similarities went. And yet she had a capacity for mercy and forgiveness which he craved for himself.

Perhaps with her guidance, he would be worthy of a woman like her.

Eryn cleared her throat beside him. "Can't you see

them clearly yet? They'll be within our range soon."

Ferris peered out over the choppy waters. Indeed, the ships had come into view.

This was his moment.

He tilted his head to gaze at the clear sky one last time, before closing his eyes fully and retreating into his mind. A low rumble of thunder could be heard overhead, which made him smile.

You could smell the dampness in the air.

He could see it in his imagination now; he didn't even need to open his eyes to confirm. His magic was working and it was more powerful than ever before.

Dense fog covered everything, from the ships to the archers to the hills and castle behind them.

The invaders were now completely blind.

CHAPTER ELEVEN

E ryn tried not to let Ferris' appearance distract her from the task at hand. The only thing disturbing the silence as they waited was the ever-increasing thump of her heart.

Whether it was nerves or excitement, she could not tell anymore. Neither did it matter.

Her instincts kicked in fast. She didn't consciously choose fight or flight. On her mind was only one thing: victory.

True to his word, as the ships approached, a mysterious fog crept up from the sea, surrounding everything and everyone.

Eryn turned around to see the extent of it. It took her breath away.

Even the worst weather these Isles had seen could not have disguised them this well.

She glanced at Ferris. He stood absolutely still, with his head tilted up toward the sky and his eyes shut. His arms were at a forty-five-degree angle to his body, with his palms facing upward. There was a slight tremble in his lip: remnants of words, not meant for anyone but himself and whatever higher power had granted him this magic.

It was probably too subdued for the human eye to see, but with her superior vision she could clearly make out a faint blue glow that surrounded his entire body.

His heartbeat was up at a feverish pace, and his breaths so shallow she could barely hear them over the crashing waves down below.

Whatever he was doing to make this happen, it was taking a toll on him.

"It better be worth it," she mumbled to herself and tightened her grip on her bow.

With an arrow lined up ready, she waited for the ships to get close enough for her to choose her first victim.

"Archers! If you have a shot, take it," she ordered.

"For victory!" one of the soldiers further down the wall called out.

"For glory!" the others responded.

A brief smile crept over Eryn's lips. This wasn't so bad, being a leader.

Hardly a minute passed before the first arrow ripped through the fog and implanted itself in the chest of an unsuspecting enemy soldier. He sunk to the ground so quickly, nobody else on board seemed to have any idea. Of course, they were at a severe disadvantage. The humans couldn't see much of anything.

One down, nine-hundred-and-ninety-nine to go, Eryn thought to herself.

She squinted and chose her own target. There was no time to think about the right or wrong of it all. She let go.

Nine-hundred-and-ninety-eight.

After this slow start, all the remaining archers let loose as well. The enemy took a heavy battering of arrows, each shot with uncanny precision. It started off as easy as shooting at the practice range. But just as soon as the humans realized what they had sailed into, things became more challenging.

Their targets were no longer stationary, and many sought shelter behind various obstacles on board their ships. Some of them even started to return fire. So far, they were ineffective, blind as they were.

All the while, the enemy ships continued to approach ever closer. But the waters were treacherous. Sharp rocks dotted the coastline.

Soon enough, the first of many ran ashore. As soon as they felt the shudder, and heard the wooden hull groaning and cracking open against the unforgiving granite rock, the enemy soldiers started to abandon ship. Once again, it was open season on them.

Kill or be killed.

Eryn lost count soon thereafter.

A quick check on her men revealed that not one had fallen so far. They were doing well.

But Eryn's optimism was short-lived.

A flash of light lit up the mist quite some distance away, followed by a deafening rumble. Had Saras joined the fight after all?

Eryn leaned forward to get a better look, when a heavy object crashed into the island several feet behind her, causing the ground to shudder.

What on earth?

What was that which had been hurtled through the sky at them? And where exactly had it come from?

Whatever it was, it was impossibly fast and it must have been large and heavy as well. Too heavy for a mere human to lift at all, never mind be able to throw. Did they possess some secret weapon as well? Magic of their own, perhaps?

Eryn tried to catch her breath and scour the incoming ships for any sign of what might have caused it, when the same thing happened again.

The flash of light nearly blinded her, and made it hard for her to pinpoint its origin as well as trajectory.

"Archers! Forget everything else, aim at the shooting light before it goes off again!" Eryn shouted.

There was yet another flash in the distance, from another direction this time. The object hit a several feet to Eryn's left, crushing one of her men, and causing a whole section of fortified wall to crumble into the sea.

What was this witchcraft?

Eryn raised her bow and aimed. She never had the chance to shoot.

The impact hit her with such intensity, it forced all the wind out of her lungs.

Oh shit. I've been struck!

Eryn let out a muffled whimper as she sunk down onto her knees.

Devoid of air, she slipped away almost instantly.

All was going perfectly. Ferris was able to maintain his focus, and the fog did not let up.

Although his body was getting tired, he willed himself to carry on.

You can rest when you're dead.

The longer he carried on, the more distant he felt. A separation formed between his physical form and mind.

The weight of his body lifted off, as though he had started to float.

As soon as he felt it was safe, he opened his eyes. It was like he was looking down on himself, just like how it was when he took over another life form.

But this time, there was no other host around. There was just him, and his body, as two separate entities.

The islanders, including Eryn, carried on like nothing had changed. At least he assumed as much. She was the only one he could see, while the rest were hidden beyond the mist.

The fight seemed to be intensifying. He could hear the whistle of arrows being set loose on either side. Further away, the clanging of iron against iron had begun. Had the ships landed yet?

It wasn't long before the cannons started to fire, just as he had anticipated. But without being able to see their targets, they were firing blind. Hopefully the islanders would be able to neutralize the cannons before long, and without suffering too many losses.

Sure, there would be some casualties. The groans and cries of injured soldiers could be heard already, along with some more feral, almost animalistic cries. Ferris had no way of knowing what side the fallen belonged to.

War was a dirty game. One had to embrace the darkness in order to win.

At least the islanders could see, somewhat, allowing them to react. It was this little glimmer of hope that Ferris held onto. They were still at an advantage here.

Ferris floated higher above his body, only to find that now he couldn't see a damn thing anymore.

Focus, he thought.

Don't let go.

A nearby moan snapped him out of his trance. Within an instant, he was sucked back into his body and opened his actual, physical eyes. Just in time to see her fall.

"No! Eryn!" he called out and quickly bridged the gap between them.

The fog lifted as quickly as it had descended initially, but he took no note. All he could see was her ashen face, as he cradled her limp body in his arms.

Tears stung in his eyes, and a rage overcame him the likes of which he'd never felt before.

He'd lost someone once. Someone who had meant everything to him. Although he had Kelly back now, the wounds of that initial loss were ripped open again.

He wasn't about to go through that again.

Ferris rose to his feet and took in the full magnitude of what he was up against. He balled his fists so hard his whole body trembled.

Curses.

"You'll pay for this. You'll pay dearly!"

He raised his hands to the sky and screamed, releasing all his remaining energy, his newfound anger and pain, all at once.

The skies turned black as night, and the roar of thunder overwhelmed his senses.

Ferris started to shiver and shake. Every last hair on his body stood up straight. He inhaled deeply and channeled his anger at whatever lay ahead.

He brought his arms down and aimed his hands at the enemy.

The clouds overhead opened, bringing forth a bolt of lightning, which crept and crackled across the air and branched off again and again until the clouds were lit up once again.

It left nothing in its wake. Ship after ship crossed its path, until the nearest dozen or so had caught alight.

Screams of terror and pain mixed in with the roaring of flames, as the mainland soldiers on the damaged vessels flung themselves overboard, hoping to escape the fire. The reflection of this unthinkable carnage lit up the sea a fiery orange. It looked like it was boiling. Angry.

The Warlock's Conquest

When it was done, he sunk onto the ground beside Eryn, completely spent.

All the anger that had seared him from within all these years, all the vengeance he had plotted since Kelly's initial disappearance, had come together. All this ugliness had culminated in this one moment.

He'd had his revenge. He had made *someone* pay.

And now, he had nothing more to give.

The last thing he saw was something he could not explain. Mainland soldiers, flailing and fighting for their lives, as they were torn to shreds by wild animals that had made their way into the water from the island. Wolves, bears, lynxes and more, all trained to kill.

He sighed deeply as he slipped into oblivion. What a strange place this was. Where animals did these people's bidding just like that. Without magic controlling them.

———— ◆ ————

Eryn couldn't see properly. Her surroundings, though vaguely familiar, were hazy. Like everything was still covered under the thick mist Ferris had conjured.

She was still on those same fortifications as a moment ago. Her bow was still drawn, with an arrow waiting to hit its aim. She could no longer see the ships, or the flashes of light of the enemy's mysterious weapons.

Where had they gone?

Forget that, where had her own people gone?

Eryn realized now that it was silent all around. Only the distant crash of waves could be heard, along with the sea winds blowing around the towers of the castle behind her. There was not even a whisper in the air otherwise. No clanging of weapons or distant flaps of enemy sails. No cries of wounded men, or whistles of arrows in the air.

She was completely alone.

It made no sense. Just a second ago, she had been fighting for her life with Ferris by her side.

She'd done the needful without hesitation; this time she hadn't failed Rhea or her training. Every arrow had hit exactly where she intended. Many enemy soldiers had fallen thanks to her.

Or had she imagined all of that?

Perhaps the fight never happened.

No, no, no! That cannot be!

Eryn called out into the silence. But no matter how hard she tried, her voice failed to make a sound.

Had she lost her mind?

A shooting pain traveled through her chest, taking her breath away, in the front and straight out the back. Eryn reached for the exact spot and rubbed to soothe the pain away. Still, her chest was so tight she couldn't breathe freely.

She let go and looked down at her hand.

In this gray, hazy world, she saw a first spot of color.

Her palm was covered in red. Blood red.

She cried out again, silently. It was no use.

Eryn stumbled, looking for someone, anyone, to help. But she was still alone, with nothing but the sea and the sky and this desolate bit of castle wall to keep her company.

Just at that moment, she was struck again, from the back this time, and sunk onto her knees.

Had she fallen in battle? Was this the end?

Finally, a sound managed to pass her lips as she whimpered in pain. It wasn't so much the injury that had hurt her. Her suffering went a lot deeper.

Regret.

For the life she would no longer get to live. The love she had denied herself, even though she realized now how much she craved it all along.

CHAPTER TWELVE

Upon opening his eyes, it took Ferris a few minutes to find his bearings. He sat up straight and had a look around. Somehow, he had ended up on an open ground near the Drawbridge that led into the castle, though the wall where his last memories placed him was still within view down below.

The battle was over. Fragments of charred wood floated in the water surrounding the island, along with more bodies than he had the courage to count.

It was carnage.

But it seemed that the worst of the battle was now over. There were no more ships as far as the eye could see. The invaders must have retreated.

"I've got a live one," someone called out.

Ferris turned to see who had said that, but he wasn't sure. Soldiers with only minor injuries, and people he assumed to be servants and workers of the castle, flitted back and forth, trying to attend to as many fallen as possible. Hardly a soul was left unscathed after the battle.

The stench of sweat and blood hung heavily in the air. It was enough to make lesser men sick, but not Ferris. This wasn't the first time he had endured horrors such as these.

He tried to get up, though his limbs were not yet cooperating with him. As he sunk back down onto the damp grass, he noticed a row of a dozen or so lifeless forms, covered in white sheets, just off to his right.

Fear gripped his heart. Was Eryn among these bodies?

Had she been discarded here, while the attendees focused on those casualties whom they could actually help?

The thought of her, alone among the dead, was enough to startle him into action. He stumbled onto his feet and began his search. Frantically he lifted sheet after sheet, only to be faced with numerous faces of soldiers she did not recognize. Interspersed among them were several wild animals as well. It was bizarre how on an island with seemingly no animal life except a handful of eagles, suddenly a whole bunch of wildlife had fallen in battle.

Yet Eryn was nowhere to be found.

"Eryn!" he called out.

His heart raced and his vision went black for a moment as he continued to limp around the mossy plateau. But when he was finally approached, it wasn't *her* face he saw.

"Not so fast," another female voice snapped.

He paused and found Rhea sitting on the ground. A familiar maidservant kneeling by her side was quickly and efficiently cleaning a nasty-looking burn on Rhea's arm. Ferris recognized her as Bree, the woman who had prepared his quarters for him the day before.

"Where is Eryn?" Ferris insisted.

Rhea glared up at him. "Forget Eryn. I knew we couldn't trust you. I knew it from the start!"

Ferris frowned. What was she trying to say? How could he forget Eryn, when she was the first and last thing on his mind right now?

"You had one job to do. *One* job! Keep us hidden, so that we could move unseen and strike at the enemy until they retreated in fear. Instead, you exposed us and damn near burned my ship down!"

Ferris opened his mouth in protest.

"Shut it!" Rhea interjected. "I'd rather cut off my ears than hear any more of the poison you spew. You think you can convince everyone, but you can no longer lie to me. I see through you, warlock!"

By now Bree had finished tying the bandage around Rhea's arm and moved away to see to someone else. Immediately, Rhea got up and glared at him with a menacing look in her eye. She meant business.

The memories of his last moments before passing out came back to Ferris. Yes, obviously he had failed to hold up his end of the bargain. As soon as he heard Eryn's cry, he'd allowed himself to become distracted. That's when the fog had dissipated.

But that had never been his intent! And it looked like the enemy had retreated anyway, despite his failure.

"I'm so sorry," Ferris mumbled. He was. But what he was most sorry for was that Eryn had been hit. His magic had failed to keep her safe. And Rhea still hadn't told him what exactly happened to her or where she was.

"You will be," Rhea said. "Guards! Take this prisoner

away and lock him somewhere where no one will think to look for him!"

"No! How was I supposed to know you were on one of the ships!" Ferris protested.

"What did you think, that I had slept through the whole battle like a coward? It's only obvious I'd be out there, fighting!" Rhea countered. "Just how your kind managed to win the mainland from us, I'll never understand."

It really had come as a surprise to him that Rhea had fought in this battle along with everyone else. Such a thing was unheard of for someone of her status, at least on the mainland. Then again, the mainland didn't have female fighters or generals either.

"At least tell me where Eryn is?" Ferris insisted.

Rhea scoffed. "Why do you care? You'll never see her again."

Ferris stumbled over his own feet as two men, each at least a foot-and-a-half taller than him, dragged him through the Drawbridge and into the castle.

He'd walked this same route before, on the day of his first arrival on Black Mountain.

It felt like a lifetime ago, even though at the most only two days had passed. And after all that he'd been through, he was a prisoner again.

Thankfully, he didn't get as far as the dungeons before his escort was intercepted by a welcome sight.

"Kelly!" Ferris called out. "Please tell these guys to let me go."

Kelly's already tense expression turned to anger. "What's the meaning of this? Where are you taking him?"

The guards stopped in their tracks and started to fumble their words. Ferris shook his head and took over the conversation.

"We have the esteemed general to thank for that. She has decided that I'm a traitor and deserve to be locked up," he explained.

Kelly shot the guards a nasty glance. "You're dismissed!"

Then she focused on Ferris again. "Rhea did this? Wouldn't be the first time."

He limbered up his arms and wrists from where the guards had held onto him. "Never mind all that. Where is Eryn?"

Kelly's face fell again. "Oh. You don't know?"

Ferris slowly shook his head as the worst possible scenarios started to play in his mind.

"Right," Kelly mumbled. "I'll take you to her."

———◆———

"How is she?" Ferris asked.

Kelly's expression had told him previously already that it was bad news.

"Please tell me she'll make it," he added. He could not

explain how he had developed such strong feelings for her in such a short time. If he lost her, now.... He couldn't bear to think about it.

Kelly shook her head. "There is no way of knowing. Frankly, I haven't seen anything like this before."

"How do you mean?" Ferris looked down at Eryn's motionless body. She was so still it looked like she was simply asleep. Except for the blood-soaked bandage wrapped around her chest, that was.

"Any fever?" Ferris asked, as he leaned down and placed his hand over Eryn's forehead.

Her skin was cold to the touch. He flinched and pulled away.

"They don't get fevers," Kelly said. "They're not like you and me. They don't get sick. They don't heal like we do either. It's much faster."

Although her words were hopeful, her tone didn't match.

"What normally happens? When someone is injured like this?" he asked.

Kelly placed her hand on his arm. "This isn't a normal injury, Ferris. I don't know how to explain it, really."

He turned to face her and look her in the eye. "Kelly. Just be honest with me."

His throat had all but closed up. For so many years he'd had only vengeance on his mind. He'd never cared for anyone else but Kelly. And now, the first other person he'd actually felt something for was on the brink of death.

"I think the first arrow hit her close to her heart. Her body can't recover as normal, at least not yet. And her mind...."

"What's wrong with her mind?" Ferris asked.

"Normally when someone is passed out, I can still enter their thoughts. She's unreachable to me. Almost like she's stuck in her own consciousness somewhere."

Ferris sank down beside Eryn's bed and kept on staring at her. Her chest was still moving up and down with shallow breaths. Her cheeks still had the faintest hint of color.

Eryn was still here. If these people indeed had extraordinary healing abilities, perhaps she'd get out of it on her own. Had fate led him here, onto this island, only to lose the first woman he'd ever truly loved? And he hadn't even had the chance to tell her so. Surely, life couldn't be so cruel?

"But if she hasn't passed yet, surely she has already begun to heal?"

Kelly carefully picked up the bandage on Eryn's chest and peered underneath.

"Maybe.... But we need both mind as well as body in order to function. If she can't find her way back...."

A sharp knock on the door interrupted the two of them.

Kelly looked up. "General Rhea."

"I've come to check on Eryn," the general said, but

then let her gaze linger on Ferris for an uncomfortable few seconds.

"What's *he* doing here?" she asked.

Kelly straightened herself. "I found out about your little scheme, Rhea. He's not going to be your prisoner, no matter what you say. Ferris is assisting me with Eryn's care."

Ferris ignored the two women and kept on watching Eryn's chest rise and fall. As long as she could breathe, there was still hope.

Beside him, Rhea leaned down over Eryn as well. "This doesn't look right."

Kelly joined them.

"I know it doesn't. There's something wrong with her that we haven't encountered before," Kelly said.

Rhea took Kelly by the hand and took her aside. Ferris could only watch as the two women spoke just out of his earshot. He couldn't be bothered to eavesdrop; he had other things on his mind.

Don't you die on me now, Eryn!

What was going on in that head of hers? He would give anything to exchange his powers with Kelly right now to find out. Perhaps he could try to decipher the mystery somehow, and help her find her way back to reality.

The door creaked open again, and yet another person entered. Ferris thought he recognized this guy from the Council meeting, though he hadn't seen him since.

"What's going on? And what's *he* doing here?" The man glared at Ferris, who merely sighed in response. Was this how it was going to go now? Every single person who burst in here seemed more interested in why Ferris was here, rather than working out how to help Eryn.

"Yorrick. We've got it under control," Kelly intervened.

"It doesn't look like it. Not with him here!"

Ferris felt his temper rise again. Did this man have some claim on Eryn which Ferris did not know about? And if so, where was *he* during the battle? Where was *he* when Eryn had needed him the most?

No, Ferris thought to himself. *If anyone has a right to be here, it's me. Not this other guy!*

"Mind yourself!" Rhea snapped as well now. "Eryn needs rest, not your drama."

Finally, Ferris could agree on something Rhea said.

"I only came to check—" the other man, Yorrick, explained.

"Stop it! I know very well what you came here for. Why don't you leave my people alone and check on your own injured? You must have some yourself."

Yorrick turned red, and for a moment Ferris thought it was going to turn into an altercation. But Rhea's authority won out this time.

They all watched as Yorrick left and closed the door behind him.

"That man is going to drive me insane one of these days," Rhea complained, then composed herself as she spotted Ferris staring at her.

"You're lucky your sister wants you here," she told him.

Ferris shrugged. "I guess I *am* lucky that way." *Especially since Kelly is queen, and you're not.* "But we do still have to figure out a way to help Eryn."

Rhea chewed on her bottom lip for a moment. She might hate Ferris, but she obviously did care for Eryn.

"We should consult the Elders," Rhea concluded finally.

Kelly nodded.

Ferris had no idea what that meant exactly, but it seemed to be their best hope.

CHAPTER THIRTEEN

W hen Eryn awoke, she was high up in the sky with no recollection of how she got there. Night had started to fall, and the clouds that surrounded her were only lit up with the faint moonlight that filtered through the haze. She circled around and headed back the same way where she had just come from.

The fog down below was still dense, making it almost impossible for Eryn to see the ground. The spires of the highest tower of the castle were the only thing that was clearly visible to her.

Just how long she had been flying for, she did not know.

She stretched her wings as wide as they would go, allowing the breeze to carry her. With the right amount of wind, it was almost effortless to fly this high.

Effortless, and blissfully quiet.

A little too quiet.

She dove down a little, and headed right for the thickest part of the fog. Still, she could detect no movement down below. Even at night, there was always someone, some guard or soldier, patrolling the castle walls.

Her very own squad ought to be around here somewhere, seeking out incoming threats from the sky.

But there was no one.

The Warlock's Conquest

Not a single sound could be heard, save for the sea and he wind itself, along with the flapping of her wings.

A sense of doom overcame her. Something was not right.

There was a tightness in her chest she could not explain. It made it hard to breathe. She closed her eyes for a moment, when a flash of a memory came to her.

Blood.

Pain.

Darkness.

Eryn's heart sped up instantly, but her breathing couldn't catch up. The tightness on her lungs worsened.

What happened to the battle she'd been in? Who won? Who lost?

What *was* this place and how did she get here?

The view beneath her changed. The once mossy hill on which the castle stood turned ashen, as the outer walls of the building began to crumble.

She averted her gaze from the nightmarish vision, only to see a dangerous orange glow in the water.

The sea had changed too. Suddenly it looked like the water had caught fire. A terrible heat rose up from it, singeing the tips of her feathers.

Eryn quickly turned back, hoping to reach the View Point before she ran out of time and air.

She had barely made it close to the correct tower when she was knocked back by a piercing sensation in her breast.

She'd been hit by something, but what?

As she looked down at herself, she lost all sense of direction. Her wings refused to cooperate any longer and she started to fall, faster and faster, rotating on her own axis as she crashed.

She never felt the impact.

Instead, she kept on falling and falling, until a familiar voice called out to her from somewhere beyond her view.

"Eryn!"

She tried to turn around, but her body was no longer able. *Ferris? Where are you?*

"**I**s it working?" Rhea asked.

Ferris frowned, but did not open his eyes or reply to her.

She's so impatient, he complained to Kelly.

That's nothing new, Kelly responded in his head. *Focus.*

He tried harder. The little veins on the side of his head began to throb and he felt a headache coming on.

But that was nothing compared to what Eryn was going through. He would endure this little discomfort if it meant there was a chance of helping her.

Beside them, Uri cleared his throat and mumbled something to Rhea which Ferris could only partially understand.

Something about focus and distraction. Rhea grumbled

an unintelligible response.

Finally, it was quiet. He inhaled deeply. The battle had all but wiped him out. Ordinarily he would have waited before attempting to perform magic again, but right now, there wasn't any time. Uri had pretty much confirmed it earlier.

If Eryn was stuck in her own version of purgatory, they had only so long to try and get her out before her mind would be lost forever.

Try to speak to her while you do it. Maybe that'll help wake her mind to your presence.

Kelly's suggestion didn't make much sense to him, but she was the mind-reading expert here; he wasn't.

As his consciousness emerged from his physical body, he could clearly see everything and everyone around him.

"Eryn, come back to us," Ferris said. As soon as he'd spoken those few words, he saw something unusual in her: a shadowy being clinging to her damaged body, which stirred at the sound of his voice.

Rhea scoffed. "This is stupid. I'm leaving. Someone, call me if this sorcery works."

Ferris breathed in and out, as deeply and slowly as he could, to maintain his fragile state of being. Suspended between life and death, he felt his body growing weaker and weaker.

"It's probably best if we all leave," Kelly whispered. "This is going to be difficult enough without all the distractions."

Uri mumbled something in agreement, and soon after, the two of them left the room. Only Eryn and Ferris remained.

He approached her and reached out for her hand. The way Kelly had explained it, she didn't have to leave her body to join another's mind. She merely heard and transmitted thoughts. Perhaps that was why she had no luck using her powers on Eryn. Her mind was too confused to allow her in.

The only thing left to try was for him to enter her, like he had done with much simpler creatures so many times before.

Out on the battlefield he had performed feats he had never thought possible. A little lighting strike was all he had achieved in the past.

Perhaps it was the thought of losing her that had sparked a greater power within him? Was there any greater motivator than fear?

Chances were that he would fail, and she would slip away. But how could he live with himself if he didn't at least try? So what if he went down with her? She was worth the sacrifice.

He gave it everything he had, and forced his soul to enter her.

Surprisingly, there was little resistance, but it wasn't an easy transition. All her pain, he felt it now. The wound in her chest was severe. Just how she could bear it, he did not know.

Was she even still in here with him?

Eryn! he thought. *Eryn, please, can you hear me?*

He tried to move, but her body wouldn't budge. He was just a helpless passenger of an incapacitated body.

Of course, moving her physical form wouldn't achieve anything. It was her mind he had to try and reach.

Eryn, damn it. Don't leave me!

The shadow he'd spotted earlier appeared again, right above her body. Strangely, it wasn't human; it was shaped like an eagle as it was trying to leave her body. He reached for its wing and held on for dear life.

Spirit to spirit, he was able to sense her fear as if it were his own.

Eryn, listen to me. You have to come back. You're not done yet with this life.

The form flapped and struggled, as it fought furiously to get away from him. With his last shred of energy, he was able to subdue it.

I'm dying, Ferris! I've been hit by the enemy! All is lost. The battle is lost.

Ferris' heartbeat surged as he sensed her response.

You're just confused. Your body has already started to heal. And we won the battle shortly after you went down.

The shadow transformed. What was once an eagle had turned into a human again. Finally, his words were getting through to her. Even the fear he'd sensed in her had subsided.

Where are you? Why am I all alone?

You're not alone, Eryn. I'm here to get you back.

As her spirit settled back into her body, Ferris was immediately expelled into the empty space between them. He exhaled slowly and focused on getting back into his own physical form.

He got up in a rush to check Eryn. Her skin was still cold, and her eyes remained closed.

Still, he'd communicated with her. He'd brought her back to her body. Surely it wasn't all for nothing?

Ferris rushed to the door, where Kelly and the others were still waiting around.

"Sis, something's happened. Please go and see if you can communicate with her now."

———◆———

Eryn awoke with a gasp and sat up straight. Everything hurt. Every breath, every movement. She immediately regretted moving at all.

When she opened her eyes, she expected to see the foggy place again. Whether in the sky or on the ground, she had always found herself in the same place. And the ordeal had always ended the same way, with what she assumed to be her own death.

But she was inside the castle, in her own room now. And there was no fog to be seen.

She wasn't alone anymore either. Surrounding her were a multitude of familiar faces.

There was Uri, who smiled down on her. "Welcome back, young Eryn."

With that same stabbing pain she'd dreamt about continuing to pierce her chest, she did not feel particularly young.

"Eryn, how do you feel?" Rhea asked. She'd never seen Rhea look this concerned before.

Eryn simply shook her head in response. Talking would hurt.

Honestly? She felt worse than she'd ever felt before.

Then, turning her head further to the right, she saw a more unexpected sight. Ferris, whose wide smile could not disguise just how terrible he looked. Had he been injured as well?

"Don't talk yet. It's alright," Ferris spoke softly.

Eryn sighed and slowly lay back down on her back. *Oh, it hurts.*

"I think let's allow her to rest. Now that she's back with us, she'll heal up fast," Uri said.

Eryn closed her eyes and tried to find a more comfortable breathing pattern. She was unsuccessful.

Footsteps shuffled away from her bed, and the door opened and closed. She sensed that everyone had left. Everyone except one person, that was.

Eryn opened her eyes again and noticed that Ferris had

sat down on a chair beside her bed. Although she couldn't voice it, she was glad he was here.

She could see in his eyes that he had gone through a fair amount of pain himself, though he seemed to be mostly intact physically. When the time was right, she would find out everything she'd missed during her absence.

He did not ask her anything, neither did she speak. But instinctively she knew that she was here now because of him somehow.

And his body had clearly paid a heavy price to make it happen.

Ferris leaned over and took her hand. It made her feel weird, but in a nice way.

He cared. Just why and how she had deserved this affection, she did not know. If she'd followed her orders rather than hesitated, she would have killed him in his sleep shortly after his capture. By all accounts, he shouldn't be alive today, yet here he was.

And words could not express how grateful she was for that.

CHAPTER FOURTEEN

Eryn's recovery was lighting fast, at least compared to what Ferris was used to.

Within a day, she was able to talk, and two days later, she was almost back on her feet.

An injury such as hers would have killed most humans; if not on the spot, then within hours.

Kelly was right. The islanders were different. They didn't get sick, and they healed extraordinarily quickly.

And as it turned out, that wasn't the only difference between them and mainlanders like Ferris himself. He was shocked to learn the reason for the strange animal appearances around the islands. The eagles overhead, and the wolves and bears he'd seen during the aftermath of the battle, were the islanders themselves.

And that eagle he had tried to possess on his first day had been Eryn all along.

It was yet another reason for Ferris to admire her.

And luckily, the feeling appeared to be mutual. She seemed to be enjoying his company, judging by the way her eyes lit up whenever he came and saw her.

But he'd been cautious not to get ahead of himself. They'd become friends, even confidantes. But he knew he wanted so much more.

After getting past the initial awkwardness between

them, Eryn had opened up to him.

They talked for hours every day, learning everything there was to know about each other.

Ferris told her about the battle, and all that had happened since. He'd tried to omit Rhea's attempt to imprison him again, but soon realized he was unable to keep too many secrets from her.

Thankfully she was in good spirits and could have a little laugh about it all.

One morning, three or four days after the battle, Ferris decided it was time to have a *real* conversation. Finally, he would know if she truly felt as he did, or if this friendship was doomed to remain only that.

"Morning, Eryn," Ferris greeted her as he entered the room.

She was sitting up in bed already, with a bowl of soup resting on her lap.

"Morning." She smiled brightly, and his nerves subsided a little.

He sat down on the chair at her bedside and folded his hands. The past seven years might have taught him a lot, but nothing that would be of use now. He hadn't the faintest idea how to proposition a woman. Worse still, he didn't know if the customs here were different.

Should he have brought her a token of some sort, to show his affection?

"You look troubled. Is something wrong?" Eryn asked.

"No, no… Nothing is wrong." Ferris' tone sounded

unconvincing even to his own ears.

Now or never!

"That day, during the battle, I made a promise to myself," Ferris began.

Eryn put her spoon down and focused solely on him.

"I said to myself, if we make it through to the end alive, I'm going to ask you something."

He leaned over and took her hand. It was warm and soft, and the feel of her skin against his made his heart beat even faster.

"Ask me what?" Eryn whispered.

The mood in the room had changed. The air had grown heavy with tension. He swallowed his fears and blurted it all out.

"Would you become my wife?"

Eryn's eyes widened as she was stunned into silence.

"I would give you a ring, or some other token to show I'm serious, but I have nothing to give but myself. I promise you'll have my loyalty for as long as I'm alive," Ferris said.

His voice had gone flat. How could it be that he'd faced off against any number of enemies, and yet speaking to this one woman had sent him into a blind panic?

He'd never been afraid of injury or death, but these stakes were higher. If Eryn refused him, he knew he would suffer gravely.

"It's not possible," Eryn stammered and pulled her

hand away. "How could we possibly do this?"

Ferris' heart all but stopped. He glanced at her, and found that she already had tears in her eyes. How could she not be interested? Had he misinterpreted the way she looked at him?

"You're..." Eryn took a deep breath. "You're the queen's brother!"

Ferris didn't know how to respond to that. What bearing did his relation to Kelly have in all of this? Finally, it dawned on him what she meant.

"I'm nobody," he said. "I'm a liar, a thief and a murderer. I almost destroyed your people in my search for revenge. Reject me on that basis, not because of Kelly."

Eryn sniffled. "But you saved us. You saved me."

"I was only trying to undo the wrong I'd caused."

Eryn stared at him. The sudden silence between them threatened to overwhelm. He wanted to scream, just to break it. But he didn't; instead he waited for her to speak first.

"I'm not worthy," Eryn finally said.

Ferris pressed his lips together, and maintained eye contact. She seemed to truly believe that. How could she possibly be serious? This woman, who was a million times better than him, was hung up on his supposed status? He hadn't earned that kind of consideration. And Kelly herself didn't care; she'd just seemed amused by the idea when she first noticed.

"You're wrong," Ferris said. "I'm the one who's

unworthy."

For days he'd watched her recover, but right now she looked more pained than she had through the worst of it. The outcome of their conversation was causing her as much grief as it was him. And all of it was completely unnecessary.

"Will you just tell me one thing?" Ferris asked. "If it were just you and me in this world, nobody else. What would your answer be?"

"That's obvious," Eryn whispered with a tremble in her voice. "I'd say yes."

Ferris stretched out his hand and watched as Eryn placed hers in his palm again. She shivered slightly as he closed his fingers gently around hers.

"Then forget about all the rest of it," Ferris said. "Kelly doesn't mind, and she can handle anyone who objects."

"But…"

Ferris placed his finger on Eryn's lips. "Trust me?"

She nodded. "I do."

"Nobody will come between us. I promise," he said.

For a change, he wasn't bluffing or exaggerating. He would move heaven and earth to get what he wanted. If he had to fight everyone on this island, from the king down to that irritating man who'd made a scene while Eryn was still unconscious, he would do it without hesitation.

She looked up at him in silence. The despair he'd just seen in her eyes was slowly dissipating. Perhaps he was getting through to her.

"Why me?" she asked. "Neither am I as good a fighter as Rhea, nor am I as pretty as the mainland girls."

Ferris smiled briefly. "Because I've never met anyone like you. You're perfect just the way you are."

Eryn smiled through her tears and bit her lip. "I've never met anyone like you either."

———◆———

Eryn couldn't believe her luck. Every day, Ferris had come to spend time with her and to care for her. She had cherished their moments together, even if she assumed it would all come to an end once she was fully recovered.

Somewhere in the back of her mind she'd always wondered, what if this was something more than just friendship? But she'd rejected the notion as quickly as it had come up.

She wasn't from one of the prominent Black Isle families like Rhea and even Yorrick. She was a commoner.

Why would he care for her like that?

But he had surprised her, despite all of her protests and concerns.

"You're perfect just the way you are." These words continued to ring in her ears, moments after he had first said them.

She was overwhelmed by the realization that all the

things she'd been trying not to think about, he'd been thinking too. The attraction she'd felt from the start, he had felt it too.

That's why he had joined her on the battlefield, when he could have performed his magic anywhere and not been so dangerously close to the action.

And it was also the reason he had avenged her injury and burned down half of the mainland's fleet of ships. After all that, he had mustered the last of his reserves to try and bring her back from the dead. She'd seen in his eyes just how close to the brink he had come. All for her.

What more could she ask for in a mate? And if the queen didn't object, then…

"Do you really think it's possible?" Eryn asked.

"Anything is possible now."

He leaned over and placed his hand on the side of her face. His touch made her cheeks burn up, and caused her breaths to quicken.

"Unless Rhea tries to arrest me again," he added.

"Don't joke," she said.

He was so close to her now, his heady perfume stirred up those same desires she'd had all along. Instinct was threatening to take over. All the things she knew her body craved; they were now within reach.

"Prove it with a kiss," she whispered.

He didn't need any more encouragement than that.

The moment their lips touched for the very first time,

she knew there was no turning back. All the tension, all the yearning she'd felt, it was all about to be unleashed.

It was the animal side of her, taking over. Just what she'd been afraid of all this time, she could no longer remember.

It felt so right; his flesh against hers.

She got onto her knees on the edge of her bed, and pulled him closer by his hand until they were more evenly matched. The taste of his lips was intoxicating.

He pulled away just enough to speak. "Tell me if it hurts."

His breath tickled her face, which sent her heart racing even faster.

"My wound healed days ago," Eryn said. "Don't worry about me."

She wrapped her arms around him and pulled him against her. This was what she had craved. It was the sort of passion that made you stupid. She'd never understood it until this very moment.

His body was firm to the touch, muscular like her own, but also very different. His skin was so smooth, she couldn't stop running her hands over him as they continued to make out.

What a beautiful man he was. He didn't have the rough edges of some of the islanders. Only a few scars adorned his skin. She touched every single one of them with the tip of her finger.

Ferris. It made her happy to say his name.

Now that she had given herself permission to feel, she was overcome with so many emotions at once. She could laugh, or cry, or both at the same time.

Was this how it felt to love?

Eryn had no idea that things would get more intense still.

Ferris joined her on the bed and guided her down on her back. His hands were on an exploratory journey of their own. Her side, her hips, her stomach and her breasts, he caressed her all over.

As he looked down on her, Eryn noticed his eyes had turned almost black with lust. She could smell the change in him, heard the racing of his heart as his body was overcome by desire.

It made her want him more.

Everything about him seemed designed to turn her on.

Ferris climbed on top of her and allowed his hand to travel downward, pushing her nightgown out of the way.

Eryn moaned and raised her hips to meet his touch.

She'd never done this before, but her body was telling her exactly what was needed.

As he lowered himself on top of her, she dug her fingernails into his shoulders. His manhood pressed up against her thigh.

"Oh please, don't hold back," she whispered impatiently.

Ferris paused and stared into her eyes. The look in his

gaze was wild. He wanted this as much as she did. Nobody could stop them now.

He let his fingers slip in between her legs.

She gasped as he found a spot most sensitive. All the pleasure in the world couldn't compare to what she felt right now.

She forced her own hand in between the two of them and touched him intimately. He shuddered as she tightened her fingers around his shaft.

Although it was her first time, she never hesitated. She guided him inside of her and cried out in pleasure as her body adjusted to him.

Just like that, they had become one.

Eryn's mind went blank. Not a doubt remained.

This was right. This was just. Nobody could take this away from her; she wouldn't allow it anymore.

Ferris rocked back and forth into her. They were different species, human and islander, but in this moment, they were exactly the same.

It did not take long for either of them to reach their peak. After trying to contain this passion for so long, their bodies simply let go.

Eryn was overcome with a wave of pleasure so strong, it knocked the wind out of her.

On top, Ferris groaned to a halt almost at the same time. He shuddered and strained as his seed flooded into her.

That's how they remained, until the fog of ecstasy lifted

enough for them to realize what had just happened.

"Well, that was unexpected," Ferris spoke as he fell back onto the bed.

Eryn chuckled. "I blame the animal in me."

"If that is your excuse, then what do I blame?" Ferris stretched out his arm and pulled Eryn's still naked body against him.

She had no answer for him; instead of talking more she rested her head on his shoulder and closed her eyes.

How warm he was. Meanwhile her own body was cool underneath the thin layer of sweat that their union had produced.

Could it be that this was her life now? He was hers and she was his, and they would sleep and wake like this, lying body to body, every night for the rest of their lives?

She wished for nothing more.

CHAPTER FIFTEEN

ays had passed since Ferris had first confessed his feelings to Eryn. Their relationship was progressing faster than he could have ever anticipated.

Now that she was fully recovered, they had become even closer, physically as well as emotionally.

But one thing still stood in the way of their future. One thing which had been playing on Ferris' mind since waking after the battle.

Despite everything, he'd failed to keep them safe.

His outburst on the battlefield had torched a bunch of the royal navy's ships, sure. But not all of them.

And although they had retreated for now, Ferris was certain a single setback like this wouldn't discourage King Harrold from trying again. The mainland army would be back, and perhaps the next time, a bit of fog might not be enough to thwart their attack.

The islanders were powerful and had many talents, but they weren't cannon-proof. Their weaponry was severely lacking as well.

He could not have any more deaths on his conscience. No, Ferris owed it to Eryn, as well as Kelly and Finlay, to redeem himself.

So, one morning he decided to discuss the matter with

King Broc.

With every passing day, the threat grew bigger. It was only a matter of time before they would be under attack again.

"My King," Ferris addressed him. "I'd like a word."

Broc greeted him with a pat on the back. "I've never had a brother-in-law before, but I'm quite sure such formalities are not required among family. Just call me Broc."

It was a relief that Broc was becoming more welcoming, but still, the ruler of the Black Isles struck an imposing figure.

"Very well…. Broc." It was odd, addressing him that way.

"What can I do for you, Ferris?" the king asked.

He was in an unusually jovial mood today. Perhaps it was still the thrill of victory.

"I mean to discuss a proposition," Ferris began.

Broc's expression sobered up. "Continue."

"As you know I was sent here as an envoy to King Harrold of the mainland. He then sent his navy after us to complete the invasion."

"Yes, and you fought them off almost single-handedly as I hear it."

Ferris shook his head. "Conjecture and exaggeration. I did what I could at the time. But I doubt we've seen the last of the mainland."

"You mean, they will attack again? Despite running away the last time, like cowards?" Broc raised an eyebrow.

"Well, I have an idea to avoid such a scenario. If you're willing to make a couple of concessions."

"Carry on."

"The Reaping, as you call it. King Harrold is using at as an excuse to motivate his army," Ferris said.

Broc scratched his beard, then looked down at Ferris again. "You mean to say that if we do away with the Reaping, his soldiers will have no more reason to fight?"

Ferris nodded. "That's exactly what I'm saying."

"We can't afford another battle. Not this quickly." Broc paced the hall as he spoke.

"I know." Ferris folded his arms in an attempt to look more confident in his plan.

The king paused and studied Ferris' face. "Are you sure this will work?"

It's going to have to. I've got nothing else. "Absolutely."

"Alright…. What's the other concession?" Broc asked.

"Let me have the prisoners. I'll return them as a gesture of goodwill."

***

"Funny, that you would turn on your own people so quickly!" King Harrold sneered, as Ferris entered the throne hall.

Ferris stared the man down. King or no king, he wasn't going to accept insults from anyone. And he certainly wasn't going to show weakness, not when he had so much riding on this moment.

"And to think I believed your story. About your missing sister, who had been chosen in the last lottery. My senses must be failing me in my advanced age that I did not predict your deceit!" King Harrold ranted on.

"Trust me, you've seen nothing much of me yet," Ferris countered.

"Apparently! I should have you executed where you stand!"

"You could try, but your men would fall before they even got close to me. Or did you not hear about what happened during the battle?" Ferris straightened himself and continued to glare directly at the king. He knew very well that he was breaking every single rule of protocol, and yet he did not care.

A murmur passed through the small group of royal advisors. Some of them shuffled uncomfortably from one foot onto the other.

Good. They *ought* to be afraid of him.

The king himself, however, remained unfazed. Either he was completely uninformed, or he knew more about Ferris and his magic than he let on.

But Ferris had come here with a clear goal in mind. If they called his bluff, so be it. He was willing to make the sacrifice.

"I haven't come here to hear your judgement. I'm more than content with the choices I have made," Ferris said.

What a joke this was. After the short time Ferris had spent on Black Mountain, he'd come to find the ways of the mainlanders to be ludicrous in comparison.

On one side there was a king who had clearly earned his place, through just rule as well as prowess in battle. Yet here sat nothing but a frail old man, and yet everyone treated him with reverence he did not deserve. What had *he* ever done for his people?

"Then what exactly are you doing here?" King Harrold folded his arms across his chest and tapped his foot impatiently.

Ferris looked at him in disgust.

How had this king ever helped Ferris and Kelly when they were growing up in West Hythe? Theirs was a life lived in poverty, with barely enough food to get by. And as soon as Ferris left to earn a little money, Kelly had been taken in the lottery.

The villagers had no idea what would happen to her, neither did they care. For all they know, she had died the day they left her on the beach.

It was pure luck that Broc had taken her in and treated her with more kindness than her own people had shown her. She had arrived in a better place, purely by chance.

Meanwhile, this supposed ruler had a limitless supply of food and all the shiny trinkets money could buy, while his advisers did nothing but brown nose him. When had he ever seen pain or sacrifice? He'd sent his soldiers off to fight a hopeless war at sea, for what?

To stop the lottery? This charlatan cared nothing about the lottery. He was in it to expand his territory.

This king had never done a single thing to deserve Ferris' respect.

"I'm here to warn you to forget about the Black Isles," Ferris spoke in a threatening tone.

Still, the man's arrogant expression remained.

"Or, what? We saw what your barbarian friends had to offer. A few soldiers, easily wiped out if I send in reinforcements." King Harrold snapped his finger to make his point.

Ferris laughed out loud. "Oh, is that what you think? I do believe you have been misinformed. What your men encountered was just a taste of what the Black Isles can unleash. Now that they're expecting a fight, they can summon an army that will put yours to shame. Perhaps question those *loyal* advisors of yours in a bit more detail."

"Are you just going to stand there while this peasant disrespects me?" the king raged. "All of you, what are you here for, exactly? Tell him!"

The small cluster of fancily-dressed men took a moment to confer, until one of them reluctantly stepped forward.

"Your Majesty, although we outnumbered them approximately four-to-one, the enemy fought with such fury, we would need to overwhelm them with troops we simply don't have," the advisor spoke in a trembling voice.

Finally, someone had stepped up against this decrepit tyrant.

The king stood up from his throne and pointed at the door. "Then go out there and get me some more men!"

"That…. I'm so sorry, Your Majesty, but even the men we currently have aren't willing to go back into battle. Not against this particular enemy."

Ferris simply watched the exchange. He'd expected to have more trouble than this. To threaten and perhaps show everyone a taste of his powers. But it seemed that the advisors were doing his job for him.

"They get a spot of bad weather during a fight and want to run for the hills?" the king raised his fist in the air. "I won't stand for this. Find me braver soldiers, then! And fire the ones we have without pay."

A spot of bad weather. This was the perfect time to teach these people a lesson.

Ferris closed his eyes and inhaled deeply. He visualized the throne room now, with a gust of wind blowing through it and extinguishing all the candles and torches at once.

Gasps and whispers could be heard from his left where the advisors stood. The cold wind tickled the hairs on his arms.

"What's the meaning of this? Stop it, right now!" the king ordered.

He was trying to maintain a brave front, but Ferris could hear fear in his voice.

Ferris opened his eyes and stared right at the king. "It's a dangerous thing, the unknown. I promise that if you face off against the Isles again, you'll encounter things you can't even imagine in your worst nightmares."

The monarch's face had turned a deep crimson. "What do you want?"

"That's all. Peace."

"And what do we get out of it? How do I justify this to the people?" the king asked.

Ferris smiled briefly. *Justify it to the people. As if he gives a damn what ordinary folk think.* "An end to the lottery. The daughters of East and West Hythe will be safe from now on."

Once again, a murmur travelled the small crowd, until the same one who had spoken up earlier approached the king again.

"Your Majesty. We believe this to be a fair deal," he whispered, though he was just loud enough for Ferris to overhear.

"So, do we have an agreement, then?" Ferris asked.

He produced the two identical scrolls Uri had prepared shortly after he'd gotten Broc's blessing. A replacement for the old treaty that had been drawn up so many centuries ago.

The king made a face, but then nodded briefly. "Very well. Prepare my seal."

Ferris watched as another one of the advisors carefully

took the scrolls from him, and stamped the royal seal onto both of them, before presenting them to the king to sign. He then rolled them up individually, and handed one back to Ferris.

"You'd better go, before he changes his mind," the man whispered fearfully.

So much fear, all for an old man who possessed neither strength nor talons or fangs. All he had in his favor was the privilege of his birth.

"A good day to you all. Your Majesty." Ferris greeted them with a comically exaggerated bow. Then he left the hall with a spring in his step.

Ferris knew he'd never to return to these lands ever again, and that was fine by him. Like Kelly, he had found a better home.

Rhea would still be skeptical of him, of course, but he could handle that.

With this achievement behind him he could honestly say he had held up his end of the deal. The war he had thrust everyone into—he had undone it as much as he possibly could.

This piece of paper, this symbol, would allow calm to return to the Isles.

And Eryn and he could live out the rest of their lives together, in peace.

EPILOGUE

"And that was the story of how I met your aunt Eryn," Ferris concluded.

The boy's eyes were wide and his lips slightly parted. He had been completely engrossed in every word so far.

"She almost died?" Finlay asked. "And you and my mom had to rescue her from the shadow world in her own mind?"

Ferris nodded. "It's true. You can ask her yourself." Although he had told the story dozens of times by now, that part still stung as though it had happened yesterday.

"I can't believe I missed the entire battle and everything!" Finlay folded his arms in frustration.

"It was for your own safety."

Finlay scoffed. "I can fight, too! Dad has been teaching me how to use a sword."

Ferris chuckled. "I don't doubt it. You'll be a great warrior one day."

"I can't wait to grow up and have adventures of my own. Then, when I come back, I'll be the one to tell you stories." Finlay smiled and Ferris' heart melted.

He was a sweet boy. He could see a lot of Kelly in him, not least because he indeed had the same eyes and the same flaming red hair.

"You'd better. You owe me a good story after all the

ones I've told you already!" Ferris laughed. "But now, I think we can all agree it's bedtime."

"No! Just one more, please, Uncle Ferris?" Finlay complained. They had this same conversation every day. And it always ended the same way.

Ferris shook his head. "You know what to do. Don't make me tell you again."

Finlay sighed and lay down flat in his cot.

"Eyes closed!" Ferris ordered.

Finlay grimaced and shut his eyes so tightly his little face was all scrunched up.

Behind him, Ferris heard the soft creak of an opening door. His senses might not be as powerful as those of the islanders, but Ferris' nose told him exactly who it was.

Her sweet perfume was unmistakable.

"Almost ready here? Broc has called us for a meeting," Eryn said. "Sweet dreams, Finlay!"

Finlay lifted his head. "Good night, Aunt Eryn!"

"You heard the lady. I've got somewhere to be. You be good now and go to sleep."

"Alright then. But tomorrow, you tell me another story."

"Of course. Any thoughts on what story you want to hear?" Ferris asked.

"I want to know how it happened that my mom and I were already here, but you came much later. Will you tell it to me?"

Ferris thought for a moment. "I think that particular

one is best told by your mother herself. You just wait. Once she's back with your little brother or sister, she'll tell you exactly what happened."

Finlay made a face. "She won't tell me. I already asked."

"Don't worry. I'll talk to her. You're a big boy now, so you're ready to hear that story as well."

"You think so?" Finlay asked.

"I know so."

With a reassured smile on his face, Finlay finally settled into his pillow and closed his eyes.

"Ok, Uncle Ferris. Good night."

"Sleep well. Little man." Ferris patted Finlay on the head, then quietly left the room and joined Eryn, who had been waiting in the hallway.

"He's going to sleep now," Ferris explained.

Eryn suppressed a smile. "If I didn't know any better, I would have thought that Ferris, the Great Warlock of the Mainland, had finally met his match. The boy's every wish is your command."

"Ha, if you say so. Though I'd argue that's true for you too."

"What is?" Eryn cocked her head to the side.

She might be tough as nails and a fearsome opponent if you met her on the battlefield. But during these little moments, they were just an ordinary couple, and she was a woman like any other. Ferris cherished this feminine side as much as the warrior in her.

He leaned over and slipped his hand across the nape of her neck. With their lips only an inch or so apart, he whispered those all-important words he knew she wanted to hear.

"Your wish is my command too."

Her eyes fluttered shut as she leaned into him, allowing their lips to touch. This right here made everything worth it. All the pain and suffering they had been through; it was meaningless now that they were together.

What had started out as mere quiet admiration on his side had awoken a burning flame of passion that he'd never expected to feel.

Her body's reaction to his touch proved that their attraction remained mutual.

Ever since he'd met her, he was willing to be a better man. A good husband. A devoted father to their children, should they have them eventually.

He had become all the things his own father had never been. All for her.

It was with great reluctance that he pulled away from their sweet kiss.

Ferris looked into Eryn's eyes and saw that she was smiling.

"What do you say, we'll pick that up later, in peace.... You said something about a meeting with the king?" Ferris asked.

Eryn nodded. "That's right. We shouldn't keep him waiting."

* * *

ABOUT THE AUTHOR

———◆———

Dear Reader,

Thanks for reading the entire Shifters of Black Isle series, a collection of stories set in a fantasy world full of mystery, magic and fantastical creatures. I hope you've enjoyed them all.

I may have only released my first book under this name in 2015, but I'm not new to writing in general. In fact, my mom still tells me to this day about how I would make up stories, and attempt to record them in my clumsy, shaky handwriting from the moment I learned to read and write. From there I went on to write fan fiction and other stuff meant for my own eyes only, until 2012, when I began to write erotica and contemporary romance.

I've always enjoyed stories of the fantastic and paranormal. Vampires, shape shifters, witches and magic, all featured in the books I loved the most, even when I was still growing up. But it wasn't until much later that I got into romance. One of the first writers (an independent author just like me!) I came across was Tina Folsom, via her Scanguards Vampire series. I was hooked. From there I went on to read more paranormal romance until I found a new kind of hero I loved: bear shifters, like the kind written by Milly Taiden, Zoe Chant, and T.S. Joyce. What I love about bears is how they can be all strong and independent, a bit reclusive, and almost grumpy, but they always end up having a heart of gold (plus they tend to know their food, and we all know that a man who can cook is doubly sexy). All that (except for the shifting into a powerful bear) almost exactly describes the sort of man I ended up falling for and marrying in real life, so it's no surprise that this is what I started my publishing career with.

To find out more, check:

LoreleiMoone.com (And why not sign up for the newsletter to be the first to find out about new releases.)

You can also get in touch with me via Facebook (search for Lorelei Moone), or email at info@loreleimoone.com

x Lorelei

Ps. If you also read contemporary / erotic romance, you might want to check out my other releases as *L. Moone.*

HAVE YOU MET THE SCOTTISH WEREBEARS?

Before there was Alpha Squad, there were the Scottish Werebears… And if you sign up for Lorelei Moone's mailing list at loreleimoone.com, you get Book 1, Scottish Werebear: An Unexpected Affair absolutely free!

Titles in the Scottish Werebears series include:

An Unexpected Affair

A Dangerous Business

A Forbidden Love

A New Beginning

A Painful Dilemma

A Second Chance

These individual books in the Scottish Werebears series are best read in order. They can also be enjoyed as part of the Scottish Werebear: Complete Collection boxed set.

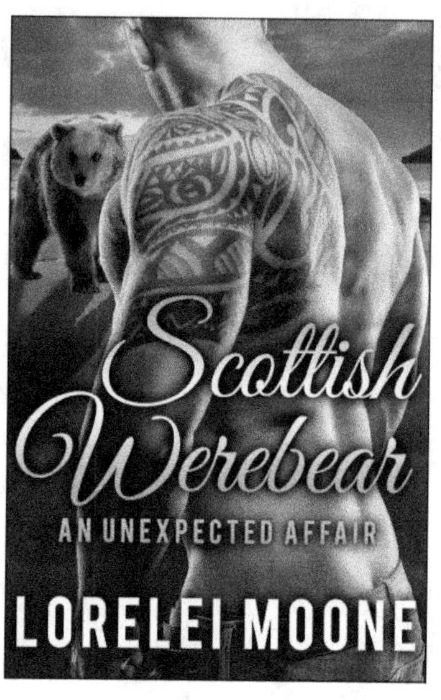

When romance novelist, Clarice Adler, hides herself away in a secluded holiday cottage to finish a book, the last thing she needs is another relationship. Imagine her surprise when she falls head over heels for the man who runs the place. Derek McMillan knows Clarice is his mate, but he's a bear shifter and she's human and the two simply don't mix. They are literally worlds apart; can they find a way to come together?

Get this book for free by joining Lorelei Moone's mailing list at loreleimoone.com!